Wolves of the Sea

Randall Parrish

Contents

WOLVES OF THE SEA

BY

Randall Parrish

FOREWORD

Anson Carlyle, aged twenty-three, the ninth in descent from Captain Geoffry Carlyle, of Glasgow, Scotland, was among the heroic Canadian dead at Vimy Ridge. Unmarried, and the last of his line, what few treasures he possessed fell into alien hands. Among these was a manuscript, apparently written in the year 1687, and which, through nine generations, had been carefully preserved, yet never made public. The paper was yellowed and discolored by years, occasionally a page was missing, and the writing itself had become almost indecipherable. Much indeed had to be traced by use of a microscope. The writer was evidently a man of some education, and clear thought, but exceedingly diffuse, in accordance with the style of his time, and possessing small conception of literary form. In editing this manuscript for modern readers I have therefore been compelled to practically rewrite it entirely, retaining merely the essential facts, with an occasional descriptive passage, although I have conscientiously followed the original development of the tale. In this reconstruction much quaintness of language, as well as appeal to probability, may have been lost, and for this my only excuse is the necessity of thus making the story readable. I have no doubt as to its essential truth, nor do I question the purpose which dominated this rover of the sea in his effort to record the adventures of his younger life. As a picture of those days of blood and courage, as well as a story of love and devotion, I deem it worthy preservation, regretting only the impossibility of now presenting it in print exactly as written by Geoffry Carlyle.

R.P.

WOLVES OF THE SEA

CHAPTER I
SENT INTO SERVITUDE

Knowing this to be a narrative of unusual adventure, and one which may never even be read until long after I have departed from this world, when it will be difficult to convince readers that such times as are herein depicted could ever have been reality, I shall endeavor to narrate each incident in the simplest manner possible. My only purpose is truth, and my only witness history. Yet, even now lately as this all happened it is more like the recollections of a dream, dimly remembered at awakening, and, perchance, might remain so, but for the scars upon my body, and the constant memory of a woman's face. These alone combine to bring back in vividness those days that were--days of youth and daring, of desperate, lawless war, of wide ocean peril, and the outstretched hands of love. So that here, where I am writing it all down, here amid quietness and peace, and forgetful of the past, I wander again along a deserted shore, and sail among those isles of a southern sea, the home for many a century of crime and unspeakable cruelty. I will recall the truth, and can do no more.

I can recall that far-away dawn now as the opening portals of a beautiful morning, although at the time my thought was so closely centered upon other things, the deep blue of the sky, and the glimmering gold of the sun scarcely left an impression on my mind. It was still early morning when we were brought out under heavy guard, and marched somberly forth through the opened gates of the gaol. There had been rain during the night, and the cobble-stones of the village street were dark with moisture, slipping under our hob-nailed shoes as we stumbled along down the sharp incline leading to the wharf. Ahead we could perceive a forest of masts, and what seemed like a vast crowd of waiting people. Only the murmur of voices greeting us as we emerged, told that this gathering was not a hostile one, and this truth was emphasized to our minds by the efforts of the guard to hasten our passage. That we had been sentenced to exile, to prolonged servitude in some foreign land, was all that any of us knew--to what special section of the world fate had allotted us remained unknown.

In spite of curses, and an occasional blow, we advanced slowly, marching four abreast, with feet dragging heavily, the chains binding us together clanking dismally with each step, and an armed guard between each file. Experiences have been many since then, yet I recall, as though it were but yesterday, the faces of those who walked in line with me. I was at the right end of my file, and at my shoulder was a boy from Morrownest, a slim, white-faced lad, his weak chin trembling from fear, and his eyes staring about so pleadingly I spoke a word of courage to him, whispering in his ear, lest the guard behind might strike. He glanced aside at me, but with no response in the depths of his eyes, in which I could perceive only a dumb anguish of despair. Beyond him marched Grover, one time butcher at Harwich, a stocky, big-fisted fellow, with a ghastly sword wound, yet red and unhealed on his face, extending from hair to chin, his little pig eyes glinting ugly, and his lips cursing. The man beyond was a soldier, a straight, athletic fellow, with crinkly black beard, who kept his eyes front, paying no heed to the cries. The guard pressed the people back as we shuffled along, but there was no way of keeping them still. I heard cries of encouragement, shouts of recognition, sobs of pity, and occasionally a roar of anger as we passed.

"Good lads! God be with yer!"

"Thet one thar is sore hurted--it's a damn shame."

"Thar's Teddy--poor laddie! Luck go with yer, Teddy."

"Ter hell with Black Jeffries, say I!"

"Hush, mon, er ye'll be next ter go--no, I don't know who sed it."

"See thet little chap, Joe; lots ther lad bed ter do with the war."

"They all look mighty peaked--poor devils, four months in gaol."

"Stand back there now. Stand back!"

The guards prodded them savagely with the butts of their musketoons, thus making scant room for us to shuffle through, out upon the far end of the wharf, where we were finally halted abreast of a lumping brig, apparently nearly ready for sea. There were more than forty of us as I counted the fellows, and we were rounded up at the extremity of the wharf in the full blaze of the sun, with a line of guards stretched across to hold back the crowd until preparations had been completed to admit us aboard. As those in front flung themselves down on the planks, I got view of the brig's gangway, along which men were still busily hauling belated boxes and barrels, and beyond these gained glimpse of the hooker's name--ROMPING BETSY OF PLYMOUTH. A moment later a sailor passed along the edge of the dock, dragging a coil of rope after him, and must have answered some hail on his way, for instantly a whisper passed swiftly from man to man.

"It's Virginia, mate; we're bound fer Virginia."

The ugly little pig eyes of the butcher met mine.

"Virginia, hey?" he grunted. "Ye're a sailorman, ain't ye, mate? Well, then, whar is this yere Virginia?"

The boy was looking at me also questioningly, the terror in his face by no means lessened at the sound of this strange word.

"Yes, sir, please; where is it, sir?"

I patted him on the shoulder, as others near by leaned forward to catch my answer.

"That's all right, mates," I returned cheerfully. "It's across the blue water, of course, but better than the Indies. We'll fall into the hands of Englishmen out there, and they'll be decent to us."

"But whar is the bloomin' hole?"

"In America. That is where all the tobacco comes from; likely that will be our job--raising tobacco."

"Have ever yer bin thar?"

"Ay, twice--and to a land beyond they call Maryland. Tis a country not so un-like England."

"Good luck that then; tell us about it, matie."

I endeavored to do so, dwelling upon what I remembered of the settlements, and the habits of the people, but saying little of the great wilderness of the interior, or how I had seen slaves toiling in the fields. The group of men within range of my voice leaned forward in breathless attention, one now and then asking a question, their chains rattling with each movement of a body. The deep interest shown in their faces caused me unconsciously to elevate, my voice, and I had spoken but a moment or two before a hard hand gripped my shoulder.

"Yer better stow that, my man," growled someone above me, and I looked up into the stern eyes of the captain of the guard "or it may be the 'cat' for ye. Yer heard the orders."

"Yes, sir; I was only answering questions."

"Questions! What the hell difference does it make to this scum whar they go? Do yer talkin' aboard, not here. So ye've been ter the Virginia plantation, hev ye?"

"Twice, sir."

"As a sailor?"

"In command of vessels."

His eyes softened slightly, and a different tone seemed to creep into his voice.

"Then ye must be Master Carlyle, I take it. I heerd tell about ye at the trial, but supposed ye ter be an older man."

"I am twenty-six."

"Ye don't look even thet. It's my notion ye got an overly hard dose this time. The Judge was in ill humor thet day. Still thet's not fer me ter talk about. It's best fer both of us ter hold our tongues. Ay, they're ready fer ye now. Fall in there--all of yer. Step along, yer damn rebel scum."

We passed aboard over the narrow gang-plank, four abreast, dragging our feet, and were halted on the forward deck, while artificers removed our chains. As these were knocked off, the released prisoners disappeared one by one down the forward hatch, into the space between the decks which had been roughly fitted up for their confinement during the long voyage. As my position was in one of the last files, I had ample time in which to gaze about, and take note of my surroundings. Except for the presence of the prisoners the deck presented no unusual scene. The ***Romping Betsy*** was a large, full-rigged brig, not overly clean, and had evidently been in commission for some time. Not heavily loaded she rode high, and was a broad-nosed vessel, with comfortable beam. I knew her at once as a slow sailor, and bound to develop a decidedly disagreeable roll in any considerable sea. She was heavily sparred, and to my eye her canvas appeared unduly weather-beaten and rotten.

Indeed there was unnecessary clutter aloft, and an amount of litter about the deck which evidenced lack of seamanship; nor did the general appearance of such stray members of the crew as met my notice add appreciably to my confidence in the voyage.

I stared aft at the poop deck, seeking to gain glimpse of the skipper, but was unable to determine his presence among the others. There were a number of persons gathered along the low rail, attracted by the unusual spectacle, and curiously watching us being herded aboard, and dispatched below, but, to judge from their appearance, these were probably all passengers--some of them adventurers seeking the new land on their first voyage, although among them I saw others, easily recognized as Virginians on their way home. Among these I picked out a planter or two, prosperous and noisy, men who had just disposed of their tobacco crop, well satisfied with the returns; some artisans sailing on contract, and a naval officer in uniform. Then my eyes encountered a strange group foregathered beside the lee rail.

There were four in the little party, but one of these was a negress, red-turbaned, and black as the ace of spades, a servant evidently, standing in silence behind the others. Another was clearly enough a Colonial proprietor, a heavily built man of middle age, purple faced, and wearing the broad hat with uplifted brim characteristic of Virginians. I passed these by with a glance, my attention concentrating upon the other two--a middle-aged young man, and a young woman standing side by side. The former was a dashing looking blade, of not more than forty, attired in blue, slashed coat, ornamented with gilt buttons, and bedecked at collar and cuffs with a profusion of lace. A saffron colored waist-coat failed to conceal his richly beruffled shirt, and the hilt of a rapier was rather prominently displayed. Such dandies were frequently enough seen, but it was this man's face which made marked contrast with his gay attire. He was dark, and hook-nosed, apparently of foreign birth, with black moustache tightly clipped, so as to reveal the thin firmness of his lips, and even at that distance I could perceive the lines of a scar across his chin. Altogether there was an audacity to his face, a daring, convincing me he was no mere lady's knight, but one to whom fighting was a trade. He was pointing us out to his companion, apparently joking over our appearance, in an endeavor to amuse. Seemingly she gave small heed to his words, for although her eyes followed where he pointed, they never once lighted with a smile, nor did I see her answer his sallies.

She was scarcely more than a girl, dressed very simply in some clinging dark stuff, with a loose gray cloak draping her shoulders, and a small, neat bonnet of straw perched upon a mass of coiled hair. The face beneath was sweetly piquant, with dark eyes, and rounded cheeks flushed with health. She stood, both hands clasping the rail, watching us intently. I somehow felt as though her eyes were upon me, and within their depths, even at that distance, I seemed to read a message of sympathy and kindness. The one lasting impression her face left on my memory was that of innocent girlhood, dignified by a womanly tenderness.

What were those two to each other? I could not guess, for they seemed from two utterly different worlds. Not brother and sister surely; and not lovers. The last was unthinkable. Perhaps mere chance acquaintances, who had drifted together since coming aboard. It seems strange that at such a moment my attention should have thus centered on these two, yet I think now that either one would have awakened my interest wherever we had met. Instinctively I disliked the man, aware of an instant antagonism, realizing that he was evil; while his companion came to me as revealment of all that was true and worthy, in a degree I had never known before. I could not banish either from my mind. For months I had been in prison, expecting a death sentence, much of the time passed in solitary confinement, and now, with that cloud lifted, I had come forth into a fresh existence only to be confronted by this man and woman, representing exact opposites. Their peculiarities took immediate possession of a mind entirely unoccupied, nor did I make any effort to banish them from my thought. From the instant I looked upon these two I felt convinced that, through some strange vagary of fate, we were destined to know more of each other; that our life lines were ordained to touch, and become entangled, somewhere in that mystery of the Western World to which I had been condemned. I cannot analyze this conception, but merely record its presence; the thought took firm possession of me. Under the circumstances I was too far away to overhear conversation. The shuffling of feet, the rattling of chains, the harsh voices of the guard, made it impossible to distinguish any words passing between the two. I could only watch them, quickly assured that I had likewise attracted the girl's attention, and that her gaze occasionally sought mine. Then the guards came to me, and, with my limbs freed of fetters, I was passed down the steep ladder into the semi-darkness between decks, where we were to be confined. The haunting memory of her face accompanied me below, already so clearly defined as to be unforgettable.

It proved a dismal, crowded hole in which we were quartered like so many cattle, it being merely a small space forward, hastily boxed off by rough lumber, the sides and ends built up into tiers of bunks, the only ventilation and light furnished by the open hatch above. The place was clean enough, being newly fitted for the purpose, but was totally devoid of furnishings, the only concession to comfort visible was a handful of fresh straw in each bunk. The men, herded and driven down the ladder, were crowded into the central space, the majority still on their feet, but a few squatting dejectedly on the deck. In the dim twilight of that bare interior their faces scarcely appeared natural, and they conversed in undertones. Most of the fellows were sober and silent, not a bad lot to my judgment, with only here and there a countenance exhibiting viciousness, or a tongue given to ribaldry. I could remember seeing but few of them before, yet as I observed them more closely now, realized that these were not criminals being punished for crime, but men caught, as I had been, and condemned without fair trial, through the lies of paid informers. I could even read in their actions and words the simple stories of their former lives--the farm laborer, the sailor, the store-keeper, now all on one common level of misfortune and misery--condemned alike to exile, to servitude in a strange land, beyond seas.

The ticket given me called by number for a certain berth, and I sought until I found this, throwing within the small bundle I bore, and then finding a chance to sit down on the deck beneath. The last of the bunch of prisoners dribbled down the ladder, each in turn noisily greeted by those already huddled below. I began to recognize the increasing foulness of air, and to distinguish words of conversation from the groups about me. There was but little profanity but some rough horse-play, and a marked effort to pretend indifference. I could make out gray-beards and mere boys mingling together, and occasionally a man in some semblance of uniform. A few bore wounds, and the clothes of several were in rags; all alike exhibited marks of suffering and hardship. The butcher from Harwich, and the white-faced lad who had marched beside me down the wharf, were not to be seen from where I sat, although beyond doubt they were somewhere in the crowd. The hatch was not lowered, and gazing up through the square opening, I obtained glimpse of two soldiers on guard, the sunlight glinting on their guns. Almost immediately there was the sound of tramping feet on the deck above, and the creaking of blocks. Then a sudden movement of the hull told all we were under way. This was recognized by a roar of voices.

CHAPTER II
THE PRISON SHIP

The greater portion of that voyage I would blot entirely from memory if possible. I cannot hope to describe it in any detail---the foul smells, the discomfort, the ceaseless horror of food, the close companionship of men turned into mere animals by suffering and distress, the wearisome days, the black, sleepless nights, the poisonous air, and the brutality of guards. I can never forget these things, for they have scarred my soul, yet surely I need not dwell upon them now, except as they may bear some direct reference to this tale I seek to tell. As such those weeks cannot be wholly ignored, for they form a part of the events to follow--events which might not be clearly understood without their proper picturing.

We were fifty-three days at sea, driven once so far to the southward by a severe storm, which struck us the second day out, as to sight the north coast of Africa before we were able to resume our westward course. To those of us who were tightly shut into those miserable quarters below these facts came only as floating rumors, yet the intense suffering involved was all real enough. For forty-two hours we were battened down in darkness, flung desperately about by every mad plunge of the vessel, stifled by poisoned air and noxious odors, and all that time without a particle of food. If I suffered less than some others it was simply because I was more accustomed to the sea. I was not nauseated by the motion, nor unduly frightened by the wild pitching of the brig. Lying quietly in my berth, braced to prevent being thrown out, amid a darkness so intense as to seem a weight, every sound from the deck above, every lift of the vessel, brought to my mind a sea message, convincing me of two things--that the *Romping Betsy* was a staunch craft, and well handled. Terrific as the gale became I only grew more confident that she would safely weather it.

Yet God knows it was horrible enough even to lie there and listen, to feel the hurling plunges downward, the dizzy upsweeping of the hull; to hear the cries, groans and prayers of frightened men, unseen and helpless in the darkness, the creaking timbers, the resounding blows of the waves against the sides, the horrid retching of the sick, the snarling, angry voices as the struggling mass was flung back and forth, the curses hurled madly into the darkness. They were no longer men, but infuriated brutes, so steeped in agony and fear as to have lost all human instincts. They snarled and snapped like so many beasts, their voices unrecognizable, the stronger treading the weaker to the deck. I could not see, I could only hear, yet I lay there, staring blindly about, conscious of every horror, and so weak and unnerved as to tremble like a child.

Yet the complete knowledge of what had actually occurred in that frightful hole was only revealed when the violence of the storm finally ceased, and the guards above again lifted the hatch. The gray light of dawn faintly illumined the inferno below, and the sweet breath of morning air swept down among us. Then I saw the haggard, uplifted faces, the arms tossed aloft, and heard the wild yell as the stronger charged forward struggling for the foot of the ladder. The place was a foul, reeking shambles, so filthy as to be positively sickening, with motionless bodies stretched here and there along the deck. Sailors and guards fought their way down among us, driving back the unarmed wretches who sought to oppose their progress, while others bore to the deck above those who were too helpless to rise. There were five dead among them, and twice as many more who had lost consciousness. These were all removed first and then, feeling helpless to resist the rush, the others were permitted to clamber up the ladder. Surging out upon the deck, we were hurdled against the lee rail, menaced by leveled guns, and thus finally fed, while the filthy quarters below were hastily cleansed.

It was a dark, lowering morning, the desolate sea still threateningly rough, the heavy clouds hanging low. The ***Romping Betsy*** was hove to, under bare poles, a bit of the jib alone showing, with decks and spars exhibiting evidence of the terrific struggle to keep afloat. I never witnessed wilder pitching on any vessel, but the fresh air brought new life to the wretches about me, and a species of cheerfulness was quickly manifested. Bad as the food was we ate it gladly, nor did the memory of the dead, already laid out on the main deck, long depress us. Why should we mourn for them? We scarcely knew any among them by name, and, facing the uncertainty of our own fate, each man secretly felt that these had possibly found the easier way. Our own misery was now greater than theirs. So we hung on to whatever would help us to keep erect, and ate the food given us like famished animals. Rough and threatening as the surroundings still were, I was seaman enough to realize that the backbone of the storm had broken, and so rejoiced when the skipper ordered sail set. In a few moments the brig was once again headed on a westerly course, and riding the heavy seas much more steadily.

We were permitted to remain on deck scarcely more than an hour, and during that time only a very few passengers made their appearance aft. Although watching eagerly I perceived no flutter of a skirt in the wind, but the Spanish looking man emerged from below, and clung to the rail for several minutes before we were ordered from deck. He spoke with the Captain, pointing and gesticulating, and the few detached words blown to me on the wind were sufficient to convince me that the fellow knew ships and the sea. I had thought him a mere dandy, but now saw in him harder stuff, even getting close enough to learn that he had visited America before, and possessed knowledge of its shores and currents. Ay, and he spoke English well, with never pause for a word, even to terms of seamanship a bit obscure.

The next few days, while uneventful, sufficed to make our discipline complete, obedience being roughly enforced by blows and oaths. At first a spirit of resistance flamed high, but the truly desperate among us were few, and without leadership, while the majority were already thoroughly cowed by months of imprisonment. Left to themselves the more reckless and criminal were soon obliged to yield to force, so that nothing more serious resulted than loud talk and threats. The hatch above remained open, but carefully guarded night and day, while we were permitted on deck for air and exercise only in squads of ten, two hours out of every twenty-four. This alone served to break the dread monotony of the voyage, for while we almost constantly encountered baffling head winds, no other storm of any magnitude obstructed our passage. The brig carried heavy canvas, and the skipper loaded her with all she could bear, but at that she was a slow sailor, dipping so deeply in a seaway as to ship considerable water even in quiet weather. From our exercise on deck we generally returned below drenched to the skin, but glad to even pay that price for two hours of fresh air, and an opportunity to gaze about at sea and sky. There was little else to witness, for in all the long voyage we encountered but one vessel in that desolate ocean, a French armed corvette, fairly bristling with guns, which ran in close enough to hail us, but seemed satisfied to permit us to pass un-visited. I clung to the rail and watched its white sails disappear until they resembled the wings of gulls, feeling more than ever conscious of our helplessness. There were few among the prisoners I had any desire to companion with--only two, as I recall now--a law clerk from Sussex, a rather bright young fellow, but full of strange notions, and an older man, who had seen service in Flanders. We messed together, and pledged mutual friendship in the new land, a pledge not destined to be fulfilled, as I never again saw nor heard of the former after we went ashore, and the last glimpse I had of the older man was as he was being loaded into a cart bound for some interior plantation. God grant they both lived, and became again free men.

How those sodden hours and days dragged! How long were those black nights, in which I lay sleepless, listening to indescribable noises, and breathing the rank, poisonous air. The short time passed on deck was my only solace, and yet even there I found little to interest, except a continuous new hope. We were herded well forward, a rope dividing us from the main deck, which space the passengers aft used as a promenade. Here, between the foremast and the cabin, someone was strolling idly about most of the time, or lounging along the rail out of the sun. In time I came to recognize them all by sight, and learned, in one way or another, something of their characteristics, and purpose in taking this voyage. They were not an unusual lot, the majority planters from the Colonies homeward bound, with occasionally a new emigrant about to try for fortune beyond seas, together with one or two naval officers. There were only three women aboard, a fat dowager, the young lady I had noticed at embarkation, and her colored maid. Many of the days were pleasant, with quiet sea and bright sunshine, and the younger woman must have passed hours on deck during so long and tedious a voyage. Yet it chanced I saw almost nothing of her. I heard her presence on board discussed several times by others of our company, but it somehow chanced that during my time in the open she was usually below. Indeed I gained but one glimpse of the lady in the first two weeks at sea, and then only as we were being ordered down to our quarters for the night. Just as I was approaching the hatch to descend, she appeared from within the cabin, accompanied by the middle-aged planter, and the two advanced toward the rail. The younger gallant, who was standing there alone, saw them the moment they emerged, and hastened forward, bowing low, hat in hand. She barely recognized him, her gaze traveling beyond the fellow toward the disappearing line of prisoners. It was an evening promising storm, with some motion to the sea, and a heavy bank of clouds visible off the port quarter, brightened by flashes of zigzag lightning. The brig rolled dizzily, so the cavalier sought to steady her steps, but she only laughed at the effort, waving him aside, as she moved easily forward. Once with hand on the rail, she ignored his presence entirely, looking first at the threatening cloud, and then permitting her gaze to rest once more upon the line of men descending through the hatch.

It had become my turn to go down, yet in that instant our eyes met fairly, and I instantly knew she saw and recognized me. For a single second our glances clung, as though some mysterious influence held us to each other--then the angry guard struck me with the stock of his piece.

"What er ye standin' thar fer?" he demanded savagely. "Go on down--lively now."

I saw her clasping fingers convulsively grip the rail, and, even at that distance, marked a sudden flame of color in her cheeks. That was all her message to me, yet quite enough. Although we had never spoken, although our names were yet un-known, I was no criminal to her mind, no unrecognized prisoner beneath contempt, but a human being in whom she already felt a personal interest, and to whom she extended thought and sympathy. The blow of the gun-stock bruised my back, yet it was with a smile and a light heart that I descended the ladder, deeply conscious of a friend on board--one totally unable to serve me, perhaps, yet nevertheless a friend. Even in our isolation, guarded in those narrow quarters, much of the ship gossip managed in some way to reach our ears. How it drifted in was often a mystery, yet there was little going on aboard we failed to hear. Much of it came to us through those detailed to serve food, while guards and sailors were not always averse to be-ing talked with. We always knew the ship's course, and I managed to keep in my mind a very dear idea of how the voyage progressed. Not a great deal of this gossip, however, related to the passengers aft, who kept rather exclusively to themselves, nor did I feel inclined to question those who might have the information. I had no wish to reveal my interest to others, and so continued entirely ignorant of the iden-tity of the young woman. She remained in my memory, in my thoughts nameless, a dream rather than a reality. I did learn quite by accident that the gay gallant was a wealthy Spaniard, supposedly of high birth, by name Sanchez, and at one time in the naval service, and likewise ascertained that the rotund planter, so evidently in the party, was a certain Roger Fairfax, of Saint Mary's in Maryland, homeward bound after a successful sale of his tobacco crop in London. It was during his visit to the great city that he had met Sanchez, and his praise of the Colonies had induced the latter to essay a voyage in his company to America. But strange enough no one so much as mentioned the girl in connection with either man.

Thus it was that the **Romping Betsy** drove steadily on her way into the west, either battered by storm, or idly drifting in calm, while life on board became a tiresome routine. The dullness and ill treatment led to trouble below, to dissatisfaction and angry outbreaks of temper. The prisoners grew quarrelsome among themselves, and mutinous toward their guards. I took no part in these affairs, which at one time became serious. Two men were shot dead, and twice afterwards bodies were carried up the ladder at dawn, and silently consigned to the sea. No doubt these tales, more or less exaggerated, traveled aft, and reached the eager ears of the passengers. They began to fear us, and consequently I noticed when on deck the promenade once so popular during the earlier days of the voyage, was almost totally deserted during our hours of recreation. So, with mutiny forward, and fear aft, the lumbering old brig, full of tragedy and hopeless hearts, ploughed steadily onward toward the sunset.

CHAPTER III
DOROTHY FAIRFAX

We were not far from two hundred miles east of the Capes, or at least so one of the mates told me, gruffly answering a question, and it was already growing twilight, the sun having disappeared a half hour before. There was but little air stirring, barely enough to keep the sails taut, while the swell of the sea was sufficient to be uncomfortable, making walking on the deck a task. We were wallowing along amid a waste of waters, the white-crested waves extending in every direction to the far horizons, which were already purpling with the approach of night. I had been closely confined to my bunk for two days with illness, but now, somewhat stronger, had been ordered on deck by the surgeon. The last batch of prisoners, after their short hour of recreation, had been returned to the quarters below, but I was permitted to remain alone undisturbed. I sat there quietly, perched on a coil of rope, with head just high enough to permit an unobstructed view over the side.

The deck aft was almost deserted, the passengers being at supper in the cabin. I could glimpse them through the unshaded windows, seated about a long table, while occasionally the sound of their voices reached me through the open companion-way. The mate was alone on the poop, tramping steadily back and forth, his glance wandering from the sea alongside to the flapping canvas above, but remained silent, as the brig was on her course. Once he clambered down the side ladder, and walked forward, shouting out some order to a group of sailors under the lee of the forecastle. It was on his return that I ventured to question him, and was gruffly answered. Something I said however, gave him knowledge that I was a seaman, and he paused a moment more civilly before resuming his watch, even pointing out what resembled the gleam of a distant sail far away on our starboard quarter. This was such a dim speck against the darkening horizon that I stood up to see better, shadowing my eyes, and forgetful of all else in aroused interest. Undoubtedly it was a sail, although appearing no larger than a gull's wing, and my imagination took me in spirit across the leagues of water. I was still standing there absorbed, unaware even that the mate had departed, when a voice, soft-spoken and feminine, broke the silence.

"May I speak with you?"

I turned instantly, so thoroughly surprised, my voice faltered as I gazed into the upturned face of the questioner. She stood directly beside me, with only the rope barrier stretched between us, her head uncovered, the contour of her face softened by the twilight. Instantly my cap was off, and I was bowing courteously.

"Most certainly," with a quick side glance toward the guard, "but I am a prisoner."

"Of course I know that," in smiling confidence. "Only you see I am rather a privileged character on board. No one expects me to obey rules. Still that does not apply to you, does it?" hesitating slightly. "Perhaps you may be punished if you talk with me--is that what you meant?"

"I am more than willing to assume the risk. Punishment is no new experience to me; besides just now I am on sick leave, and privileged. That accounts for my being still on deck."

"And I chanced to find you here alone. You have been ill?"

"Not seriously, but confined to the berth for a couple of days. And now the doctor prescribes fresh air. This meeting with you, I imagine, may prove even of greater benefit than that."

"With me? Oh, you mean as a relief from loneliness."

"Partly--yes. The voyage has certainly proven lonely enough. I have made few friends forward, and am even bold enough to say that I have longed for a word with you ever since I first saw you aboard."

"Why especially with me?"

"Rather a hard question to answer at the very beginning," I smiled back at her. "Yet not so difficult as the one I shall ask you. Except for a fat matron, and a colored maid, you chance to be the only woman on board. Can you consider it unnatural that I should feel an interest? On the other hand I am only one of fifty prisoners, scarcely cleaner or more reputable looking than any of my mates. Yet surely you have not sought speech with these others?"

"No."

"Then why especially with me?" Even in the growing dusk I could mark a red flush mount into the clear cheeks at this insistent question, and for an instant her eyes wavered. But she possessed the courage of pride, and her hesitancy was short.

"You imagine I cannot answer; indeed that I have no worthy reason," she exclaimed. "Oh, but I have; I know who you are; my uncle pointed you out to me."

"Your uncle--the planter in the gray coat?"

"Yes; I am traveling home with him to Maryland. I am Dorothy Fairfax."

"But even with that explanation I scarcely understand," I insisted rather stubbornly. "You say he pointed me out to you. Really I was not aware that I was a distinguished character of any kind. How did he happen to know me?"

"Because he was present at your trial before Lord Jeffries. He merely chanced to be there when you were first brought up, but became interested in the case, and so returned to hear you sentenced. You are Geoffry Carlyle, in command of the ship that brought Monmouth to England. I heard it all."

"All? What else, pray?"

Her eyes opened widely in sudden surprise and she clasped and unclasped her hands nervously.

"Do you really not know? Have you never been told what happened?"

"Only that I was roughly forbidden to speak, called every foul name the learned Judge could think of, and then sentenced to twenty years penal servitude beyond seas," I answered soberly. "Following that I was dragged from the dock, and flung into a cell. Was there anything else?"

"Why you should have known. Lord Jeffries sentenced you to death; the decree was signed, to be executed immediately. Then influence was brought to bear--some nobleman in Northumberland made direct appeal to the King. That was what angered Jeffries so."

"An appeal! For me? Good God! not Bucclough--was it he, the Duke?"

"Yes; it was whispered about that the King was in his debt--some word of honor, and dare not refuse. The word of mercy came just in time, ordering Jeffries to commute your sentence. At first he swore he'd hang you, King or no King, but his nerve failed. My uncle said he roared like a bull. This Bucclough; is he not your friend?"

I hesitated for an instant of indecision, looking into her face, but the truth would not be denied.

"Scarcely that," I said soberly. "Nor can I solve entirely his purpose. He is my brother, and I am the next in line. We are not even on speaking terms; yet he is childless, and may feel some measure of dislike to have the family end in a hangman's knot. I can think of no other reason for his interference. I knew nothing of his action."

"I am glad it became my privilege to tell you. Besides, Captain Carlyle," simply, "it may also help you to understand my interest. If you are of the Carlyles of Bucclough, how happened it that you went to sea?"

"Largely necessity, and to some extent no doubt sheer love of adventure. I was a younger son, with very little income. There were then two lives between me and the estate, and the old Duke, my father, treated me like a servant. I always loved the sea, and at fourteen--to get me out of his sight, I think largely--was apprenticed to the navy, but lost my grade in the service by a mere boyish prank. His influence then would have saved me, but he refused to even read my letter of explanation. I dare not return home in such disgrace, and consequently drifted into the merchant service. It is a story quickly told."

"Yet not so quickly lived."

"No, it meant many hard years, on all the oceans of the world. This is the first message reaching me from the old home."

"I have seen that home," she said quietly, "and shall never forget the impression it made on me. A beautiful place. I was there on a coaching party, the first summer I was in England. I was a mere girl then, and everything seemed wonderful. I have been away from Maryland now for three years."

"At school?"

"Of course; nothing else would satisfy father. Maryland is only a Colony, you know."

"Yes, I understand. A great many over there send back their sons and daughters to be educated. Your home is at Saint Mary's?"

"Lower down the Potomac. Have you ever been there?"

"Twice; once as mate, and the last time as master of a ship. My latest voyage in these waters was made nearly two years ago."

She was silent for several moments, her face turned away from me, her eyes gazing out across the waste of waters which were already growing dark. Her clear-cut profile against the yellow light of the cabin windows appeared most attractive.

"It is not so strange then, is it, that I should have felt interested in you?" she asked suddenly, as though justifying herself. "When Uncle Roger first told me who you were, and then explained what had occurred at your trial, naturally you became to me something entirely different from the others."

"Certainly I am not inclined to condemn."

"I never once thought of speaking to you--truly I did not," she went on simply. "But when I saw you sitting here all alone, the impulse came suddenly to tell you how sorry I was. You see," and she paused doubtfully, "girls brought up in the Colonies, as I have been, are--are not quite so careful about whom they talk with as in England--you know what I mean; we always have indentured servants, and become accustomed to them. It--it is quite different out there."

I laughed, thinking only to relieve her embarrassment.

"Believe me, Miss Dorothy, there is no thought in my mind that you have done wrong," I insisted swiftly. "That would be very ungrateful, for you have brought me new heart and hope."

"Then I am not sorry. Were you actually with Monmouth?"

"In sympathy, yes; but I had no hand in the actual fighting. I was not even ashore until it was all over with. Still I shall pay my share of the bill."

"And you know what that means, do you not? What will happen when we reach Virginia?"

"Perfectly; I have no illusions. I have seen just such ships as this come in. We are to be advertised, and sold to the highest bidder. A week from now I shall probably be out in the tobacco fields, under the whip of an overseer, who will call me Jeff. All I can hope for is a kind-hearted master, and an early opportunity to escape."

"Oh, no!" and in her eagerness her hands actually clasped mine, where they clung to the rope between us. "It is not going to be quite so bad as that. That is what I wanted to tell you. That is what gave me boldness to come across here to you to-night. It has all been arranged."

"Arranged?"

"Yes--everything. You are not going to be sold on the block with those others. Uncle Roger has already contracted with the Captain for your services. You are going north with us to Maryland."

I stared through the dusk into her animated face, scarcely comprehending.

"Do you not understand, yet?" she asked. "The Captain of this brig is the agent; he represents the government, and is obliged to find places for the prisoners."

"Yes; I know that. We are billed like so much livestock; he must account for every head."

"Well, Uncle Roger went to him yesterday, and made a bid for you. Finally they came to terms. That is one reason why you are left alone here on deck tonight. The officers are no longer responsible for you--you are already indentured."

I drew a deep breath, and in the sudden impulse of relief which swept over me, my own fingers closed tightly about her hands.

"You tell me I am to accompany your party up the Chesapeake?"

"Yes."

"I owe this to you; I am sure I must owe this to you--tell me?"

Her eyes drooped, and in the dim light I could mark the heaving of her bosom, as she caught her breath.

"Only--only the suggestion," she managed to say in a whisper. "He--he was glad of that. You see I--I knew he needed someone to take charge of his sloop, and--and so I brought you to his mind. We--we both thought you would be just the one, and--and he went right away to see the Captain. So please don't thank me."

"I shall never cease to thank you," I returned warmly, conscious suddenly that I was holding her hands, and as instantly releasing them. "Why, do you begin to understand what this actually means to me? It means the retention of manhood, of self-respect. It will save me the degradation which I dreaded most of all--the toiling in the fields beside negro slaves, and the sting of the lash. Ay, it means even more--"

I hesitated, instantly realizing that I must not utter those impetuous words leaping to my lips.

"More!" she exclaimed. "What more?"

"This," I went on, my thought shifting into a new channel. "A longer servitude. Up to this moment my one dream has been to escape, but I must give that up now. You have placed me under obligations to serve."

"You mean you feel personally bound?" "Yes; not quite so much to your uncle, perhaps, as to yourself. But between us this has become a debt of honor."

"But wait," she said earnestly "for I had even thought of that. I was sure you would feel that way--any gentleman would. Still there is a way out. You were sentenced as an indentured servant."

"I suppose so."

"It is true; you were so entered on the books of this ship. Uncle Roger had to be sure of all this before he paid his money, and I saw the entry myself. It read: 'Geoffry Carlyle, Master Mariner, indentured to the Colonies for the term of twenty years, unless sooner released; crime high treason.' Surely you must know the meaning of those words?"

"Servitude for twenty years."

"'Unless sooner released.'"

"That means pardoned; there is no hope of that."

"Perhaps not, but that is not all it means. Any indentured man, under our

Maryland laws, can buy his freedom, after serving a certain proportion of his sentence. I think it is true in any of the Colonies. Did you not know that?"

I did know it, yet somehow had never connected the fact before directly with my own case. I had been sentenced to twenty years--twenty years of a living death--and that alone remained impressed on my mind. I could still see Black Jeffries sitting on the bench, glaring down at me in unconcealed anger, his eyes blazing with the fury of impotent hate, as he roared, that, by decree of the King, my sentence to be hung was commuted to twenty years of penal servitude beyond seas. It had never even seemed an act of mercy to me. But now it did, as the full truth suddenly came home, that I could buy my freedom. God! what a relief; I stood up straight once more in the stature of a man. I hardly know what wild words I might have spoken had the opportunity been mine; but at that instant the figure of a man crossed the deck toward us, emerging from the open cabin door. Against the gleam of yellow light I recognized the trim form advancing, and as instantly stepped back into shadow. My quick movement caused her to turn, and face him.

"What!" he exclaimed, and evidently surprised at his discovery. "It is indeed Mistress Dorothy--out here alone? 'Twas my thought you were safely in your cabin long since. But--prithee--I mistake; you are not alone."

He paused, slightly irresolute, staring forward beyond her at my dimmer outline, quite uncertain who I might be, yet already suspicious.

"I was preparing to go in," she answered, ignoring his latter words. "The night already looks stormy."

"But your friend?"

The tone in which he spoke was insistent, almost insolent in its demand, and she hesitated no longer in meeting the challenge.

"Your pardon, I am sure--Lieutenant Sanchez, this gentleman is Captain Geoffry Carlyle."

He stood there stiff and straight against the background of light, one hand in affected carelessness caressing the end of a waxed moustache. His face was in shadow, yet I was quite aware of the flash of his eyes.

"Ah, indeed--some passenger I have not chanced to observe before?"

"A prisoner," she returned distinctly. "You may perhaps remember my uncle pointed him out to us when he first came aboard."

"And you have been out here alone, talking with the fellow?"

"Certainly--why not?"

"Why, the man is a felon, convicted of crime, sentenced to deportation."

"It is not necessary that we discuss this, sir," she interposed, rather proudly, "as my personal conduct is not a matter for your criticism. I shall retire now. No; thank you, you need not come."

He stopped still, staring blankly after her as she vanished; then wheeled about to vent his anger on me.

"Carlyle, hey!" he exclaimed sneeringly. "A familiar sound that name in my ears. One of the brood out of Bucclough?"

"A cadet of that line," I managed to admit, wonderingly. "You know of them?"

"Quite as much as I care to," his tone ugly and insulting. Then an idea suddenly occurred to his mind. "Saint Guise, but that would even up the score nicely. You are, as I understand it, sent to Virginia for sale?"

"Yes."

"For how long a term?"

"The sentence was twenty years."

"Hela! and you go to the highest bidder. I'll do it, fellow! To actually own a Carlyle of Bucclough will be a sweet revenge."

"You mean," I asked, dimly grasping his purpose, "that you propose buying me when we reach shore?"

"Why not? A most excellent plan; and I owe it all to a brat I met in London. Egad! it will be some joke to tell when next I visit England. 'Twill count for more than were I to tweak the Duke's nose."

I stopped his laughter, smiling myself grimly in the darkness.

"A very noble plan for revenge," I admitted, enjoying the swift check-mating of his game. "And one which I am not likely to forget. Unfortunately you come too late. It happens, Senor, that I am already safely indentured to Roger Fairfax."

"To Fairfax? She told you that?"

"Who told me can make no difference. At least I am out of your hands."

I turned away, but he called angrily after me:

"Do not feel so sure of that, Carlyle! I am in the game yet."

I made no answer, already despising the fellow so thoroughly as to ignore his threat. He still stood there, a mere shadow, as I disappeared down the ladder, and I could imagine the expression on his face.

CHAPTER IV
THE SHORES OF VIRGINIA

I rested quietly in my berth for a long time, staring blankly up at the dark deck above, unable to sleep, and endeavoring to figure out the true meaning of all these occurrences. It began to rain, torrents sweeping the planks overhead, while vivid flashes of lightning illumined the open hatch, before it could be hastily closed, revealing the squalidness of the interior in which we were quartered. Then someone, growling and stumbling through the darkness, lit a slush lantern, dangling from a blackened beam, its faint flicker barely discernible. The hole became foul and sickening, men tossing and groaning in their uneasy sleep, or prowling about seeking some measure of comfort. There was no severe wind accompanying the storm, and the flurry of rain soon swept by, leaving an ugly swell behind, but enabling the guard to again uplift the hatches.

Immersed as I was in thought, all this left but small impress on me. I felt that I could understand the interest exhibited by Dorothy Fairfax, and, greatly as I already admired her, I was not egotist enough to even imagine that her effort to serve me had basis in any personal attraction. My connection with Bucclough, coupled with her uncle's report of my conviction, had very naturally aroused the girl's sympathy in my behalf. She felt a desire to lighten my sorrows as much as possible, and, under the existing circumstances, had found it comparatively easy to persuade the good-natured planter to acquiesce in her suggestion. In all probability he really had need of my services, and was therefore glad enough of this opportunity to secure them. This part of the affair I could dismiss without giving anyone undue credit, although I deeply appreciated the kindness of heart which had led her to interpose, and which later led her to tell me so quickly what had occurred. Her purpose, however, was fairly clear.

But what about Lieutenant Sanchez? Why was this unknown Spaniard already so openly my enemy? There was no doubting his position, and there surely must be some reason for it outside of anything which had occurred on board the ***Romping Betsy***. His words had given me some inkling of the cause--a past quarrel with the Duke of Bucclough, in England, in which he must have been worsted, and which had left in his mind a lurking desire for revenge. He dreamed of striking his enemy through me, because of relationship, a cowardly blow. Yet this, by itself alone, was scarcely a reason why he should have thus sought me out for a victim. No sane man would deliberately visit the sins of my brother on me. Nor had this been deliberate; it was the mere outburst of sudden passion, arising through my intercourse with the young woman. Otherwise it might never have occurred to him. So there was seemingly but one answer--Sanchez used this merely as an excuse for the conceal-ment of his real object. What could that object be? Could it be Dorothy Fairfax? I was a long while in actually convincing myself of this probability, and yet no other satisfactory explanation offered itself. She had exhibited an interest in me from the very first, and he had endeavored to win her attention elsewhere. Even that day when we first came aboard in chains, he had plainly evinced this desire, and, since then, the girl had never appeared on deck, without his immediately seeking her company. I felt finally that I had the clue--jealousy, the mad, unreasoning jealousy of his race. He fiercely resented her slightest interest in anyone--even a prisoner--as against his own attractions. He was incapable of appreciating friendly sympathy, and already held me a dangerous rival. Then, possibly, it had not been a mere idle desire to visit the Colonies, which had originally led to his prompt acceptance of Roger Fairfax's invitation to make one of their party; the real attraction was the charms of Dorothy--her girlish beauty, coupled, no doubt, with her father's wealth. The fellow was in love, impetuously in love, resenting blindly the slightest advance of any other.

The thought rather pleased me, largely because of its absurdity. It was, in my case at least, so utterly false, and unjustifiable. To the ordinary mind, indeed, any such connection would be practically unthinkable. Even had I been wild enough to dream of such a thing, the gulf existing between myself and Dorothy Fairfax was far too deep and wide ever to be spanned. I had before me twenty years of servi-tude, and an unknown future; nor could I even conceive the possibility of any such thought ever entering her mind. The very opposite was what gave her courage to serve me. I had no false conception as to this; no vagrant thought that her interest in me was any more than a passing fancy, born of sympathy, and a desire to aid. Nevertheless, as she had thus already served me, I now owed her service in return, and here was the first call. If conditions made it possible it was my plain duty to place myself between these two. I felt no hatred toward the man, no desire to do him a personal injury; but I did dislike and distrust him. This feeling was instinctive, and without the slightest reference to his seeking intimacy with the girl. From the first moment I had looked upon his face there had been antagonism between us, a feeling of enmity. Whether this arose from his appearance, or actions, I could not determine--but the fellow was not my kind.

In the intensity of my feelings I must have unconsciously spoken aloud, for a shaggy head suddenly popped out from the berth beneath where I lay, and an interested voice asked solicitously:

"Hy, thar; whut's up, mate? Sick agin?"

"No," I answered, grinning rather guiltily, "just thinking, and letting loose a bit. Did I disturb you?"

"Well, I reckon I wa'n't exactly asleep," he acknowledged, without withdrawing his head. "Ye wus mutterin' 'way thar an' not disturbin' me none, till ye got ter talkin' 'bout sum feller called Sanchez. Then I sorter got a bit interested. I know'd thet cuss onct," and he spat, as though to thus better express his feelings. "The damned ornary pirate."

I laughed, my whole mental mood changed by this remark.

"It is not very likely we have the same party in mind, Haley. You see Sanchez is a decidedly common name among Spaniards. I've known two or three of that name myself. You were not referring to anyone on board, were you?"

"I sure hope not," he scratched his head, staring up at me through the dim light, wakefulness encouraging him to talk. "They tell me ye are a sea-farin' man. Well, I wus a Deal fisher, but hev made a half dozen deep-sea v'y'ges. Thet's how I hed the damn luck ter meet up with this Sanchez I was a speakin' 'bout. He's the only one ever I know'd. I met up with him off the isle o' Cuba. Likely 'nough ye know the devil I mean?"

The question served to center my memory suddenly on a dim remembrance of the past.

"No, unless you refer to 'Black Sanchez.' I 've heard of him; were you ever in his hands?"

"Wus I!" he laughed grimly. "I hed eight months of it, mate, and a greater demon never sailed. The things I saw done ye 'd never believe no human bein' could do. If ever thar wus two people in one skin, sir, it's thet Black Sanchez. When he's playin' off fer good he's as soft an' sweet as a dandy in Picadilly, an' when he's real he's like a devil in hell."

"Was you a prisoner--or did you sail under him?"

"Both, fer the matter o' thet. He give me the choice ter serve, er walk the plank. I wus eighteen, an' hed an ol' mother at Deal."

"I see; but later you got away?"

"Ay, I did thet," chuckling over the recollection. "But I hed ter wait eight months fer the luck. Hev ye ever been sea-farin' down in them waters, off the West Indies?"

"No."

"Well, they're all studded over with little islands--cays, they call 'em down thare; an' it's in among them thet the buccaneers hide away, an' sorter rest up after a cruise. Thar's a lot o' 'em too; whole villages hid away on some o' them cays, with women an' children--every color ye ever saw. Sanchez he made his headquarters on a cay called Porto Grande. He hed three ships, an' maybe a hundred an' fifty men 'bout the time I got away. The last I saw o' him wus at sea. He'd overhauled an English ship, an' sunk her; an' then the next mornin' we took a Dutch bark in ballast. She wus such a trig sailor Sanchez decided to keep her afloat, an' sent a prize crew aboard ter sail her inter Porto Grande. I wus one o' the fellers picked fer thet job, an' we wus told off under a nigger mate, named LaGrasse--he wus a French nigger from Martinique, and a big devil--an' our orders wus ter meet Sanchez three days later. His vessel wus a three-masted schooner, the fastest thing ever I saw afloat, called the ***Vengeance***, an' by that time she wus chock up with loot. Still at that she could sail 'bout three feet to our one. Afore night come we wus out o' sight astern. Thar wus eight o' us in the crew, beside the nigger, an' we had twelve Dutchmen under hatches below. I sorter looked 'round, an' sized up four o' that crew ter be good honest sailormen, who'd been shanghied same as I wus. So, long about midnight, I 'd got ter talk with all these fellers, an' when LaGrasse went down below ter take a snooze in the cabin, we hoisted them Dutchmen on deck, flung a couple o' hell-hounds overboard, an' just naturally took control. The mate wus a dead nigger afore he ever knew whut wus up. When daylight come we wus streakin' it eastward by compass, an' every damn sail set. Thet wus the easiest part of it. Them Dutchmen could n't talk nuthin' but their own lingo; an' thar wa'n't a navigator aboard, fer Sanchez hed kept all the offercers with him, an' the end wus about a week later, when we piled up against an island off the African coast, an' only one boat load of us got ashore. Thet's whut I know about Sanchez."

"I had a shipmate once," I observed, interested in his story, "who claimed to have seen the fellow; he described him as being a very large man, with intensely black hawklike eyes, and a heavy black beard almost hiding his face."

Haley laughed.

"Maybe he looked like that when he saw him, but he ain't no bigger man than I am; he won't weigh as much by fifteen pound. Fact is he mighty seldom looks the same, fer thet's part o' his game. Them whiskers is false, an' so is the saller look to his face. I 've seen him in all sorts o' disguises. It's only his eyes he can't hide, an' thar's been times when I thought they wus the ugliest eyes ever I saw. He's sure an ornary devil, an' when he gits mad, I'd rather be afront of a tiger. Besides fightin's his trade, an' no weaklin' ain't goin' ter control the sort o' chaps he's got ter handle. Most of 'em would murder him in a minute if they dared. Oh, he's bad all right, but yer wouldn't exactly think so, just ter look at him, I've run up agin a lot o' differ-ent men in my time, thet I 'd naturally sheer off from a blame sight quicker than I would from him."

"You mean that when he is not in disguise he does not appear dangerous. What then does he really look like?"

Haley spat again onto the deck, and scratched his shock of hair as though thus to stimulate his memory.

"Oh, a sorter swash-bucklin' Spanish don--the kind whut likes ter dress up, an' play the dandy. He's got a pink an' white complexion, the Castilian kind yer know, an' wears a little moustache, waxed up at the ends. He's about two inches taller than I am, with no extra flesh, but with a hell of a grip in his hands. As I said afore, if it wa'n't fer his eyes nobody'd ever look at him twice. All his devilishness shows thar, an' I've seen 'em laugh like he didn't have a care on earth."

"How old a man is he?"

"How old is the devil? I heard he wus about forty-five; I reckon he must be thet, but he don't look older than thirty. He ain't the kind yer can guess at."

We talked together for quite a while longer, our conversation gradually drifting to the recounting of various sea adventures, and my thoughts did not again recur to Sanchez until after I rested back once more in my berth, endeavoring to fall asleep. Haley must have dropped off immediately, for I could distinguish his heavy breathing among the others; but my mind continued to wander, until it conjured up once again this West India pirate. His name, and the story of his exploits, had been familiar to me ever since I first went to sea. While only one among many operating in those haunted waters, his resourcefulness, daring and cruelty had won him an infamous reputation, a name of horror. In those days, when the curse of piracy made the sea a terror, no ordinary man could ever have succeeded in attaining such supremacy in crime. No doubt much that had been reported was either false, or exaggerated, yet there flashed across my memory numberless tales of rapine, outrage and cold-blooded cruelty in which this demon of the sea had figured, causing me to shudder at the recollection. To my mind he had long been a fiend incarnate, his name a horror on the lips. Black Sanchez--and Haley pictured him as a dandified, ordinary appearing individual, with white and red complexion, a small moustache, and flashing dark eyes--a mere Spanish gallant, without special distinction. Why, that description, strangely enough, fitted almost exactly this fellow on board, this other Sanchez. I leaned over the edge of my bunk, and looked down on Haley, half resolved to ask if he had ever noticed this lieutenant, but the man was already sound asleep. The suspicion which had crept into my mind was so absurd, so unspeakably silly and impossible, that I laughed at myself, and dismissed the crazy thought. What, that fellow Black Sanchez! Bah, no! He had been at sea, of course; there was no denying that fact, for he knew ships, and spoke the lingo of blue water; but the very idea that that blood-stained buccaneer, whose hated name was on the lips of every sea-faring man of Britain, would ever dare openly to visit England, and then sail under his own name on board an English vessel for Virginia, was too preposterous for consideration. Why, it would be sheer madness. The knowledge that such a possibility ever had flashed into my mind became amusing, and chuckling over it, I finally fell asleep.

It was noon, the sky overcast, the wind blowing strong from the southeast, when the Virginia coast was first sighted from our mast-head. An hour later it became plainly visible from the deck below, and the prisoners were routed out from their quarters, and the shackles, removed from limbs when we first arrived on board, were again riveted in place, binding them together in fours, preparatory to landing. I, with one or two others, already disposed of, and in control of masters, were spared this indignity, and permitted to move about as we pleased within the narrow deck space reserved for our use. The last meal was served in the open, the men squatting on the deck planks, endeavoring to jest among themselves, and assuming a cheerfulness they were very far from feeling. The long hardships of the voyage had left indelible marks on the majority, and they were by now a woebegone, miserable lot, who had largely abandoned themselves to despair.

The Monmouth campaign had been brief, but no less disastrous to the men engaged in it. Those who survived the one battle, wounded and fugitive, had been hunted down remorselessly like so many wild beasts. Escape from the pursuit of soldiers was almost impossible, and they had been brutally beaten and bruised by infuriated captors; and then, uncared for, nor shown the slightest mercy, had been thrust into loathsome gaols to helplessly await trial, and a certain conviction. No pen could adequately describe the suffering and horror of those months of waiting, while the unfortunate victims lived in crowded, dirty cells, subjected to every conceivable indignity and insult from brutal guards, half starved, and breathing foul, fetid air--the breath of sickness, the stench of unclean wounds. Dragged forth at last, one by one, into a court organized for condemnation, presided over by a foul-mouthed brute, whose every word was insult, denied all opportunity for defense, they had later been shackled together as felons, and driven aboard ship like so many head of cattle. Herded below deck, tossed about for weeks on a stormy sea, uncared for, and half starved, scarcely realizing their destination, or knowing their fate, seeing their dead dragged out from their midst with each dawn, and flung carelessly overboard, cursed at and struck by their guards, they now dragged their aching bodies about in half dead despair, the chains clanking to every movement of the limbs, their dull, lackluster eyes scarcely discerning the darkening line of coast toward which the **_Romping Betsy_** steered.

With what depth of pity I looked at them, my glance gladly straying from their downcast faces toward the group of passengers gathered eagerly along the poop rail to welcome joyfully the approach of land. These were all animation, excitement, talking eagerly to each other, and pointing out familiar headlands as they emerged through the thin mists. Their thoughts were all centered on home, or the promises of this new land they were approaching, and so deeply interested that scarcely an eye turned toward those miserable wretches grouped on the forward deck, being borne into slavery and disgrace. It was a contrast between hope and despair. As these passengers moved restlessly back and forth, from rail to rail, I easily recognized among them every face grown familiar to me during the course of the voyage, excepting the two I most eagerly sought; and became convinced that neither Roger Fairfax nor his niece had yet come upon deck. Sanchez was there, however, standing alone and silent, seldom lifting his eyes to the changing view ahead, but apparently buried in his own thoughts. Once our glances accidentally met, and I could but observe the sudden change in the man's expression--a change sinister and full of threat. Whatever the original cause might be, his personal feeling toward me was undoubtedly bitter and unforgiving, and he possessed no wish to disguise it. The new life in the new world had already brought me both friend and enemy before I had as yet touched foot on land.

CHAPTER V
THE WATERS OF THE CHESAPEAKE

The brig, with all sails set, and favored by a strong wind, drew rapidly in toward the point of landing. The great majority of the prisoners remained on deck, chained together and helpless, yet surrounded by armed guards, while the few who had already been purchased by passengers, humbly followed their new masters ashore the moment the gang-plank touched the soil of Virginia. There were five of us altogether thus favored, but I was the only one owing allegiance to Roger Fairfax. The rude landing wharf along which we lay was already densely crowded with men, their appearance and dress largely proclaiming them to be planters from the interior, either gathered to inspect the consignment of prisoners, or eager to purchase at low prices the stores hidden away in the vessel's hold. Some among the concourse, however, were undoubtedly present to welcome friends and relatives among the passengers. Altogether it was a bustling scene, full of change and color, the air noisy with shouting voices, the line of wharves filled with a number of vessels, either newly arrived, or preparing to depart. Servants both white and colored were busily at work, under the command of overseers, loading and unloading cargoes, while the high bank beyond was crowded with vehicles of various kinds. News of the arrival of the **Romping Betsy** had evidently spread widely, together with the rumor that she brought a number of prisoners to be auctioned off. It was a good-natured, restless crowd, especially anxious for any news from abroad, and eager to benefit from the sale. The majority of the men I judged to be landowners, hearty, whole-some looking fellows, whose lives were passed out-of-doors, dressed in their best in honor of the occasion. The prevailing fashion was a broad-leafed, felt hat with one side looped up to the crown by a brilliant metal button, a velvet coat with long, voluminous skirts, wide sleeves, metallic buttons as large as a Spanish dollar, short breeches, and long stockings with gold or silver knee and shoe buckles. Many wore swords, while those who did not bore about with them enormous gold or silver-headed canes. The smoking of pipes was common, and thoughtless profanity was to be heard on all sides as an ordinary part of speech. It was with no small difficulty we succeeded in forcing our way through this jostling throng until we attained to an open space ashore.

I followed closely behind the three composing our party, Roger Fairfax, and Sanchez, with the laughing girl between them for protection, pressing a passage forward. Even had I not been laden with packages my general appearance and dress would doubtless have proclaimed my position, and aroused passing interest. I heard voices calling attention to me, while curious eyes stared into my face. Fairfax was evidently well known to a number present, for he was being greeted on all sides with hearty hand-shakes, and words of welcome.

"Ah, back again, Roger; and what fortune in London?" "A fair price for the crop?"

"Is the lad trailing behind ye one o' Monmouth's men?"

"Any news, friend, in Parliament? What is the latest on the tax?"

"And pray who is this damsel, Roger; not Hugh Fairfax's girl? Ay, quite the woman now."

"Your men? They're over there, across the road. Of course I know; did I not come from the dock with them?"

There were two of them, both negroes, but one, addressed by Fairfax as Sam, was much the lighter in color, and far more intelligent of face. A few words of instruction dispatched these back to the **Romping Betsy** for the luggage yet remaining on board, while our own party continued to advance along the water front toward where Sam had designated the Fairfax boat would be found awaiting us, fully prepared to depart up the Chesapeake. When finally attained this vessel proved to be a goodly sized sloop, of a type familiar to those waters, containing a comfortable small cabin forward, a staunch, broad-beamed craft, but with lines indicating sailing qualities, while requiring only a small crew. Several similar vessels--doubtless owned and operated by planters residing along the shore of the Bay--were anchored in the basin, or fastened at the dock, but the **Adele** had been warped in against the bank, which at this point was high enough to enable us easily to step aboard over the low rail. A dingy looking white man, quite evidently from his appearance an indentured servant, was in charge, He greeted us rather surlily, staring at me with almost open hostility, yet responded swiftly enough to Fairfax's orders.

"Here, Carr, stow these packages away. Yes, you better help with them, Carlyle. The other bags will be along directly--Sam and John have gone after them. Put these forward, under cover. Has everything been seen to, so we can start at once?"

"Ay, ay, sorr," was the gruff response, in a strong Irish brogue. "Lord knows we've hid toime enough, fer we've bin waitin' here fer yer a wake, er more. It's a month since the lether came."

"We have had a slow voyage, Carr. So all I ordered is aboard?"

"She's full oop ter the hatches; bedad I hope thar ain't no more."

"Good; we ought to get as far as Travers' by dark then. Hurry along, and stow that stuff away; here come the others now."

The three found comfortable seats along the opposite rail, and sat there watching us hastily bring aboard the various articles which the two negroes, assisted by a boy and a cart, had transported from the brig. I worked along with the others, under the orders of Sam, who seemed to be in charge, already feeling somewhat deeply the humiliation of my position, but nevertheless realizing the necessity of prompt obedience. The knowledge that I was now a slave, on a level with these others, compelled to perform menial labor under the very eyes of Dorothy Fairfax and that sneering Spaniard, cut my pride to the quick. In my trips back and forth I kept my eyes averted, never once venturing to glance toward them, until this work had been accomplished. But when we stood idle, while Sam went aft for instructions, I had recovered sufficient nerve to turn my eyes in that direction, only to observe that the young woman sat with head turned away, gazing out over the rail at the shore, her chin cupped in her hands, her thoughts apparently far away. Strange as it may seem her obvious indifference hurt me oddly, my only comprehension being that she did not in the least care; that in fact she had already entirely dismissed me from her mind. This supposition, whether true or false, instantly hardened me to my fate, and I stared at Sanchez, meeting his eyes fairly, at once angered by the sneer on his lips and the open insult of his manner. He turned toward her, fingering a cheroot, and said something; but, though she answered, her head remained motionless, her eyes searching the shore indifferently. A figure or two appeared along the summit of the bank, voices calling to Fairfax, who stood up as he replied, ending the conversation with a wave of the hand to Sam, who had taken position at the wheel. The latter began shouting orders in a shrill voice. Carr cast off, and, with the negro and myself at the halliards, the mainsail rose to the caps, while we began gliding out from the shore into the deeper water. By the time we had hoisted the jib, and made all secure, we were out far enough to feel the full force of the stiff breeze, the *Adele* careening until her rail was awash, the white canvas soaring above us against the misty blue of the sky.

There was little to be done after the ropes had been coiled away, and we were fairly out into the broader reaches of the Bay. The wind held steady, requiring no shifting of canvas, so Sam, having dispatched the negro below to prepare lunch, and stationed Carr forward as lookout, called me aft to the wheel. He was a rather pleasant-faced fellow, yellow as saffron, with rings in his ears, and a wide mouth perpetually grinning.

"Massa Fairfax he say you real sailorman," he began, looking me over carefully, with a nod of his head toward the group at the rail. "Dat so?"

"Yes; I have been a number of years at sea."

"Dat what he say; dat he done bought yer fer dat reason mostly. Ah reckon den ye kin steer dis boat?"

"I certainly can."

"So? Den Ah's sure goin' fer ter let yer try right now. Yer take hol', while Ah stand by a bit."

I took his place, grasping the spokes firmly, and he stood aside, watching every movement closely, as I held the speeding sloop steadily up to the wind, the spray pouring in over the dipping rail forward. The grin on his lips broadened.

"What is the course?" I asked curiously.

"'Cross ter dat point yonder--see, whar de lone tree stan's; we done 'round dat 'bout tree hunder' yards out, an' then go straight 'way north."

"You use no chart?"

He burst into a guffaw, as though the question was a rare joke.

"No, sah; I nebber done saw one."

"But surely you must steer by compass?"

"Dar is a little one somewhar on board, and Ah done ain't seed it fer mor 'n a yare, Ah reckon. 'Tain't no use enyhow. Whut we steer by is landmarks. Ah sure does know de Chesapeake. Yer ever bin up de Bay?"

"Yes, twice, but out in the deep water. I suppose you hug along the west shore. How is the sloop--pretty heavily loaded?"

He nodded, still grinning cheerfully over the ease with which I manipulated the wheel.

"Chuck full ter de water line; we've done been shovin' things inter dat hold fer a week past, but she's sure a good sailor. Whut wus it Massa Roger say yer name wus?"

"Carlyle."

"So he did; don't ever recollect hearin' dat name afore. Ye's one of dem rebels ober in England?"

"I got mixed up in the affair."

"An' whut dey done give yer?"

"My sentence, you mean--twenty years."

"Lordy! dat's sure tough. Well, I reckon yer done know yer job all right, so I'll just leave yer here awhile, an' go forrard an' git a snack. Ain't eat nuthin' fer quite a spell. Ah'll be back afore yer 'round de point yonder."

I was alone at the wheel, the sloop in my control, and somehow as I stood there, grasping those spokes, the swift boat leaping forward through the water, leaning recklessly over before the force of the wind, the numbing sense of helpless servitude left me in a new return of manhood and responsibility. It was a scene of exhilaration, the sun, still partially obscured by misty clouds already well down in the western sky, with the tossing waves of the Bay foam-crested. The distant headlands appeared spectral and gray through the vapor, while the waters beyond took on the tint of purple shadows. The *Adele* responded to the helm gallantly, the spreading canvas above standing out like a board, a broad wake of white foam spreading far astern. Not another sail appeared across that troubled surface of waters, not even a fisherman's boat, the only other vessel visible along our course being a dim outline close in against that far-away headland toward which I had been instructed to steer. I stared at this indistinct object, at first believing it a wreck, but finally distinguishing the bare masts of a medium-sized bark, evidently riding at anchor only a few hundred yards off shore.

Satisfied as to this, my glance shifted to our own decks, feeling a seaman's admiration for the cleanliness of the little vessel, and the shipshape condition of everything aboard. The decks had more the appearance of a pleasure yacht, than that of a cargo carrier, although the broad beam, and commodious hatches bespoke ample storage room below. Apparently all this hold space had been reserved for the transportation of goods, the passenger quarters being forward, with the cook's galley at the foot of the mast. Where the crew slept I was unable to discern, but they were few in number, and as Sam had disappeared up a short ladder, and then across the roof of the cabin, it was highly probable there would be a compact forecastle nestled between the bows. The blacker negro was busily engaged in the galley, his figure occasionally visible at the open door, and a column of black smoke poured out through the tin funnel. The deck planks were scrubbed white, and the handrails had been polished until they shone.

The three passengers still remained seated together, the men conversing, and occasionally pointing forth at some object across the water, but, while I watched the little group, the girl made no movement, nor attempt at speech. None of them even so much as glanced toward me, and I felt that, already, I had been dismissed from their thought, had been relegated to my proper position, had sunken to my future place as a mere servant. Finally Mistress Dorothy arose to her feet, and, with a brief word of explanation to her uncle, started forward in the direction of the cabin. A sudden leap of the boat caused her to clutch the rail, and instantly Sanchez was at her side, proffering assistance. They crossed the dancing deck together, his hand upon her arm, and paused for a moment at the door to exchange a few sentences. When the Spaniard came back he pointed out to Fairfax the position of the still distant bark, which however was by this time plainly revealed off our port quarter. The planter stood up in order to see better, and then the two crossed the deck to a position only a few yards from where I stood at the wheel, and remained there, staring out across the intervening water.

"Surely a strange place in which to anchor, Lieutenant," said Fairfax at last, breaking the silence, his hand shading his eyes. "Bark rigged, and very heavily sparred. Seems to be all right. What do you make of the vessel?"

The Spaniard twisted his moustache, but exhibited little interest, although his gaze was upon the craft.

"Decidedly Dutch I should say," he answered slowly, "to judge from the shape of her lines, and the size of her spars. The beggars seem quite at home there, with all their washing out. Not a usual anchorage?"

"No, nor a particularly safe one. There are some very heavy seas off that point at times, and there is no plantation near by. Travers' place is beyond the bend. We'll put up with him tonight; he owns that land yonder, but his wharf is several miles up the coast. Damn me, Sanchez, I believe I 'll hail the fellow, and find out what he is doing in there."

Sanchez nodded, carelessly striking flint and steel in an effort to relight a cheroot, and Fairfax turned his head toward me.

"Oh, is that you, Carlyle? Where is Sam?"

"Gone forward, sir, half an hour ago. He decided I was safe."

The planter laughed, with a side glance toward Sanchez, who gave no sign that he overhead.

"No doubt he was right. Port your helm a little, and run down as close as seems safe to that fellow out yonder, until I hail him."

"Very well, sir."

We came about slowly, tossed a bit by the heavy swell, the ponderous boom swinging, and permitting the loosened canvas to flap against the ropes, until the sloop finally steadied onto the new tack. The distance to be covered was not great, and in less than ten minutes, we were drawing in toward the high stern of the anchored vessel. She was larger than I had thought, a lumping craft for those days, bark rigged, with lower spars the heaviest I had ever seen. No evidence of life appeared on board, although everything looked shipshape alow and aloft, and a rather extensive wash flapped in the wind forward, bespeaking a generous crew. There was no flag at the mizzen to signify nationality, yet there was a peculiar touch to the rig which confirmed in my mind the truth of Sanchez's guess that she was originally Dutch. A moment later this supposition was confirmed as my eyes made out the name painted across the stern--NAMUR OF ROTTERDAM.

Fairfax leaned far out across the rail, as we swept in closer, his eyes searching the stranger's side for some evidence of human presence aboard, but the Spaniard exhibited no particular interest in the proceedings, standing motionless, the smoke of the cheroot blown idly from his mouth, The fellow's face was turned from me, yet I could not help note the insolence of his attitude, in spite of my occupation at the wheel. A hundred feet distant, I held the dancing sloop to mere steerage-way, while Fairfax hailed in a voice which went roaring across the water like a gun.

"Ahoy, the bark!"

A red-faced man with a black beard thrust his head up above the after rail, and answered, using English, yet with a faint accent which was not Dutch. What he looked like below the shoulders could not be discerned.

"Veil, vat's vanted? Vos anyding wrong?"

"No, not aboard here," returned Fairfax, a bit puzzled at the reply, "We ran down to see if you were in any trouble. This is a strange place to anchor. What are you--Dutch?"

The fellow waved his hands in a gesture indicating disgust. "Dat's eet. Ve're out ov Rotterdam--you see ze name ov ze sheep. But ve not sail frum thar dis time--no. Ve cum here from ze Barbadoes," he explained brokenly "wiz cane-sugar, an' hides. Ve vait here for our agent."

"But why anchor in a place like this? Why not go on up to the wharfs?"

"Vye not? For ziz--I no trust my crew ashore. Zay Vest Indy niggers, an' vud run avay ven ze chance cum. I know vat zay do."

In spite of my efforts the two vessels were drifting rapidly apart, and this last explanation came to us over the water in a faint thread of sound barely discernible. I asked if I should tack back, but Fairfax shook his head, and in a moment more we were beyond reach of the voice. Dorothy appeared at the door of the cabin and stood there, gazing in surprise at the bark, while the moment he caught sight of her Sanchez went hastily forward, removing his hat with so peculiar a flourish as he approached as to cause me to notice the gesture. Fairfax remained beside the rail, staring out across the widening water, clearly dissatisfied, but finally waved his hand in a command to me to resume our course. Shortly after he crossed the deck to the wheel, and stood there beside me, still watchful of the dwindling vessel already far astern.

"What do you make of her, Carlyle?" he asked finally, turning slightly to glance at my face. "I believe that fellow lied."

"So do I, sir," I answered promptly. "Whatever else he may be, he's no peaceful Dutch trader. The bark is Dutch built all right, and no doubt once sailed out of Rotterdam; but that fellow got his accent from South Europe."

"Damn me, that's just what I thought."

"Nor is that all, sir. If he was loaded with cane-sugar and hides for market, he wouldn't be nearly so high out of water. That bark was in ballast, or I miss my guess. Besides, if he was a trader, where was his crew? There wasn't a single head popped over the rail while we were alongside; and that isn't natural. Even a West India nigger has curiosity. I tell you the men on board that hooker had orders to keep down."

Fairfax stroked his chin, his eyes shifting from the distant vessel to Dorothy and Sanchez who were now making their way slowly aft, the latter grasping the girl's arm, and smirking as he talked rapidly.

"By God! but I believe you are right," he admitted frankly, "although it had not occurred to me before. There is something wrong there. I'll tell Travers, and have him send a runner overland to give warning below."

CHAPTER VI
FAIRFAX SPEAKS WITH ME

Sanchez drew a chair into the slight shade cast by the mainsail, and induced his reluctant companion to sit down. He remained bending over her, with his back turned toward us chattering away, although she only answered in monosyllables, seldom glancing up into his face. With hands gripping the spokes of the wheel, and my attention concentrated on the course ahead, I could yet notice how closely Fairfax was observing the two, with no pleasant expression in his eyes, and, forgetful that I was merely a servant, I ventured a question.

"You have known Senor Sanchez for some time, sir?"

He started in surprise, yet answered as though the unexpected query had been merely an echo of his own thoughts.

"No," he admitted frankly. "Indeed I hardly know how it happened that I invited him to join our party. It seemed natural enough then, but lately I confess to having taken a dislike to the fellow, and have begun to imagine that he even pushed his way on me. But," he stopped, suddenly realizing what he was saying, "why do you ask?"

I was not wholly prepared to say, yet as instantly comprehended the prompt necessity of advancing some reasonable explanation. There came to me swiftly, from the sharpness of his question, the paralyzing knowledge that I was a servant addressing my master.

"Of course it is no business of mine," I confessed, rather lamely, "who your guests are. I'm sorry I spoke."

"It is altogether too late to say that," he insisted. "Some thought prompted the inquiry. Go on. See here, Carlyle, you are no nigger or white thief. I know the difference, and recognize that you are gentleman born. Because I've bought your services for a term of years, is no reason why you cannot talk to me like a man. Do you know anything about this Spaniard?"

"Not very much, sir. He has seen fit to threaten me, on account of some row he has had with a brother of mine in England."

"In England! The Duke of Bucclough?"

"Yes. I haven't the slightest knowledge of what it was all about, but evidently our Spanish friend got the worst of it. He planned to buy me in at the sale; but, fortunately for me, you gained possession ahead of him."

"Do you mean to say that he told you all this?"

"It came out in a moment of anger."

Fairfax looked at me incredulously.

"See here, Carlyle," he exclaimed bluntly, "I am not questioning your word, but it is a bit difficult for me to understand why a guest of mine should indulge in angry controversy with a government prisoner, sent overseas for sale as an indentured servant. There must have been some unusual cause. Haven't I a right to know what that cause was, without using my authority to compel an answer?"

I hesitated, but only for a moment. He undoubtedly was entitled to know, and besides there was nothing involved I needed to conceal.

"It is my impression, sir, that Mistress Dorothy was the unconscious cause. She chanced to discover me alone on deck the night before we landed, and hastened to tell me of your purchase. It was merely an act of kindness, as we had never spoken together before. We were still talking across the rope, when Sanchez came out of the cabin, and joined us. I imagine he may not have liked the interest both you and the young lady had shown in me since we came aboard. Anyway when he found us there, he was not in good humor. Mistress Dorothy resented his language, treated him coldly, and finally departed, leaving him decidedly angry. He merely vented his spite on me."

"But he said nothing about himself--his motives?"

"Not a word, sir; yet it is plain to be seen that he is deeply interested in your niece."

Fairfax frowned, ignoring the remark.

"But do you know the man--who he is?"

I shook my head, the memory of Haley flashing into my mind, but as instantly dismissed as worthless. Fairfax would only laugh at such a vague suspicion. Yet why should the planter ask me such a question? Could it be that the Spaniard was equally unknown to himself?

"But if he has quarreled with your brother," he insisted, unsatisfied "you perhaps know something?"

"I have not seen my brother in years. I doubt if I would know him if we met face to face. As to this man, my knowledge of him is only what little I have seen and heard on board the **Romping Betsy**," I answered soberly. "I confess a prejudice; that I am unable to judge him fairly. In the first place I do not like his race, nor his kind; but I did suppose, of course, that, as he was your guest, you considered him a man worthy your hospitality."

Fairfax's face reddened, and he must have felt the sting of these words, uttered as they were by the lips of his bondman. I thought he would turn abruptly away, leaving them unanswered, but he was too much of a gentleman.

"Carlyle," he said brusquely, "you have touched the exact point--I do not know. I thought I did, of course, but what has occurred on the voyage over has led me to doubt. I met Sanchez at the Colonial Club in London. He was introduced to me by Lord Sandhurst as a wealthy young Spaniard, traveling for pleasure. It was understood that he brought letters of introduction to a number of high personages. He knew London well, enjoyed a wide circle of acquaintants, and we became rather intimate. I found him companionable and deeply interested in America, which he said he had never visited. Finally I invited him to accompany me as a guest on my return."

"He accepted?"

"No, not at once; he doubted if he could break off certain business engagements in England. Then, at a reception, he chanced to meet my niece, and, a little later, decided to undertake the voyage. I am inclined to believe she was the determining factor."

"Very likely," I admitted, deciding now to learn all possible details. "However, that is not to be wondered at. Mistress Dorothy is an exceedingly attractive young woman."

The look he gave me was far from pleasant.

"But she is not a girl for any swash-buckling Spaniard to carry off as prize," he burst out hotly. "God's mercy! Her father would never forgive me if that happened."

"Never fear," I said dryly, "it is not going to happen."

"Why do you say that?"

"Because I have seen them together, and am not entirely blind, Watch them now--she scarcely responds to his words."

His eyes rested for a moment on the two, but he only shook his head moodily.

"No one knows what is in the heart of a woman, Carlyle. Sanchez is fairly young, handsome in a way, and adventurous. Just the sort to attract a young girl, and he possesses an easy tongue. More than that, I have lost faith in him. He is not a gentleman."

"You surely must have reason for those words, sir," I exclaimed in surprise. "He has revealed to you his true nature during the voyage?"

"Unconsciously--yes. We have had no exchange of words, no controversy. He is even unaware that I have observed these things. Some were of very small moment, perhaps unworthy of being repeated, although they served to increase my doubt as to the man's character. But two instances remain indelibly stamped on my mind. The first occurred when we were only three days at sea. It was at night, and the two of us chanced to be alone, on deck. I was reclining in the shadow of the flag locker, in no mood for conversation, and he was unaware of my presence as he tramped nervously back and forth. Suddenly he stopped, and reached over into the quarter-boat, and when he stood up again he had the Captain's pet cat in his hands. Before I dreamed of such a thing he had hurled that helpless creature into the water astern."

"Good God! an act of wanton cruelty."

"The deliberate deed of a fiend; of one who seeks pleasure in suffering."

"And the other incident? Was that of the same nature?"

"It was not an incident, but a revelation. The fellow is not only, beneath his pretense of gentleness, a fiend at heart, but he is also a consummate liar. He led me to believe in London--indeed he told me so directly--that he was totally unacquainted with America. It is not true. He knows this entire coast even better than I do. He forgot himself twice in conversation with me, and he was incautious enough to speak freely with Captain Harnes. The Captain told me later."

"This begins to sound serious, sir," I said, as he ceased speaking. "Do you suspect him of any particular purpose in this deceit?"

"Not at present; I can only wait, and learn. As a Spanish naval officer he may have obtained some knowledge of this coast--but why he should have deliberately denied the possession of such information is unexplainable at present. I shall watch him closely, and have told you these facts merely to put you on guard. I know you to be a gentleman, Carlyle, even though you are temporarily a servant, and I feel convinced I can trust in your discretion."

"You certainly can, sir. I appreciate your confidence in me." "Then keep your eyes and ears open; that's all. Dorothy is calling, and yonder comes Sam."

We had yet a full hour of daylight, during which little occurred of special interest. Sam took the wheel, while I ate supper, sitting with Carr on the deck behind the galley. Fairfax and his guests, were served at a table within the small cabin, and we had a glimpse of them, and their surroundings, the table prettily decorated with snowy linen, and burnished silver, while John, in a white jacket, waited upon them obsequiously, lingering behind his master's chair. The Lieutenant seemed in excellent humor, laughing often, and talking incessantly, although it occurred to me the man received scant encouragement from the others. After taking back to the galley my emptied pewter dish, and not being recalled aft to the wheel, I was glad to hang idly over the rail, watching the shore line slip past, and permit my thoughts to drift back to my conversation with Fairfax. Carr soon joined me, rather anxious to continue our talk, and ask questions, but not finding me particularly responsive, finally departed forward, leaving me alone.

The sun by this time was rapidly sinking below the fringe of tall trees on the main-land, but the fresh breeze held favorably, and the little *Adele* was making most excellent progress, the water being much smoother since we had rounded the point. We were already beyond view of the anchored bark. All about was a scene of loneliness, whether the searching eyes sought the near-by shore, apparently a stretch of uninhabited wilderness, densely forested, or the broad extent of the Bay, across which no white gleam of sail was visible. All alike was deserted, and becoming gloomy in the closing down of night. Dorothy remained hidden in the cabin, until about the time of our approach to the rude landing at Travers' plantation. Whether this isolation arose from an effort to make herself more presentable, or a desire to avoid further contact with the Spaniard, was a question. When she finally emerged at Roger Fairfax's call, and crossed the deck to where the men were, there was no alteration in her dress, but by that time I was busily engaged with Carr in reefing the mainsail, and she passed me by without so much as a glance of recognition. Meanwhile Fairfax and Sanchez paced restlessly back and forth, conversing earnestly as they smoked, only occasionally pausing to contemplate the shore past which we were gliding in silence, the only sound the ripple of water at our stem.

Where I leaned alone against the rail, my eyes followed the Spaniard in doubt and questioning, nor could I entirely banish from mind Haley's description of that buccaneer, bearing a similar name, under whom he had been compelled to serve through scenes of crime. Yet, in spite of my unconscious desire to connect these two together, I found it simply impossible to associate this rather soft-spoken, effeminate dandy with that bloody villain, many of whose deeds were so familiar to me. The distinction was too apparent. Beyond all doubt this fellow concealed beneath his smiles a nature entirely different from the one he now so carefully exhibited. He could hate fiercely, and nourish revenge, and he was capable of mean, cowardly cruelty. His threat toward me, as well as that strange incident Fairfax had observed on the deck of the ***Romping Betsy***, evidenced all this clearly, yet such things rather proved the man a revengeful coward instead of a desperate adventurer. Black Sanchez, according to all accounts, was a devil incarnate, and no such popinjay as this maker of love, could ever be changed into a terror of the sea. He was not of that stern stuff. That it was perfectly easy for him to lie--even natural--was no surprise to me. This seemed to accord with his other characteristics; nor was it altogether strange that he should be fairly familiar with these waters. If, as he claimed, he had once been connected with the Spanish navy, which quite likely was true, even if he had never visited this coast in person, he might have had access to their charts and maps. It was well known that early Spanish navigators had explored every inch of this coast line, and that their tracings, hastily as they had been made, were the most correct in existence. His memory of these might yet retain sufficient details through which he could pretend to a knowledge much greater than he really possessed.

No, I would dismiss that thought permanently from my mind, as being quite impossible. I felt that I had learned to judge men; that my long years at sea, both before the mast, and in supreme command, had developed this faculty so as to be depended upon. I believed that I knew the class to which Lieutenant Sanchez belonged--he was a low-born coward, dangerous only through treachery, wearing a mask of bravado, capable enough of any crime or cruelty, but devoid of boldness in plan or execution; a fellow I would kick with pleasure, but against whom I should never expect to be obliged to draw a sword. He was a snake, who could never be made into a lion--a character to despise, not fear. And so I dismissed him, feeling no longer any serious sense of danger in his presence, yet fully determined to watch closely his future movements in accordance with my promise.

It was already quite dusk when we finally drew in beside Travers' wharf, and made fast. Our approach had been noted, and Travers himself--a white-haired, white-bearded man, yet still hearty and vigorous, attired in white duck--was on the end of the dock to greet us, together with numerous servants of every shade of color, who immediately busied themselves toting luggage up the steep path leading toward the house, dimly visible in the distance, standing conspicuous amid a grove of trees on the summit, of the bank. The others followed, four fellows lugging with difficulty an iron-bound chest, the two older men engaged in earnest conversation, thus leaving Sanchez apparently well satisfied with the opportunity alone to assist the girl. Except to render the sloop completely secure for the night, there remained little work for us to perform on board. Sam found an ample supply of tobacco and pipes, and the four of us passed the early evening undisturbed smoking and talking together. The fellows were not uninteresting as I came to know them better, and Carr, who I learned had been transported three years before for robbery, having at one time been a soldier, was prolific of reminiscences, which he related with true Irish wit. Sam contented himself with asking me numerous questions relative to the Duke of Monmouth, whose effort to attain the throne interested him greatly, and I very gladly gave him all the information I possessed. So the time passed quickly, and it must have been nearly midnight before we brought out blankets from the forecastle, and lay down in any spot we chose on deck.

It was a fair, calm night, but moonless, with but little wind stirring, and a slight haze in the air, obscuring the vision. The windows of the great house above, which earlier in the evening had blazed with lights, were now darkened, and the distant sounds of voices and laughter had entirely ceased. The only noise discernible as I lay quiet was the soft lapping of waves against the side of the sloop or about the piling supporting the wharf to which we were moored. The others must have fallen asleep immediately, but my own mind remained far too active to enable me to lose consciousness. At last, despairing of slumber, and perchance urged by some indistinct premonition of danger, I sat up once more and gazed about. The three men were lying not far apart, close in to the galley wall, merely dark, shapeless shadows, barely to be distinguished in the gloom. With no longer any fear of disturbing them, I arose to my feet, and stepping carefully past their recumbent forms, moved silently aft toward the more open space near the wheel. I had been standing there hardly a minute, staring blankly out into the misty dimness of the Bay, when my startled eyes caught glimpse of a speck of white emerging from the black shadows--the spectral glimmer of a small sail. I was scarcely convinced I had seen it, yet as swiftly crouched lower, hiding myself behind the protection of the rail, instantly alert to learn the meaning of this strange apparition. An instant told me this was no deceit. The strange craft swept past, so far out that those on board no doubt believed themselves beyond sight from the shore, heading apparently for a point of land, which I vaguely remembered as jutting out to the northward. Even my eyes, accustomed to the darkness, and strained to the utmost, could detect scarcely more than the faintest shadow gliding silently by, yet sufficient to recognize the outlines of a small keel boat, propelled by a single lug sail, and even imagined I could discern the stooped figure of a man at the helm.

CHAPTER VII
THE LIEUTENANT UNMASKED

I had in truth hardly more than grasped the reality of the boat's presence--it seemed so spectral a thing amid the mists of the night--when it had vanished utterly once more behind the curtain of darkness. There was no sound to convince me my eyes had not deceived; that I had actually perceived a boat, flying before the wind, under complete control, and headed to the northward. No echo of a voice came across the water, no slight flap of sail, no distant creak of pulley, or groaning of rope--merely that fleeting vision, seemingly a phantom of imagination, a vision born from sea and cloud. Yet I knew I was not deceived. Where the craft could be bound; for what secret purpose it was afloat; who were aboard, were but so many unanswerable questions arising in my mind. I stared vainly into the darkness, puzzled and uncertain, impressed alone by the one controlling thought, that some mysterious object, some hidden purpose alone could account for that swift, silent passage. Where could they have come from, unless from that strange Dutch bark riding at anchor off the point below? The passing craft had impressed me as a ship's boat, and no craft of fishermen; and if it really came from the ***Namur of Rotterdam***, had it been sent in answer to some signal by Sanchez? I could think of nothing else. They must have chosen this late hour purposely; they had doubtless endeavored to slip past us unobserved, seeking some more desolate spot on the coast where they might land unseen. Possibly, deceived by the night, the helmsman had approached closer to the wharf than he had intended; yet, nevertheless, if he held to his present course, he must surely touch shore not more than five hundred yards distant. In all probability that was his purpose.

I stood up, tempted at first to arouse Sam, but deciding almost as quickly that at present this was unnecessary. I had no wish to be the occasion for laughter; it would be better first to ascertain who these parties were, rather than create an unwarranted alarm. The reasonable probability was they composed merely a party of innocent fishermen, returning home after a day of sport--plantation servants possibly, who having stolen away unobserved, were now endeavoring to beach their stolen boat, and reach quarters without being seen. This theory appeared far more reasonable than the other, and, if it proved true, to arouse the sleepers on deck, would only result in making me a butt for ridicule. It appeared safe enough for me to adventure alone, and I was at least determined to assure myself as to the identity of these strangers. If they had actually landed it would require only a few moments to ascertain the truth, and I could accomplish this fully as well by myself, as though accompanied by others--indeed with less danger of discovery. I quietly lowered my body over the rail, and found footing on the wharf.

My knowledge of the path to be pursued was extremely vague, for our arrival had been in the dusk of the evening, so that any observation of the shore lines had been quite casual. I merely remembered that the bluff rose rather steeply from the water's edge, the path leading upward toward the house crowning the summit, turning and twisting in order to render the climb easier, and finally vanishing entirely as it approached the crest. Beside this, leading downward straight to the shore end of the wharf, was the broad slide, along which the bales and hogsheads of tobacco were sent hurtling on their way to market. My impression remained that the strip of beach was decidedly narrow, and generally bordered by a rather thick growth of dwarfed shrub. The point of land beyond clung dimly in my memory as sparsely wooded, tapering at its outer extremity into a sand bar against which the restless waves of the Bay broke in lines of foam. The only feasible method of approach to the spot I now sought would be by following this narrow strip of beach, yet this might be attempted safely, as my movements would be concealed by the darker background of the high bluff at the left.

In spite of the unfamiliarity of this passage, I succeeded in making excellent progress, advancing silently along the soft sand, assured I was safe from observation by reason of the intense darkness. The waves lapping the beach helped muffle my footsteps, but no other sound reached my ears, nor could my eyes perceive the slightest movement along the water surface within reach of vision. The distance proved somewhat greater than anticipated, because of the deep curve in the shore, and I had nearly reached the conclusion that the boat must have rounded the point and gone on, when suddenly I was brought to a halt by a voice speaking in Spanish--one of those harsh, croaking voices, never to be reduced to a whisper. Imperfect as was my knowledge of the tongue, I yet managed a fair understanding of what was being said.

"Not the spot, Manuel? Of course it is; do you not suppose I know? The cursed fog made me run in close ashore to where I could see the sloop, so as not to mistake. This is the place, and now there is nothing to do but wait. The Senor--he will be here presently."

"Ay, unless you misread the signal," a somewhat more discreet, but piping voice replied doubtfully. "I saw nothing of all you tell about."

"Because you knew no meaning, nor read the instructions," a touch of anger in the tone. "I tell you it was all written out in that letter brought to me from England on the *Wasp*. They were his last orders, and it was because of them that we anchored off the point yonder, and explored this coast. You saw the Senor touch the handkerchief to his cheek?"

"As he went forward alone--yes, surely."

"It was that motion which bade us come here, Manuel. Once for each cursed plantation along this west coast from the point. He touched the cloth to his cheek but the once, and this is the first. I watched for the sign with care for he is not one with whom to make a mistake."

"Dios de Dios! Do I not know, Estada? Have I not a scar here which tells?"

"True, enough; and have I not received also my lesson--eight hours staked face upward in the sun. So 'tis my very life wagered on this being the place named. Besides 'tis proven by the sloop lying there by the wharf."

"Where then is the Captain?" perversely unsatisfied.

"At the house yonder on the hill--where else? He knew how it would be, for this is not his first visit to the Bay. 'Twas because of his knowledge he could plan in England. Tis the custom of these planters to stop by night along the way, and go ashore; not to camp, but as guests of some friend. Only beforehand it was not possible for him to know which plantation would be the one chosen. That was what he must signal. You see it now?"

"Clearly, Estada; he is the same wary fox as of old."

"Never do they catch him napping," proudly. "Santa Maria! have I not seen it tried often in ten years?"

"About his plan here? He wrote you his purpose?"

"Not so much as a word; merely the order what to do. Dios! he tells nothing, for he trusts no man. A good thing that. Yet I have my own thought, Manuel."

"And what is that?"

The other hesitated, as though endeavoring to rearrange the idea in his own mind, and possibly doubtful of how much to confide to his companion. When he finally replied his words came forth so swiftly I could scarcely grasp their meaning with my slight knowledge of the tongue.

"'Tis no more than that I make a guess, friend, yet I have been with the Captain for ten years now, and know his way. This planter Fairfax is rich. The letter says nothing of that--no, not a word; but I made inquiries ashore. There is no one more wealthy in these Colonies, and he returns now from London, after the sale of his tobacco crop. No doubt he sold for his neighbors also. 'Tis the way they do, form a combine, and send an agent to England to get the best price. He will surely bear back with him a great sum. This the Senor knows; nor is it the first time he has done the trick, Manuel. Santa Maria! 'tis the easiest one of all. Then there is the girl."

"The one who was aboard the sloop?"

"Of course. I knew nothing of her, but I have keen eyes, and I have been long with the Senor. Marked you not how he approached her? No sea rover ever had greater desire for women, or won them easier. 'Tis a bright eye and red lip that wins him from all else. Even to me this one looked a rare beauty; yet am I sorry he found her, for it may delay the task here."

"Why must you fear that?"

"Bah! but you are stupid. Who will take by force what may be won by a few soft words?" He paused suddenly, evidently struck by a new thought. "Yet I think, Manuel, the Captain may have failed in this case. I watched their greeting, and her's was not that of love. If this be true, we strike at once, while it is safe."

"Here, you mean--tonight?"

"And why not here, and tonight? Is there a better spot or time? With another night the sloop will be far up the Bay, while now from where we are anchored, we could be beyond the Capes by daybreak, with the broad ocean before us. We are five--six with the Senor--and our ship lies but a short league away, ready for sea. There are only four men on the sloop, with some servants above--spiritless fellows. Why else should he have signaled our coming, unless there was work to do? That will be the plan, to my notion--the money and the girl in one swoop; then a quick sail to the southward. Pist! 'tis boys' play."

The other seemed to lick his lips, as though the picture thus drawn greatly pleased him.

"Gracioso Dios! I hope 'tis so. It has been dull enough here this month past. I am for blue water, and an English ship to sack."

"Or, better yet, a week at Porto Grande--hey, Manuel? The girls are not so bad, with clink of gold in the pocket after a cruise. Wait, though--there is someone coming down."

I crouched backward into the bushes, and, a moment later, the newcomer moved past me scarcely a yard distant, along the narrow strip of sand. He appeared no more than a black shadow, wrapped in a loose cloak, thus rendered so shapeless as to be scarcely recognizable. Directly opposite my covert he paused peering forward in uncertainty.

"Estada." He spoke the name cautiously, and in doubt.

"Ay, Captain," and another figure, also shapeless, and ill-defined, emerged noiselessly from the gloom. "We await you."

"Good," the tone one of relief. "I rather questioned if you caught my signal. I was watched, and obliged to exercise care. How many have you here?"

"Four, Senor, with Manuel Estevan."

"Quite sufficient; and how about the others?"

"All safely aboard, Senor; asleep in their bunks by now, but ready. Francois LeVere has charge of the deck watch."

"Ah! how happens it the quadroon is with you? A good choice, yet that must mean the *Vengeance* is still at Porto Grande. For what reason?"

"Because of greater injuries than we supposed, Captain. There were two shots in her below the water line, and to get at them we were obliged to beach her. Le-Vere came with us, expecting this job would be done before now, for by this time the schooner should be in water again, her sides scraped clean of barnacles, fit for any cruise. We have been waiting for you along this coast for several weeks."

"Yes, I know. The boat we intended to take met with an accident, while the one we did take proved the slowest tub that ever sailed. How is it here? Are there suspicions?"

"None, Senor. We have cruised outside most of the time. Only once were we hailed; while Manuel, with a boat crew, was ashore for nearly a week, picking up such news as he might. There is no warship in these waters."

"So I discovered on landing; indeed I was told as much in England. However your disguise is perfect."

Estada laughed.

"There is no mistaking where the *Namur* came from, Senor; she's Holland from keel to topmast, but the best sailing Dutchman I ever saw. You said you were being watched on the sloop. Are you known?"

The other uttered an oath snarling through his teeth.

"'Tis nothing," he explained contemptuously. "No more than the bite of a harmless snake in the grass. A dog of a servant who came over with us--one of Monmouth's brood. He has no knowledge of who I am, nor suspicion of my purpose. It is not that, yet the fellow watches me like a hawk. We had some words aboard and there is hate between us"

"If he was indentured, how came he on the sloop?"

"Fairfax bought him. The fellow won the interest of the girl coming over, and she interceded in his behalf. It was my plan to get him into my own hands. I'd have taught him a lesson, but the papers were signed before we landed. Yet the lad is not through with me; I do not let go in a hurry."

"May I ask you your plans, Senor?"

"Yes, I am here to explain. Are we out of ear-shot?"

"None can hear us. Manuel has gone back to the boat."

"Then listen. This planter, Fairfax, has returned from England with a large sum. It is in gold and notes. I have been unable to learn the exact amount, but it represents the proceeds in cash of the tobacco crop of himself, and a number of his neighbors. They pooled, and made him their agent. Without doubt, from all I could ascertain, it will be upward of fifty thousand pounds--not a bad bit of pocket money. This still remains in his possession, but a part will be dispersed tomorrow; so if we hope to gain the whole, we must do so now."

"Fifty thousand pounds, you say? Gracioso Dios! a sum worth fighting for."

"Ay; we've done some hard fighting for less. It is here under our very hands, and there could be no better place than this in which to take it. Everything is ready, and there is not the slightest suspicion of danger--not even a guard set over the treasure. I assured myself of this before coming down."

"Then it is at the house?"

"In an iron-bound chest, carried up from the sloop, and placed in the room assigned to Fairfax for the night. He considers it perfectly safe under his bed. But before we attempt reaching this, we must attend to those men left below on the boat. They are the only dangerous ones, for there are none of the fighting sort up above. Only two servants sleep in the main house, the cook, and a maid, both women. The others are in the slave quarters, a half mile away. Fairfax is vigorous, and will put up a fight, if he has any chance. He must be taken care of, before he does have any. Travers is an old man, to be knocked out with a blow. All we have to fear are those fellows on the sloop, and they will have to be attended to quietly, without any alarm reaching the house. I am going to leave that job to you--it's not your first."

"The old sea orders, Captain?"

"Ay, that will be quicker, and surer," The voice hardened in gust of sudden ferocity. "But, mark you, with one exception--the Englishman is not to be killed, if he can be taken alive. I would deal with him."

"How are we to recognize him from the others?"

"Pish! a blind man would know--he is the only one of that blood on board, taller, and heavier of build, with blond hair. A mistake, and you pay for it. Besides him there are two negroes, and an Irish fool. It matters not what happens to them; a knife to the heart is the more silent; but I would have this Geoffry Carlyle left alive to face me. You will do well to remember."

"I will pass the word to the men."

"See that you do. Then after that," Sanchez went on deliberately, as though murder was of small account, "you will follow me up the bluff. Who are the others with you?"

"Carl Anderson, Pedro Mendez, and Cochose."

"Well chosen; Mendez is the least valuable, and we will leave him with the prisoner at the boat. The big negro, Cochose, together with Manuel, can attend to Travers, and the two negresses--they sleep below. That will leave you and the Swede to get the chest. No firearms, if they can be avoided."

"You are certain of the way, Senor--in the dark?"

"I have been over the house, and drawn a rude diagram. You can look it over in the cabin of the sloop, after affairs have been attended to there. The stairs lead up from the front hall. I will go with you to the door of Fairfax's room."

Estada hesitated, as though afraid to further question his chief, yet finally, in spite of this fear, the query broke from his lips.

"And you, Senor--the girl?"

"What know you of any girl?"

"That there was one on the deck of the sloop--an English beauty. It was when you turned to greet her that you gave me the signal. I merely thought that per-haps--"

"Then stop thinking," burst forth Sanchez enraged. "Thinking has nothing to do with your work. If there is a girl, I attend to her. Let that suffice. Dios! am I chief here, or are you? You have my orders, now obey them, and hold your tongue. Bring the men up here."

Without a word, evidently glad to escape thus easily, Estada vanished into the gloom, leaving behind only the vague figure of Sanchez pacing the sands, his lips muttering curses. I dared not move, scarcely indeed to breathe, so closely did he skirt my covert. To venture forth would mean certain discovery; nor could I hope to steal away through the bushes, where any twig might snap beneath my foot. What could I do? How could I bring warning to those sleeping victims? This heartless discussion of robbery and murder left me cold with horror, yet helpless to lift a hand. I had no thought of myself, of my possible fate when once delivered into the hands of this monster, this arch villain, but all my agony of mind centered on the imminent danger confronting Dorothy Fairfax, and those unsuspecting men. All my preconceived impressions of Sanchez had vanished; he was no longer in my imagination a weakling, a boastful, cowardly bravado, a love-sick fool; but a leader of desperate men, a villain of the deepest dye--the dreaded pirate, Black Sanchez, whose deeds of crime were without number, and whose name was infamous. Confronted by Fairfax's ill-guarded gold, maddened by the girl's contemptuous indifference, no deed of violence and blood was too revolting for him to commit. What he could not win by words, he would seize by force and make his own. As coolly as another might sell a bolt of cloth, he would plan murder and rape, and then smilingly watch the execution. And I--what could I do?

The little band of men emerged from the concealment of the fog noiselessly, and gathered into a group about the figure of Sanchez, where he stood motionless awaiting them. I could distinguish no faces, scarcely indeed the outlines of their separate forms in the gloom, but one was an unusually big fellow, far taller and heavier than his companions. When he spoke he possessed a negro's voice, and I recognized him at once for Cochose. The Captain swept his impatient eyes about the circle.

"Lads," he said, incisively, a sharper note of leadership in the tone "it has been a bit quiet for you lately; but now I am back again, and we'll try our luck at sea once more. There must be many a laden ship waiting for us. Does that sound good?"

There was a savage growl of response, a sudden leaning forward of dark figures.

"I thought it would. We'll begin on a job tonight. There are fifty thousand pounds for us in that house yonder, and I waive my share. Estada will explain to you the work I want done; see that you do it quietly and well. By daylight we shall be on blue water, with our course set for Porto Grande. How is it, bullies, do you sniff the salt sea?"

"Ay, ay, Captain."

"And see the pretty girls waiting--and hear the chink of gold?"

"Ay, Senor."

"Then do not fail me tonight--and remember, it is to be the knife. Estada."

"Here, Senor."

"I have forgotten one thing--scuttle the sloop before joining me. 'Tis better to make all safe; and now, strong arms, and good luck. Go to your task, and if one fails me, it will mean the lash at the mast-butt."

They moved off one by one, Estada leading, along the narrow strip of sand, five of them, on their mission of murder. The leader remained alone, his back toward where I crouched, his eyes following their vanishing figures, until the night had swallowed them.

CHAPTER VIII
A VICTORY, AND A DEFEAT

I arose silently to my feet, conscious of possessing no weapon, yet fully aware that all hope of thwarting this villainy lay in immediate action. But I must await the right moment. Even with the advantage of surprise, there would inevitably be the noise of struggle. I had in the past despised Sanchez, but I had never yet tested him as a fighting man, and, indeed, no longer considered the fellow to be a mean antagonist. Remembering who he was, I now realized fully the desperate nature of my attempt, the need of quick, remorseless action. Nevertheless I dared not attack until assured that those men he had just dispatched were safely beyond ear-shot. I could hear or see nothing of them; they had vanished utterly, and the soft sand returned no echo of their footsteps. Time alone gave me judgment as to the distance they would travel. If I yielded too much of this, they might attain the sloop before I could sound an alarm; while if I moved too quickly the noise would bring them back to the rescue. The moments were agony, as I bent tensely forward, poised for a leap. God! I could wait no longer!

Sanchez had turned slightly, apparently immersed in thought, and stood with his face toward the Bay. Even in that darkness his position was that of a man intently listening for the slightest sound to reach him out of the black night. I ventured a cautious step forward, and stood on the open sand, scarcely a yard to his rear, every nerve throbbing, my lips still silently counting the seconds. I could not, I dared not wait longer. Some vague sense of my presence must have influenced the man, for he swung suddenly about, uttering a stifled cry of startled surprise, as we met face to face. For an instant we were locked so closely within each other's desperate grip, his head bent beneath my arm, with my fingers clutching at his throat to block any call for help, that he possessed no knowledge of his assailant's identity. But the man was like a tiger, possessed of immense strength encased in a wiry frame. The surprise of attack was to my advantage, yet almost before I realized what was being done, he had rallied, broken my first hold, and his eyes were glaring straight into mine. Then he knew me, signaling his discovery with an oath, his free hand instantly grasping at the knife concealed beneath his loose cloak. Even as he jerked it forth, I crushed his wrist within my fingers, forcing his fore-arm back. Breast to breast we wrestled for mastery, every muscle strained, our feet firm planted on the sand. There was no outcry, no noise, except that of our heavy breathing, and trampling feet. Personal hatred had ascendancy in both our hearts--I doubt if he ever thought of aught else but the desire to kill me there with his own hands. Only once did he even utter a word, hissing out the sentence as though it were a poison:

"To hell with you, you sneaking English cur!"

"Then I travel that road not alone," I muttered back. "There will be one less of the devil's brood afloat."

What followed has to me no clearness, no consistency. I remember, yet it is as though memory played me a thousand tricks. Never have I fought more wickedly, nor with deeper realization that I needed every ounce of strength, and every trick of wit and skill. I had not before dreamed he was such a man; but now I knew the fellow possessed greater knowledge of the game than I, and a quicker movement; I alone excelled in weight of body, and coolness of brain. His efforts were those of an infuriated animal, his uncontrolled outburst of hatred rendering him utterly reckless of results in his struggle to overcome me at any cost. It was this blind blood-lust which gave me victory. I know not clearly how it was done; my only memory being his frantic efforts to drive home the knife point, and mine to defeat the thrust. Twice he pricked me deep enough to draw blood, before I succeeded in twisting backward the arm with which he held the blade. It was a sailor's trick of last resort, heartlessly cruel in its agony, but I felt then no call to mercy. He met the game too late, falling half back upon one knee, hoping thus to foil my purpose, yet my greater weight saved me. There was the sharp crack of a bone, as his useless fingers let the knife drop, a snarled curse of pain, and then, with the rage of a mad dog, Sanchez struck his teeth deep into my cheek. The sharp pang of pain drove me to frenzy, and for the first time I lost all control, my one free hand seeking to reach the lost knife. With a thrill of exultation I gripped it, driving instantly the keen blade to its hilt into the man's side. He made no cry, no struggle--the set teeth unlocked, and he fell limply back on the sand, his head lapped by the waves.

I remained poised above him, spent and breathless from struggle, scarcely conscious even as to what had occurred so swiftly, the dripping knife in my hand, blood streaming down my cheek, and still infuriated by blind passion. The fellow lay motionless, his face upturned to the sky, but invisible except in dim outline. It did not seem possible he could actually be dead; I had struck blindly, with no knowledge as to where the keen blade had penetrated--a mere desperate lunge. I rested my ear over his heart, detecting no murmur of response; touched the veins of his wrist, but found there no answering throb of life. Still dazed and uncertain, I arose staggering to my feet, conscious at last that the man must actually be dead, yet, for the moment, so surprised by the discovery as to scarcely realize its significance. Not that I regretted the act, not that I experienced the slightest remorse, yet, for an instant, the shock seemed to leave me nerveless and unstrung. Only a moment since I was engaged in desperate struggle, and now I could only stare down at the dark lines of that motionless body outstretched upon the sand.

Then I remembered those others--the unconscious sleepers on the deck of the sloop; those blood-stained villains creeping toward them through the black shadows of the night. The memory was like a dash of water in the face. With the death-dealing knife still gripped in my hand, I raced forward along the narrow strip of sand, reckless of what I might encounter, eager only to arrive in time to give utterance to a shout of warning. I could not have covered more than half the distance when the first sound of attack reached me--far-off, gurgling cry of agony, which pierced the darkness like the scream of a dying soul. The heart leaped into my throat, yet I ran on, unhalted, unseen, until the planks of the wharf were beneath my feet, the low side of the sloop looming black before me. There was confusion aboard, the sounds of struggle, mingled with curses and blows. With one upward swing of my body I was safely aboard, knife still in hand, peering eagerly forward. Through the gloom concealing the deck, I could perceive only dim figures, a riot of men, battling furiously hand to hand, yet out of the ruck loomed through the darkness in larger outline than the others---Cochose, the negro. I leaped at the fellow, and struck with the keen knife, missing the heart, but plunging the blade deep into the flesh of the shoulder. The next instant I was in a bear's grip, the very breath crushed out of me, yet, by some chance, my one arm remained free, and I drove the sharp steel into him twice before he forced the weapon from my fingers. Through a wrestler's trick, although my wrist was as numb as if dead from his fierce grip, I thrust an elbow beneath the brute's chin, and thus forced his head back, until the neck cracked.

This respite served merely for the moment, yet sufficiently long to win me a firm foot-hold on deck, and a breath of night air. He was too strong, too immense of stature. Apparently unweakened by his wounds, the giant negro, thoroughly aroused, exerted his mighty muscles, and, despite my utmost effort at resistance, thrust me back against the stern rail, where the weight of his body pinned me helplessly. With a roar of rage he drove his huge fist into my face, but happily was too close to give much force to the blow. My own hands, gripping the neck-band of his coarse shirt, twisted it tight about the great throat, until, in desperation, panting for breath, the huge brute actually lifted me in his arms, and hurled me backward, headlong over the rail. I struck something as I fell, yet rebounding from this, splashed into the deep water, and went down so nearly unconscious as to make not even the slightest struggle. I had no strength left in me, no desire to save myself, and I sank like a stone. And yet I came up once more to the surface, arising by sheer chance, directly beneath the small dory--which my body must have struck as I fell--towing by a painter astern of the sloop, and fortunately retained sense enough to cling desperately to this first thing my hands touched, and thus remained concealed.

This occurred through complete exhaustion, rather than the exercising of any judgment, for, had it not been for this providential support, I would surely have drowned without a struggle. Every breath I drew was in pain; I felt as though my ribs had been crushed in, while I had lost sufficient blood to leave me as weak as a babe. I simply clung there desperately, hopelessly, yet the salt water soon served to revive me physically, and even my brain began to arouse from its daze to a faint realization of the conditions. The small dory to which I clung, caught in some mysterious current, floated at the very extremity of its slender towline, and in consequence the sloop appeared little more than a mere smudge, when my eyes endeavored to discover its outlines. Evidently the bloody work had been completed, for now all was silent on board. I could not even detect the sound of a footstep on the deck. Then, clear enough to be distinctly heard across the narrow strip of water, came the voice of Estada, in a gruff inquiry:

"So you are hiding here, Cochose? What are you looking for in the sea?"

"What? Why that damned Englishman." The response was a savage growl, intensified by husky dialect. "Mon Dieu! He fought me like a mad rat."

"The Englishman, you say? He was here then? It was he you battled with? What became of the fellow?"

"He went down there, Senor. The dog stabbed me three times. It was either he or I to go."

"You mean you threw him overboard?"

"Ay, with his ribs crushed in, and not a breath left in his damned body. He's never come up even--I've watched, and there has not been so much as a ripple where he sank."

The two must have hung in silence over the rail staring down. I dared not advance my head to look, nor even move a muscle of my body in the water, but both were still standing there when Estada finally gave utterance to an oath.

"How know you it was the man?"

"Who else could it have been? You have the others."

"Ay, true enough; yet it will go hard with you, Cochose, when the Captain learns of this--he would have the fellow alive."

"As well attempt to take a tiger with bare hands--see, the blood yet runs; a single inch to the left, and it would be I fed to the fishes. Pah! what is the difference, Senor, so the man dies?"

"Right enough, no doubt; anyway it is not I who must face Sanchez, and it is too late now to change fate. Let's to the rest of our task. You can still do your part?"

The giant negro growled.

"Ay; I have been worse hurt, yet a bit of cloth would help me."

"Let Carl see to that, while I gain glimpse at this map of the house up yonder.

Come forward with me to the cabin, till I light a candle. How came you aft here?"

"Because that fellow leaped the rail from the wharf. I saw him, and we met at the wheel."

"From the wharf, you say? He was not aboard then? Santa Maria! I know not what that may mean. Yet what difference, so he be dead. Anderson, Mendez, throw that carrion overboard--no, bullies, never mind; let them lie where they are, and sink an auger in the sloop's bottom. That will settle the whole matter. What is that out yonder, Cochose?"

"A small boat, Senor--a dory, I make it."

"Cut the rope, and send it adrift. Now come along with me."

The darker loom of the sloop vanished slowly, as the slight current sweeping about the end of the wharf drifted the released boat to which I clung outward into the Bay. The faint echo of a voice floated to my ears across the widening expanse of water, and then all was silent as the night closed in darkly between. There was scarcely a ripple to the sea, and yet I felt that the boat was steadily drifting out into deeper water. I was still strangely weak, barely able to retain my grasp, with a peculiar dullness in my head, which made me fearful that at any moment I might let go. I was not even conscious of thinking, or capable of conceiving clearly my situation, yet I must have realized vaguely the immediate necessity of action, for finally I mustered every ounce of remaining energy in one supreme effort, and succeeded in dragging my body up out of water over the boat's stern, sinking helplessly forward into the bottom. The moment this was accomplished every sense deserted me, and I lay there motionless, totally unconscious.

I shall never know how long I remained thus, the little dory in which I lay rocked aimlessly about by the waves, and constantly drifting in the grasp of unseen currents farther and farther out into the Bay. The blackness of the night swallowed us, as tossed by wind and sea, we were borne on through the waste unguided. Yet this time could not have been great. As though awakening from sleep a faint consciousness returned, causing me to lift my head, and stare hopelessly about into the curtain of mist overhanging the water. At first, with nothing surrounding to awaken memory into action, only that dull vista of sea and sky, my mind refused to respond to any impression; then the sharp pain of my wounds, accented by the sting of salt water, brought me swift realization of where I was, and the circumstances bringing me there. My wet clothing had partially dried on my body as I lay there motionless in the bottom of the boat, and now, with every movement, chafed the raw spots, rendering the slightest motion a physical agony. I had evidently lost considerable blood, yet this had already ceased to flow, and a very slight examination served to convince me that the knife slashes were none of them serious. Beyond these punctures of the flesh, while I ached from head to foot, my other injuries were merely bruises to add to my discomfort--the result of blows dealt me by Sanchez and Cochose, aggravated by the bearlike hug of the giant negro. Indeed, I awoke to the discovery that I was far from being a dead man; and, inspired by this knowledge, the various incidents of the night flashed swiftly back into my mind. How long had I been lying there unconscious, adrift in the open boat? How far had we floated from land? Where were we now, and in the meantime what had occurred ashore?

These were questions impossible to answer. I could not even attempt their solution. No gleam of light appeared in any direction; no sound echoed across the dark waste of water. Far above, barely visible through a floating veil of haze, I was able to detect the faint gleam of stars, and was sailor enough to determine through their guidance some certainty as to the points of compass; yet possessed no means by which to ascertain the time of night, or the position of the boat. With this handicap it was clearly impossible for me to attempt any return to the wharf through the impenetrable black curtain which shut me in. What then could I do? What might I still hope to accomplish? At first thought the case appeared hopeless. Those fellows had swept the sloop clean, and had doubtless long ago scuttled it. This ruthless deed once accomplished, their orders were to raid the house on the bluff. But would they go on with their bloody work? They would suddenly find themselves leaderless, unguided. Would that suffice to stop them? The vivid memory came to me anew of that arch villain, Sanchez, lying where I had left him, his head resting in the surf--dead. Would the discovery of his body halt his followers, and send them rushing back to their boat, eager only to get safely away? This did not seem likely. Estada knew of my boarding the sloop from the wharf, and would at once connect the fact of my being ashore with the killing of Sanchez. This would satisfy him there was no further danger. Besides, these were not men to be easily frightened at sight of a dead body, even that of their own captain. They might hesitate, discuss, but they would never flee in panic. Surely not with that ruffian Estada yet alive to lead them, and the knowledge that fifty thousand pounds was yonder in that unguarded house, with no one to protect the treasure but two old men asleep, and the women. The women!--Dorothy! What would become of her? Into whose hands would she fall in that foul division of spoils? Estada's? Good God--yes! And I, afloat and helpless in this boat, what could I do?

CHAPTER IX
A SWIM TO THE NAMUR

All was black, hopeless; with head buried in my hands I sat on a thwart, dazed and stupefied, seemingly even unable to think clearly. Before me, pleading, expressive of agonized despair, arose the sweet face of Dorothy Fairfax. Nothing else counted with me at that moment but her safety--the protecting her from the touch of that blood-stained brute. Yet how, and through what means, could such rescue be accomplished? No doubt by this time all was over--the dead body of Sanchez discovered, the projected attack on the house carried out, the two old men left behind, either dead or severely wounded, and the girl borne off a helpless prisoner, together with the treasure of fifty thousand pounds. Even if I knew where the drifting boat had taken me, which way to turn to once again attain the wharf, the probability remained that I should arrive altogether too late to be of slightest service--the dastardly deed had already been accomplished. Ay, but this I knew; there was only one place to which the villains might flee with their booty--the *Namur of Rotterdam*. Only on those decks, and well at sea, would they be safe, or able to enjoy their spoils. The thought came to me in sudden revelation--why not? Was not here a chance even yet to foil them? With Sanchez dead, no man aboard that pirate craft would recognize me. I felt assured of this. I had fought the giant negro in the dark; he could not, during that fierce encounter, have distinguished my features any more clearly than I had his own. There was no one else to fear. Although I had been stationed at the wheel of the sloop as we swept past the *Namur* while at anchor the day before, yet Estada, watching anxiously for the secret signal of his chief, would never have accorded me so much as a glance. His interest was concentrated elsewhere, and, in all probability, he could not swear whether I was black or white. If others of that devilish crew had been secretly watching our deck it was with no thought of me; and not one of them would retain any memory of my appearance. If only I might once succeed in getting safely aboard, slightly disguised perhaps, and mingle unnoticed among the crew, the chances were not bad for me to pass undetected. No doubt they were a heterogeneous bunch, drawn from every breed and race, and in no small force either, for their trade was not so much seamanship as rapine and fighting. Such ships carried large crews, and were constantly changing in personnel. A strange face appearing among them need not arouse undue suspicion. From what Estada had reported to Sanchez, I knew boats had been sent ashore on this coast. What more likely then than that some new recruit had returned to the bark, attracted by a sailor's tale? Who would know how the stranger came among them, or question his presence, unless suspicion became aroused? Even if questioned, a good story, easily told, might win the trick. Before daylight came, and already well at sea beyond pursuit, inconspicuous among the others, accepted as mate by the men, unrecognized even by the officers, there was scarcely a probability that anyone aboard would note, or question my presence.

And I felt convinced I could locate the *Namur*. Ay, even in that darkness I could find the bark, if the vessel yet swung at her former anchorage. The task would not even be a difficult one. The stars gave me the compass points, and I recalled with some clearness the general trend of the coast line as we came up. But could I hope to attain the ship in advance of the returning party of raiders? To succeed in my object this must be done, because the moment these reached the deck the bark would hastily depart for the open sea. And if I was to accomplish this end it must be attempted at once. The call to action, the possibility of thus being of service to Dorothy, seemed instantly to awaken all my dormant energies; the painful chafing of my wounds was forgotten, while new strength returned miraculously to my bruised body. God helping me, I would try! My brain throbbed with fresh resolution--the call to action.

There were oars in the boat. I had noticed these dumbly before, but now I drew them eagerly forth from the bottom, and quickly fitted them into the oarlocks. They were stout, ashen blades, unusually large for the craft in which they had been stowed, yet workable. The boat itself was a mere shell, scarcely capable of sustaining safely more than three persons, but with lines of speed, its sharp prow cutting the water like a knife blade. I shipped the useless rudder inboard, and chose my course from the stars. The north star was completely obscured by thick clouds, but the great dipper gave me my bearings with sufficient accuracy. To attain again to the west coast not far from where the great point projected outward into the Bay, and behind which the bark swung at anchor, required, according to my under-standing of our present position, that I head the boat toward the southwest. I bent earnestly to the oars, and the speed of the craft was most encouraging, especially as my strength and energy seemed to increase with each stroke. My mind brightened also quite perceptibly, as the violent exercise sent the blood coursing anew through my veins. Before I realized the change I had become thoroughly convinced that the course I had chosen was the wisest one possible.

It was wild, and desperate, to be sure. I was not blind to its danger, and yet nothing else offered any solution. The only probable chance now for me to prove of direct service to the captive girl lay in being near her while she remained with these men. If, by any good fortune, she had thus far succeeded in escaping from Estada and his gang of ruffians, I would learn this fact more surely aboard the *Namur* than in any other way; and, once assured as to this, could certainly find some means of early escape from the ship. While, if she was captured and taken aboard, as was most probable, for me to be left behind on shore would mean her total abandonment. Better any risk of discovery than that. To be sure I had no plan of action devised, no conception of how a rescue could be effected. Yet such an opportunity might develop, and my one hope lay in being prepared, and ready. With the death of Sanchez, his second in command would undoubtedly succeed him; but would that be Estada, or would it be this other, the mulatto, Francois LeVere? More likely the former, for while buccaneers had operated under colored chiefs, a crew of white men would naturally prefer to be led by one of their own color. Indeed it was even possible that a controversy might arise, and a divided authority result. Discipline among such as these depended entirely on strength and ferocity. The most daring and resourceful became the chosen leaders, whose only test was success. Perhaps, in the turmoil, and uncertainty, arising from a knowledge of Sanchez's death, and the jealousy thus aroused between those who would succeed him in command, I might discover the very opportunity I sought. These were some of the thoughts which animated me, and gave new strength to my arms, as I sent the dory flying through the water.

My boat, unguided, had drifted considerably farther out into the Bay than I had supposed, and it required a good half hour of steady toil at the oars before I sighted ahead of me the darker outlines of the shore. Nothing had crossed our path, and no unusual sound had reached my ears along the black water. If the *Namur's* boat had already returned to the bark, its passage must have been made during the period of my unconsciousness, and this seemed to me utterly impossible. The course I had followed thus far took me directly across the water which they would be compelled to traverse, and they could not have passed unnoticed. No, they were surely yet in the neighborhood of Travers' plantation. The men engaged in that night's bloody business, would have been compelled to carry it out under many obstacles; they would be delayed by consternation at the discovery of their dead leader lying on the sand, and by their lack of knowledge regarding the interior of the house on the summit of the bluff. Quite likely also this lack of a guide would result in an alarm, and consequent struggle, perhaps even in the serious injury of some among them before they secured possession of the money, and the girl. In any case it must have resulted in delay. Convinced of this, and confident that I was already well in advance of them, I drew in as closely as I dared to the dim outline of shore, and studied it carefully, in an endeavor to learn my exact position.

Although the sloop in its voyage up the Bay had never been out of sight of this coast, had indeed skirted it closely all the way, yet my memory of its more prominent landmarks was extremely vague. I had made no effort to impress them on my mind. Therefore at first I could identify nothing, but finally, out of the grotesque, shifting shadows, dimly appearing against the slightly lighter sky beyond, there suddenly arose, clearly defined, the gaunt limbs of a dead tree, bearing a faint resemblance to a gigantic cross. I recalled that Sam had chanced to point this out to me on our upward voyage, and this glimpse obtained of it again now told me exactly where I had made shore. This peculiar mark was at the extremity of the first headland lying north of the point itself, and consequently a straight course across the Bay, would land me within five hundred yards of where the *Namur* had last been seen at anchor.

To a degree my immediate plan of action had been definitely mapped out within my own mind while toiling at the oars. At least I had arrived at certain conclusions. The one immediate object before me was to attain the bark in advance of Estada. I now was convinced that thus far I was safely ahead. The night wind was light, and baffling, not greatly affecting my own progress, but of a nature to retard considerably the sail-boat, and compel a series of wide tacks, so as to enable those on board to round the point. All this distance I could avoid by beaching my dory, and striking out on foot directly across the narrow neck of land. The *Namur*, unless her position had been changed since darkness set in, was not so far out from shore as to make swimming to her a dangerous feat; and I could approach and board her with far less chance of discovery in that manner, than by the use of a boat. The watch on deck would undoubtedly be a vigilant one, yet no eye could detect through that darkness--unless by sheer accident--a submerged swimmer, cautiously advancing with silent strokes. The greater danger would come after I had attained the deck, wet to the skin.

The sharp bow of the dory ran up on the soft sand of the beach, and I stepped ashore, hauling the light boat after me beyond the reach of the waves. The night remained calm and still, although the scudding clouds were thickening overhead, until scarcely a single star remained visible. The sea behind me was overhung by a black curtain, yet, by bending low, I could look along the surface for some distance where the heaving water reflected from wave to wave what little light there was. The beach was a narrow one, and only a few feet away the neck of land became elevated into a leveled crest, thickly covered with trees, their upper branches dimly visible from where I stood. Judging from the trend of the coast, it would be necessary for me to strike directly across to the opposite shore, but in this journey special caution was not required. There would be no one in the midst of this desolate region to interfere with my progress, or be alarmed by any noise I might make. Close to shore as the *Namur* lay, no ordinary sound from the land could be heard aboard, even in the silence of night, nor was it likely the crew would be watchful in that direction. Unquestionably the entire attention of the deck watch at this hour would be concentrated on the expected return of their expedition around the distant point--seeking the glimpse of a white sail above the black water.

To the best of my recollection the bark floated with bow pointing toward the open sea. The sweep of the current about the point was inshore, making the drift of the vessel strong against the anchor hawser. This would naturally bring her with broadside to the eastward, from which direction the absent boat must return. If this proved correct then, in all probability, the deck watch would largely be gathered on that side, even the attention of the officer more or less drawn in that direction. No doubt they had orders to be ready for instant departure the moment the approaching boat was sighted, and the lookout for it would be keen. It was, as I stood there, revolving these matters in my mind, with eyes endeavoring to pierce the surrounding darkness, and ears strained to detect the slightest sound, that there came to me the first real consciousness of the reckless nature of this adventure upon which I had so lightly embarked. Surely it was but the dream of a crazed man, foredoomed to failure. As I faced then the probabilities, there scarcely seemed one chance in a hundred that any such scheme as I proposed would succeed. And yet I must admit there was the one chance; and in no other action could I perceive even that much encouragement. If Dorothy Fairfax was already in the hands of these men, then my only opportunity for serving her lay in my being close at hand. No alternative presented itself; no other effort could be effective. It was already too late to attempt the organization of a rescue party; there was no warship on the coast, and the authorities of the Colony possessed no vessel fitted for pursuit. Long before daylight came, or I might hope to spread an alarm abroad, the *Namur* would be safely at sea. No, the only choice left was for me either to accompany the girl, or else abandon her entirely to her captors. I must either face the possibility of discovery and capture, which as surely meant torture and death, or otherwise play the coward, and remain impotently behind. There was no safe course to pursue. I believed that I could play my part among the crew, once securely established among them; that I could succeed in escaping recognition even on the part of Cochose. If this was true, then, to a stout heart and ready hand, a way might open even aboard the bark to protect her from the final closing of the devil's jaws. I had nothing to risk but my life, and it had never been my nature to count odds. I would act as the heart bade, and so I drove the temptation to falter away, and strode on up the bank into the black shadow of the trees.

I found extremely hard walking as I advanced through tangled underbrush, over unlevel ground, the night so dark in those shadows I could but barely perceive the outlines of a hand held before the eyes. Fortunately the distance was even shorter than I had anticipated, but, when I finally emerged upon the opposite beach, it was at once quite evident that the sea beating upon the sand was decidedly heavier than higher up the Bay, the white line of breakers showing conspicuously even in the night, while their continuous roar sounded loud through the silence. It was not until after I had advanced cautiously into the water, and then stooped low to thus gain clearer vision along the surface, that I succeeded in locating the vessel sought. Even then the *Namur* appeared only as a mere shadow, without so much as a light showing aboard, yet apparently anchored in the same position as when we had swept past the previous afternoon. The slightly brighter sky above served to reveal the tracery of bare poles, while the hull was no more than a blot in the gloom, utterly shapeless, and appearing to be much farther away than it was in reality. Indeed, as the sky gradually darkened the entire vision vanished, as though it had been one of those strange mirages I had seen in the African deserts. Yet I knew with certainty the ship was there, had sufficient time in which to mark its position accurately, and rejoiced at the increase of darkness to conceal my approach. Guided by this memory I waded straight out through the lines of surf, until all excepting the head became completely submerged. If I was to reach the bark at all, this was the one opportunity.

I stood there, resisting the undertow tugging at my limbs, and barely able to retain my footing, intent upon my purpose. Full strength had come back to my muscles, and my head was again clear. The imminent sense of danger seemed to bring me a feeling of happiness, of new confidence in myself. The die was cast, and whatever the result, I was going ahead to accomplish all that was humanly possible. From now on there was to be no doubting, no turning back. A voice, high-pitched, echoed to me across the water, reaching my ears a mere thread of sound, the words indistinguishable. It must have been an order, for, a moment later, I distinguished the clank of capstan bars, as though men of the crew were engaged in warping the vessel off shore for greater safety. The movement was too deliberate and noiseless to mean the lifting of the anchor, nor was it accompanied by any flapping of sail, or shifting of yards to denote departure. Nevertheless even this movement decided me to delay my attempt no longer, and, with strong, silent strokes I swam forward, directly breasting the force of the incoming sea, yet making fair progress. Some unconsidered current must have swept me to the right, for, when the outlines of the bark again became dimly visible through the night, I found myself well to starboard of the vessel, and quite likely would have passed it by altogether, but for the sudden rattle of a block aloft, causing me to glance in that direction. As my eyes explored the darkness, yet uncertain that I really beheld the *Namur*, a light flared for a brief instant, and I had glimpse of a face illumined by the yellow glare, as the single spark of flame ignited a cigarette. It was all over with so swiftly, swallowed up in that blackness, as to seem a vision of imagination. Yet I knew it to be real. Stroking well under water, and with only my eyes exposed above the surface, I changed my course to the left, and slowly and cautiously drew in toward the starboard bow. A few moments later, unperceived from above, and protected from observation by the bulge of the overhang, and density of shadow, my hands clung to the anchor hawser, my mind busy in devising some means for attaining the deck.

CHAPTER X
ON THE DECK OF THE NAMUR

It was here that fortune favored me, strengthening my decision, and yielding a fresh courage to persevere. The pounding of the seas against the bow rendered other sounds, for the moment, unnoticeable, while the current swept so strongly against my submerged body as to compel me to cling tightly to the swaying rope to prevent being overcome. Close as I was the bark appeared scarcely more than a dense shadow swaying above me, without special form, and unrevealed by the slightest gleam of light, merely a vast bulk, towering between sea and sky. Forking out, however, directly over where I clung desperately to the wet hawser, my eyes were able to trace the bow-sprit, a massive bit of timber, with ropes faintly traced against the sky, the rather loosely furled jib flapping ragged edges in the gusts of wind. Suddenly, as I stared upward, I became aware that two men were working their way out along the foot-ropes, and, as they reached a point almost directly over my head, became busily engaged in tightening the gaskets to better secure the loosening sail. The foot of one slipped, and he hung dangling, giving vent to a stiff English oath before he succeeded in hauling himself back to safety, The other indulged in a chuckling laugh, yet was careful not to speak loudly.

"Had one drink too many, Tom?" he asked. "That will pay yer fer finishin' the bottle, an' never givin' me another sup."

The other growled, evidently not in any too good humor after his mishap.

"You, hell! Yer bed the fu'st ov it. Thar's no sorter luck yer don't git yer fair share of, Bill Haines--trust yer fer thet. What I ain't got straight yet, is whar thet stuff cum from so easy. Thet wus the real thing."

Haines laughed again, working carelessly. As the men advanced along the spar I could distinguish their forms more clearly.

"That wus part o' the luck, Tom," he acknowledged, his accent that of a cockney. "Did yer git eyes on thet new feller Manuel Estevan brought back with him in the boat?"

"The one you and Jose carried aboard?"

"He's the lad. Thar wa'n't nuthin' the matter with the cove, 'cept he wus dead drunk, an' he hed a bottle o' rum stowed away in every pocket. But Manuel, he never knew thet. It wus just 'bout dark when he cum staggerin' down ter the boat. We wus waitin' on the beach fer Estevan, an' three fellers he hed taken along with him inter town, ter cum back--the nigger, Jose, an' me--when this yere chap hove 'longside. He never hailed us, ner nuthin'; just clim over inter the boat, an' lay down. 'Whar ye aimin' ter go, friend?' ses I, but by then the cove wus dead asleep. I shook him, an' kicked him, but it wa'n't no use; so we just left him lie thar fer Manuel ter say whut wus ter be done with him. Only Jose he went thru his pockets, an' found three bottles o' rum. We took a few drinks, an' hid whut wus left in the boat locker."

"So that's how yer got it! Who wus the party?"

"Thet's mor'n I'll ever tell yer. I never got no sight o' him, 'cept in the dark. 'Bout all I know is he wus white, an' likely a sailor, judgin' frum the feel o' his hands. Maybe he thought that wus his boat he'd stumbled inter--thar wus quite a few 'long the beach. Enyhow, when Manuel got back, he just took a look at him in the dark, an' then told us to haul the lad forrard out o' the way, an' fetch him along. So we pulled out with the feller cuddled up in the bow. He was drunk all right."

"I never seed nuthin' more of him after he was hauled aboard," commented Tom, as the other ceased speaking. "Whut become o' the lad?"

"Him? Oh, Jose an' me carried him inter the for'cassel, an' shoved him inter a berth ter sleep off his liquor. Thet wus the last I ever see, er hear o' him fer 'bout six hours. I'd fergot all 'bout the feller--er wud have, if it hadn't been fer the rum. Manuel went off in the long-boat with Estada, an' when my watch went below, I stowed myself away back o' the bow gun fer a few drinks. I hadn't been thar mor'n ten minutes, when this yere feller must a woke up in the for'cassel sum crazy. He cum a chargin' out on deck, whoopin' like an Indian, wavin' a knife in his hand, intendin' fer ter raise hell. I cudn't see then who the lad wus, but it must o' been him, fer when I went down later he wusn't whar we'd put him. Well, it happened thet the fu'st feller he run up against wus LeVere, who wus cumin' forrard fer sumthin', an' fer about a minute thar was one hell ov a fight. Maybe LeVere didn't know et onct just whut hed happened, but he wusn't almighty long finding out his job, an' the way he started in fer ter man-handle the cuss, wus worth seein'. It was so damn dark thar by the foremast I couldn't tell whut did happen, but it wus fists mostly, till the mate drove the poor devil, cussin' like mad, over agin the rail, an' then heaved him out inter the water 'longside. I heerd the feller splash when he struck, but he never let out no yell."

"What did LeVere do?"

"Him? Hell, he didn't do nuthin'. Just stared down over the rail a bit, an' then cum back, rubbin' his hands. Never even asked who the feller wus. Thar ain't nuthin' kin skeer that black brute."

"By God--no! He ain't got no human in him. It's hell when English sailormen has got ter take orders frum a damned nigger, an' be knocked 'round if they don't jump when he barks. He's goin' ter get a knife in his ribs sum day."

"Maybe he is; but yer better hold yer tongue, Tom. Sanchez don't stand fer thet talk, an' he's back o' LeVere. Let's go in; them gaskets will hold all right now--cum 'long."

The two vaguely distinguishable figures disappeared, clambering awkwardly over the rail, and as instantly vanishing into the blackness of the bark's deck. An unsecured bit of canvas continued to flap noisily above me, and the constant surge of water pounded against the bow, but I could perceive now clearly the character I was destined to assume when once safely aboard the *Namur*. Such an assumption would involve but slight danger of discovery. It was as though a miracle had opened the way, revealed to me by the unconscious lips of these two half-drunken, gossiping sailors. The story told fitted my necessities exactly. Had I planned the circumstances myself, nothing could have been better prearranged. No one on board had seen the missing man by daylight; if an impression of his features remained in any individual mind, it must be extremely vague, and valueless. Bill's conviction that the man was English, and probably a sailor, was the most definite, and he had had greater opportunity closely to observe the stranger than anyone else. LeVere had obtained no more than a glimpse of his opponent, during their struggle in the dark, and while fighting for his life. Surely it would be easy enough to obscure any faint impression thus acquired. And the fellow had been heartlessly flung overboard; was believed to have sunk without a struggle, too drunk to save himself; was scarcely given another thought. Yet no one knew positively that this was so, because no one cared. The death of the lad had simply been taken for granted, when LeVere failed to see his body rise again to the surface. Yet it was quite within the realm of possibility for the fellow to come up once more in that darkness, beyond LeVere's range of vision, and even to have remained afloat, buoyed up by clinging to the anchor hawser, until strong enough to return on board. At least there was no one aboard the *Namur* able to deny that this had been done.

Satisfied by this reasoning of being able to pass myself off as the dead man, with small danger of detection, and likewise assured--so far at least as eyes and ears testified--that none of the crew were grouped on the forecastle, to be attracted by my movements, I began, slowly and cautiously, to drag myself up the taut hawser, hoping thus to attain a position from which to gain hand-hold on the rail, and thus attain the deck unseen. While my explanation might suffice, I greatly preferred having to present it only as a last resort. I would much rather slip quietly aboard, and mingle unnoticed with the crew for the next few hours, than be haled at once before LeVere, and endure his scrutiny and possible violence. The fellow was evidently a brute, and a hard master. Seemingly I had chosen a fortunate moment for my effort; no one heeded the little noise I made, and, when I finally topped the rail, and was able to look inboard, it was to discover a deserted fore deck, with the watch all engaged at some task amidships. There was no gleam of light, but I could hear the patter of feet, and imagined seeing dim moving figures. A rather high-pitched voice was giving orders, and enough of his words reached me to convince that other men were aloft on the main yard. Believing my best policy would be to join those busied on deck, just as though I belonged among them, I crept down the forecastle ladder, and worked my way aft beneath the black shadow of the port rail, until able thus to drift unnoticed into a group tailing on to a mainsail halliard. The fellow next to me, without releasing his grip, turned his head and stared, but without discerning my features.

"Whar the hell did yer cum' frum?" he growled, and I as instantly recognized Bill Haines. "Been sojerin', have yer? Well, now, damn yer eyes! lay too an' pull."

Before I could attempt an answer, a tall figure loomed up before us, the same high-pitched voice I had noticed previously calling out sharply:

"There, that's enough, men! Now make fast. We can head the old girl out from here in a jiffy, if it really begins to blow. Jose, you stand by at the wheel, in case you're needed; some of the rest ship the capstan bars, and remain near for a call."

Discipline on board must have been somewhat lax, or else Haines held some minor official position which gave him unusual privilege, for, while the others instantly separated to carry out these orders, he remained motionless, confronting the man I supposed to be the mulatto, LeVere. My own position was such I could not press past the two without attracting attention.

"What are ye swingin' the yards fer, enyhow?" asked the sailor insolently. "Just fer exercise?"

The other, who already had started to turn away, stopped, and took a step backward toward his questioner.

"Because I am a sailor, Haines," he replied angrily. "Anyhow it is none of your business; I was left in command here. Those clouds don't look good to me; there is going to be a blow before morning."

"Then it's yer intention ter work out'er this yere berth?"

"It's my intention to be ready, if it becomes necessary. There is no regular officer left aboard, but, just the same, I am not going to let this bark pile up on those rocks yonder. We'll hang on here for another half hour, maybe, and then, if the long-boat don't show up, we'll work further off shore until daylight. That's sensible, isn't it?"

Haines growled something, inaudible to me, but evidently accepted as an assent, and LeVere, still in no good humor from the questioning, wheeled sharply about to go forward. This movement placed him face to face with me.

"What are you loafing here for?" he burst forth, no doubt glad to thus vent his anger on someone. "Who the hell are you?"

"Joe Gates, sir," I answered quickly, mouthing the first name which came to my lips.

"Gates--Joe Gates?" peering savagely into my face, but unable to distinguish the features. "I never heard of anybody on board by that name. Who is the fellow, Haines?"

The Englishman gripped me by the sleeve to whirl me about, but as his fingers touched the soaked cloth of my jacket, he burst forth with an oath.

"By God! but he's wet enough to be the same lad you chucked overboard an hour ago. Damn me, I believe he is. Say, mate, are you the gay buck we hauled aboard drunk, and dumped inter the for'cassel?"

"I dunno, sir," I answered dumbly, believing it best not to remember too much. "I couldn't even tell yer whut ship this is, ner how I signed on. Last I seem ter remember I wus ashore frum the schooner *Caroline*; but this yere is a bark."

Haines laughed, already convinced of my identity, and considering it a good joke.

"Well, my buck, I'll tell yer whar yer are, an' likewise how yer got yere," he chuckled. "I wus one of a party frum this hooker ashore 'bout dusk, when yer hove in sight 'bout as drunk as a sailorman kin get. Fact is yer wus so soused yer stumbled inter the wrong boat, and went ter sleep. We're allers ready fer ter take on a new hand er two, so we just let yer lie thar, an' brought yer aboard. 'Bout an hour ago yer must a had a touch o' tremens, fer, all at onct yer cum chargin' out on deck, an' tried ter knife LeVere, an' he flung yer overboard. We sorter figured thet yer went down, an' never cum up agin."

LeVere broke in with a savage snarl.

"What's all that? Do you mean, Haines, that this is the same damned scamp who tried to stick me?"

"No doubt of it. But he never knew what he was dloin'--he wus crazy as a loon. There's nuthin' fer yer ter fuss over now. Tell us about it, Gates--the bath must have sobered yer up?"

I watched LeVere, but he remained motionless, a mere shadow.

"I suppose it must have been thet, sir," I confessed respectfully, "if things happened as you say they did. I haven't any memory o' tryin' ter slash nobody. Leastwise I seemed ter know whut I wus about when I cum up. I don't remember how I got ther; furst I knew I wus slushin' 'round in the water, a tryin' ter keep afloat. It wus so blame dark I cudn't see nuthin', but sumhow I got grip on a hawser, an' hung on till I got back 'nough strength ter clime on board. I knew this wa'n't my ship, so I just lay quiet awhile, figurin' out whar I wus."

"Yer English?" "Born in Bristol, sir, but I wus workin' on the *Caroline*--she's a Colony schooner, in the fish trade."

"Sailor?"

"At sea since I wus twelve. What's this yere bark--Dutch, ain't she?"

"Once upon a time; just now we are flying whatever flag cumes handy. We ain't got no prejudice in flags."

"Is thet a gun forrard, covered with taupalin?"

"Yes, an' yer might find another aft, if yer looked fer it. Mor'n thet, we know how ter use 'em. Now see here, Gates; thar's no reason why we should beat about the bush--fact is we're sea rovers."

"Sea rovers--pirates, sir?"

"Bah! what's a name! We take what we want; it's our trade, that's all. No worse than many another. The question is, are yer goin' ter take a chance 'long with us? It's the only life, lad--plenty of fun, the best of liquor and pretty girls, with a share in all the swag."

"What is the name of this bark?"

"The *Namur*--sailed out o' Rotterdam till we took her."

"Whut wus yer in when ye took her?"

"The *Vengeance*, a three-masted schooner, the fastest thing afloat. She's south in West India waters."

"Who's the captain?"

"Silva Sanchez."

"Gawd! Sanchez--not--not 'Black Sanchez?'"

"That's him; so yer've heerd o' 'Black Sanchez?' Well, we're sailin' 'long with him, all right, mate, an' yer ought ter know whut thet means fer a good man."

I hesitated, yet only long enough to leave the impression I sought to make on them both.

"Likely thar ain't no sailor but whut has heerd o' him," I said slowly. "Enyhow, I sure have. I can't say thet I have any special hankerin' after bein' a pirate, an' I never aimed ter be one; but, seem' as how I am yere on this bark, an' can't easy get away, it don't look like thar wus much choice, does it?"

LeVere appeared amused in his way, which was not a pleasant one.

"Oh, yes, friend, there is choice enough. Bill, here, had exactly the same choice when he first came--hey, Bill? Remember how you signed on, after we took you off the *Albatross*? This is how it stands, Gates--either go forrard quietly yerself, er the both of us will kick you there. We never give an order twice on the *Namur*. That will be enough talk. If you do your work, all right; and if you don't, then look out, my man--there will be plenty of hell waiting for you. Go on, now."

It was a curt dismissal, coupled with a plain threat, easy to understand. I obeyed the order gladly enough, slinking away into the black shadows forward, realizing my good fortune, and seeking some spot where I could be alone. The result was all that I could have hoped for; my position on board was assured; my story had been accepted without awakening the slightest suspicion; and it was perfectly clear that no one on board the *Namur* possessed the slightest memory of the personal appearance of the poor fellow who had been thrown overboard, and drowned. Even Haines believed me to be the man. Of course I should be watched to some extent for a few days, my willingness to serve noted, and my ability as a seaman put to the test; but in this I had nothing to fear. I could play the assumed character with little danger of any mishap. The only remaining peril of discovery would come with the return of the absent boat, and the necessity of my encountering the giant negro. Yet I was convinced even this would not prove serious. If Cochose had glimpsed my features at all during the course of our desperate struggle on the deck of the sloop, the impression made on his mind must have been merely momentary; and, besides, he would never once conceive it possible that the same man could have reached the bark ahead of his return. Even if such a suspicion dawned, I was now in a position to positively establish my arrival aboard the *Namur* early the evening previous, and before their expedition had departed.

I felt so safe, and so content with my success thus far, as to already believe thoroughly in the final result of my mission. This confidence developed almost into sheer recklessness. There were some difficulties ahead, to be sure. I remained sane enough to recognize these, yet I had already conquered easily, what at first had appeared insurmountable, and, in consequence of this good luck, these others yet to be met, seemed far less serious. The same happy fortune which had opened the way for me to board the *Namur* must also intervene to aid me in solving future problems. Mine was the philosophy of a sailor, to whom peril was but a part of life. All I seemed to require now was a sufficiency of courage and faith--the opportunity would be given. In this spirit of aroused hope, I continued to stare out into the black night, watchfully, the shrouded deck behind me silent, and seemingly deserted, except for the steady tramp from rail to rail of LeVere, keeping his lonely watch aft. The crew had disappeared, lying down no doubt in corners out of the wind. And this wind was certainly rising, already attaining a force to be reckoned with, for the boom of waves hurled against the bows of the laboring bark, was steadily becoming more noticeable, while overhead the ropes sang dismally. I wondered that LeVere hung on so long in his perilous position, although, in spite of the increased strain, the anchor still clung firmly. Quite probably he had received stern orders not to shift from his present position until the boat returned, yet surely his judgment as a competent seaman, left in command, must make him aware of the threatening danger. He would never wreck his vessel merely because he had been instructed to remain at that particular spot. It seemed to me that no hawser ever made could long withstand the terrific strain of our tugging, as the struggling bark rose and fell in the grip of the sea. To him must have come the same conviction, for suddenly his high-pitched voice sang out from the poop:

"Stand by, forrard, to lower the starboard anchor; move lively, men. Everything ready, Haines?"

"All clear, sir. Come on the jump, bullies!"

"Then let go smartly. Watch that you don't get the line fouled. Aloft there! Anything in sight, Cavere?"

From high up on the fore-top yard, the answer, blown by the wind, came down in broken English:

"Non, M'sieur; I see nottings."

"Well, don't go to sleep; keep both eyes open!"

I had already joined the watch forward, aware only of the numerous dim, and shapeless figures about me, busily employed in straightening out the kinks in the heavy cable. The number of men on deck was evidence of a large crew, there being many more than were necessary for the work to be done. Most of them appeared to be able seamen, and Haines drove them mercilessly, cursing them for lubbers, and twice kicking viciously at a stooping form. There was no talking, only the growl of an occasional oath, the slapping of the hawser on deck, and the sharp orders of Haines. Then the great rope began to slip swiftly through the hawse hole, and we heard the sharp splash as the iron flukes struck the water, and sank. Almost at that same instant the voice of Cavere rang out from the mast-head:

"A sail, M'sieur--a sail!"

"Where away?"

"Off ze port quarter. I make eet to be ze leetle boat--she just round ze point"

CHAPTER XI
THE RETURN OF THE BOAT

Receiving no other orders, the moment all was secure, the crew eager to welcome back the boat party, and learn the news, hurried over to the port rail. Beyond doubt most of those aboard realized that this had been an expedition of some importance, the culmination of their long wait on the coast, part of some scheme of their chief, in the spoils of which they expected to share. It was for this end they had been inactive for weeks, hiding and skulking along shore; now they hoped to reap their reward in gold and silver, and then be permitted to return to the wilder, more adventurous life they loved on the high seas. Moreover this boat approaching through the darkness was bringing back their leader, and however else they might feel toward him, the reckless daring, and audacious resourcefulness of Sanchez meant success. These fellows, the scum of the seven seas, whom he had gathered about him, might hate and fear, yet were glad to follow. They had learned on many a bloody deck the merit of their chief, and in their way were loyal to him.

I was made to comprehend all this by the low, muttered utterances of those crowding near me, spoken in nearly every language of the world. Much I could not even translate, yet enough reached my ears to convince me of the temper of the crew--their feverish eagerness to be again at sea, under command of a captain whom they both hated and feared, yet whom they would follow to the very gates of hell. Even as they cursed him with hot oaths, in memory of some act of discipline, there came into their voices a tinge of admiration, which furnished me an accurate etching of the man. They knew him, these hell-hounds of the sea, and from out their mouths I knew him also for what he was--a cruel, cold-blooded monster, yet a genius in crime, and a natural leader of such men as these. ***Black Sanchez!*** All the unspeakable horror which in the past had clung to that name came back again to haunt me; I seemed to hear once more the tales of men who had escaped from his grip alive; to see again the scenes they had witnessed. It could not seem possible that I was actually upon one of his ships, in the very midst of his wild crew. I listened to their comments, their expectations, with swiftly beating heart. I alone knew what that boat was bringing. And when it arrived, and they knew also, what would these sea wolves say? What would they do? What would be the result when the dead body of their leader came up over the rail?

For a few moments we could perceive nothing through the black night. The clouds were rolling low, thickened by vapor, and the increasing wind had already beaten the waves into crests of foam. We could hear them crash against the stout sides of the bark, which leaped to their impetus, yet was held in helpless captivity by the two anchors. The deck under foot tossed dizzily, the bare masts swaying above, while our ears could distinguish the sullen roar of breakers tumbling up on the sand just astern. Overhead ropes rattled noisily, the sound mingling with the flapping ends of loosened sails beating against the yards. LeVere shouted an order, and a sudden flare was lighted amidships, the circle of flame illumining a part of the deck, and spreading out over the wild expanse of water. The seaman holding the blazing torch aloft, and thrusting it forth across the rail, took on the appearance of a black statue, as motionless as though carved from ebony, while in the gleam the various groups of men became visible, lined up along the port bulwarks, all staring in the one direction, eagerly seeking a first glimpse of the approaching craft.

Scarcely had a minute elapsed before it came sweeping into the radius of light--at first a dim, spectral shadow, scarcely to be recognized; then, almost as suddenly, revealed in all its details--a boat of size, flying toward us under a lug sail, standing out hard as a board, keeling well over, and topping the sea swells like a bird on wing. 'Twas a beautiful sight as the craft came sweeping on before the full weight of the wind, out from that background of gloom into the yellow glare of the torch, circling widely so as to more safely approach the bark's quarter. LeVere called for men to stand by, the fellows rushing past me to their stations, but, in the fascination of the moment, I failed to move. I could do nothing but stare out across the intervening water, with eyes fastened on that swiftly approaching boat. I must see. I must know the message it brought; what story it held of the tragedy. At first I could only barely distinguish the figures of those aboard, yet these gradually assumed recognizable form, and finally the faces also became dimly visible. Manuel held the tiller, with Estada seated beside him, leaning forward, and gesticulating with one hand, as he directed the course. I had never seen these two, yet I knew them beyond a doubt. Mendez and Anderson (at least I supposed these to be the two) were poised at the sail halliards, ready to let the straining sheet down at a run, while Cochose crouched low in the bow, his black hand uplifted, gripping a coil of rope. Their faces were all turned forward, lighted by the flare from our deck, and I felt a shudder of fear run over me--no expression on any countenance spoke of defeat; even the ugly features of the negro beamed with delight.

But was that all? Was that all? Surely not, yet the boat had to leap forward, and then turn broadside too, as it swept aft toward the main chains, before I succeeded in seeing what remained partially concealed between the thwarts in its bottom. Forward of the single mast was stowed the chest, which Travers' slaves had borne with such care up the bluff; while in the open space between the helmsman and the two sailors were stretched two motionless bodies. LeVere, gripping a stay-rope, and leaning well out, hailed in Spanish.

"Ahoy, the boat--there is not too much sea? You can make it?"

"Ay!" came back Estada's voice, swept aside by the wind, yet still audible. "Stand by to fend us off. Call all hands, and break anchor as soon as we are aboard."

"Very well, sir. Where is Captain Sanchez?"

Estada pointed downward in swift, expressive gesture.

"Here at my feet--badly hurt, but will recover. Send two men down to help when we make fast. Now, Cochose--let go of your rope; watch out above!"

I stood, gripping hard at the rail, and staring down at the scene below, as the men in the boat made fast. I felt paralyzed, and helpless, unable to move. I had no business to remain there; every prospect of security depended on my joining the crew, but it was not in my power to desert my position. I could hear the hurrying feet of the watch tramping across the deck in response to LeVere's orders; the heavy pounding of a marling-spike on the forecastle hatch, as Haines called for all hands. I was aware that men were already mounting the ratlines, and laying out on the upper yards to make sail, while the capstan bars began rattling. Yet only one thought gripped me--***Sanchez was not dead***! I had believed he was; I had staked all on his death as a certainty. But instead, the man was lying there in the boat, helpless at present, sorely wounded perhaps, yet still alive. Estada even said he would surely recover. And that other body? That of Dorothy Fairfax, without doubt, yet certainly not lifeless. Those fellows would surely never bring back to the ***Namur*** the useless, dead form of one of their victims. That was unthinkable, impossible. If their prisoner was the girl--and who else could it be?--she remained alive, helplessly bound to prevent either struggle, or outcry, and destined to a fate far worse than death.

This revelation struck me like a blow. I had anticipated the possible capture of the young woman, but not the return of Sanchez. His living overthrew all my plans. There was no hope in the narrow confines of the ship for me to remain long out of his sight, once he became able again to reach the deck. And he would instantly recognize me in any guise. Every hope of rescue had vanished, every faith that I could be of aid. My own life hung in the balance--nay, rather, my doom was already sealed. There, seemingly was but one chance for escape left--that was to drop silently overboard, amid the confusion of getting under way, and make the desperate attempt to reach shore unseen before the crew could lift anchor, and set sail. This possibility came to me, yet I continued to cling there, dazed and helpless, staring dully down, lacking both physical and mental energy to put the wild scheme into execution. God, no! that would be the craven act of a coward. Better far to stay, and kill, or even be killed, than to be forever cursed by my own conscience. The fellow might die; some fatal accident befall the ***Namur***; why a hundred things might occur before Sanchez was capable of resuming command, or could attempt any serious injury to Dorothy.

The fellows sent down from the main chains to the boat brought the injured Captain up first. This required the services of three men, his body hanging limp between them, his upturned face showing ghastly in the flaming of the torch thrust out over the rail. To every appearance it was apparently a corpse they handled, except for their tenderness, and a single groan to which the white lips gave utterance, when one of the bearers slipped, wrenching the wounded body with a sharp pang of pain. Once safely on deck, the three bore him across to the after cabin, in which a swinging lantern had been lighted, and was by then burning brightly, and disappeared down the steps. My eyes followed every movement, as I forgot for the instant the boat and its occupants still tossing alongside on the waters below. As I turned back, awakened by some cry, I saw that Estada had already swung himself up into the chains, while Anderson and Mendez were lifting the girl to her feet, and rather roughly urging her forward. Her hands and limbs had been set free, but she swayed back and forth in the grasp of the two men, as though unable to support herself alone, her face upturned into the flare of light, as she gazed in terror at the black side of the bark towering above. Her eyes reflected all the unutterable horror which for the moment dominated her mind, while her loosened hair, disarranged by struggle, only served to intensify the pallor of her face. Yet in spite of this evident despair, there was still strength and defiance in the firm closing of her lips, and her efforts to stand alone, uncontaminated by the touch of the sailors' hands.

"Hustle her along lively, boys," shouted back Estada coarsely. "If she won't move, give her a shove. Then tie her up again, and take the turn of a rope 'round her. What do you think this is--a queen's reception? Move lively, Senorita," in mock sarcasm.

Her gaze settled on him, where he hung far out, grasping a backstay, watching the movements below, and her slender form straightened as by the acquisition of new strength.

"If these creatures will take their hands off me," she said, using their tongue without a tremor in the clear voice. "I can easily go up alone. What is it you are so afraid of--a woman?"

The expression of Estada's face promised an outburst of profanity, but, instead of giving it utterance, he lifted his cap in a sudden pretense at gallantry.

"Your pardon, Senorita," he said in a tone of humble mockery. "If you have come to your senses at last, it is well. No one can be happier than I. Leave her alone, men. Now, my beauty, I am taking you at your own word--a step, and then the protection of my hand. We welcome you, as a guest aboard."

A moment and she had attained the deck. Where she stood I could no longer see her face, yet she remained there silent and motionless, rather stiffly erect as she faced him. Frightened, and helpless as she was, yet her very posture seemed to express the detestation she felt for the man. But Estada, apparently pleased with his performance thus far, chose to continue playing the fool.

"Thanks, Senorita--thanks," he began softly, and again bowing before her, cap in hand. "We greet you with due honor aboard the *Namur*--"

"Enough of that, you coward, you murderer," she broke in coldly. "Do not touch nor speak to me."

She turned her back on him, thus coming face to face with LeVere, who stood enjoying the scene, a wide grin on his dark face, revealing a row of white teeth under a jet-black moustache.

"You, sir--you are an officer?"

"I have charge of the deck."

"Then where am I to go?"

The mulatto, surprised by the sudden question, glanced inquiringly toward Estada, who had already completely lost his sense of humor.

"Go!" the latter growled. "Where is she to go? Why send the wench below. I'll see to her later, and teach her who is the master here. She will not queen it long on these decks, I warrant you. Off with her now, but be back quickly." He leaned out over the rail, sending his gruff voice below. "Send up that chest, you men--careful now not to let it drop overboard. Yes, that's better. Hook on the boat, Manuel, and let her drag; we must get out of here in a hurry. All ready, aloft?"

"Ay, ay, sir."

"Then sheet home; how is it forrard?"

"Both anchors apeak, sir."

"Smartly done--hard down with your helm there! That's it; now let her play off slowly."

He must have caught sight of me through the gloom, for he strode furiously forward, giving utterance to a bristling Spanish oath. All the savage brutality of his nature had been brought to the surface by Dorothy's stinging words, and he sought now some fit opportunity to give it vent. Before I could move, he had gripped me by the collar, and swung me about, so that the light streaming out from the cabin fell directly on my face.

"What the devil are you doing, loafing aft here?" he demanded roughly, staring into my eyes. "Didn't you hear the orders, you damned shirker? I've seen you hanging about for ten minutes, never lifting a hand. Who the hell are you anyhow--the captain?"

"Joe Gates, sir."

"Gates--another damned Englishman! How did you ever get aboard here?"

It was the returning LeVere who made explanation before I could reply.

"Manuel brought him on board last night. Picked him up drunk ashore."

Estada's ugly eyes roved from face to face, as though he failed to fully comprehend.

"Well, does he imagine he is going to be a passenger? Why hasn't he been taught his place before this? It's about time, LeVere, for this drunken sailor to be given a lesson to last him for awhile; and, by God, if you won't do it, I will. Step over here, Gates."

I took the necessary step forward, and faced him, expecting the rabid tongue lashing, which I rather felt I deserved.

"Now, my man, do you know what this bark is?"

"I think so, sir--Mister LeVere explained that to me."

"Oh, he did? Well, he must have failed to make clear the fact that we enforce discipline aboard. The next time you neglect to jump at an order, you are going to taste the cat. You understand me? You speak Spanish?"

"Yes, sir; I lived two years in Cuba."

"I see; well now, do you happen to have any idea who I am?"

"No, sir--only that you are one of the officers."

"Then I will enforce the information on your mind so that you are not liable to forget; also the fact that hereafter you are to jump when I speak. I am the first officer, and in command at present. Pedro Estada is my name. Now, you damned English whelp, remember that!"

Before I even suspected what was coming, his unexpected action as swift as the leap of a poised tiger, he struck me fairly between the eyes with the butt of a pistol, and I went down sprawling onto the deck. For a moment I seemed, in spite of the viciousness of the blow, to retain a spark of consciousness, for I knew he kicked me savagely with his heavy sea boots; I felt the pain, and even heard the words, and curses, accompanying each brutal stroke.

"You drunken dog! You whelp of a sea wolf! You English cur! Take that--damn you! And that! You'll not forget me for awhile, That's it--squirm, I like to see it. When you wake up again, you'll remember Pedro Estada, How did that feel, you grunting pig? Here, LeVere, Manuel, throw this sot into the forecastle. Curse you, here is one more to jog your memory."

The heavy, iron-shod boot landed full in my face, and every sensation left me as I sank limply back, bloody and unconscious.

CHAPTER XII
A FRIEND IN THE FORECASTLE

I slowly and regretfully opened my eyes, aroused perhaps by a trampling of feet on the deck above, to find myself lying in an upper bunk of the forecastle. I was partially covered by a ragged blanket, but for a few moments remained unable to comprehend the situation. Yet the vivid memory soon returned, stimulated no doubt by the continuous aching of my body where Estada had so brutally kicked me with his heavy boots. The first recollection of that assault brought with it a dull anger, strangely commingled with a thought of Dorothy Fairfax, and a sense of my own duty. The heavy rolling of the bark clearly evidenced that we were already at sea, and bucking against a high wind. Occasionally a monster wave broke over the cats-head, and struck thunderingly on the deck above me, the whole vessel trembling to the shock. Oilskins hung to the deck beams, swung here and there at strange angles, while the single slush lantern dangled back and forth like the pendulum of a clock.

It was a dark, dismal, smelly interior, amply large enough, but ill ventilated, and inexpressibly dirty. Every stench under heaven seemed to assail my nostrils, so compounded together, as to be separately indistinguishable, although that of stale bilge water strongly predominated. The only semblance of fresh air found entrance through the small, square scuttle hole, attainable by means of a short ladder, and staring up at this, I was able to perceive the light of day, although so little penetrated below, the swaying slush light alone served to illumine the place, and render its horrors visible. It was day then, and we were well out at sea. I must have been lying unconscious for several hours. In all probability, finding it impossible to arouse me, the brutes had finally left me alone, to either recover, or die, as fate willed. I rested back, feeling of the numerous bruises on my body, and touching gingerly the dried blood caked on my face. No very serious damage seemed to have been done, for I could move without great pain, although every muscle and tendon appeared to be strained and lacerated. My head had cleared also from its earlier sensation of dullness, the brain actively taking up its work. Clinching my teeth to keep back a groan, I succeeded in sitting upright, my head touching the upper deck, as I undertook to survey my surroundings. They were gloomy and dismal enough. The forecastle, in true Dutch style, had been built directly into the bows, so that the bunks, arranged three tiers high, formed a complete half circle. The single lantern, flickering and flaring as it swung constantly to the sharp pitching of the vessel, cast grotesque shadows, and failed entirely to penetrate the corners. The deck below me was littered with chests, sea boots, and odds and ends of clothing, while farther aft considerable water had found entrance through the scuttle hole, and was slushing back and forth as the bark rolled. About half the bunks seemed to be occupied, the figures of the sleeping men barely discernible, although their heavy breathing evidenced their presence, and added to the babel of sound. Every bolt and beam creaked and groaned in the ceaseless struggle with the sea.

The bunk in which I had awakened was situated almost at the apex of the half circle, so that I had a clear view of the wider open space. Those beneath me contained no occupants, nor, at first, could I distinguish any in the tier directly opposite. Evidently the watch off duty preferred to seek their rest as far away as possible from those waves pounding against the bow. However, as I sat there, staring about at this scene, and uncertain as to what my next move should be, there was a stir within the upper berth on my own level, and a moment later, an uplifted face appeared suddenly in the yellow flare of light. It was manifestly an English face at first glance, rosy of cheek, with chestnut beard, and light, tousled hair. A pair of humorous, gray eyes surveyed me silently, and then, apparently satisfied by the scrutiny, the owner sat up in the bunk, revealing powerful shoulders, and a round, bull neck.

"Ahoy, mate," he said pleasantly, endeavoring to speak low, the effort resembling the growl of a bear. "How do you feel--pretty sore?"

"Ache from head to foot," I answered, immediately feeling his friendliness. "But no harm done."

"I saw part of it. The damn black brute kicked savagely enough, but at that you're lucky; it's the Spanish style to use a knife. I've seen that cock slash a man into ribbons for nothing at all--just to show he was bad. Haines tells me your name is Gates, and that you are English."

"That's right; I shipped first out of Bristol."

"So did I, mate--twenty years ago though, and I never went back since. My name is Tom Watkins. Let's shake; there is quite a sprinkling of us Britishers aboard, and we ought to hang together."

He put out a big, hairy fist, and I gripped it heartily, decidedly liking the man as his eyes frankly met mine. He appeared honest and square, a fine type of the English seaman.

"Tom Watkins, you said. May I ask if you were out on the bow-sprit along with Haines last night?"

"Just afore the long-boat come in? Yes, we were there."

"Well, I was down below, hanging to the cable, and overheard you two talking together. Somehow, Watkins, you do not seem to me to fit in exactly with this gang of pirates; you don't look to be that sort. How long have you been with them?"

He glanced about warily, lowering his voice until it became a hoarse whisper.

"Three years, mate, and most of that time has been hell. I haven't even been ashore, but once, and that was on an island. These fellows don't put any trust in my kind, nor give them any chance to cut and run. Once in awhile a lad does get away, but most of them are caught; and those that are sure get their punishment. They never try it again. I've seen them staked out on the sand, and left to die; that ain't no nice thing to remember."

"But how did you come into it?" "Like most of the rest. I was second mate of the *Ranger*, a Glasgow brig. We loaded with sugar at Martinique, for London. These fellows overhauled us at daybreak about a hundred miles off the east end of Cuba. They had a swift schooner, and five guns, one a Long Tom. All we had to fight them with was about fifteen men, and two brass carronades. Our skipper was Scotch, and he put up some fight, but it wasn't any use. There was only three of us left alive when the pirates came aboard. One of these died two days later, and another was washed overboard and drowned down in the Gulf. I am all that is left of the **Ranger**."

"You saved your life by taking on?"

"Sanchez had the two of us, who were able to stand, back in his cabin. He put it to us straight. He said it was up to us whether we signed up, or walked the plank; and he didn't appear to care a damn which we chose. The cold-blooded devil meant it too, for he was raging mad at getting only five hundred pounds off the brig. Well, Jack and I looked at each other--and then we signed."

"And you say others of this crew have been obtained in the same manner?" I questioned, deeply interested, and perceiving in this a ray of hope.

"Not exactly--no, I wouldn't precisely say that. It's true, perhaps, that most of the Britishers were forced to join in about the same way I was, and there may be a Scandinavian, or two, with a few Dutch, to be counted in that list; but the most of these cusses are pirates from choice. It's their trade, and they like it. Sanchez only aims to keep hold of a few good men, because he has got to have sailors; but most of his crew are nothing but plain cut-throats."

"Where does he find them?"

"Where? Why the West Indies are full of such devils; been breeding them down there for two hundred years---Indians and half-breeds, niggers, Creoles, Portuguese, Spanish, and every damned mongrel you ever heard of. Sanchez himself is half French. The hell-hound who kicked you is a Portugee, and LeVere is more nigger than anything else. I'll bet there is a hundred rats on board this **Namur** right now who'd cut your throat for a sovereign, and never so much as think of it again."

"A hundred? Is there that many aboard?"

"A hundred an' thirty all told. Most o' 'em bunk amidships. They're not sailormen, but just cut-throats, an' sea wolves. Yer ought ter see 'em swarm out on deck, like hungry rats, when thar's a fight comin'. It's all they're good fer."

"Watkins," I said soberly, after a pause during which he spat on the dirty deck to thus better express his feelings "do you mean to say that in three years you've had no chance to escape? No opportunity to get away?"

"Not a chance, mate; no more will you. The only place I've put foot ashore has been Porto Grande, where we run in to refit. That's a worse hell than the ship itself."

"But Haines goes ashore; he was with Manuel's boat yesterday."

The big fellow laughed grimly.

"Bill rather likes the job, an' they know it. He's a boatswain, an' gets a big share of the swag. He's the only Britisher aboard who wouldn't cut and run in a minute; besides he's got a girl at Porto Grande."

"And that fellow Anderson who was with Estada?"

"The lowest kind of a Swede cur--he'll do more dirt than a Portugee. I know what yer thinkin' 'bout. I had them notions too when I fu'st come aboard--gettin' all the decent sort tergether, and takin' the vessel. 'Twon't work; thar ain't 'nough who wud risk it, and if thar wus, yer couldn't get 'em tergether. Sanchez is too damn smart fer thet. Every damn rat is a spy. I ain't hed no such talk as this afore in six months, Gates; the last time cost me twenty lashes at the mast-butt."

"Is there any chance of our being overheard now?"

"No; these near bunks are all empty, an' the damn noise drowns our voices. What'd yer have in your mind, mate?"

"Only this, Watkins. I've got to do something, and believe I can trust you. You are a square English seaman, probably the only one aboard I can repose confidence in. I don't blame you for sticking, for I suppose likely I'd do the same if I was in your case. But I ain't--it's not my life I'm thinking about, but that of a woman."

He stared at me across the narrow space separating our bunks, the shadows from the swinging lantern giving his features a strange expression.

"A woman! Hell, lad; not the one brought aboard last night?"

"Exactly; now listen--I'm going to tell you my story, and ask your help. Do you know what Estada went after in the long-boat?"

"Well, there's been plenty o' talk. The cook brought us some stories he heard aft, an' we knew we wus driftin' along the coast, waitin' fer Sanchez ter cum back. I suppose he'd got onto some English gold--in that chest they slung aboard, wasn't it?"

"Yes; that was the main object. My name is not Gates, at all, and I am not the man Mendez brought aboard drunk, and who was thrown over the rail by LeVere. That fellow was drowned."

"Well, by God!"

"I am Geoffry Carlyle, an English skipper. There has been a revolution in England, in which I became involved. When the attempt failed, I was taken prisoner and deported to America for twenty years servitude. I came over with a bunch of others on the same ship with Sanchez."

"The **Romping Betsy**?"

"Yes. There was a rich planter, and his niece also aboard. He was coming home with a chest of money--fifty thousand pounds--realized from a big sale of tobacco in London, and the young woman was returning from attending school in England. Sanchez was aboard to gain possession of both."

Watkins nodded, too deeply interested in the narrative to interrupt.

"He pretended to be of the Spanish nobility, an ex-naval officer, and tried all the way over to make love to this Dorothy Fairfax. He got along all right with the uncle, and was invited to visit him, but the girl was not so easy. He must have had it all planned out how he was to get the gold, Fairfax carried--that was what the **Namur** was waiting for--and when he found that the young woman could not be won by fair means, he decided to take her by force."

"It's not the first time for the black-hearted devil. But how did you happen to come along?"

"Fairfax bought me to run his sloop. Perhaps it was the girl who won him over. Anyhow this arrangement angered Sanchez, and we had words. You know the rest, or, at least, the main facts. Sanchez and the boat crew held rendezvous at the first landing up the Bay. It was prearranged, but it was my fortune to meet the Captain alone on shore in the dark, where we fought."

"It was you then who drove the knife in? God!" excitedly, "but I would give ten years for such a chance. Ay, and, they say, you came within an eighth of an inch of sending him to hell."

"I knew not where I struck; 'twas a death struggle in the dark. I thought him dead when I left him, and ran to warn the others. But for this I was too late. The moment I set foot on the sloop's deck it was to close in battle with the big negro."

"Cochose? He saw you then?"

"No, only as a shape. He can have no better memory of me, than I of him. We fought as demons, until his giant strength forced me over the rail. He has no knowledge that I ever rose again."

"And then--what?"

"Oblivion; nothing. Only what I saw in the return of the boat tells me what followed. I came back to consciousness in a small dory, afloat on the Bay, with but one thought in my mind--to save the girl. How? It was too late to return, even had I known the way; but I could come here, to this ship. So here I came."

"But how, in advance of those in the long-boat?"

"By cutting across the point; the coast to the north is a wide circle. Besides the discovery of Sanchez sorely wounded left the others without a leader. Fairfax and his niece together with the treasure, were in Travers' house, at top of the bluff. They had to carry out an attack there, which probably meant more fighting. What really happened there, of course, I do not know."

"It can be easily imagined," said Watkins soberly. "Estada has no mercy; he is a born devil. I have seen him kill just for the pleasure of it. With Sanchez to avenge he would be an unleashed demon. But it is not the fate of those men to consider now; it is what will befall this girl prisoner. You have no plan?"

"None; to become a member of the crew was my only thought. But I must act, if at all, before the Captain recovers. He would recognize me at sight. You will aid, advise me?"

The sailor sat silent; the former expression of humor in his face vanished.

"That is easier to ask, than answer, mate," he admitted finally. "I am an English seaman, and will do my duty, but, so far as I can see, there is no plan we can make. It is God who will save the girl, if she is to be saved. He may use us to that end, but it is wholly beyond our power to accomplish it alone. The only thing I can do is to sound out the men aboard, and learn just what we can expect of them if any opportunity to act comes. There are not more than a dozen at most to be relied upon."

"And my part?"

"Do nothing at present. Play your part, and keep quiet. If you can let her know of your presence aboard without discovery it might be best--for if she saw you suddenly, unprepared, she might say or do something to betray you. There are other reasons why it may be best for her to know she is not entirely deserted."

He leaned over, motioning me toward him, until his lips were at my ear.

"It may not prove as hopeless as it appears now," he whispered confidentially. "I helped carry Sanchez to his stateroom, and washed and dressed his wound. There is no surgeon aboard, but I have some skill in such matters. He has a bad cut, and is very weak from loss of blood. The question of our success hinges on Pedro Estada."

"What he will do, you mean?"

"Yes; this is a chance which I happen to know he has long been waiting for. The only question is, has he the nerve to act. I doubt if he has alone, but LeVere is with him, and that half-breed would cut the throat of his best friend. You understand?-- the death of Sanchez would make Estada chief. The two men hate each other--why not? There was a plan before which failed; this time it may not fail."

"But," I interposed, "in that case what would the crew do?"

"Accept Estada, no doubt; at least the cut-throats would be with him, for he is of their sort. All they care for is blood and booty. But Sanchez's death would save you from discovery, and," his voice still lower, so that I barely distinguished the words, "in the confusion aboard, if we were ready, the *Namur* might be so disabled as to compel them to run her ashore for repairs. That would give you a chance. If once we reach Porto Grande there is no hope."

A marling-spike pounded on the scuttle, and Haines' voice roared down.

"Port watch! Hustle out bullies!"

CHAPTER XIII
I ACCEPT A PROPOSAL

I went on deck with the watch, and mingled with them forward. No one in authority took any particular notice of me, and I was permitted to take hold with the others at the various tasks. A Portuguese boatswain asked me who I was, and later reported my presence to LeVere, who had charge of the deck, but the only result was my being set at polishing the gun mounted on the forecastle. The mulatto did not come forward, and I rejoiced at having my status aboard so easily settled, and being permitted to remain in the same watch with Watkins.

It was a dull gray morning, the gloominess of the overhanging clouds reflected in the water. Men on lookout were stationed in the fore-top and on the heads, yet the sharpest eyes could scarcely see beyond a half mile in any direction. The sea came at us in great ocean swells, but the stout bark fought a passage through them, shivering with each blow, yet driven forward on her course by half-reefed sails, standing hard as boards in the sweep of the steady gale. Two men struggled at the wheel, and there were times when LeVere paused in his promenade from rail to rail to give them a helping hand. His anxiety was evidenced by his hailing the mast-head every few moments, only to receive each time the same response. The mist failed to lift, but seemed to shut us in more closely with every hour, the wind growing continually more boisterous, but LeVere held on grimly. I was kept at the guns during the entire time of our watch. Besides the Long Tom forward, a vicious piece, two swivel guns were on each side, completely concealed by the thick bulwarks, and to be fired through ports, so ingeniously closed as to be imperceptible a few yards away. All these pieces of ordnance were kept covered by tarpaulin so that at a little distance the **Namur of Rotterdam** appeared like a peaceful Dutch trader.

There was a brass carronade at the stern in plain view, and so mounted as to be swung inboard in case of necessity. Its ugly muzzle could thus rake the deck fore and aft, but the presence of such a piece would create no suspicion in those days when every ship was armed for defense, and consequently no effort was made for its concealment. I was busily at work on this bit of ordnance, when Estada came on deck for a moment. After staring aloft, and about the horizon into the impenetrable mist, he joined LeVere at the port rail in a short earnest conversation. As the two worthies parted the fellow chanced to observe me. I caught the quick look of recognition in his eyes, but bent to my work as though indifferent to his presence, yet failed to escape easily.

"You must be a pretty tough bird, Gates," he said roughly, "or I would have killed you last night--I had the mind too."

Something about his voice and manner led me to feel that, in spite of his roughness, he was not in bad humor.

"That would have been a mistake, sir," I answered, straightening up, rag in hand, "for it would have cost you a good seaman."

"Hoila! they are easily picked up; one, more or less, counts for little in these seas."

He looked at me searchingly, for the first time perhaps, actually noting my features. In spite of my dirty, disheveled appearance and the bruises disfiguring my face, this scrutiny must have aroused his curiosity.

"Why do you say that, my man?" he questioned sharply. "You were before the mast and drifted aboard here because you were drunk--isn't that true?"

"Partially, yes. It was drink that put me before the mast." I explained, rejoicing in his mood, and suddenly hoping such a statement might help my status aboard. "Three years ago I was skipper on my own vessel. It was Rum ruined me."

"Saint Christopher! Do you mean to say you can read charts, and take observations?"

I smiled, encouraged by his surprise, and the change in his tone.

"Yes, sir; I saw ten years' service as mate."

"What was your last ship?"

"The **Bombay Castle**, London to Hong Kong; I wrecked her off Cape Mendez in a fog. I was drunk below, and it cost me my ticket."

"You know West Indian waters?"

"Slightly; I made two voyages to Panama, and one to Havana."

"And speak Spanish?"

"A little bit, sir, as you see; I learn languages easily."

He stared straight into my face, but, without uttering another word, turned on his heel and went below. Whether, or not, I had made an impression on the fellow I did not know. His face was a mask perfectly concealing his thought. That he had appeared interested enough to question me had in it a measure of encouragement. He would surely remember, and sometime he might have occasion to make use of me. At least I would no longer remain in his mind as a mere foremast hand to be kicked about, and spoken to like a dog. I went back to my polishing of brass in a more cheerful mood--perhaps this would prove the first step leading to my greater future liberty on the *Namur*. I had finished my labor on the carronade, and was fastening down securely the tarpaulin, when a thin, stoop-shouldered fellow, with a hang-dog face crept up the ladder to the poop, and shuffled over to where LeVere was gazing out over the rail, oblivious to his approach.

"Mister LeVere, sir," he spoke apologetically, his voice no more than a wisp of sound.

The mulatto wheeled about startled.

"Oh, it's you! Well, what is it, Gunsaules?"

"Senor Estada, sir; he wishes to see a sailor named Gates in the cabin."

"Who? Gates? Oh, yes, the new man." He swept his eyes about, until he saw me. "Gates is your name, isn't it?"

"Yes, sir."

"Follow the steward below; Senor Estada wishes to see you--go just as you are."

"Very good, sir--is this the steward?"

The fellow led the way, amusing me by the peculiar manner in which his long legs clung to the ladder, and then wobbled about on the rolling deck until he attained the protection of the companion-way. A half dozen broad, uncarpeted steps led down into the after cabin, which was plain and practically without furniture, except for a bare table suspended from the upper beams and a few chairs securely resting in chocks. The deck was bare, but had been thoroughly scrubbed, the water not entirely dried, and forward there was a rack of small arms, the polished steel shining in the gray light of the transom overhead. The Dutch character of the bark was very apparent here, in the excessively heavy deck beams, and the general gloom of the interior, finished off in dark wood and ornamented with carved paneling. Filled with wonderment as to why I had been sent for, I halted at the foot of the steps gazing about the dreary interior, surprised at its positive dinginess. There were evidently six staterooms opening on the main cabin, and these must be little more than boxes to judge from the breadth of the vessel. What was farther aft I could not determine because of a lack of light, but as no stern ports were visible, it was to be assumed that this gave space for two more larger staterooms directly astern--occupied probably by the Captain and his first officer. There was no one in the main cabin, although a cat lay asleep on one of the chairs, and after a moment's hesitancy, I followed the beckoning steward, who rapped with his knuckles on one of the side doors. Estada's voice answered.

"Who is it?"

"Gunsaules, Senor; I have with me the sailor." "Open the door, and let him in; I would see him here. Come inside, Gates." His eyes surveyed us both in the narrow opening. "That will be all Juan; no one is to be admitted until I tell you--and, 'twill be well for you to remain by the stairs on guard, you understand?"

"Si, Senor."

"Another thing," sternly, "don't let me catch you listening outside the door; if I do God have mercy on you."

"Si, Senor."

I stepped inside, doubtful enough of what all this might mean, yet quite prepared to accept of any chance it might offer. Gunsaules closed the door softly, but I had already visioned the apartment in all its details. It was small, and nearly square, a swinging lantern in the center, a single bunk on one side, and a small table on the other, screwed to the wall, and covered with charts and various papers. A few books were upon a shelf above this, and a sea chest was shoved under the bunk. Some oilskins, together with a suit of clothes dangled from wooden pins, while the only other furniture consisted of a straight-backed chair, and a four-legged stool. The round port stood partly open, and through it I could see the gray expanse of water.

All these I perceived at a glance, but the instant the door closed behind me my entire attention concentrated on Estada. He sat upright in the chair gazing straight at me, his own face clearly revealed in the light from the open port. It seemed to me I was looking at the man for the first time, and it was not a pleasant picture. His face was swarthy, long and thin, with hard, set lips under a long, intensely black moustache, his cheeks strangely crisscrossed by lines. The nose was large, distinctively Roman, yielding him a hawklike appearance, but it was his eyes which fascinated me. They were dark, and deeply set, absolute wells of cruelty. I had never before seen such eyes in the face of a human being; they were beastly, devilish; I could feel my blood chill as I looked into their depths, yet I held myself erect, and waited for the man to speak. It seemed a long delay, yet doubtless was scarcely more than a moment. Then his lips curled in what was meant to be a smile, and he waved his hand.

"Sit down on the stool, Gates. Have you any knowledge of Portuguese?"

"None whatever, sir."

"Nor do I English; so we shall have to rely on the language of Spain."

"I am hardly expert in that" I explained. "But if you do not talk too fast, I can manage fairly well."

"I shall speak simply. Wait a moment."

He arose, stepped quietly to the door, and glanced out, returning apparently satisfied.

"I don't trust that damned steward," he said, "nor, as a matter of fact, anyone else wholly." He paused, and stared at me; then added: "I've never had any faith in your race, Gates, but am inclined to use you."

"I do not know any special reason why you should sir."

"No more do I. Every Englishman I ever knew was a liar, and a sneaking poltroon. I was brought up to hate the race, and always have. I can't say that I like you any better than the others. By God! I don't, for the matter of that. But just now you can be useful to me if you are of that mind. This is a business proposition, and it makes no odds if we hate each other, so the end is gained. How does that sound?"

I shifted my position so as to gain a clearer view of his face. I was still wholly at sea as to what the fellow was driving at--yet, evidently enough he was in earnest. It was my part to find out.

"Not altogether bad," I admitted. "I have been in some games of chance before."

"I thought as much," eagerly, "and money has the same chink however it be earned. You could use some?"

"If I had any to use; after a sailor has been drunk there is not apt to be much left in his pockets."

He reached across into the upper bunk, and brought forth a bottle and glass, placing these upon the table at his elbow.

"Have a drink first," he said, pouring it out. "It will stiffen your nerve."

"Thanks, no, Senor. I have nerve enough and once I start that sort of thing there is no stopping. Take it yourself and then tell me what is in the wind."

"I will, Gates," affecting cordiality, although I somehow felt that my refusal to imbibe had aroused a faint suspicion in his mind. "But I would rather you would show yourself a good fellow. I like to see a man take his liquor and hold it."

He sat down the emptied glass, and straightened back in the chair, his eyes searching as ever.

"The fact is," he began doubtfully, "what you just said to me on deck chanced to be of interest. You were not boasting?"

"I answered your questions truthfully, if that is what you mean."

"You are a navigator?"

"I was in command of ships for four years, Senor; naturally I know navigation."

"Do you mind if I test you?"

"Not in the least; although it will have to be in English; as I do not know the Spanish sea terms."

"Let that go then; I will soon learn if you have lied, and that will be a sorry day for you. I'll tell you, Gates, how matters stand aboard, and why I have need of your skill. Then you may take your choice--the forecastle, or the cabin?"

"You invite me aft, Senor?"

"I give you a chance to move your dunnage, if you will do my work," he explained seriously. "Listen now. Sanchez has been badly hurt. It may be weeks before he leaves his cabin, if, indeed, he ever does. That leaves me in command with but one officer, the mulatto, LeVere. This might answer to take us safely to Porto Grande, as we could stand watch and watch, but Francois is no sailor. It was his part on board to train and lead the fighting men--he cannot navigate. Saint Christopher! I fear to leave him alone in charge of the deck while I snatch an hour's sleep."

"I see," I admitted. "And yourself, Senor? You are a seaman?"

He hated to confess, yet my eyes were honest, and met his squarely.

"Enough to get along, but not quite sure as to my figures. I have taken no sights, except as we came north, on this trip. 'Tis for this reason I need you--but you will play me no smart English trick, my man, or I'll have you by the heels at once. I know enough to verify your figures."

"I thought of no trick, Estada." I said coldly, now satisfied as to his purpose, and confident of my own power. "English, or otherwise. It is well we understand each other. You would have me as navigator, very well--at what terms?"

His eyes seemed to narrow, and become darker.

"With rating as first officer, and your fair proportion of all spoils."

"You mean then to continue the course? To attack vessels on the high seas?"

"Why not?" sneeringly. "Are you too white-livered for that sort of job? If so, then you are no man for me. It is a long voyage to Porto Grande, and no reason why we should hurry home; the welcome there will be better if we bring chests of gold aboard. Ay, and the thought will put hope into the hearts of the crew; they are restless now from long waiting."

"But Captain Sanchez? You have no surgeon I am told. Will he not suffer from neglect of his wound?"

"Suffer? No more than under a leech ashore. All that can be done, has been. There are men aboard able to treat any ordinary wound. His was a clean knife thrust, which has been washed, treated with lotion, and bound up. No leech could do more."

"And my quarters--will they be aft?"

"You will have your choice of those at port. Come now--have you an answer ready?"

"I would be a fool not to have," heartily. "I am your man Estada."

CHAPTER XIV
I WARN DOROTHY

The Portuguese, evidently well pleased at my prompt acceptance of his proposal, talked on for some time, explaining to me something of the situation aboard the *Namur*, and pointing out what he believed to be our position on the chart. I asked a few questions, although I paid but little attention to what he said, my mind being busied with searching out his real purpose. No doubt the situation was very nearly as he described it to be--LeVere was no navigator, and Estada himself only an indifferent one. Yet at that the course to the West Indies was not a long one, and, if the Portuguese had been able to bring the bark from there to the Chesapeake, the return voyage should not terrify him greatly. No, that was not the object; he was planning to keep at sea, to waylay and attack merchant ships, and then, after a successful cruise, arrive at Porto Grande, laden with spoils, and hailed as a great leader. His plan was to dispose of Sanchez--even to permit the Spaniard to die of his wounds; possibly even to hasten and assure that death by some secret resort to violence. No doubt LeVere was also concerned in the conspiracy, and would profit by it, and possibly these two were likewise assured of the cooperation of the more reckless spirits among the crew. I remembered what Watkins had whispered to me forward--his suspicions of them both. He had been right; already the fuse was being laid, and, very fortunately, I happened to be chosen to help touch it off. The chance I had sought blindly, was being plainly revealed.

It was evident enough, however, that Estada had no intention of trusting me immediately with his real motives. His confidence was limited, and his instructions related altogether to mere matters of ship routine. I asked a few questions, and twice he lied coolly, but I dared not mention the girl in any way, for fear that even a casual reference to her presence on board, might arouse his suspicions of my interest. We were at sea, and my presence aft gave me opportunity to observe all that was going on in the cabin. I could await developments. But I was becoming wearied by the man.

"I understand perfectly, Senor," I broke in at last impatiently. "You will have to take for granted that I can enforce sea discipline, and navigate your boat to whatever part of the ocean you desire to sail. All I need is your orders. This, I take it, is all you require of me?"

"Yes; I plan, you execute."

"Very good; now about myself," and I arose to my feet, determined to close the interview. "I would study these charts, and figure out our probable position by dead reckoning--there is little chance of having glimpse of the sun today; the fog out there grows heavier. You say I may choose any stateroom on the port side?"

"They are all unoccupied, except one, used by the steward as a storeroom."

I opened the door, and stepped out into the main cabin, the roll of charts under my arm. The place was deserted, and, with a glance about, met Estada's eyes observing me closely. He didn't wait for me to question him.

"Captain Sanchez's stateroom is aft," he said, with a wave of the hand.

"The entire width of the bark?"

"No, there are two rooms."

"He is left alone?"

"Jose is with him--a negro, with a knack at nursing."

"Who else is quartered aft here?"

He ignored the one thing I most desired to learn, but I did not press it, believing I knew the answer already.

"LeVere has this middle stateroom, and Mendez the one forward."

"What rank has Mendez?"

"Third officer, and carpenter. Just at present with LeVere required on deck, he has charge of the men below."

"The crew, you mean?"

"Not the working crew; they are quartered in the forecastle, and are largely English and Swede. But we have to carry extra men, who bunk amidships--hell-hounds to fight; damn mongrels of course."

"You keep them below, all through the voyage?"

"They are allowed on deck amidships when we are at sea, but are not encouraged to mingle with the sailors. We're over a powder magazine all the time, Gates--any spark might set it off."

I opened one of the doors opposite, and glanced within. The interior differed but little from that of the stateroom occupied by Estada, except it was minus the table. No doubt they were all practically alike.

"This will do very well," I said, quietly. "Now how about clothes? These I wear look rather rough for the new job."

"I'll send you the steward; he'll fix you out from the slop-chest. We're always well supplied."

I was glad to see him go and closed the door on him with a sigh of relief. His eyes seemed to exercise a peculiar influence over me, a snakelike charm, against which I had to constantly battle. I threw the bundle of charts into the upper bunk, and unscrewed the glass of the port to gain a view without, and a breath of fresh air. There was nothing to see but a small vista of gray sea, blending into the gray mist, and the waves on this side ran so high I was compelled to close the port to keep out the spray. I sat down on the stool, staring about the compartment, realizing suddenly how well fortune had served my cause--the chance to impersonate the drunken sailor; the meeting with Watkins, my chance words to Estada on deck, and now this translation from forecastle to cabin. It had all occurred so quickly, almost without effort on my part, I could do little but wonder what strange occurrence would be next. What, indeed, was there for me to do except to await developments? Only one thing occurred to me--I must discover some means immediately of communicating with Dorothy Fairfax.

The importance of this could not be overestimated. With myself quartered aft, and eating in the cabin, we were bound to meet sooner or later; and the girl must previously be warned of my presence aboard, or in her first surprise at the recognition, I should be instantly betrayed. Nothing would escape Estada, and the slightest evidence that we two had formerly met, would awaken his suspicion. My only hope of success lay in my ability to increase his faith in my pledges. The necessity of having a competent navigator aft alone accounted for my promotion. The Portuguese neither liked nor trusted me; he hated and despised my race; he would have me watched, and would carefully check over my figures. I should be compelled to serve him faithfully and without arousing the slightest question in his mind, in order to establish myself in his esteem, or gain any real freedom aboard. Yet, if I was to serve the girl, there must be, first of all, intelligent cooperation between us. She must not only know of my presence on the *Namur*, but also the purpose actuating me. I had reached this conclusion, when a light hesitating knock sounded on the door.

"Who is there?"

"The steward, Senor, with your clothes?"

"Bring them in."

Gunsaules entered, the garments over his arm, and shuffled in his peculiar gliding manner across to the bunk where he laid out the pieces carefully one by one, evidently proud of his selection.

"Quite a beautiful piece of goods, Senor," he ventured, speaking so softly I could barely distinguish the words above the crash of the waves on the ship's side. "And most excellently tailored. I do not remember whether these came out of the *Adair* or *La Rosalie*--the French ship most likely, for as you see, Senor, there is quite the Parisian cut to this coat. I mark these things for I was once apprenticed to a tailor in Madrid."

He stood fondling the garment lovingly, the expression of his face so solemnly interested, I had difficulty in suppressing a laugh.

"Some change in your trade, Gunsaules. Did you take this one up from choice? You do not look to me like a fighting man."

He glanced apprehensively at the open door, speaking even lower than before, if possible.

"No more am I, Senor. The blood make me faint. I go hungry in Santo Domingo--God forgive me for ever going there!--and, to keep from starving I took this job."

"With Sanchez, or before the bark was captured?"

"Before, Senor. The captain's name was Schmitt. Not since have I been ashore, but they spare me because I was Spanish."

I would have asked the fellow more, perhaps even have tested him in his loyalty to his new masters; but I felt this was neither place nor time. Estada might return, and besides the man was evidently a poor-spirited creature, little apt to be of service even if he so desired.

"The clothes seem to be all right, Steward," I said rather briskly, "and I judge will fit. Now hunt me up first of all something to shave with, then some tobacco and a pipe and--yes, wait a second; writing materials."

"Yes, Senor."

"And, by the way, there are two staterooms astern. Who occupies the one to starboard--Senor Estada?"

"No Senor; it is the young lady."

"Oh, the one brought aboard last night. Have you seen her?" "Si, Senor; she is English, and good to look at, but she sit and stare out the stern port. She will not speak or eat. I take in her breakfast, but she touch not a morsel. So I tell Senor Estada, and he say, 'then bring her out to dinner with me; I'll make the hussy eat, if I have to choke it down her dainty throat,'"

"Good; I'll have a look at her myself then. Now hurry up those things, Steward, and remember what I sent you after."

He brought the shaving set, and writing materials first, explaining that he would have to go down into the lazaret, and break open some packages for the tobacco and pipe. The moment the fellow disappeared I grasped the opportunity. Where Estada had gone, whether back into his stateroom, or on deck, I had no means of knowing. In fact this could make little difference, for it was not likely he would leave me alone for any great length of time. It must already be approaching the end of LeVere's watch, and I would certainly be called upon to relieve him. And, following my turn on deck would be dinner in the cabin, and the probable encounter with Dorothy. This clearly meant that I must communicate with the girl immediately, or not at all. I dashed off a note hurriedly--a brief line merely stating my presence on board, and begging her not to exhibit surprise at meeting me. I had no time in which to explain, or make clear the situation. With this folded and concealed in my hand, I silently pushed open the door, and took a hasty glance about the cabin.

It was unoccupied, yet I must move with caution. It was possible for one on deck to look down through the skylight, and even if Estada was not in his own room, the nurse assigned to Sanchez might be awake and appear at any moment. The risk was not small, yet must be taken, and I crept swiftly forward following the circle of the staterooms, until I came to the closed door of the one I sought aft. I bent here an instant, listening for some sound from within, but heard none. I dared not remain, or even venture to test the lock. Gunsaules had said this was her place of confinement, and there was seemingly no reason why she should have been given a guard. Beyond doubt the girl was within and alone, and I must trust her quick intelligence to respond to my written message. I thrust it through the narrow opening above the sill, and the moment it disappeared within, stole swiftly back to my own room. The action had not been seen, and yet I had scarcely a moment to spare. Before I could lather my face, standing before a small cracked mirror, bracing myself to the roll of the bark, the steward returned, bearing in his hands tobacco and pipe.

Estada, however, remained away longer than I had anticipated he would, and I was fully dressed and comfortably smoking before he came down from the deck and crossed the cabin to my partially open door.

"The starboard watch has been called," he said, "and you are to take charge of the deck, relieving LeVere. I waited to explain the situation to the men before you appeared. I suppose you are ready?"

"Ay, ay, Senor," knocking the ashes out of my pipe, and rising. He eyed my clothes disapprovingly.

"Rather a fancy rig, Gates, for a first officer on duty." "Some style I admit, Senor, but they were all the steward offered me."

"You'll have to carry a hard fist, my man, to back up that costume aboard the *Namur*," he said coldly. "Those black devils are apt to mistake you for a plaything."

"Let them test it once; they will soon find I have the hard fist. I've tamed wild crews before today and it might as well be first as last. I suppose half measures do not go with these lads."

"Santa Maria---no! It is kill, or be killed, in our trade, and they will try out your metal. Come on now."

I followed him up the stairs to the deck. His words had in no way alarmed me, but served rather to harden my resolve. I looked for trouble, and was inclined to welcome it, anxious indeed to prove to Estada my ability to handle men. Nothing else would so quickly appeal to him, or serve so rapidly to establish me in his esteem; and to win his confidence was my chief concern. Nothing occurred, however, to cause any breach of authority. A few fellows were lounging amidships and stared idly at us as we mounted to the poop deck. These were of the fighting contingent I supposed, and the real members of the crew were forward. LeVere was still on duty, and came forward and shook hands at my appearance.

"Rather glad I didn't drown you," he said, intending to be pleasant. "But hope you'll not run amuck in the after cabin."

"I shall try not too, unless I have cause," I answered, looking him square in the eyes, and determining to make my position clear at once. "Senor Estada tells me I am to relieve you. What is the course?"

"Sou'west, by half sou'."

"We might be carrying more canvas."

"There is nothing to hurry about, and the fog is thick."

"That will probably lift within an hour. Do you know your position?"

"Only in a general way. We have held an east by south course since leaving the Capes, until an hour ago, making about ten knots."

"Very well, I will figure it out as best I can, and mark it on the chart. There is nothing further to report?"

"No Senor; all has been as it is now."

He glanced toward Estada, not greatly pleased I presume with my brusqueness, yet finding nothing in either words or manner from which to evoke a quarrel. The latter had overheard our conversation, but he stood now with back toward us looking out on the sea off the port quarter. His silent indifference caused LeVere to shrug his shoulders, and disappear down the ladder on his way below. I turned my face to the man at the wheel--it was the giant negro--Cochose.

CHAPTER XV
THE CABIN OF THE NAMUR

Both huge black hands grasped the spokes, and it was evident that it required all his giant strength to control the bucking wheel. He was an ugly-looking brute, the lower portion of his face apelike, and the wool growing so low as to leave him scarcely an inch of forehead. His eyes lifted an instant from the binnacle card to glance at me curiously. They exhibited no flash of recognition. With sudden relief, and a determination to thoroughly assure myself, I stepped forward and accosted him.

"Little heavy for one man, isn't it?"

"Oh, Ah don't mind, boss," his thick lips grinning. "Ah's bin alone worse tricks den dis."

"You seem to be holding the course, all right--sou'west, by sou', Senor LeVere says."

"Yas, Senor."

"What is your name?"

"Cochose, Senor; Ah's a French nigger."

"Very good, Cochose; my name is Gates, and I am the new first officer. If you need any help, let me know."

He nodded, still grinning, to let me realize he understood, and I stepped aside, confident that the fellow retained no recollection of my features. The relief of this knowledge was considerable, and I gazed over the bark forward with a new feeling of security. Thus far I had successfully passed the test, and been accepted by all on board. The only remaining danger of recognition lay in the early recovery of Sanchez, and, as I glanced aside at Estada the conviction became fixed in my mind that such recovery was doubtful. I felt that I had already penetrated the cowardly plan of the Portuguese, but felt no inclination to interpose. Indeed I had more occasion to dread the return of Sanchez to command than did Estada himself. With me life was at stake; while with him it was but the goal of ambition and power. Brutal and evil minded as Estada undoubtedly was, I had taken his measure, and felt confident of being able to outwit him; but Sanchez would prove a different problem, for he possessed brains and cool, resourceful courage. Of the two he was far more to be feared.

For half an hour Estada hung about aft, apparently paying no attention to me, and yet watching my movements closely. There was little to be done, but I thought it best to keep the watch reasonably busy, so they might thus learn that I knew my work. They proved prompt and capable enough, although I was eyed with some curiosity when I went forward, and, no doubt was very thoroughly discussed behind my back. The idlers amidships were a totally different class--a mongrel scum, profanely chatting in Spanish, or swaggering about the deck, their very looks a challenge. However they kept out of my way, and I found no occasion to interfere with their diversions. After Estada left the deck the majority amused themselves gambling, and as I had received no orders to interfere, I permitted the games to proceed. Mendez interfered only once on occasion of a brief fight. My only instructions from the Portuguese on his going below was to call him at once if a sail was sighted. Apparently he was satisfied of my ability to command the deck.

No occasion to call him arose during my watch. The mist of fog slowly rose, and drifted away, leaving a wide view of ocean, but revealed no glimpse of any other craft. The white-crested waves gleamed in the sun, as we plowed bravely through them, and the wind steadily decreased in violence. I had the crew shake out reefs in jib and foresail, and was surprised myself at the sailing qualities of the bark. In spite of breadth of beam, and heavy top-hamper, she possessed speed and ease of control, and must have been a pretty sight, as we bowled along through that deserted sea. Before my watch was up I could see Gunsaules through the skylight busily preparing the table in the cabin below. It was still daylight, but with a purple gleam across the waters, when LeVere arrived on deck for my relief. We were talking together abaft the wheel when Estada appeared in the companion-way.

"Every promise of a clear night," he said, glancing about at the horizon. "Better change the course two points east LeVere; we are lying in too close to the coast for our purpose. The table call will come very shortly, Senor Gates."

I washed up hastily in my stateroom, and came out into the cabin perplexed as to what might occur within the next few moments. Yet whatever the result, there was no avoiding it. Would the girl be called to join us, as the Portuguese had threatened? Had she received my note of warning? And if so, would she have the strength to play her part so as to avoid suspicion? Those keen searching eyes of Estada's would note every movement, observe every fleeting expression. He had no present doubt of me, only the caution natural to one leading his life of danger. He believed my story, and nothing thus far had arisen to bring him the slightest doubt. To his mind I was a reckless adventurer, ruined by drink, a drifting derelict, so glad to be picked up, and given rank, as to be forever grateful and loyal to the one aiding me.

While his instinct made him distrust an Englishman, he already had some measure of faith in me personally, yet this confidence was still so light as to be completely shattered by the slightest mishap. My every move must be one of extreme caution.

He and Estevan were awaiting me, the latter all rigged out, and with smooth black hair oiled and plastered down upon his forehead. I never beheld a more disagreeable face, or one which so thoroughly revealed the nature of a man. As I touched his hand, at Estada's brief introduction, it was as if I fingered a snake, and expected to be greeted with a kiss. Gunsaules hovered about an open door leading forward, and the table had been set for four. As I knew LeVere had eaten alone, before coming to my relief, the only conclusion was that the Portuguese intended that we be joined by the prisoner. Indeed he gave me little time for doubt.

"This is your chair, Gates, and you will find we live well aboard the *Namur*--wine, women and song--hey, Manuel! Why not, when all are at command? Steward, you told the lady what my orders were?"

"Si, Senor."

"Then bid her join us."

We stood in silence, as Gunsaules crossed the deck, and inserted a key in the afterstateroom door. Manuel was grinning in full enjoyment, but the expression on the face of Estada was that of grim cruelty. Evidently he expected a scene, an outburst of resentment, pleading and tears, and was ready enough to exercise his authority. Perhaps he meant all this as a lesson to me; perhaps it was no more than a natural exhibition of his nature. Yet his purpose to conquer was clearly depicted in his features---this woman would be made to obey, or else ruthlessly crushed. I felt my hands grip like iron on my chair back and my teeth clinch in restraint. God, but I would have liked to grip the fellow where he stood--all the bottled-up hatred in my soul struggling for action. Yet that would only mean the death of all hope, and I turned my eyes away from him, and stared with the others at the opening door. I failed to catch the words Gunsaules uttered, but they were instantly responded to. Out into the full light of the cabin the woman came, and halted, barely a step in advance of the steward, her head uplifted proudly, her eyes on us. Never before had I realized her beauty, her personality, as I did then. The glow of the light was upon her face, and there was color in her cheeks, and a strange appealing look in her eyes. Her posture was not that of defiance, nor of surrender; she stood as a woman defending her right to respect, sustained by a wonderful courage. I caught her glance, but there was no recognition in it; not by the flicker of an eyelid did she betray surprise, and yet in some mysterious manner a flash of intelligence passed between us. It was all instantaneous for her gaze seemed to concentrate on Estada as though she knew him as leader.

"You sent for me? For what?" she asked, her Spanish clear and well chosen.

"To join us at meal," he answered unmoved. "It is better than to remain alone."

"Better! You must have a strange opinion of me to believe I would sit with murderers and thieves."

"Harsh words, Senorita," and Estada grinned grimly. "Yet I expected them. There are many trades in the world by which men are robbed. We only work at the one we like best; nor will I discuss that with you. However, Senorita, I can say that we have taken no lives in this last affair."

"No lives!" in sudden, incredulous surprise. "You mean my uncle lives?"

"If you refer to Fairfax--the one in whose room the chest was hidden, I can reply truthfully that he lives. One of my men struck him down, but it was not a death blow. If that be the reason of your disdain, there is no cause. This chair is held for you."

"But why was I brought away a prisoner? To be a plaything? A sport for your pleasure?"

"That was but the orders of our chief; we await his recovery to learn his purpose."

"Sanchez! was he your chief? A pirate?"

"A buccaneer; we prey on the enemies of Spain," he explained, apparently believing his own words. "It is war with us, without regard to treaties. We rob only that we may carry on the war. They have robbed us, and now it has become our turn. It was at Captain Sanchez's orders we waited the arrival of your vessel from England. It seems he met you on the voyage."

"Yes," breathlessly.

"He loved you; he would, no doubt, have dealt with you honorably: I have reason to believe that to be his purpose now. To this end you gave him no encouragement--is not this true?"

"I--I did not like him."

"Yet it was his will that you should. Nothing will change his purpose. He is that kind, and he has the power. He determined that if you would not come to him by choice, you should be made to by force. You are here now by his orders and will remain until you consent to his purpose--all that remains for you to decide is whether you choose to be prisoner, or guest aboard."

Her questioning, perplexed eyes turned from face to face, as though she could not grasp fully the purpose of what was said.

"He--he is still alive--this Captain Sanchez?"

"Yes, with a chance to survive."

"And if he lives I am to be at his disposal?"

"He is the chief here; his will is law aboard."

"And if he should die?"

Estada shrugged his shoulders indifferently.

"Who knows!"

Her lips tightened as though to hold back a cry while one hand pressed to the open door steadied her. The cheeks were no longer flushed, and there was a look in the searching eyes I did not like to see. It was a moment before she could control her voice.

"I have heard them call you Estada," she said finally, determined to learn the whole truth. "Of what rank in this company are you?"

"I am Pedro Estada, formerly the first officer, now, by occasion of Captain Sanchez's wound, in full command. These are two of my officers--Senor Gates, one of your own countrymen, and Manuel Estevan."

"You are pirates?"

He laughed unpleasantly, as though the word had an ugly sound even to his ears.

"Rather call us sea rovers, Senorita. It better expresses our trade. Enough to admit that we serve under no flag, and confess no master. And now, that I have answered your questions, what is it to be between us--peace or war?"

Her eyes drooped, and I could distinctly note the trembling of her slender figure. When she slowly raised her glance once more it rested on my face as though seeking approval, guidance.

"If there be only the one choice," she said quietly. "I accept peace. I cannot live locked in that room alone, haunted by my thoughts and memories. If I pledge you my word, Senor, am I to enjoy the freedom of this cabin and the deck?"

Estada looked at us, a shade of doubt in his eyes. I made no sign, but Manuel nodded.

"Why not?" he asked in his harsh croak of a voice. "So long as we be at sea? What harm can the girl do?"

"Perhaps none; I will take a half chance, at least. You shall have the freedom of the cabin. So long as you keep your word, while as to the deck we will consider that later. Prove you mean what you say by joining us here."

My recollection of that meal is not of words, but of faces. I do not even clearly recall what it was we talked about, although it included a variety of topics, limited somewhat by lack of knowledge on the part of Estada and Manuel. The former attempted conversation, but soon gave up the effort in despair. His eyes, however, sought constantly the girl's face and to my consternation exhibited an interest in her personality which promised trouble. I know not whether she noticed this awakening admiration, but she certainly played her part with quiet modesty, speaking just enough to entertain, and hiding the deep anxiety against which she struggled. I believe that even the Portuguese reached the conclusion that she was not altogether regretful for this adventure and that it was safe for him to relax some degree of vigilance. His manner became more gracious and, long before the meal ended, his language had a tendency to compliment and flatter. I contented myself with occasional sentences. The young woman sat directly across from me, our words overheard by all, and as I knew both men possessed some slight knowledge of English, I dare not venture beyond commonplace conversation in that tongue. With quick wit she took her cue from me, so that nothing passed between us, either by word of mouth or glance of eye, to arouse suspicions.

Believing the feeling of confidence would be increased by such action, I was first to leave the table, and it being my watch below, immediately retired to my room, noisily closing the door after me, yet refraining from letting the latch catch, thus enjoying a slight opening through which to both see and hear. Manuel did not linger long, making some excuse to go forward, but Estada remained for some time, endeavoring to entertain. She laughed at his efforts and appeared interested in encouraging him, so that he kept his spirit of good humor even amid these difficulties. His egotism made a fool of the man, yet even he finally became discouraged of making her comprehend his meaning, and lapsed into a silence which gave her an excuse to retire. This was accomplished so graciously as to leave no sting, the fellow actually accompanying her to the door of her stateroom, bowing his compliments as she disappeared within. The fool actually believed he had made a conquest and preened himself like a turkey cock.

"Gunsaules."

"Senor."

"You need not lock the Senorita in her room or guard her in any way hereafter. She is permitted to come and go as she pleases aboard."

"Si, Senor."

"You have served the Captain and Jose? Yes--did the wounded man eat at all?"

"A little soup, Senor; he would taste nothing else."

Estada entered his own stateroom, leaving the door ajar. When he came out he had exchanged his coat for a rough jacket. Thus attired for a turn on deck, he disappeared through the companion.

CHAPTER XVI
IN DOROTHY'S STATEROOM

I stood crouched, with eye at the crack watchful of every movement in the lighted cabin, my own decision made. I must see and talk with Dorothy. We must understand each other, and the earlier we could thus begin working together in unison, the better. Gunsaules bore a tray of dishes from the Captain's room and then, after carefully wiping up the main table, and sliding it up out of the way on its stantions, placed a bottle of brandy and some glasses on a swinging shelf. Apparently satisfied that his work there was completed he turned down the light, and departed along the passage leading amidships. A moment later I heard the sound of dishes grinding together preparatory to being washed. No better opportunity for action was likely to occur, although the situation was not without peril. Jose might emerge at any instant from Sanchez's cabin, while I had no reason to be assured that Estada would remain long on deck. Even if he did, any movement below could be observed through the overhead glass. Indeed it might be with this purpose in view that he had gone outside. However I felt compelled to accept the chance. The light was so dim that I believed I could steal cautiously along in the deeper shadows without attracting attention from the deck, even if someone stood there on watch.

I moved noiselessly leaving my own door slightly ajar, and crept along close to the side walls until I attained my destination. Nothing occurred causing me to fear my movements were detected. To have knocked at the closed door however softly might be overheard, so knowing it to be unlocked I merely lifted the latch noiselessly, and slipped quickly within. There was no light, except a glimmer of stars through a large after port, but against this faint radiance she stood vaguely revealed. Evidently the girl had been standing there, gazing out at the waters, and had turned swiftly about at my entrance, aroused by some slight sound. Her first thought must have been Estada, for there was a startled note of fear in her challenge.

"Who are you? Why do you come here?"

"Speak low," I cautioned. "You must know my voice."

"Geoffry Carlyle!"

"Yes, but do not use that name--all hope depends on my remaining unknown. You welcome me?"

She came straight forward through the dim star-shine, a spectral figure, with both hands outstretched.

"Welcome!" her tone that of intense sincerity. "Your presence gives me all the strength I have. But for you I should throw myself through that port into the sea. But I know not how you came here--tell me, you are not really one of these wretches?"

"No; you must believe that first of all, and trust me."

"I do--but--but tell me all you can."

"Is there a divan here, or anywhere we can sit down together? I can see nothing in this darkness."

"Yes, hold my hand while I guide you; we can sit here." It was a couch of some kind against the outer wall. She did not release her grasp, seemingly gaining courage from this physical contact, and my fingers closed warmly over her own.

"Now please," breathlessly, "how is it possible you are aboard this vessel--an officer?"

I told her the strange story, as swiftly and simply as possible, speaking scarcely above a whisper, feeling as I progressed that I related a dream rather than a series of facts. It seemed to me she could scarcely be expected to believe the truth of what I said, and yet she did, almost unquestioningly, the clasp of her fingers perceptibly tightening as I proceeded. The soft light from the open port touched her face slightly, enough to reveal its outline and she sat so close beside me, her eyes uplifted to mine, that I could feel her breath upon my cheek.

"Why, if---if you had not told me this yourself I could hardly believe such a tale," she exclaimed. "Yet it must be true, miraculous as it seems. But what is to be the ending? Have you any plan of escape?"

"Hardly a plan. I have had no opportunity even to learn the true nature of the crew. Watkins is an honest sailor, and he has told me of others on whom I could rely. There are those aboard--but I do not know how many--who would mutiny if they had a leader, and a reasonable chance of success. I must reach these and learn who they are. Fortunately the voyage promises to be long enough to enable me to plan carefully."

"You have discussed the voyage with this man--Estada?" "He told me what he had decided upon; not to return to their rendezvous until after they had captured some prizes, and could go with gold chinking in their pockets."

"They have gold already--the chest taken from my uncle."

"That only serves to make such as these more greedy."

"Where is their rendezvous?"

"An island in the West Indies, probably not on the chart. They call it Porto Grande."

"And they will sweep the ocean between here and there, seeking victims? Unarmed merchantmen to rob and sink? And you--you will be compelled to take part in such scenes, such acts of pillage and perhaps murder. Is this true?"

"I presume I must seem to be one of them to avoid suspicion. There is some hope in my mind that we may chance to run into an English or French warship. Quite a few must be cruising in these waters. But these are only contingencies; they may happen and they may not. How we are to act under such conditions will have to be decided later. Now we must be content to seek release through our own efforts. Have you any suggestions?"

She was silent for a long moment, during which she withdrew her hand, pressing it over her eyes as though thus to better concentrate her thoughts.

"There is conspiracy on board already," she said finally "that you may not know about."

"You mean to depose Sanchez?" I questioned in surprise.

"Yes; you had suspicioned it? They thought me unconscious in the boat, and talked among themselves--the two at the stern, Estada and that beast, Manuel. I did not understand all they said, only a word or two, but I do not think they intend the Captain shall recover."

"You think it best that he should?"

"Oh, I do not know; there is no best that I can see. Yet I would have more faith in being spared disgrace if at the mercy of Sanchez, than his lieutenant. Both may be equally guilty, equally desperate, but they are not the same men."

"True, but I know not which is to be most feared."

"I may be wrong," she insisted, "for I judge as a woman, yet I would feel safer with Sanchez. He cares not much for me, perhaps, yet enough so that I possess some power over him. The other does not--he merely desires with the passions of a brute. No appeal would reach him; he would laugh at tears and find pleasure in suffering. I do not quite believe this of Sanchez."

"Perhaps not---the other may be the greater beast."

"I know he is; the proof is in those horrid eyes. What is the man? Of what race?"

"Portuguese, I am told, but likely a half-breed."

"Ugh! it makes me shudder to even look at him; and yet you would have me appear friendly?"

"We cannot permit him to feel that either of us are enemies. He is the power aboard; our lives, everything are in his hands. If he means to be rid of Sanchez, the man is doomed, for he will find a way to accomplish his purpose at whatever cost; murder means nothing to these men."

"Of course you are right," she acknowledged. "Our case is so desperate we must resort to any weapons. You believe it will serve the possibility of escape if I permit this monster to imagine that I have some interest in him?"

"To do so might delay the explosion," I replied gravely, "and just now any delay is welcome. I know how such an effort will try you, but the end may be well worth the sacrifice. I doubt if even Estada will resort to force on board; indeed force will be the very last card he will care to play in your case. He is a brute, and capable of any crime, yet at heart a coward. There is reason why he will fear to assault you. You are English and all the practical seamen on board are from northern Europe--English and Scandinavian. These men are not pirates from choice--they are prisoners who have taken on to save their own lives. With his bullies and cut-throats amidships he can compel them to work, but he dare not go too far. Once these fellows unite in mutiny they could take the ship. An assault on you would be dangerous."

"It is these men you count on?"

"Yes; but for me to gain their confidence and leadership will require time. I must reach them all secretly and alone. Not more than half are in my watch, and Watkins must approach the others. A plan for concerted action will have to be arranged, and every precaution taken. The slightest slip would mean failure, and merciless punishment. Even if I succeed in gathering together all these better elements on board, we shall yet be outnumbered two to one, perhaps more, and our only hope rests in surprise. At best the situation is absolutely desperate--but I see no other solution."

"And my service is deceit--the acting of a part to blind the eyes of Estada?"

"I sincerely believe your greater chance of security lies in this course. The fellow is a supreme egotist; opposition will anger him, while flattery will make him subservient. You have the wit and discretion to hold him within certain limits. It is a dangerous game, I admit, and a disagreeable one, but the case requires desperate remedies."

She lifted her eyes, searching my face through the dim light.

"Geoffry Carlyle," she said, at last, a tremor in the low voice, "there is no sacrifice I would not make to preserve my honor. I hate this man; I dread his touch; I shrink from contact with him, as I would from a snake, but I am not going to refuse to do my part. If you say this is right, and justified, I will consent."

"I believe it is."

"And you will not lose faith in me?" she questioned earnestly. "It will not lower your belief in my womanhood?"

"Nothing could do that. Mistress Dorothy, I want you to realize the depth of my interest and respect. Your friendliness has meant much to me, and I would never urge you to lower your ideals. But we must face this situation as it is. You cannot cling now to the standards of London, or even Maryland. We are on the ocean, upon a pirate ship, surrounded by men utterly devoid of all restraint--hellhounds of the sea, who live by murder and pillage. We possess but two weapons of defense--deceit, or force. A resort to the latter is at present impossible. I cannot conceive that you are lowering yourself in any way by using the power you possess to escape violence--"

"The power I possess?"

"Yes--beauty and wit. These are your weapons, and most effective ones. You can play with Estada and defeat him--temporarily at least. I confess there is danger in such a game--he is a wild beast, and his evil nature may overcome his discretion. You are armed?"

"No; I have never felt the need."

"Then take this," and I thrust a pistol into her hands. "I took it from the rack in the cabin, and can get another. It is charged; keep it hidden about your person, but use it only when all else fails. Do you see this necessity now from my standpoint?"

"Yes," hesitatingly, "all that you say is true, but--but the thought frightens me; it--it is like creeping into a lion's cage having only a fan with which to defend myself."

I smiled at her conceit.

"A fan rightly used is no insignificant weapon. In the hands of a woman it has won many a victory. I have faith in your wielding it to the best effect--the lasting discomfiture of Senor Estada."

"You laugh," indignantly, "believing me a coquette--a girl to play with men?"

"No; that misconstrues my thought. I believe you a true woman, yet possessing the natural instincts of your sex, and able to use your weapons efficiently. There is no evil in that, no reproach. I would not have you otherwise, and we must not misunderstand each other. You retain faith in me?"

"Implicitly."

"And pledge yourself to your part, leaving me to attend to mine?"

Her two hands clasped my fingers, her eyes uplifted.

"Geoffry Carlyle, I have always believed in you, and now, after the sacrifice you have made to serve me, I can refuse you nothing you ask. I will endeavor to accomplish all you require of me. God knows how I hate the task; but--but I will do my best. Only--only," her voice sank, "if--if the monster cannot be held, I will kill him."

"I hope you do."

"I shall! If the beast lays hands on me he--he pays the price. I could not do otherwise. Geoffry Carlyle--I am a Fairfax."

Satisfied with my mission, and confident nothing more need be said, I arose to my feet.

"Then we can do nothing further, until I learn the disposition of the crew," I said quietly. "Estada is not likely to resort to extreme measures at present. He has two objects before him---to permit Sanchez to die of his wounds, if that is at all probable; and to win the men by some successful capture. These fellows only retain command by success. The taking of a rich ship will make Estada a hero, while a defeat would mean his overthrow, and the ascendancy of someone else. There is no other test of a robber chief. Estada knows this, and will not dare act until he has put clinking coin in the pockets of his men. That is why I believe you are comparatively safe now--his own position of command is in the balance."

"I am glad you explained that to me, The knowledge will give me more confidence."

"Do not rely too much on his control of himself. There is no trust to be put in such a man. I must go now, and endeavor to reach my quarters unseen."

"I will see you again?"

"Perhaps not here; it is too dangerous, but I will find means to communicate with you. Possibly the steward can be trusted as a messenger; I will talk with him and make sure. Meanwhile we must not appear interested in each other. Good-bye."

We stood with hands clasped in the darkness. I thought she was going to speak again, but the words failed to come. Then suddenly, silently, the door opened a mere crack, letting in a gleam of yellow light from the main cabin, while the crouching figure of a man, like a gliding shadow slipped through the aperture, closing the door behind him as softly as he had opened it. I heard her catch her breath, and felt her hands grasp my sleeve, but I never stirred. The fellow had neither seen nor heard us, and I stared into the black curtain, endeavoring to locate him by some sound of movement.

Who could he be? What might be the purpose of his entrance? But one answer occurred to me--Pedro Estada, driven by unbridled passions to attack the girl. Mad as such an act would be, yet no other explanation seemed possible. I thrust her behind me, and took a step forward, with body poised for action. I was unarmed, but cared little for that in the swift desire felt to come to hand grips with the brute. I could hear him now, slowly and cautiously feeling his way toward us through the darkness.

CHAPTER XVII
A MURDER ON BOARD

The fellow made scarcely a sound as he advanced, yet, as I waited breathlessly, I felt assured of his stealthy approach. To be certain of free space I extended one hand and my fingers came into unexpected contact with the back of a chair. Without moving my body I grasped this welcome weapon of defense and swung it above my head. Whoever the invader creeping upon us might prove to be, he was certainly an enemy, actuated by some foul purpose, and, no doubt armed. To strike him down as quickly and silently as possible was therefore the plain duty of the moment. I had no other thought.

The slowness with which he groped his way forward indicated unfamiliarity with the apartment, although his direct advance proclaimed some special purpose. Clearly he had no fear of attack, believing no one more formidable than a girl was there to oppose him. The darkness, perhaps, and silence, convinced the fellow that she had already retired. He would have his grip on her, before she could even dream of his presence. Then there would be no scream, no alarm. I could determine almost his exact position as his advancing foot felt cautiously along the deck, seeking to avoid striking any obstacle in the darkness. He came forward inch by inch, and I had the sensation of awaiting the spring of some creeping animal, about to leap upon me. With tense muscles, the heavy chair poised for a blow, I measured the distance as indicated by faint, shuffling sounds, perceptible only because of the profound stillness.

I could not see, but I knew; I felt his presence; in imagination I pictured him, with arms outstretched, barely beyond my reach, deliberately advancing one foot for yet another step forward. With all my force I struck! Blindly as it had been delivered, the blow hit fair; there was a thud, an inarticulate groan, and the fall of a body onto the floor--beyond that nothing. I waited breathlessly, the chair back gripped in my hands, anxiously listening for the slightest movement. There was none to be distinguished; not so much as the quiver of a muscle. I felt Dorothy touch my shoulder, and caught the sound of her voice, trembling at my ear.

"What it is? What did you do?"

"I struck him with a chair; he lies there on the deck. Wait where you are until I learn what has happened."

I bent over and touched him, dropping to my knees, every nerve tingling as my hands felt of the recumbent body. The fellow lay in a heap, his flesh warm, but with no perceptible heart-beat, no semblance of breathing. My fingers sought his face, and I could scarcely suppress a cry of surprise--he was not Estada. Who then was he? What could have been his purpose in thus invading this stateroom? All I could grasp was the fact that the fellow was not the Portuguese--he possessed a smooth face, long hair, and was a much smaller man. It must have become overcast without, for the star-gleam was no longer visible through the after port, and yet a faint light entered, sufficient for my purpose. I dragged the body that way, dropping it where the slight illumination fell directly on the upturned face. The features revealed were unfamiliar--those unquestionably of a half-breed Indian. Dorothy crossed to my side, her foot striking a knife, which came glimmering into the narrow range of light. She stared in horror at the ugly weapon, and then at the ghastly countenance.

"Who is he? Do you know?"

"One I have never seen before; he must belong to the gang amidships--an Indian."

She shuddered, her voice trembling.

"He came to murder! See his knife lies there. Why should he have sought to kill me?"

"It is all mystery," I admitted, "and too deep for me. Perhaps it was a mistake, or the fellow thought you had jewels. Anyway he will never try that trick again--see, my blow crushed his skull."

"He is actually dead?"

"Beyond doubt. The chair was a heavy one, and I struck with all my strength. What shall be done with the body? It cannot be left lying exposed here; no one would believe you killed him, and my presence must not be suspected."

"Could it," she suggested, "be dropped astern through the port?"

"Ay, that might be done; it was dull of me not to think of that. Yet we must not risk a splash to be overheard on deck. Is there a rope of any kind to be had?"

"Only this curtain cord; it is not large, but strong." "That ought to do, if long enough; there must be a twenty-foot drop to the water. Yes, splice the two together; let me have them."

She shrank back from touching the inanimate figure, her face very pale in the dim light, yet it required the combined efforts of both to force the stiffening body through the port hole, and then lower it slowly to the surging water below. The cord cut our hands cruelly, but it held, and the dead man sank beneath the surface, and was swept swiftly astern, into the black depths. We could distinguish footsteps on the deck above, but these were regular and undisturbed--the slow promenade from rail to rail of the officer on watch. Clearly nothing had been heard, or seen, to awaken suspicion. I turned back, as the released body vanished, to look into her face, which was scarcely visible.

"If you should be questioned tomorrow you had best know nothing," I said gravely. "I do not think you will be, for surely such an attack can be no plan of Estada's. It could gain him no advantage. The fellow was pillaging on his own account; if he is missed it will be supposed he fell overboard, and no one will greatly care."

"You will be able to learn? I--I shall feel better if I know the truth."

"Possibly; however it will be safer for me not to ask questions. I am not myself in too good repute aboard. You are not afraid to remain here alone?"

"No; I am not greatly frightened but shall try and bar the door with a chair. I have no key."

"Then I'll leave you; half of my watch below must be gone by now. I'll take the fellow's knife along, as it must not be found here."

We parted with a clasp of hands, as I opened the stateroom door, and slipped out into the cabin. To my surprise the light over the table had been extinguished, rendering the cabin so black I held to actually feel my way forward. This struck me as very strange, particularly as I recalled clearly that a stream of light had flashed into the after stateroom with the entrance of the prowler. The lantern must have been put out since then by some confederate. Gunsaules would be soundly asleep long ago, and the light was supposed to burn until morning. However there was no noise, other than the creaking and groaning of the ship's timbers, mingled with the steady tread of LeVere on the upper deck. So, after a moment of hesitation, I found my way across to my own stateroom and pressed open the door.

A misty light came in through the port, sufficient to show me all was exactly as I had left it, and I flung off my jacket preparatory to lying down for a short rest before being recalled for the watch on deck. The hilt of the knife in my belt attracted my attention, and I drew it forth, curious to learn if it bore any mark of ownership. Whether it did, or not, I shall never know, as my eyes were instantly attracted to a dark stain on both hilt and blade. I held it to the light--it was the stain of blood, and my hands were also reddened by it. In that first instant of horror, I hurled the weapon out through the open port into the sea. Blood! human blood, without doubt! There had been murder committed on board, and the fellow I had struck down was seeking refuge, endeavoring to find concealment following his crime. Ay, but what about the light in the cabin? It had been extinguished after the fleeing fugitive had entered Dorothy's stateroom. Did this mean that the slayer had an accomplice? If so, then the killing was not the result of a mere personal quarrel amidships, or in the forecastle; but the result of some conspiracy. I thought of Sanchez, and of Estada's plan to obtain control of the ship. Could this be its culmination? And was the Spaniard already lying dead in his cabin? This was the only solution of the mystery which seemed probable, and yet this did not wholly satisfy my mind. Not that I questioned the fiendishness of Estada, or his coconspirator, Manuel, or their unwillingness to commit such a crime, but it seemed so unnecessarily brutal. Why should they stab a man already so severely wounded as to be threatened with death? he was helpless, and in their power; neglect, or at most a simple reopening of his wounds, would be sufficient for their purpose. To attack him anew would only mean exposure, and perhaps awaken the enmity of the crew.

Nothing came of my thought--only confusion; nor did I dare investigate for fear of becoming more deeply involved in the tragedy. There had been no alarm; everything aboard was going on as usual; I could hear LeVere tramping the deck, and occasionally catch the echo of his voice, as he hailed the main-top, or gave some order to the men forward. No, there was nothing to be done; my safety, and the safety of the girl depended on our apparent ignorance of what had occurred. We must have no part in it, no knowledge or suspicion. There was nothing to do but wait the revelation of the morning. Convincing myself of this, I washed the blood stains from my hands, and lay down in the bunk, fully dressed to await my call. Evidently the wind had decreased, as the *Namur* pitched but little in the sea, and I could hear the scuffling of feet indicating a new spread of canvas above. The night air, blowing in through my open port became so chill that I covered myself with a blanket. The vessel creaked and groaned in every joint, some of the sounds actually startling me with their resemblance to cries of human agony. I tossed about, occasionally sitting upright to peer around in the darkness, my body bathed in cold perspiration, yet must have dropped finally off into an uneasy sleep. A sharp rapping of knuckles on the door awoke me with a start.

"Starboard watch, Senor."

"Will be on deck at once."

"Ay, ay, Senor."

I drew on a heavy pea jacket of leather, fastening it securely at the throat, and donned a wool cap. The lantern in the cabin had been relighted, and was burning brightly, and my anxious glance about the interior revealed nothing out of place. The only door open led to the steward's storeroom. Feeling it best to be prepared for any eventuality, I selected a pistol from the rack, saw to its loading, and slipped the weapon into my pocket. Except for one man busily engaged coiling a rope, the main deck was deserted, and I climbed the short ladder to the poop, meeting LeVere as I straightened up. The sea was a gentle swell, the sky clear above, but with a mass of dark clouds off the port quarter. A glance aloft revealed a full spread of canvas. The air contained a nip of frost.

"All set, I see, LeVere?"

"Si, Senor, and at that we barely move. The bark needs a gale o' wind to make any headway."

"You have no fear of the storm yonder?"

He glanced aside at the mass of cloud.

"No, Senor. It hung just there an hour past--not come here, but creep around."

"Your course?"

"Still to the sou' o' east, Senor." He bent down to glance at the card and I saw his dark face in the gleam of the binnacle light. He was not bad looking, but for the continuous gleam of prominent teeth. He straightened up.

"Who put out the cabin light, Senor?"

"I am sure I don't know; was it out?"

"Yes, Senor. I never knew that to happen before."

"An accident, no doubt. The steward probably left some near-by port open, and a gust of wind did the business. That's nothing to worry over."

He shook his head as though far from satisfied by my theory, but went below without attempting to reply. I watched him through the skylight, but he merely gulped down a glass of liquor, and entered his stateroom.

My watch was uneventful. The fellow at the wheel was unfamiliar to me, and rather surly in his answers, to the few questions I put to him. As he could speak nothing but Spanish I soon left him alone, and fell to pacing the deck, immersed in my own thoughts. These were far from pleasant ones, as I reviewed again the strange situation in which I found myself. Circumstances had played me a sorry trick. Without plan, almost without effort, I had drifted into a position of utmost delicacy. Any accident or mistake might lead to disastrous results. Not only my own life, but the life of the young woman below, could be endangered by a single careless word, or act. The whole affair seemed more a nightmare than a reality. I was actually serving as first officer on a pirate ship in search of vessels to rob on the high seas, commanding a crew of West Indian cut-throats--the very scum of hell, and under the order of a Portuguese devil, whose ambition coolly plotted murder. I was sailing under the black flag, to be hung if captured, compelled to act out the masquerade, a satellite of the most infamous villain who ever sacked a merchant-man. Why, the very name of Sanchez had been horror to me in the past--yet here I actually was in charge of the deck of his death ship, searching for new victims, and only hoping that the arch villain might live to overthrow the even fouler demon who would succeed him if he died. Already I knew murder had been done; that the coming morning would reveal some hideous tragedy, on which, perhaps my fate would depend. Somewhere below in the dark lay a dead man, his sightless eyes staring upward. The curse of crime was upon the vessel, and this, possibly, was only the beginning, whose end could not be foreseen. And for what was I there? The answer was not upon my lips, but in my heart--Dorothy Fairfax. I bowed my head on the rail, and stared out over the dark water, but I saw only her face. No, I would not turn back; would not fail her. Let the end be death, and disgrace, I meant to fight grimly on until that end came. In that hour I knew she was more to me than life, or even honor. Far more than mere duty bound me; I was prisoner to love.

The dawn came cold and gray, but with clearing skies. The force of the wind increased, becoming unsteady, and causing a choppy sea, so that I felt impelled to lower the topsails and take a reef in the larger canvas. Nothing was reported in sight, but to reassure myself, I climbed into the main crosstrees, and swept the horizon with a glass. Not so much as a speck rewarded my efforts, and I descended the ratlines, shouting to the boatswain to call the port watch. Watkins came aft to the wheel, and I sent the fellow thus relieved down into the cabin to rout out LeVere. The two returned to deck together, the negro glancing about curiously without mounting the ladder.

"You call Senor Estada yet?" he questioned.

"No; I had no orders to do so."

"He tol' me call him at daylight. Here you, Amada; go wake up the Senor."

The seaman disappeared grumbling, while LeVere crossed the poop deck, and stood beside me looking out across the expanse of sea.

"No sail--hey? We hav' bad luck--too far north."

"And west; we are out of the sea lanes; but if it keeps bright I'll take an observation at noon."

Amada emerged from the companion, and stared up at us, shading his mouth with one hand as he spoke.

"He answer nothing, Senor LeVere."

"You rapped on the door?"

"Si, Senor; I strike with my fist, and my boot, but he never wake up."

"Was the door locked?"

"I know not, Senor; I not try open it."

LeVere gave utterance to an oath.

"The pig-headed swine," he said fiercely. "I suppose I'll have to go myself."

Our eyes met, and something seemed to bid me accompany him.

"We'll go down together, Senor," I said quietly. "Estada must be sick; I could hear the rumpus Amada kicked up even on deck here. No man could sleep through that racket."

CHAPTER XVIII
A NEW CONSPIRACY

The interior of the cabin appeared more desolate than ever in the gray light of dawn. The swinging light yet burned, but was now useless, all the dismal horrors of the place revealed by the slowly increasing gleam of day stealing down from above. Gunsaules had not appeared, and LeVere's stateroom door remained ajar, giving glimpse of the disarranged bunk within. The other doors were tightly closed. Le-Vere rather held back, not noticeably so, perhaps, yet enough to give me the lead, and, with one swift glance about, I led the way directly to Estada's stateroom.

Something sinister had occurred during the dark hours of the night. Of that I was convinced, and I believed we were now about to lift the veil hiding the tragedy. My heart pounded like a hammer as I rapped on the wooden panels and waited some response from within. There was no answer, no sound of movement, and I rapped again more loudly, my questioning eyes seeking LeVere's face. He was listening as intently as myself, his eyes expressing anxiety. If I had felt some suspicion of the man before, this lack of faith vanished---he certainly was concerned in no plot involving the life of the Portuguese.

"There is something wrong, Senor," he whispered, "for he was ever a light sleeper."

"Then we will find out what it is."

The door was unlocked, the latch yielding instantly to the hand, and I stepped within. A glance told everything. The port was closed, but through the thick glass sufficient light found entrance to reveal the interior. The chair before the table was overturned, and there were papers scattered about the deck. Estada lay in his bunk, with one leg dangling outside, and his head crooked against the side wall. His very posture was that of sudden death, even had it not been pictured by the ghastly face, peculiarly hideous in the gray light which stared at us, and the dark pool of blood underneath. I heard an exclamation from LeVere, and stood for an instant utterly unable to move. The only sound audible was the steady drip of blood. I knew already what I should find, yet finally forced myself forward--he was stone dead, pierced with three knife thrusts. I stood up and faced the mulatto, whose countenance was fairly green with horror.

"What do you know about this, Senor LeVere?" I asked sternly. "The man has been murdered, knifed. Who did it--and why?"

He could scarcely answer, gripping at the table for support, and never removing his gaze from the face of the dead man. Yet I believed his words; was convinced this was not the terror of guilt.

"My God! I cannot tell; I have never dreamed of this--that is true, Senor."

"Had the man enemies. Anyone you would suspect?"

"Enemies? Ay, plenty of them; we all have. We expect that in our trade. This ship is full of devils ready enough to do such a job; but I could not name the one who did do it. I know of no cause. I have heard nothing."

"I believe you, LeVere," I said, when his voice ceased, yet unwilling even then to trust him fully. "All that rules here is strength. Murder is but a weapon, and hate struck this blow."

"What can we do, Senor?"

"Do! we must talk that over first. Open the port there and let in some fresh air. That is better; but we cannot think, looking at that ghastly face, and hearing the blood drip onto the deck. We'll leave him here and talk over the affair in the cabin."

"But the men will think it strange," he protested, "if I do not return to the deck; some may know what lies here."

"We cannot help that, LeVere. We cannot meet this thing until we are prepared; until we talk it over, and decide what to do. It is not the men on deck, the watch, I fear, but those fellows amidships--they are the ones to be afraid of; is that not so?"

"Si, Senor."

"Then come; there is more danger in hasty action than anything else."

I shut the door behind us, and turned the key. It was a relief to get outside, even into that dismal cabin, beyond view of Estada's dead face. The vessel rolled considerably, and LeVere, who had evidently lost his nerve, sank into a chair as though no strength remained in him.

"You fear an uprising, a mutiny?" I questioned, "when this is reported?"

"What will prevent?" he asked. "The Captain cannot stir; the mate dead; the men already crazed because we take no prizes. They will murder us also, and take control."

"Who will? Those devils amidships?"

"Ay; they care only to fight for gold--it is their trade."

"And who leads them? Who would they make captain?"

"Manuel Estevan," he whispered, "he would be the one."

"I thought as much. Then it is Manuel Estevan we must secure first--before they know. 'Tis my thought he is at the bottom of it all, and our hope lies in our early discovery. If we can act before he does, we may thwart his plan. Listen, Le-Vere; I will speak low for that forward stateroom is his. He has not supposed we would discover the murder so quickly, for he knew nothing of Estada's request that he be called at daylight--is this true?"

"Si, Senor; it was his last order when he went below."

"Good; then we must organize before he can act. We have that one chance left. Whatever his men may know of what has occurred they will make no move until they get his orders. We must stop the possibility of his issuing any. Without a leader, the advantage is ours."

"You mean to kill him?"

"Only as a last resort. I am no murderer, although there is enough at stake here to make me willing to take life. There is no good feeling between those quartered amidships, and the crew?"

"No, Senor; it is hate generally, although they are not all alike. The real sailors are mostly captured men; they serve to save their lives, and only for these others on board could not be held long. We do not arm them or use them to board prizes.

It's those devils amidships who loot; that is all their work to fight and guard these others. Naturally there's no love lost between them. Your plan, Senor, is to set the one against the other?"

"Yes, if possible; I know no other way. These sailor men are of all races. Can they be trusted?"

He sat bending forward, his hands on his knees, his dark face far from pleasant. I had every reason to know the fellow to be criminal, desperate, guilty of everything in the calendar, and yet I must place confidence in him. Only as we worked together now was there any prospect of success.

"Some might be; it is hard to tell how many. It is not the race which counts so much, Senor. There are those among them who would not care to return to honesty."

"And you, LeVere?"

He spread his hands, and shrugged his shoulders.

"There is no hope of me; I was born to the free life."

"What then is it with you?"

"Hate, Senor--revenge," and his teeth gleamed savagely. "I would spit on this Manuel who seeks to be chief. I can never be---no; I am of black skin, with negro blood in my veins, and white men would never have it so. But I can hate, Senor. That is why I am with you now, if the devil so will. Your plan might work--tell me more of it."

"It is simple enough, LeVere, and came to me but now as I looked upon Estada lying there dead. Treachery killed him, and that treachery must have purpose behind it. You believe this to be the ambition of Manuel Estevan to become chief, and that in this he is backed by those buccaneers amidships whom he commands. But to accomplish this end there must soon be other murders aboard--the Captain Sanchez, and possibly our own as well, although 'tis likely he may offer us life to join him. But I doubt if the fellow be ready yet to throw off the mask and openly declare himself. He will claim the murder of Estada to be the act of some fiendish member of the crew, and wait until things aboard ripen to his purpose. He is not likely to dream that we suspect him. This gives us our chance--we can act before he does."

"But if the men are with him?"

"What are the odds, say you--thirty to a hundred? Ay, but surprise will overcome that. My plan is this; first, for you and I to secure Manuel, as quietly as possible, but at whatever cost. Surely that can be done. With him in our hands, or dead, the buccaneers have no leader. What then? There are men in the crew on deck and in the forecastle to be trusted--Watkins is one, and he will know others, a dozen, no doubt. They will be enough. We will whisper the truth to these, and have them ready for a signal. The forward door from amidships is closed by iron bars--is it not?"

"Si, Senor," his eyes again sparkling with interest. "The men quarreled, and there was fighting."

"Then there is no escape in that direction and it can be no great task to close any passage leading aft. Lower the deck hatch, and we have those devils below caged like so many rats. There need be no fighting; starvation will bring them to terms."

"But, Senor, you forget--your dozen men cannot guard the buccaneers below, and also manage the bark at sea. The crew are not all lambs--many will sympathize with those thus locked beneath deck. Cochose is bad, and a friend of Manuel. He will fight, and there are others to back him."

"I know that, LeVere. The whole plan is desperate, but there is no other possible. Here is my scheme. There is a gun rack in the cabin, containing enough weapons to arm the dozen men we can trust. The others have nothing but their sheath knives. The buccaneers can be secured below, before these other lads ever realize what is happening--many will be asleep in the forecastle. As soon as we have control of the ship we'll round them up forward. They won't dare face the guns. I'll give them their choice, and, as for Cochose, I've taken his measure once already, and am ready to try it again."

"And what will you tell them, Senor?"

I caught my breath, conscious of his meaning. My secret hope could not be revealed to this fellow. However hate and ambition might sway him, and however personal fear might influence him, at the moment, his purpose and mine were entirely different. Piracy was his life; he knew and cared for nothing else. In innate savagery he was not better than any of the others, and must be dealt with accordingly. Just now I must have him on my side, and conditions had delivered him into my hands. But I could only hope to retain him through self interest. The mulatto had little faith in me; I was a stranger, an Englishman, unknown and untried. Naturally we were enemies. He would make use of me for the present if he could, and as smilingly knife me tomorrow if it served his turn. I felt confident of that, and in consequence the answer came quickly to my lips.

"The whole truth, Senor LeVere--that Manuel conspired to seize the bark through a mutiny of the buccaneers; that these were to be turned loose with license to kill anyone on board who opposed them; that their real purpose was to divide among themselves all the treasure below; then wreck the vessel, and escape with it. That to this end Estada had already been foully murdered and that they also intended to take the lives of the other officers so as to be free to do as they pleased. I shall explain that we discovered this conspiracy just in time to save them from butchery, and that they must stand by us, or else submit to those hell-hounds. I'll put it strong."

"And after that, Senor?"

"Why Porto Grande, of course," I admitted heartily. "It is not a long voyage, and if we bring the boat in safely the treasure is ours. The men will understand what that means--a handful of gold for each of them and a run ashore. Why, LeVere, they will make more apiece than by looting a half dozen ships, and with no fighting. It will be a fortune for you and me."

His somber eyes lighted up, startled by this new idea, and he sprang to his feet, swaying before me to the pitch of the deck.

"You mean that, Senor! We divide what is below, and sail for Porto Grande? I hear you right? You not mean surrender? You stay pirate?"

I laughed, my nerves tingling to the success of my ruse--he had taken the tempting bait like a hungry fish.

"Why of course; so that was the trouble. Hell! man, I am not such a fool as to throw away this chance. I came aboard here without a dollar, drunk, a sailor before the mast. Look at me now---shoved into a job as first officer, with my full share of all we can lay hands on. Do you suppose I'm going back to the forecastle, and a bit of silver? Not me! I'm for all I can get, and with no care how I get it. This is our chance, LeVere. If we put the *Namur* into Porto Grande, with Sanchez on board and alive, and those hell-hounds locked below, we'll get anything we ask for. We'll be the cocks of the walk. If he shouldn't live through, why then we'll have a ship, and can run the game alone. Either way, if we win, the prize is ours--and, by God! if we stick together we win."

My apparent enthusiasm caught the fellow. I could read the working of his mind in his face. This was a new view of the situation, a new vision. It appealed to him from every standpoint--it promised wealth, power, the total defeat of Estevan; everything he most desired. And as I pictured it, the result seemed easy of attainment. His eyes gleamed lightning.

"You think Senor Sanchez live?"

"What difference? If he lives he owes his life to us. If he dies the bark is in our hands, and the treasure. The thing to consider now is how to get control. Once we have won, we care nothing if he live or die. Come, we have wasted time enough in talk; it is action that counts--what say you? Are we together in this?"

He thrust out a lean, yellow hand, and I gripped it firmly.

"Si, Senor; you speak right. To do this we must act. I am with you."

"You pledge your word, Francois?"

"I pledge it, Senor."

"Good! and you have mine. Now to the work--first Manuel Estevan, and then the men on deck. 'Tis his stateroom yonder."

CHAPTER XIX
LAYING THE TRAP

Our first job was executed much more easily than I had anticipated. We caught Manuel sound asleep, and LeVere had sinewy hands at his throat before the fellow could grasp a weapon, or even clearly comprehend the nature of the attack. The narrowness of the stateroom prevented my taking much part in the affair, but the mulatto needed no help, as he dragged the cursing Spaniard from his bunk to the deck and throttled him savagely. Indeed he would have killed the fellow had I not interfered and twisted his hands loose, leaving Estevan barely conscious. A blanket ripped into strips served to bind him securely enough for the present, but I thought it best to lock the door, and keep the key in my own pocket. LeVere would have knifed him even as he lay there helpless, but for my threat and insistence. Once back in the cabin my eyes distinguished the frightened face of the steward peering forth at us from out the dark of the passage leading forward.

"Come here, Gunsaules," I said sternly. "Step lively, lad; there's nothing for you to fear."

"Yes, Senor--yes," and; he crept forth from his partial cover, glancing fearfully from face to face as he advanced.

"Senor Estada has been killed during the night, and we have just captured his murderer," I explained hastily. "There is reason to believe this act was part of a conspiracy to seize the ship."

"By Senor Manuel?" his eyes staring at me from out a white face.

"Yes, in connection with those fellows amidships. Does that passage lead to their quarters?"

"It did once, Senor, but now there is a closed door. The Captain Sanchez had it so arranged to prevent the men from coming aft."

"What kind of a door?"

"Of oak, studded with iron, not only locked, but barred on this side."

"You have no key?"

"No, Senor; there are but two--one for the Captain and the other for him who commands the buccaneers."

"Manuel?"

"Si, Senor."

I stood there a moment silent, considering this information, and rapidly arranging in mind our future operations. The only way the mutineers could reach the cabin then would be from the deck, descending through the companion. So long as they remained unaware of the capture of Manuel there was little danger of their taking such action. My faith in Gunsaules was not great, yet the probability was that he would remain loyal to whichever party held the upper hand. That was ever the way with these men.

"Very well, steward," I said. "You go on about your work as though nothing had happened. If any word of this affair gets to the crew, or to those fellows forward, I'll hold you responsible. Understand that!"

"Si, Senor."

"You are not to leave this cabin without my permission, nor speak to anyone.

LeVere."

The mulatto faced me respectfully enough, and I had a feeling he would obey orders, largely because he dare not rebel.

"Si, Senor."

"They will be wondering why you are not on deck. It will be better for you to take charge of the watch at once, and keep the men busy. Relieve Watkins at the wheel and send the man down to me. He can choose the fellows who will stick better than you could, and then can circulate among them without arousing suspicion. Send him down at once quietly."

He disappeared through the companion, while Gunsaules vanished within the storeroom, where I could hear him rummaging noisily about. I sat down to wait the appearance of Watkins, satisfied that matters were already safely in my control. That the English sailor would cooperate, I had no doubt, and as to LeVere, he had already gone too far to openly play the traitor. It was full daylight now, and evidently a bright morning, although the swell of the sea remained heavy, and I judged there must be a strong wind. Watkins, muffled to the ears in a heavy jacket, and with cap pulled down so I could scarcely see his face, shuffled down the steps. He whipped off the cap and stood waiting.

"The officer of the deck sent me here, sir."

"I asked for you; did LeVere tell you why?"

"No sir; only that I was to come at once and quietly." I put my hand on his shoulder. "Tom," I said soberly, but so low I felt sure even Gunsaules would not overhear, "we are in the same boat, and understand each other. The chance has come for both of us, if we play the cards right. Listen while I tell you the situation, and what I plan doing."

I told it briefly, wasting no words, yet relating every fact, even including my visit and conversation with Dorothy, and the throwing of the body through the after port. He listened eagerly, but without interruption until the end.

"What do you make of it?" I asked, irritated by his silence.

"About what you do, sir. I knew there was something of the kind going on-- some of the men forward are in on it. You've got the ring-leader."

"Manuel, you mean. Who did he count on for help in the forecastle?"

"Cochose, and a handful of others, niggers and Spaniards, mostly. They even tried out one or two white men. That's how I heard of it, through Jack Jones, but they never told him enough to make the plan clear. However, with what you've just said I've got a pretty fair understanding. They meant to pull the affair off either today or tonight. What sorter lookin' chap was the fellow you knocked out, sir?"

"I scarcely saw his face--a half-breed I should say; rather short, but stout, with long hair."

"Jose; he is the one Manuel would choose for such a job. But why he got into the girl's room is more than I know. However, if he is dead, and Manuel a prisoner, it gives us a fair chance, sir. It leaves those fellows amidships without a leader. A dozen good men on deck might do the business."

"But are there a dozen aboard to be trusted?"

He hesitated, running the names over in his mind, evidently weighing each one carefully.

"Well, yes sir. I rather think there are," he said finally. "It won't do for to make any mistake here, but I'm pretty sure of these fellows. I'd say that in both watches there's maybe fourteen to be relied on. There's one or two others in the starboard watch who are likely enough all right, but I don't get to see them alone much."

"Who do you pick out?"

"In my watch there's Jones, Harwood and Simms, either English or Welsh. They're all right. Then there's a nigger named Sam; Schmitt, a Dutchman, with his partner, whose name I don't know, and two Frenchies, Ravel and Pierre. That makes eight, nine counting myself. Then in the starboard watch I'd pick out Jim Carter and Joe Cole, two Swedes, Carlson and Ole Hallin, and another nigger. Then there are a couple of Finns who ought to be with us, but I can't talk their lingo. That would give us sixteen out of thirty, and it's quite likely some of the others would take a hand with us, if they thought it was safe. I have'nt any use though, sir, for Francois LeVere. There ain't a worse scamp aboard."

"I know that," I admitted, "but he had to be used. It was through him that Estada's murder was discovered. But he is safe enough for the present, for he made the attack on Manuel, and so will not dare go back on us. His life is in the balance. But wait, Tom; don't breathe in his ear our real purpose; I've convinced him that we mean to keep in the trade, dividing the treasure aboard, and sailing the bark to Porto Grande."

"Oh, so that's the game? And what is my part now?"

"This is my watch below, and it will be best for me to keep off the deck until all is prepared. Besides I am afraid to leave the cabin unguarded. There is no knowing what Gunsaules might do. You sound these men and get them together; wake up the ones in the starboard watch you feel sure are all right, and have them slip quietly on deck. LeVere will understand what you are up to, and will make no objection. As soon as you have everything ready, let me know."

"We are none of us armed, sir."

"That is what I was coming to. When you are sure of your men, and have them on deck, I'll get LeVere to send them all aft on some pretext or other. I'll think up a way to do this without creating any suspicion. Then we'll get these arms in the rack here, and be ready for business--the rest will be done in a hurry. You have it all clear?"

"Yes, sir."

"Then I'll wait here for your report."

At the very best Watkins could scarcely perform the task assigned him in less than an hour. No doubt there were those on his list whom he would have to approach with great caution, while there was always danger that some word might be dropped to awaken suspicion. The success or failure of our effort depended entirely upon taking these fellows by complete surprise. If it came to an open fight our cause was hopeless, for that would mean fourteen or fifteen men unarmed, pitted against over a hundred, thoroughly equipped and trained fighters. To be sure these were at present, without a leader, yet their force alone was sufficient to overcome us, and some one among them would doubtless assume leadership in an emergency. Only by confining them below, with hatches battened down, and a carronade trained upon them, would we be safe.

I sat where I could watch the stairs, and the entire forward part of the cabin. Gunsaules lowered the table, and began preparing the morning meal. He glanced at me each time he passed, but ventured on no questioning, although it was quite evident the fellow was nearly bursting from curiosity. I lit my pipe, endeavoring to appear entirely at ease, as I turned over and over again in mind every detail of the contemplated action. With each review the result seemed more certainly assured, and my courage revived. Except for some accident, or act of treachery, I could perceive no reason why my plan should not work perfectly. It was evident that LeVere was endeavoring to keep the watch on deck busy. I could hear his voice frequently, calling out orders and occasionally singling out some man for a special task. A slushing of water proved that the deck amidships was being washed down, and twice, at least, men were sent aloft to make some change in the spread of canvas.

I stepped across into my stateroom to gain a glimpse out through the port. Narrow as the vista was it yet revealed a beautiful sea view, the waves running high, but in long billows, with bright sunshine glowing along their crests, the hollows a deep purple. Above the sky was a pale blue, with scarcely a fleeting cloud visible, and the bark was sailing free, laying well over to the fresh breeze, evidently carrying all the spread of canvas possible. As I returned to the cabin, Gunsaules awaited me to announce breakfast.

"What already?"

"It is six-thirty, Senor. Those were my orders."

"Very well; I suppose Estada and Manuel usually eat first?"

"Si, Senor."

"That leaves me alone; suppose you rap on the lady's door yonder, and ask if she will join me. Say your message is from Senor Gates."

She came forth immediately fully dressed, but bearing herself with reserve. On my part I made no effort at greeting, not certain as to what eyes might be observing us through the deck light above, or, for the matter of that, unwilling to face the curiosity of the watchful steward.

"I had you called," I explained, "because of a disinclination to eat entirely alone. You were evidently awake?"

"Yes; I have not undressed. I felt no desire to sleep, although, no doubt I dozed. The call to breakfast was quite welcome."

She seated herself opposite me, and we spoke of the weather while Gunsaules served with some skill. He was still hovering about, but my anxiety to enjoy a word with her alone caused me to send him on a task elsewhere.

"Has Captain Sanchez been attended to yet?" I asked sharply. "No; then see to him at once. I have reason to believe he is alone this morning, and will need you. Yes, we can get along very nicely."

We waited until he disappeared within the after stateroom, bearing a tray; then her eyes suddenly lifted to mine, filled with questioning.

"Tell me what has happened?" She breathed eagerly. "I heard the noise of a struggle out here, and voices conversing. Why are you alone?"

I leaned over to speak in as low a tone as possible.

"I can only explain very briefly. The man who came into your room last night had just murdered Estada. LeVere and I found the mate's body at daylight. His killing was part of a plot by Manuel, and the buccaneers quartered amidships, to seize the bark. We have Manuel already prisoner and are preparing to gain possession of the boat ourselves."

"Who are planning? You have found friends on board?"

"I have made LeVere believe his only safety lies in assisting me. I told you about Watkins and the other men forward. He has picked out a dozen, or so, in whom he has confidence, English sailors mostly and is sounding them out. I expect him back with a report at any minute."

"And then what?" her excitement visible in her eyes. "What can a dozen men do?"

"Our main weapon is surprise of course. By acting quickly we can gain control of the deck. If Watkins' estimate is correct, nine out of the port watch now on duty will be with us. If he can add to these five or six from the starboard watch below this will make a total, not counting LeVere and myself, of fifteen. There would be only five left to oppose us on deck and probably two of these would be on watch aloft. Once we gain control of the deck we can lock the others below, and negotiate with them at our leisure. The plan looks to me quite possible."

She sat silently gazing at me across the table, seemingly failing to quite comprehend, her parted lips trembling to an unasked question. Before she could frame this in words, the door to the companion opened, and Watkins descended the stairs. At sight of her he whipped off his cap, and stood motionless, fumbling it awkwardly in his hands.

"You may speak freely," I said. "This is the young lady I told you about, and of course she is with us. Only talk low, as the steward is in the stateroom yonder."

"Yes sir," using a hoarse whisper, and fastening his gaze on me. "It's all right, sir."

"They are with us! How many?"

"Eight sure from my watch, sir. Harwood is in the fore-top and couldn't be seen, but I'll answer for his bein' all right. There was only four I could get word to in the forcastle, but there's others there who'll give us help soon as they know what's goin' on."

"That makes twelve of the men, fifteen of us altogether. Are the four from the starboard watch on deck?"

He nodded, clutching and unclutching his hands nervously, scarcely able to restrain himself.

CHAPTER XX
THE DECK IS OURS

I had the next step carefully outlined in my own mind, and yet I hesitated a moment, glancing into the two faces before me, with a sudden realization of what the contemplated action would mean to all of us, if by any chance it should fail of success. Our lives certainly hung in the balance, for these fiends would show no mercy, if once they gained power to strike back. Yet how could we fail? Only through treachery, or some unforseen accident. And, moreover, it was too late for retreat. The one chance, desperate as it appeared, must be taken. I managed to speak cheerfully, putting a ring of confidence into my voice.

"Then the sooner we act the better. Watkins have LeVere order these men aft. Let him say that Senor Estada wishes them to break out some stores in the lazaret. That will create no suspicion. They need be here only long enough for us to distribute these arms among them, and for me to speak a word of instruction to them. Are you ready?"

"Ay, ay, sir."

As he vanished, I turned to the girl, who had arisen to her feet, one hand grasping the edge of the table to balance herself against the pitching of the deck.

"It is a desperate chance, is it not?" She questioned anxiously. "Yes," I admitted. "Fifteen of us against a hundred and fifteen, but worth taking and such an opportunity may never occur again. I believe the plan will work; its greatest weakness is, I do not know the men on whom I must rely. If there should be a traitor among them we are done for. I mean to work so fast no one man will be able to spread the news."

"But have I no part? Is there no way in which I can help?"

"You have your pistol?"

"Yes."

"Then remain here. I shall have to go on deck with the men, and will not dare leave them a moment until the ship is absolutely secure. Manuel is locked in that stateroom, but must not be communicated with by anyone. I hardly believe Gunsaules will attempt anything, but it is not safe to trust him alone. It will be your part to see that the fellow neither enters that passage leading amidships, nor approaches this door. Keep him in sight. You can do this?"

"Of course I can."

"Then you will do most valuable service, and save us a man. Wait here now until I see how securely this passage forward is closed."

It was as described to me--a heavy oaken door, nail studded, not only locked, but held firmly in place by a stout iron bar. There was not the faintest possibility of any entrance aft, except through assistance from this side. As I returned to the cabin, Gunsaules came out of the Captain's room and crossed the deck. At sight of me he stopped instantly, holding his tray in front of him.

"Gunsaules," I said, wasting no words, "you are to remain in this cabin until I give the word. The lady here has a pistol, and orders to shoot if you attempt to either enter this passage, or approach the door of Manuel's stateroom."

"Yes, Senor," his face like chalk, and his eyes rolling.

"How did you find Sanchez?"

"Sitting up in his bunk, Senor, and able to eat."

"Does he know what is occurring on board?"

"No, Senor. He questioned me, but I only told him everything was all right, so far."

In my heart I believed the fellow deliberately lied, but there was no opportunity to question him further, for at that moment the door of the companion opened and a miscellaneous group of men thronged down the stairs. They were a rough hairy lot, here and there a sturdy English countenance meeting my gaze, but the faces were largely foreign, with those of two negroes conspicuous. I felt my heart beat furiously at sight of such poor material, and yet many a ship's crew appeared worse. The fellows grouped themselves awkwardly behind Watkins.

"Twelve here, sir; I couldn't get Harwood down from the fore-top."

"And there are others below who will join us?"

"Yes sir; six more I count on."

"Which means lads, that with Harwood, Senor LeVere, and myself, we'll total twenty-one in this shindy. Now I'll tell you what is up. Watkins gave you some of it no doubt, but a word from me will make it clearer. I'm no pirate; I'm an English sailor, shanghied on board. Estada named me first officer because I understand navigation."

I stopped speaking, staring at one of the faces before me; all at once it appeared familiar.

"What is your name, my man?"

"Jim Carter, sir."

"You were in the crew of the *Sinbad*, three years ago?"

"I was that, Mister Carlyle," he answered grinning. "I know'd you the minute I cum down yere."

"Then that is all I need say on that line. Here's one of your mates, lads, who will vouch for me. Now, as I've been told, you are all of you in the same boat--you are prisoners on board, cowed by those mongrel devils amidships. Do you understand what I say?"

"If ye'd put it in Spanish, sir," said Carter respectfully, "an' talk kinder slow, they'd most ov 'em catch the meanin'. That's 'bout all the lingo we've heard lately."

"Very well; now listen closely, all of you. Luck has given us a chance to make a break, and get away. Captain Sanchez is wounded and helpless. Pedro Estada is dead, and I've got Manuel locked in that stateroom. His cut-throats are all below, and now all we've got to do is clap on the hatch and keep them there."

"What 'bout the nigger on watch?" broke in Jones hoarsely. "I'd like ter crook him, by God."

"He's with us so far. I'll answer for him. Now, what I want to know is are you fellows with me?"

Watkins answered up promptly; then Carter; the others joining in with less heartiness, the different accents revealing their nationalities. I knew sailors well enough to feel assured they would follow their leaders once the game started.

"That's good enough; now we've got to hit hard and quick, lads. There are six men on deck who are not with us. Watkins will take care of them with those fellows I don't assign to other work. Jones, you and Carter make straight for the forecastle and don't let anyone come up the scuttle. One of you had better drop down below, and prevent any of those lads from unbarring the door leading amidships. Who is the best for that job?"

"Let Carlson do it. He belongs to the starboard watch."

"All right--Carlson it is then. You Frenchmen, and the two negroes, your part will be to ship the main hatch. Do a quick job, and clamp it down tight. Do you all understand just what you are to do?"

The responses satisfied me.

"I'll come down to you, Carlson, as soon as we have the deck. It ought not to take more than five minutes to handle those lads, and slew around a carronade. Now don't be afraid to hit hard. Watkins, you and Carter hand out the cutlasses from the rack; you boys will handle those better than firearms. Good; now are you all ready?"

There was a low murmur of voices, the faces watching me showing their increasing excitement and eagerness. Our little talk had served to arouse their confidence in my leadership, and with gleaming weapons in their hands they became self-reliant volunteers. Once turned loose my greatest difficulty might be to restrain them, rather than urge them on. Revenge for past wrongs was in each heart, and they welcomed a chance to strike and kill.

I whispered a parting word of admonition into the ear of Dorothy, receiving in return a glance from her eyes, which gave a new throb to my heart; then straightened up, and pistol in hand, pushed my way through the throng of sailors to the foot of the stairs.

"Follow me, lads," I said quietly, "and every man do the particular thing assigned him. Don't pay any attention to your mates--do your part, and then wait for orders. Come on now."

We emerged through the companion, and I stepped aside as the others rushed by. There was no shout, no cheer, the fellows seeming to realize the desperate nature of their work, and the importance of surprise. They were outnumbered five to one, and their only hope of success lay in rendering their opponents helpless before they could rally to a defense. All the pent-up hate of years was in their hearts, blazed madly in their eyes; they were tigers leaping at the throat of their prey, yet sane enough to comprehend even in their blood-rage that they must act together. It was over so quickly I scarcely saw it all; my memory now is of a clear sky, a deck almost deserted, its brass work glowing in the sun, the white sails above bellowing out to the pressure of a strong wind, and the blue sea, crested with white, stretching about us in desolate grandeur. LeVere stared down over the poop rail, behind him the motionless figure of the wheelsman, his hands gripping the spokes, while across the open deck the speeding mutineers leaped to their several posts, with bare cutlasses shining in the sun. And they did their work. My eyes swept from group to group--the four toiling at the cover of the main hatch; the fellows racing toward the forecastle; and Watkins' squad driving straight into the grouped watch beyond the foremast. It was smartly done; Watkins had taken no cutlass, but went in with both fists, asking no questions, but battering right and left, his men surging after, with steel blades flaming in the sunlight. The astounded watch, cursing and fighting grimly, held for a moment, and then went staggering back against the port rail, unable to stem the rush, and roaring for mercy. I had view of Carlson dropping recklessly down the forecastle scuttle, and then sprang forward myself to give a hand to the four wrestling with the main hatch. Together we dragged it into position, forcing relentlessly back as we did so, a dozen struggling figures frantically endeavoring to reach the deck. Shots were fired, the bullets whistling through the opening, the flare lighting up the black depths below, revealing vaguely a mass of frantic men staring up, and cursing us fiercely in a dozen languages; but, in spite of them, we clamped the hatch down tight, and locked it securely into place with an iron bar. Even through this cover the sound of smothered yells reached our ears, mingled with blows of gun-butts, as the fellows vainly endeavored to break out from their prison. The negro Sam grinned from ear to ear, executing a jig, as he flashed his cutlass above his head.

"Stay here, all four of you," I commanded sharply. "This job is well done. Now let me see about the others."

Watkins needed no help; he had his party rounded up, and in complete control,

the fellows begging for mercy, as they crouched before the cutlasses of their assailants. To my orders they were driven into the cook's galley and a guard stationed at
the door. Then I turned to the more serious work confronting me in the forecastle.
What lay before me in facing the members of the starboard watch it was impossible
to conceive, but they had to be sorted out, and it was my task. We must have men
enough to sail the bark, and if I was to command them, I must first of all prove my
courage and enforce authority. The whole success of our effort depended on this.

"What's going on below?" I asked.

"Cursin' mostly," answered Carter, peering down through a slight uptilting of
the scuttle. "They don't just know what's happening yet, but the big nigger seems
ter be raisin' hell. Carlson is a holdin' him back with his cutlass."

"Open up and let me down."

I fell, rather than clambered along the rungs of the ladder, coming to my feet
on deck in the midst of a group of angry men, who had Carlson pinned against the
bulkhead. The light was so poor I could scarcely see their faces; a babel of voices greeted me, and more than one hand gripped me fiercely as the excited owner
yelped a demand to know what in hell we were up to. I roughly cleared a space,
aided by Carlson's cutlass, and fronted them defiantly. Towering above them all,
his black apelike face, distorted with rage, I distinguished the giant Cochose, his
immense hands grasping a wooden bar ripped from a bunk. Plainly enough he was
the leader, the one man whose ascendency I must crush, and I meant to do it, then
and there. This was no job I could turn over to others; if I was to rule, this black
brute must be conquered at the very start, conquered by my own hands, and in the
presence of his mates. Here, in this black forecastle, we must fight it out, breast to
breast, as savagely as beasts of the jungle, to the bitter end. I made the resolve, with
teeth clenched, and every muscle throbbing with eagerness.

"Stand back there lads," I said sternly, my eyes searching their faces, and with
pistol poised threateningly. "Give us room. I'll explain all that has happened presently, but first I am going to lick that black brute within an inch of his life. Step out
of there, Cochose."

He came grinning widely, balancing the heavy club in his hands.

"You mean me, sah? You all think yer kin lick me?"

"Yes, I think so; I'll try it anyway. Here Carlson, take this pistol and sheath knife. If anyone interferes shoot him. All I ask is fair play. Drop that club, Cochose, and throw away your knife. You and I will fight this out with bare hands."

His dull brain worked slowly, and he stared at me, his eyes ugly, his grin becoming savage with a display of teeth. His silence and lack of response, awoke a growl from the impatient circle of men behind. One fellow kicked the club out of his hand contemptuously, and another plucked the knife from his belt.

"You big skulker," the latter said, with an oath of derision, "go on, and fight! What in hell are you afraid of?"

"What for Ah fight this white man? Ah don't even know who he is."

"Then I'll tell you. Estada is dead; Manuel is a prisoner. I'm in command of this bark, and I am going to give you a lesson for the benefit of the crew. You are a big, boasting cur! I heard what you said when I came down, and now I'll make you prove it. You other fellows stand back--I'll make this beast fight."

I took two steps forward, my advance so swift and unexpected, the big negro had not even time in which to throw up an arm in defense. With open hand I struck him squarely across the face, an insulting, stinging blow.

CHAPTER XXI
IN FULL POSSESSION

A roar of delight mingled with the negro's snarl of rage at this action. For an instant the fellow appeared too completely surprised for movement, although an angry oath burst from his lips, and the grin of derision faded from his face. I knew sailors, and felt that these men would not differ greatly from the occupants of other forecastles on the seven seas. They would welcome a fight like this and their immediate sympathy would be with me for starting it. More than that, this black bully, ruling over them by brute force, could be no favorite. They might fear him, but with that fear would be mingled hate, and a delight in his downfall.

The respite was short, yet in that instant, although I cannot recall removing watchful eyes from the negro's face, I received an impression of my surroundings never to be erased from memory. The grim picture arises before me now, distinct in every detail, the gloomy interior, the deck, foul, littered with sea boots, and discarded clothing, and the great beams overhead blackened by smoke. The rays of the swinging slush lantern barely illuminated the central space, the rows of bunks beyond remaining mere shadows, yet this dim, yellowish light, fell full upon the excited, half circle of men who were roaring about the negro, and had already pressed him forward until he stood confronting me, his grin of derision changed into a scowl of hate. They were a rough, wild lot, bearded and uncombed, ranging in color from the intense black of Central Africa to the blond of Scandinavia, half naked some, their voices mingling in a dozen tongues, their eyes gleaming with savagery. They impressed me as animals of the jungle, thirsting for blood, and I knew the man who came victorious from this struggle would be their leader. The thought stiffened my muscles, and strengthened my determination to win.

I know not whether Cochose lunged forward of his own volition, or was pressed on from behind, yet suddenly he was within reach of me, and the battle was on. It was short and fierce, his object evidently being to crush me in his giant grip, mine to oppose science to strength, and avoid his bear-hug. We swayed back and forth to the sharp pitching of the ship, barely able to keep our feet, sparring for some advantage. Once he would have had me, but for a lunge of the vessel which sent him sprawling on hands and knees; yet, before I could recover, the man was up again, furious with anger. This time, he sprang straight at me, uttering a growl of rage, determined to smash me to the deck by the very power of his onslaught. But I side-stepped him, getting in two swift blows, which rocked his head, and tore open one cheek, from which blood trickled. Yet he kept his feet, blindly gripping for me, driven almost crazy by the pain of my last blow, and the jeers of his mates.

I evaded his clutch by leaping aside, but the space was far too small to permit these tactics to carry long, and finally he had me. Yet, even as he seemingly crushed the very breath out of me, his giant strength met with a resistance which increased his fury. Already the fellow had lost his head, but I fought coolly, putting my skill against brute force, every wrestler's trick I knew flashing into my brain. Breathless, my flesh scraped and bruised, I wriggled partly free, and tripped him, his great body striking the deck with a thud. I fell with him, dragged down by his desperate grip, but was first upon my feet, saluted by a roar of delight from the lips of those crowding about us. As he staggered up also, cursing fiercely, his lips drawn back in a snarl, his brutal face, that of a wild animal, I struck him again, a blow which would have ended the game, had not my foot slipped on the reeling deck. As it was it drove him to his knees, groggy, and with one eye half closed, yet with strength enough left to regain his feet as soon as I. This time he charged me like a wild bull, froth whitening his lips, scarcely appearing human in the yellow light. In mad rage he forgot all caution, all pretense at defense, his one thought to reach me with his hands, and throttle me into lifeless pulp. Here was where skill and coolness won. I fought him back, driving blow on blow through his guard, sidestepping his mad rushes, landing again and again on his body. Twice I got in over his heart, and at last, found the chance I sought, and sent a right jab straight to the chin. All the force of one hundred and eighty pounds was behind the clinched fist, and the negro went down as though floored by a poleaxe. Once weakly he endeavored to rise, but this time I used my left, and he never stirred again, lying there with no sign of life except the quivering of the huge body. Assured that he was down and out, I stood above him, gazing into the ring of excited faces.

"That's one attended to," I said shortly. "Now is there any more of you who would like to fight this out?"

There was no answer although the ring widened under the threat of my eyes, and I met sullen faces here and there. I was in no mood to take chances.

"Carlson," I said, glancing back at him. "You know all these men?"

"Yes, sir."

"Pick out those you can trust, and have them stand over there to the right. Call them out by name; be lively now."

They stepped forth eagerly enough, and ranged themselves before the bunks, the faces mostly those of northern Europe, although a negro or two was among them. As the Swede ceased calling, six or seven yet remained clustered in front of me, a motley lot, one of them an Indian, the others mostly half-breeds. I glanced from face to face inquiringly.

"How about it, you?" I asked. "Are there any more of you fellows who take a chance with us? This is my last offer?"

"What's the game?" asked a sullen voice in English, and a bearded fellow burned black, pushed his way to the front. I had not noted his presence before, but instantly recognized his character.

"Are you English?"

"No; I used ter be Scotch; now I'm damned if I know what I am. One flag is as good as another ter me--only I want to know what sorter game I'm playin' in. Who the hell are yer? An' whar'd yer cum frum?"

"I am an English seaman," I answered shortly, "and how I came aboard makes no difference. Right now I am the only navigator on the *Namur*."

"What's happened ter Estada?"

"He's dead--knifed last night by one of the buccaneers. Manuel Estevan had a hand in the business, and he's safely locked in a stateroom aft. Captain Sanchez is wounded and helpless, and those cut-throats amidships are battened down below hatches. LeVere and I are the officers left, and we control the deck. We had to fight it out, or likely it would be our turn next."

"Yer mean those fellers were aimin' ter take the ship?"

"Exactly that; now where are you lads? With Manuel and his bunch of pirates? Or with us?"

"What er yer going ter do with us, an' this ship? That's the fu'st question."

I had not decided that even in my own mind, but the answer came promptly enough, as my eyes swept the faces fronting me.

"What's your name?"

"Ben MacClintock."

"Well, MacClintock. I am going to leave that to the crew. As soon as we have all secure, I'll have every man on deck, and then we'll talk it over. That's fair enough isn't it?"

"It looks fair. Come on, mates; I'm fer the Englishman."

Only one followed him, however, a sheep-faced boy; the others remained sullen, and defiant. Likely enough they failed to understand what had been said, but I had no further time to waste in explanations. I glanced up at Carter's face framed in the scuttle hole.

"Your guard there?"

"Ay, ay, sir."

"Pass these men up and take them forward with the others. Turn them over to Watkins. Then come back here, and report to me."

"Ay, ay, sir."

They went up the ladder one by one, and disappeared onto the deck above, the majority cheerful enough, although a few of the faces were scowling darkly as they passed me. Carlson and I watched the others, the Swede still retaining his pistol in hand, until Carter stuck his head once again through the opening.

"All safe, sir--they was like lambs."

"Very well; stand by to help. Now you lads, lift this black brute and shove him up to where they can get hold above. Step lively unless you want trouble. Show them the way Carlson."

It was some heavy job, but they finally hoisted the unconscious form up the ladder and forced it through the hole onto the deck. At my stern command the others also crawled forth into the sunlight, where Carlson and I followed them, leaving the forecastle deserted. I felt that I must dispose of these fellows before attempting anything else, and scarcely took time to glance about. They were huddled in a little bunch around the outstretched body of Cochose, helpless from lack of leadership.

"Pick up the negro; yes, you fellows. Now aft with him--all of you." We halted at the main hatch, and I had the cover slipped to one side, the armed sailors gathering close about the edge, as I peered down. It was a scene of pandemonium, revealed in the yellow flame of slush lanterns, a group of white faces showing clearly, as the prisoners below struggled forward, gesticulating and shouting. The glow of light glistened on a variety of weapons, but I dare not send men below, into the midst of those shrieking devils to disarm them. Nor was I greatly afraid of the result at present. They must still be in total ignorance of what had occurred on board, and why the hatch had been fastened down. Indeed this was plainly evidenced by their cries and threats. They were leaderless, confused, unable to determine what to attempt. While they remained in that condition they could not greatly endanger my plan. Later, with a body of armed seamen behind me, I would compel the surrender of weapons, but now I must hold them as they were, quarreling among themselves, and take time to strengthen my authority on deck. With this in mind, ignoring their mad roaring, and the threat of leveled guns, I stared down at the infuriated faces, until the clamor ceased sufficiently to let my voice be heard. I used Spanish, my lack of facility in that tongue rendering my speech slow. The instant silence proved my words understood.

"What are you men trying to do, frighten me? You might as well stop that. This opening is lined with guns, and if one of you fire a shot we'll pour lead into you.

More than that; if you attempt to climb out, you'll meet a hot reception. There is a brass carronade trained on the hatch to sweep you to kingdom come. So listen!"

Several voices shouted up inquiries, but one, shrill and insistent, rose clearly above the others.

"What's happening? What yer going to do with us?"

I thought I located the questioner among the jumbled mass below, and with my eyes on him, answered for all his mates.

"We are in control of the ship," I called back, "and mean to keep it. The old officers are either dead or prisoners. What we do with you will depend on your actions, but we're ready to kill if necessary. If you keep quiet down there, and obey orders, you'll be fed, and treated decently enough. Pass up your arms."

There was no movement, only a glare of hostile eyes, an indistinguishable growl of voices.

"Kneel down, lads and cover those fellows," I ordered sternly drawing my own pistol. "Now you below there, this is my last word. I'll count ten, and you'll either pass up those weapons or we'll pour our fire into you. If your miserable lives are worth anything to you, the quicker you move the better. Take aim, boys."

There was a moment of deathly silence, except for my counting and the heavy breathing of the trapped prisoners. One man uttered a curse, and the jam of figures at the foot of the ladder endeavored to work back out of range, yet, before I had spoken the word eight, guns were held aloft, and poked up within reach, and at this sign of surrender even the most desperate lost heart and joined the more cowardly. It was a strange collection of weapons stacked on the deck--guns, cutlasses, knives and pistols of every description, relics of many a foray, some apparently very old. Probably all had not been delivered, yet there was such a pile, I felt no further fear of the few pieces remaining hidden. It was not my intention that the villains should have the slightest chance to use the weapons, so when the stream finally ceased, I asked no questions, although I gave no orders to the guard to withdraw. I had the fellows cowed, and meant to keep them so.

"That's all, is it? Very well--now you men at the foot of the ladder take care of this big nigger we're sending down; no, he is not dead, only stunned. Let him have a bucket of water, and he'll be all right. Now stand aside while a few of your friends join you; they'll tell you what's up. Make room there?"

We passed the forecastle scum down one after the other, and as the last of these merged into the scarcely distinguishable mass below, I gave vent to a sigh of relief, and straightened up, with pistol still grasped in my hand. They were now bunched together, all of them, and confined where they would prove the least possible danger. Desperate and reckless as many of them were, we had them now safely in our own hands--disarmed and imprisoned within narrow limits. To be sure they might wreck the bark by fire, or otherwise, but that would only peril their own lives, and, no matter how willing some might be to accept this hazard of fortune, there would be more to oppose the proposition--forcibly, if necessary. For them to escape the only means was through treachery, and against that possibility I must guard. I knew little of the men who had responded to my call, and chosen me as leader. Some among them I could trust, but others were merely with me while I retained power--would desert at the first doubt. I must rely on the judgment of Watkins as to whom among them I could safely depend upon, and suspicion and watch the rest. It was no pleasant position, yet success thus far had come so easily the knowledge was no discouragement.

"When we goin' ter be fed?" yelled a voice from below.

"Presently," I answered. "As soon as the cook has it ready. Shove the hatch cover back into place, lads--yes it will be safer fastened down; they'll get air enough through treachery, and against that possibility I must caged."

Satisfied that every precaution had been taken, and ignoring the indignant roar of voices which greeted this order, I watched the men shift the heavy hatch cover into place, and then permitted my eyes to survey the deck, as I hastily considered our next action.

CHAPTER XXII
THE CREW DECIDES

Except that many of the men remained armed there was no suggestion of violence visible, no reminder of the fact that we were mutineers. But for the gleaming carronade trained on the main hatch, and the small group of gunners clustered about it, the scene was peaceable enough, resembling the deck of some merchant ship. The bark held steadily to her course, with practically every inch of canvas set, the wind steady, and only a single hand at the wheel. LeVere stood motionless at the poop rail, staring down, as though scarcely realizing what had transpired on board, and some way his very attitude and expression of face aroused within me a doubt of the man, a determination to put him to the test. Evidently he had held aloof and cautiously refrained from taking even the slightest part in our activities. The men themselves were mostly forward, grouped together and still excitedly discussing the situation. That all among them were not satisfied was indicated by their gestures, and the fact that Watkins, and others of the more loyal, were passing from group to group combating their arguments. Plainly enough I must have a heart-to-heart talk with the fellows, outlining a plan of escape, and leaving them to imagine their choice in the matter would be followed. But, in the meanwhile action of some sort would be most apt to overcome their dissatisfaction and prevent discussion.

The sky overhead was a pale blue, the sun shining, but as through a slight haze, while a heavy cloud of vapor obscured the western horizon. Although this promised fog rather than storm, yet the sea had a heavy swell and I accepted this threat of a change in weather to employ the men in reducing sail. It pleased me to note how swiftly they responded to the sound of my voice.

"Stand by to reef topsails," I shouted. "We're all one watch now. Go at it lively, lads, and when the job is over we'll eat, and decide together what's our next move. Two of you will be enough to guard the hatch and you Carter, go into the cabin and relieve the girl there. Keep your eyes open. I'll be down presently. Aloft with you and see how quick a job you can make of it."

Watkins led the way up the main-mast ratlines, and Cole was first into the fore shrouds, the others following eagerly. I watched them lay out on the yards and was heartened to hear the fellows sing as they worked, the canvas melting away as if by magic. Only three men remained in sight on the main deck, the two guarding the closed hatch, and one watching the open scuttle leading into the deserted forecastle. Back and forth in the galley the cook and his assistant passed the open door and Carter had disappeared through the companion. I climbed the ladder to where LeVere stood on the poop, but carefully ignored his presence, my gaze on the scene aloft. Twice I gave orders, changing the steering direction slightly, and commanding the lower sails reefed. The mulatto scowling, joined me at the rail.

"Main-top there!" I called sharply. "Anything to report?"

"No, sir; all haze off the port quarter, and nothing showing to starboard."

"Keep a lookout; let the others lay down."

LeVere fronted me.

"What's all this about?" he asked. "That's no storm cloud yonder."

"There is always danger in fog," I answered coldly, "and besides there is no use carrying on until we know where we are bound. My purpose is to keep the men busy, and then talk the situation over with them. Have you any criticism of this plan, Senor LeVere?"

He hesitated, but his eyes were narrowed, and ugly.

"You'll do as you please, but you told me we sailed for Porto Grande. Was that a lie?"

"Not necessarily," and I smiled grimly. "Although I should not have hesitated to tell one under the circumstances. I mean to leave that decision to the men themselves. It is their lives that are in danger."

"That damn scum! half of them are English and French. All they want is to get away; they will never go back to Porto Grande without you make them."

"How make them?"

"By false observations; there is no navigator forward. It is a trick easy enough to play with a little nerve. I would never have taken part in this mutiny if I had supposed you meant to play into the hands of the men."

"It is very little part you took Senor LeVere, judging from what I saw. You seemed quite content to stand aft here and look on. However you are in it just as deeply as I am, and are going to play the game out with me to the end. Do you understand that?"

"What you mean, Senor--play it out?"

"Go on with the rest of us; take your chance with the men and do your duty. I am captain here, and I know how to handle insubordination. The first sign of treachery on your part, will send you below with those others. I don't trust you, and all I want is an excuse to put you out of the way--so be careful what you do."

I turned and walked away from him toward the forward rail. The men were still aloft but coming in from off the yards. Below me in the door of the companion, stood Dorothy, her eyes peering curiously about the deserted deck. She glanced up, and saw me, the whole expression of her face changing.

"May I come up there?" she asked.

"Certainly; let me help you. Stand here beside me, and you can see all that is being done. That's all, lads; breakfast is ready; lay down all except the lookout."

We watched while they streamed down the ratlines and gathered forward of the galley, squatting in groups on the deck. To all appearances the fellows had not a care in the world, or any thought of the stirring scenes just passed through. The girl's hand touched my sleeve, and I turned and looked into her face.

"A happy-go-lucky lot," I said pleasantly. "Real sailormen. As long as they are fed and housed why worry about tomorrow. I'll put this job up to them presently."

"The sailor who came into the cabin told me about your fight with the negro; you were not hurt?"

"Oh, I did not escape entirely free, but received no serious injury. It is not to be thought about now, with all the work ahead."

"The ship is safely in your hands?"

"I can hardly affirm that, Miss Dorothy. The vessel is in our control, and the worst of the gang secured below. I have confidence in the loyalty of only a very few of these fellows, and the others will have to be watched day and night as long as we remain afloat. Those are desperate men locked below, and are bound to make some effort to free themselves. If there is any treachery on deck it may lead to their release."

"You were talking with Senor LeVere; I overheard a word or two. He is not with you willingly?"

"No," and I swept the deck seeking him, fearful what I said might be overheard. "I distrust him more than any of the others. Those men forward are seamen, and will abide by their mates. Moreover they are accustomed to taking orders, and doing what they are told. I believe I can handle them, with what help I have. But the mulatto is different. He belongs with the worst element on board, and only joined us from fear of being killed just as Estada was. He has no heart in this job, and would accept any chance to square himself with those cut-throats below. I'll have trouble with him before we are done, but prefer to catch the man red-handed."

"But what do you mean to do next?" she asked anxiously. "There cannot be a moment of safety with those horrible creatures aboard."

"True; yet with the material I am dealing with, I dare not venture too far. Probably in that bunch forward there are men guilty of every crime in the calendar; as depraved as any we have below. They have joined us for various reasons, but would desert and become ugly in an instant, if they suspected we might turn them over to the authorities. There is only one safe course for me to pursue under these conditions; let them decide by vote what should be done."

"What do you imagine such a vote will show?"

"That the vessel be beached on some remote coast, all the spoils aboard divided, and then the crew permitted to go where they please. There will be some who may prefer continuing the cruise before destroying the bark, but I believe there are enough fairly honest fellows among them eager to escape this sort of life, to control."

"But the wretches below? Surely you would not leave them to drown?"

"No; they would have to be released with the others, after the division had been made."

"That would leave us at their mercy?"

"Yes," I whispered, "if we waited until that time. I do not propose taking any such chance. Here is my plan, and it seems the only feasible one left us. We are helpless if these men revolt, and they certainly will unless given their own way. I have no doubt but what their decision will be practically as I have outlined. Very well, I will acquiesce in it cheerfully enough to arouse no suspicion. I am the only navigator on board; the only one with any knowledge even of where we are. Not even LeVere could check up on me. The night the vessel is to be beached Watkins and Carter, with one or two they select, will get off in a small boat, carefully provisioned, and thus make our own landing. We'll not worry about what fate awaits the others."

Her eyes sought mine anxiously, full of questioning.

"You are confident of being able to accomplish this without detection?"

"Yes; we can choose the right moment. With not men enough on deck to prevent our lowering a boat, and a dark night, the escape will not prove difficult. No one aboard except myself will know where we are."

"Have you considered Captain Sanchez?"

"Why no," in surprise, "he is helpless below, badly wounded."

"Not so badly as you suppose," she said swiftly. "He is able to be up and about his stateroom. I heard him moving, and I believe the steward has told him what has occurred on board, and endeavored to bear a message from him to those men amidships."

"You believe this? What did you do?"

"I held my pistol to his head and locked him in the pantry. He is there now, with the sailor you sent on guard. That is what I came on deck to tell you."

"But Sanchez! You saw nothing of him?"

"No; but there was certainly movement in his room after the man Gunsaules came out. I went over to the door and listened, but there was no way for me to lock him in. Surely it must have been him moving, as he was alone there."

I stood silent, my eyes first on the forward deck, and then sweeping about the horizon. The view by then was very narrow, the gathering clouds of mist so dense as to obscure everything, leaving a mere gray trail of sea revealed, scarcely a hundred yards in extent in any direction. I hardly perceived even this as my thought centered on this new peril. Yet why should I hold it a peril? The ending of it was in my hands, I need not await action, or permit him opportunity. The warning had come in ample time. Sanchez was still in my power, separated from his followers, incapable of doing us any serious harm. All that was needed for me to do was to keep him in close confinement. We were surely not far from the coast; twenty-four hours, perhaps twelve, would suffice, to make our escape from this cursed ship possible. I must get an observation so as to know our exact position; after that the course would be figured definitely, and I would then know the time required. My eyes again sought her face.

"He is a danger, of course, but not a serious one," I said confidently. "It is safe enough to leave him undisturbed at present with Cole on guard. The first thing I need do is to satisfy those men. I'll attend to that now, and then see to the proper securing of Sanchez."

"Shall I remain here?"

"You told the man Cole what you heard?"

"Yes, I explained everything to him before I came on deck."

"Then you are not needed in the cabin. He is a reliable man. Remain here with LeVere while I go forward, and watch that he does not attempt to go below."

The fellows had not finished mess, but I felt the danger of further delay, and talked to them as they sat on deck, explaining briefly the entire situation, and the causes leading up to the mutiny. I dealt with the matter in plain terms, making no apparent effort to influence them, yet forcibly compelling each individual to realize what would be the result of our recapture. They listened earnestly, asking an occasional question, and passing comments back and forth freely among themselves.

I shall never forget that scene, the decks already wet with fog, which swirled about us in an impenetrable cloud of vapor, utterly blotting out the sea, and even rendering our faces strange and indistinct. The foremast disappeared at the lower fore-yard, while aft of the cook's galley the bark was entirely invisible. We rolled heavily in the swell of the heaving water, barely retaining steerage-way, the closely reefed sails aloft flapping against the masts, the straining deck beams creaking noisily to every roll of the vessel. The sailors stared up at me, rough dressed and hairy, yet not a bad-looking lot as sailors go, but with here and there a face to be distrusted. I sent Watkins to the cabin for a roll of charts, and spreading these out, endeavored as well as I could, to make clear our probable position and the nearest point of land. This was largely guesswork, but I approximated distances and made the situation fairly clear. When I had completed the explanation, and stood before them awaiting decision, it was Haines who acted as their spokesman.

"This yere is Cape Howarth?" he asked, a grimy thumb on the point indicated. "An' yer say it's 'bout a hundred and fifty miles west?"

"Yes, about that."

"An' thar's no settlement?"

"Some colonists fifty miles north is all." "That's 'bout right." He turned to the others. "Say mates, this is how I figure. We can't go on no long cruise with all those bloody rats in the hold. They're bound ter find some way out if we give 'em time 'nough. Fer as I'm concerned, I'm fer dividin' up whut we've got, and ter hell with piratin'. What 'er yer say, mates? Shall we run the ol' hooker ashore, an' leave her thar, while we tramp the coast? We're just a ship-wrecked crew."

"What 'bout them fellers down below?"

"Ter hell with 'em! Let 'em take keer o' 'emselves. Thet's the way they'd treat us."

"He's bloody well right, mates," said a loud voice heartily. "There's plenty o' swag aboard ter give us all a fist full. I'm fer a division, an gettin' out with our lives--what say yer?"

There was a chorus of approval sufficient in volume to satisfy me, and I accepted this as a decision.

"All right, lads," I said briefly. "In my judgment your choice is a wise one. I'll have an observation as soon as the fog clears and we'll head in for the Cape."

"When do we divide the swag?"

"Fifty miles off the coast. That's fair enough, isn't it? And my share goes to you."

There was a straggling cheer, but I broke it up with a sharp order.

"Now stand by for work, all of you. Watkins and Carter I want you aft."

CHAPTER XXIII
THE PRISONERS ESCAPE

The two men followed me silently as far as the companion, where we paused a moment staring blindly about us into the fog. Even the guard at the main hatch was invisible.

"This can scarcely last long," I remarked, "but there may be a storm brewing."

"I don't think so, sir," one of the men answered civilly. "I've run in to these yere mists afore 'long this coast; it's liable ter be all clear 'fore the sun goes down."

"Well we'll make the ship safe first Carter, you are an able seaman?"

"Yes, sir."

"Guard this after deck until Watkins and I come back. Under no circumstances permit LeVere to enter the cabin. You understand?"

He grinned appreciatively.

"That nigger ain't likely ter get by me, sir; I'd just like for ter take one whack at him."

"Don't be rough, if you can help it. As far as I know now he is with us, and ranks second officer. My only orders are--see that he remains on deck while we are below."

"Ay, ay, sir; he'll stay thar." With the door closed, we were plunged into a darkness which rendered the interior invisible. I wondered dimly why the man on guard had not lighted the swinging lantern but before I could call out to the fellow, Watkins whispered.

"What's up? Anything wrong in here?"

"Not that I know of, but the young lady reported Sanchez moving about in his stateroom and I think it safer to see to him at once."

"It's blacker than hell down thar."

"Yes; I don't understand it--wait here a minute until I strike a light."

I stumbled over something on the deck, as I groped forward, but with mind centered on the one object, did not pause until I had located the lantern. It blazed up brightly enough, its yellow flame illuminating the cabin, and the first thing I saw was the outstretched figure of the sailor almost between my feet. I sprang back, giving utterance to a cry, which brought Watkins to me, and the two of us stared at the grewsome object and then about into the wavering shadows. There was nothing to see but the dead man, lying on his face motionless, blood still oozing from an ugly knife wound in his back. We needed to ask no questions, imagine nothing--the overturned chair, the stricken sailor told the whole story. He had been treacherously stuck from behind, the blade driven home by a strong hand, and was dead before he fell to the deck. It had been silent, vengeful murder, and the assassin had left no trace. Who could it have been? Not Gunsaules surely--the steward lacked both nerve and strength for such a deed. Then there was but one to suspect--Silva Sanchez! I stood there dumb, gazing at the dead man, realizing all this dimly, yet conscious only of thankfulness that the victim had not been Dorothy Fairfax.

"He's dead, sir," growled Watkins, turning the fellow over with his foot, until the ghastly face stared up at the deck beams overhead. "Stabbed to the heart frum behind. Look a yere--that wus sum slash. Who, the hell do yer suppose did it?"

"That is ours to find out. The deed has just been done, for blood is still flowing. Let him alone Watkins and come with me--the murderer can't be far off."

I flung open the pantry door, but one glance inside told me that Gunsaules had vanished. On the deck lay the strands of rope with which he had been secured--- they had been severed by a sharp knife, the ends discolored with blood stains. I held these out to Watkins.

"Cut since the murder," I said harshly, "and by the same knife."

"Who was in here, sir."

"The steward, Gunsaules. He didn't do the job, but I believe I know who did. We'll try the port stateroom aft. Stand by; there's likely to be two of them."

The door was unlocked and opened noiselessly, but I took no chances, thinking this possibly a ruse. Gloomy as the interior appeared in the weird light with banks of fog driving against the ports, a single swift glance convinced me it was deserted. There was no place for a man to hide, yet I could not convince myself of its emptiness until I peered into the disarranged bunk, and surveyed every shadowed corner. Watkins watched me curiously, turning his head occasionally to stare out into the lighted cabin behind. The situation baffled me completely--that Sanchez had done the deed, informed by the steward of what was occurring on board and rendered desperate by that report, was clear enough in my mind; but what had become of the man? He could not have escaped overboard, as the ports were screwed down, and his appearance on the open deck above would have surely been observed. His place of concealment must remain aft in the cabin, and if so, he must be discovered by immediate search. I ordered Watkins to take the lantern from the rack and follow me from stateroom to stateroom. We began with Dorothy's, finding none of them locked until we came to where Manuel was held prisoner. All were empty and in disorder, while bending my ear to the locked door, I could distinguish the heavy breathing of its inmate, the fellow was evidently sound asleep.

"What do you make of it, Tom?" I asked, facing him in the dim halo of light.

"Well, sir," scratching his head with his disengaged hand, "Thar ain't but two more places ter look--the cuss is either in the lazaret, er' else hidin' in the passage forward; more likely the last."

"Why not the lazaret?"

"Cause thar wouldn't be no object fer him to go thar. He dudn't get out agin with the kiver shut down. The thing he'd most likely try fer wud be ter release them lads amidships--that'd give him a gang o' bullies ter fight with. My idea is, sir, he thought he'd have time ter git the bulkhead door open, before anybody cum below--he an' the steward, who'd know what the tools wus. That wus the scheme, only we busted in too quick. That whar they both are--skulkin' back in them shadows."

He fitted the smoking lantern back onto the shelf to have his hands free for action, and drew a cutlass out of the arm rack, running one leatherly thumb along the blade to test its sharpness. His eyes sought mine questioningly.

"Probably your guess is the right one," I said soberly. "We'll give it a trial, and should need no help to handle the two of them."

The deck under our feet was fairly steady, the vessel having barely steerageway, rolling slightly to the heave of the sea. No sound readied us from above, and the silence of the cabin was profound. Indeed the stillness irritated me with its mystery, rendered me reckless to penetrate its meaning. Murder had been committed for a purpose--it was the first step in an effort to retake the ship. If we were to retain our advantage there was no time to be lost; we were pitted now against Silva Sanchez, and he was a leader not to be despised or temporized with; no cowardly, brainless fool.

The passage leading forward was wide enough to permit of our advancing together and for a few steps the light dribbled in past us, quite sufficient for guidance, although our shadows were somewhat confusing. There were closed doors on either side, evidently locked, as they refused to yield to the hand. I took these to be storerooms, possibly containing spoils of the voyage, but gave them little other thought, my whole interest centered on the intense blackness ahead. I had been down this tunnel once before, and knew the bulkhead was not far away, but the few steps necessary plunged us into profound blackness, through which we advanced cautiously with outstretched hands. No slightest sound warned of danger and I was already convinced in my own mind that the refugees were not hiding there, when it happened. Within an instant we were fighting for our lives, fronted not by two men, but by a score, who flung themselves cursing upon us. Their very numbers and the narrowness of the passage was our only salvation. At first our resistance was blind enough, guided only by the senses of touch and sound. We could see nothing of our antagonists, although their fierce rush hurled us backward. I fired into the mass, as Watkins slashed madly with his cutlass, both managing in some way to keep our feet. Hands gripped for us, a bedlam of oaths splitting the air; yet, even in that moment of pandemonium, I was quick to realize the fellows were weaponless, seeking only to reach and crush us with bare hands. The same discovery must have come to the mind of the sailor, for he yelled it out defiantly, every stroke of his blade drawing blood. I joined him, striking with the butt of the pistol, feeling within me the strength of ten men, yet the very weight of them thrust us remorselessly back. We killed and wounded, the curses of hate changed into sharp cries of agony, but those behind pressed the advance forward, and we were inevitably swept back into the light of the cabin lamp.

Then I saw faces, hideous in the glare, demonical in their expression of hatred--a mass of them, unrecognizable, largely of a wild, half-Indian type, with here and there a bearded white. Nor were they all bare-handed; in many a grip flashed a knife, and directly fronting me, with a meat cleaver uplifted to strike, Sanchez yelled his orders. Ignoring all others I leaped straight at him, crying to Watkins as I sprang.

"Back lad; dash out that light; I'll hold these devils here a minute!"

I did---God knows how! It was like no fighting ever I had done before, a mad, furious melee, amid which I lost all consciousness of action, all guidance of thought, struggling as a wild brute, with all the reckless strength of insanity. It is a dim, vague recollection; I am sure I felled Sanchez with one blow of my pistol-butt, stretching him apparently lifeless at my feet; in some way that deadly cleaver came into my hands and I trod on his body, swinging the sharp blade with all my might into those scowling faces. They gave sullenly backward; they had to, yelping and snarling like a pack of wolves, hacking at me with their short knives. I was cut again and again, but scarcely knew it. I stood on quivering flesh, driving my weapon from right to left, crazed with blood, and seeking only to kill. I saw faces crushed in, arms severed, men reeling before me in terror, the sudden spurting of blood from ghastly wounds. Oaths mingled with cries of agony and shouts of hate. Then in an instant the light was dashed out and all was darkness.

It was as though my brain snapped back into ascendency. I was no longer a raging fury, mad with the desire to kill, but cool-headed, planning escape. Before a hand could reach me in restraint, I sprang backward and ran. In the darkness of the cabin I collided with the table, and fell sprawling over a stool. The noise guided pursuit, yet, wedged together as those fellows still were in the narrow passage, fighting each other in the black gloom, gave me every advantage and so unhalted, I stumbled up the stairs leading to the companion. The vague glimmer of daylight showing through the glass, revealed the presence of Watkins. I heard him dash the door wide open, call to those on deck, and then saw him wheel about to again confront the devils plunging blindly forward toward us through the dark cabin. We could hold them here for a time at least, yet I had the sense to know that this check would prove only temporary. They outnumbered us ten to one, and would arm themselves from the rack. Yet the greater danger lay in the loyalty of my own men. A dozen of us might hold these stairs against assault, but treachery would leave us helpless. And the very thickness of the fog without invited to treachery. If one among them, and there were many capable of such an act, should steal below forward, and force open the door from the forecastle, we would be crushed between two waves of men, and left utterly helpless. I saw the whole situation vividly, and as quickly chose the only course to pursue, the one hope remaining.

"Here lads," I called sharply back over my shoulder, "five or six of you are enough to hold back this scum. Watkins!"

"Ay, sir."

"Bend down here--now listen. Get the boats ready--two will be enough--and be lively about it. We'll hold these fellows until you report. You know the lads to be trusted. Put two of them at the forecastle scuttle, and then rout everybody out from below. Who is here now?"

"Name yerselves, bunkies--I can't see yer."

"Simmes."

"Schmitt."

"Ravel DeLasser."

"Carter."

"Jacob Johansen."

"Sam."

"That's enough; you lads remain here with me. Have Harwood watch LeVere, while the rest of you get out the boats."

"How many, sir?"

"The two quarter-boats will hold us all. Knock out the plugs in the others--and Watkins!"

"Ay, ay, sir."

"See that Miss Fairfax is placed safely in the after-boat, and then stand by. Send me word the moment all is ready. That's all--we're going to be busy here presently."

I had glimpse of the thick fog without as he pushed through the door, and of a scarcely distinguishable group of men on the deck. Those about me could only be located by their restless movements. I stepped down one stair conscious of increasing movement below, the meat cleaver still gripped in my hands.

"Any of you armed with cutlasses?"

"Oui, M'Sieur, Ravel DeLasser."

"Stand here, to right of me, now another at my left. Who are you?" "Jim Carter, sir."

"Good; now strike hard, lads, and you others be ready."

"What's up, sir?" asked a gruff voice. "Has they busted out from between decks?"

"That's what's happened. The cabin is full of 'em, and it is your life and mine in the balance. If we can get away in this fog they'll never find us, but we've got to hold them here until the boats are ready."

"Is it Sanchez?"

"It was Sanchez, but I killed him. That is where we've still got them huskies, without a leader."

"But they've got arms."

"Only hand weapons," broke in Carter contemptuously. "We're as good as they are--thar ain't no powder."

"Sure of that?"

"Course I am. I cleaned up that rack two days ago. There's ball in the bandoliers, but no powder. I wus goin' ter break open a cask, but Estada put me at another job."

"Then that leaves us on even footing, lads, we ought to be equal to them with the cold steel--can any of you see below?"

CHAPTER XXIV
IN CLASP OF THE SEA

The sound of voices, of moving bodies and bits of furniture overturned were plainly discernible, but the darkness was far too dense below to permit the eye perceiving what was taking place. Yet I could picture the scene, the leaderless mob surging blindly forward, each man vocal in his own tongue, swaying with rage, many smarting with wounds, uncertain where we had disappeared, yet all alike crazed with a desire to attain the open deck. The rattle of steel, the curses, told me some among them had reached the arm rack, and seized whatever weapons they found there. In their struggle the rack was overturned, and suddenly, amid the din, a shrill, penetrating voice yelled something in Spanish, which seemed to hush the clamor. There followed a shuffling of feet, and the crash of wood as though the butt of a gun had splintered a door panel. Then the same voice again pierced the babel. My mind gripped the meaning of it all; they had found a leader; they had released Manuel Estevan. Now the real fight was on!

We stooped low, to escape as much as possible from the dim revealing light streaming through the glass at our backs, and waited, staring into the black depths of the cabin, and listening for every sound. The release of Manuel, the very knowledge of his presence had changed the mob into dangerous fighters. The roar of voices died away with the noise of confusion. I could hear the fellow question those about him, seeking to learn the situation, but the delay was short, and no inkling of his quickly conceived plan of attack was revealed. Yet he saw us and understood; his eyes, long trained to darkness, must have already marked our dim outlines, for his first order evidenced his purpose.

"Who have cutlasses? So many! a dozen form with me. Now bullies, they are on the stairs there, and that is the only way to the deck. We'll show those damned traitors what fighting means. Now then---to hell with 'em!"

We met them, point to point, our advantage the narrow staircase and the higher position; theirs the faint glimmer of light at our backs. The first rush was reckless and deadly, the infuriated devils not yet realizing what they faced, but counting on force of numbers to crush our defense. Manuel led them yelling encouragement, and sweeping his cutlass, gripped with both hands, in desperate effort to break through. DeLasser caught its point with his blade while my cleaver missing him with its sharp edge, nevertheless dealt the fellow a blow which hurled him back into the arms of the man behind. I saw nothing else in detail, the faint light barely revealing indistinct figures and gleam of steel. It was a pandemonium of blows and yells, strange faces appearing and disappearing, as men leaped desperately at us up the steps, and we beat them remorselessly back. I saw nothing more of Manuel in the fray, but his shrill voice urged on his followers. It was strike and parry, cut and thrust. Twice I kicked my legs free from hands that gripped me, and DeLasser fell, a pike thrust through him. Who took his place I never knew, but a stout fighter the lad was, wielding his cutlass viciously, so that we held them, with dead men littering every step to the cabin deck.

But they were of a breed trained to such fighting, and the lash of Manuel's tongue drove them into mad recklessness. And there seemed no end of them, sweeping up out of those black shadows, with bearded or lean brown savage faces, charging over the dead bodies, hacking and gouging in vain effort to break through. I struck until my arms ached, until my head reeled, scarcely conscious of physical action, yet aware of Manners shouts.

"Now you hell-hounds--now! once more, and you have them. Santa Maria! you've got to go through, bullies---there is no other way to the deck. Think of the yellow boys below; they are all yours if you strike hard enough. Rush 'em! That's the way! Here you--go in outside the rail! Broth of hell! Now you have him, Pedro!"

For an instant I believed it true; I saw Jim Carter seized and hurled sideways, his cutlass clashing as it fell, while a dozen hands dragged him headlong into the ruck beneath. But it was only an instant. Before the charging devils could pass me, a huge figure filled the vacant space, and the butt of a gun crashed into the mass. It was the Dutchman, Schmitt, fighting like a demon, his strength that of an ox. They gave way in terror before him, and we went down battering our way, until the stairs were clear to the deck, except for the dead under foot. When we stopped, not a fighting man was left within the sweep of our arms. They had scurried back into the darkness like so many rats, and we could only stare about blindly, cursing them, as we endeavored to recover breath. Schmitt roared like a wild bull, and would have rushed on, but for my grip on his shirt.

"Get back, men!" I ordered sharply. "There may be fifty of them yonder. Our only chance is the stairs. Do as I say, Schmitt, or fight me. Back now!"

We flung the bodies on one side, and formed again from rail to rail. Below us there was noise enough, a babel of angry voices, but no movement of assault. I could see nothing, although the uproar evidenced a large number of men jammed together in that blackness beneath. What they would do next was answered by a blaze of light, revealing the silhouette of a man, engaged in touching flame to a torch of hemp. It flung forth a dull yellow glare, and revealed a scene of unimaginable horror. Our assailants were massed half way back, so blended together I could not judge their number, many between us and the light with faces darkened by shadow. Between us, even ten feet from the stairs, the deck was littered with bodies, ghastly faces staring up, with black stains of blood everywhere. It was Manuel's hand which had kindled the light, and the first croak of his voice told his purpose.

"Now you sculking cowards," he yelled pointing forward, "do you see what you are fighting? There are only five men between you and the deck. To hell with 'em! Come on! I'll show you the way!"

He leaped forward; but it was his last step. With one swing of my arm I sent the cleaver hurtling through the air. I know not how it struck him, but he went down, his last word a shriek, his arms flung out in vain effort to ward off the blow. Schmitt roared out a Dutch oath, and before I knew fully what had happened, his gun, sent whirling above me, had crashed into the uplifted torch. Again it was black, hideous night, through which the eye could perceive nothing. Even the noise ceased, but a hand gripped my shoulder.

"Who are you?"

"Nigger Sam, sah. Mistah Watkins sez it's all done fixed."

"Where is he?"

"Here," answered Watkins himself in a hoarse whisper. "The boats are ready."

"Afloat?"

"Yes, sir. The one forward has pushed off loaded. The after-boat is alongside. There is such a hell of a fog, sir, yer can't see two fathoms from the ship."

"All the better for us; is the girl in the boat?"

"Safe, sir; but LeVere ain't."

"What do you mean? That he has got away? I ordered you to have Harwood watch him."

"Yes, sir; but the mate slipped out o' sight in the fog. He's somewhar aboard, but we ain't been able ter put hands on him nowhar yet."

"Never mind him; the fellow can do no harm now. Move back slowly lads. Schmitt and I will be the last ones out. Pick up that cutlass, Schmitt. We must act before those devils down there wake up again."

We closed the companion door as silently as possible and for the moment there was no sound from within to show that our cautious withdrawal had been observed. I stared about, but was able to perceive little beyond the small group awaiting my orders. The fog clung thick and heavy on all sides, the lungs breathed it in, and the deck underfoot was as wet as though from heavy rain. Moisture dripped from yards and canvas, and it was impossible for the eye to penetrate to either rail. Fortunately there was no weight of sea running, and the bark swung gently, still retaining steerage-way, but with not wind enough aloft to flap the sails. The silence and gloom was most depressing.

"Is there a hand at the wheel, Watkins?"

"No sir; it's lashed."

"And the quarter-boat?"

"There, sir, below the mizzen-chains."

"Then there is nothing more to keep us aboard lads. Stow yourselves away and hang on; I'll wait here until you are all over."

They faded away into the mist, dim spectral figures, and I remained alone, listening anxiously for some hostile sound from below. Had I chosen the right course? I was not altogether sure, yet we had gone too far now to decide on any other. Perhaps if I had called on those men up on deck, who had loaded guns, we might have forced the escaped prisoners back into their place of confinement, and thus kept control of the vessel. Yet at that it would only mean a few hours more on board amid constant danger of revolt. It might have enabled us to salvage the gold hidden below, but I was not greatly concerned for this, as my one and only purpose was the preservation of Dorothy. The men might prove ugly when they awoke to the loss, but I had little fear of them, once we were at sea in the small boats, and their lives depended on my seamanship. Unless a storm arose our lives were in no great peril, although I would have preferred being closer to the coast before casting adrift. I wondered what could be the meaning of that silence below. True the fellows were leaderless and defeated, yet they were desperate spirits, and fully aware that they must attain the open deck in order to recapture the vessel. They would not remain quiet long, and once discovering our retirement, would swarm up the stairs animated with fresh courage. Satisfied that the lads were safely over the rail and the decks clear, I turned toward the ship's side. As I did so a yell reached my ears from the blackness below--the hounds had found voice.

I ran through the fog in the direction the others had disappeared, and had taken scarcely three steps when I collided against the form of a man, whose presence was not even noticed until we came together. Yet he must have been there expectant and ready, for a quick knife thrust slashed the front of my jacket, bringing a spurt of blood as the blade was jerked back. It was a well-aimed blow at the heart, missing its mark only because of my outstretched arms, and the rapidity of my advance. Even as my fingers gripped the uplifted wrist, 'ere he could strike the second time, I knew my antagonist. I knew also this was a fight to the death, a sharp remorseless struggle to be terminated before that unguarded crew below could attain the deck. It was LeVere's life or mine, and in the balance the fate of those others in the waiting boat alongside. The knowledge gave me the strength and ferocity of a tiger; all the hate and distrust I felt for the man came uppermost. In that moment of rage I did not so much care what happened to me, if I was only privileged to kill him. I ripped the knife from his fingers, and we closed with bare hands; our muscles cracking to the strain, his voice uttering one croaking cry for help as I bore in on his windpipe. He was a snake, a cat, slipping out of my grip as by some magic, turning and twisting like an eel, yet unable to wholly escape, or overcome, my strength and skill. At last I had him prone against the rail, the weight of us both so hard upon it, the stout wood cracked, and we both went over, grappling together until we splashed into the water below. The shock, the frantic effort to save myself, must have loosened my hold, for, as I fought a way back to the surface, I was alone, lost in the veil of mist.

Blinded by fog, the water dripping from my hair, weakened by struggle and loss of blood, my mad rage against LeVere for the moment obscured all else in my mind. What had become of the fellow? Had he gone down like a stone? Or was he somewhere behind this curtain of fog? A splash to the right led me to take a dozen strokes hastily, but to no purpose. The sound was not repeated and I no longer retained any sense of direction to guide me. The sea was a steady swell, lifting my body on the crest of a wave, to submerge it an instant later in the deep hollow. I could feel the motion, but scarcely perceived it otherwise, as the thick gray mist obscured everything three feet away. It deadened and confused sound also. Again and again I felt I located the near presence of the *Namur*, the sound of feet on deck, the shout of a voice, the flapping of canvas against the yards; but as I desperately turned that way, the noise ceased, or else apparently changed into another point of compass. Once a cry reached me, thrilling with despair, although I could not catch the words, and again came to me plainly enough the clank of an oar in its rowlock. I struck out madly for the point from whence it came, only to find the same rolling water, and obscuring fog. My strength began to fail, hope left me as I sank deeper and deeper into the remorseless grip of the sea. There was nothing left to fight for, to struggle after; the fog about me became red and purple before my straining eyes, and then slowly grew black; my muscles refused to respond to my will; I no longer swam, but floated so low in water the crest of the waves swept over my face. I no longer cared, gripped by a strange, almost delicious languor. I was not afraid; my lips uttered no cry, no prayer--I drifted out into total unconsciousness and went down.

CHAPTER XXV
THE OPEN BOAT

I came back to a consciousness of pain and illness, unable at once to realize where I was, or feel any true sense of personality. I seemed to be floating through the air, aware dimly of suffering, but helplessly in the grasp of some power beyond all struggling against. Then slowly I comprehended that I rested in a boat, tossed about by a fairly heavy sea; that it was night and there were stars visible in the sky overhead. I stared at these, vacant of thought, wondering at their gleam, when a figure seemed to lean over me, and I caught the outline of a face, gazing eagerly down into my own. Instantly memory came back in a flash--this was not death, but life; I was in a boat with her, I could not move my hands, and my voice was but a hoarse whisper.

"Mistress Fairfax--Dorothy!"

"Yes--yes," swiftly. "It is all right, but you must lie still. Watkins, Captain Carlyle is conscious. What shall I do?"

He must have been behind us at the steering oar, for his gruff, kindly voice sounded very close.

"Yer might lift him up, miss," he said soberly. "He'll breathe better. How's that, Captain?"

"Much easier," I managed to breathe. "I guess I am all right now. You fished me out?"

"Sam did. He got a boat hook in your collar. We cast off when yer went overboard, and cruised about in the fog hunting fer yer. Who was it yer was fightin' with, sir?"

"LeVere."

"That's what I told the lads. He's a goner, I reckon?"

"I never saw him after we sank. Are all the men here?"

"All but those in the forward boat, sir. They got away furst, an' we ain't had no sight ov 'em since. Maybe we will when it gets daylight."

"Who had charge?"

"Harwood, sir; he's the best man o' ther lot, an' a good sailor, I give him a compass, an' told him ter steer west. Wus thet right?"

"All I could have told him," I admitted, lifting myself on one elbow to look about. "I haven't had an observation, and it is all guesswork. I know the American coast lies in that direction, but that is about all. I couldn't tell if it be a hundred, or a hundred and fifty miles away. So the fog has lifted without a storm?"

"Yes, sir, but left an ugly sea. There has been plenty o' wind somewhere, but we seem to be out of it. Must a bin midnight when the mist lifted."

"Is it as late as that? I must have been in bad shape when you pulled me in?"

"We thought you was gone, sir. You was bleedin' some too, but only from flesh wounds. The young lady she just wouldn't let yer die. She worked over yer for two or three hours, sir, afore I hed any hope."

Her eyes were downcast and her face turned away, but I reached out my hand and clasped her fingers. They remained quietly in my grasp, but neither of us spoke. The boat lay before me a black shadow under the stars, flung up on the crests of the waves and darting down into the hollows. It required all of Watkins' skill to keep it upright, the flying spray constantly dashing against our faces. The men were but dimly revealed, sitting with heads lowered beneath the slight protection afforded by the lug sail, although one was upon his knees, throwing out the water which dashed in over the front rail. He was succeeding so poorly I called to another to help him, and the two fell to the job with new vigor. I could not distinguish the faces of the fellows, but counted nine altogether in the boat, and felt assured the huge bulk at the foot of the mast was the Dutchman Schmitt. Beyond these dim outlines there was nothing for the eye to rest upon, only a few yards of black sea in every direction, rendered visible by the reflected star-shine and the dull glow of crested waves. It was dismal, awe inspiring, and I felt that I must speak to break the dreadful silence. My eyes sought the averted face beside me, and for a moment in peculiar hesitancy, observed the silhouette of cheek and form. She rested against the gunwale, her eyes on the dark vista of sea, her chin cupped in her hand. The mystery of the night and ocean was in her motionless posture. Only as her hand gently pressed mine did I gain courage, with a knowledge that she recognized and welcomed my presence.

"Watkins says I owe my life to you," I said, so low the words were scarcely audible above the dash of water alongside. "It will make that life more valuable than ever before."

She turned her head, and I felt her eyes searching the dim outline of my face questioningly.

"Of course I did everything I knew," she replied. "Why should I not? You are here, Captain Carlyle, for my sake; I owe you service."

"And must I be content merely with that thought?" I urged, far from pleased. "This would mean that your only interest in me arises from gratitude."

"And friendship," her voice as confidential as my own. "There is no reason why you should doubt that surely."

"It would be easier for me to understand, but for the memory of what I am--a bond slave."

"You mean the fact that you were sold to my uncle remains a barrier between us?"

"To my mind, yes. I hope you forget, but I cannot. If I return to Virginia, it is to servitude for a term of years. I am exiled from my own country by law, and thus prevented from following a career on the sea. I belong to Roger Fairfax, or, if he be dead, to his heirs, and even this privilege of being the property of a gentleman is mine through your intercession. I know your sympathy, your eagerness to help-- but that is not all of friendship."

"Your meaning is that true friendship has as a basis equality?"

"Does it not? Can real friendship exist otherwise?"

"No," she acknowledged gravely. "And the fact that such friendship does exist between us evidences my faith in you. I have never felt this social distinction, Captain Carlyle, have given it no thought. This may seem strange to you, yet is most natural. You bear an honorable name, and belong to a family of gentlemen. You held a position of command, won by your own efforts. You bore the part of a man in a revolution; if guilty of any crime, it was a political one, in no way sullying your honor. I have every reason to believe you were falsely accused and convicted. Consequently that conviction does not exist between us; you are not my uncle's servant, but my friend--you understand me now?"

"I have trained myself so long to another viewpoint, Mistress Dorothy," I admitted, still speaking doubtfully, although impressed by her earnestness, "I know not how to accept this statement. I have not once ventured to address you, except as a servant."

"I know that, and have regretted it," she interrupted. "But not until now have I been able to correct your impression."

"And you would actually have me speak with you as of your own class--a free man, worthy to claim your friendship in life?"

"Yes," frankly, her face uplifted. "Why should it be otherwise? It has been our fortune to meet under strange conditions, Captain Carlyle--conditions testing us, and revealing the very depths of our natures. Concealment and disguise is no longer necessary between us. You have served me unselfishly, plunging headlong into danger for my sake. I shudder at the thought of where I would be now, but for your effort to save me. No man could have done more, or proved himself more staunch and true. We are in danger yet, adrift here in the heart of this desolate sea, but such peril is nothing compared with what I have escaped. I am glad, sincerely glad; I have prayed God in thankfulness, I feel that your skill and courage will bring us safely to land. I am no longer afraid, for I have learned to trust you."

"In all ways?"

"Yes; as gentleman as truly as sailor. You possess my entire confidence."

Cordial and earnest as these words were, they failed to yield me sufficient courage to voice the eager impulse of my heart. There was a restraint, some memory of the past, perhaps, which fettered the tongue. Yet I struggled to give my desire utterance.

"But do you understand fully?" I questioned anxiously. "All I have done for you would have been done for any other woman under the same conditions of danger. I claim no reward for that--a plain duty."

"I am sure that is true."

"It is true, and yet different. Such service to another would have been a duty, and no more. But to be with you, aiding and protecting, has been a delight, a joy. I have served Dorothy Fairfax for her own sake--not as I would any other."

"Did you not suppose I knew?"

Her glance flashed into mine through the star-gleam, with a sudden message of revealment.

"You knew--that--that it was you personally I served?"

"Of course I knew. A woman is never unaware of such things. Nor is there reason now--here in this boat, with you as my only protector--why I should pretend otherwise. Neither of us know what the end may be; we may sink in these waters, or be cast ashore on a desolate coast to perish miserably, and it is no moment for concealment. Now, if ever, I must tell you the truth. I know you care for me, and have cared since first we met. An interest no less fateful has led me to seek your acquaintance, and give you my aid. Surely it is not unmaidenly for me to confess this when we face the chance of death together?"

"But," I stammered, "I can scarcely believe you realize your words. I--I love you Dorothy."

"And is it not also possible for me to love?"

"Possible--yes! But why should you? Forgive me, but I cannot drive away memory of the gulf between us. I would not dare speak such words of my own volition, they seem almost insult. You are rich, with position and friends of influence, while I at best am but a merchant skipper, in truth a bond servant, penniless and disgraced. In the eyes of the world I am not fit to touch the hem of your garment."

"Is it the eyes of the world, or my eyes into which you look?"

"Yours! I am selfish enough, I fear, to find my happiness there--but it is not right, not just."

"Can you not permit me to be the judge as to that?" she asked seriously. "I know your story, and have seen you in stress and storm. Am I one, think you, to love any man for wealth or position. If I possess these things they are to share, not to hoard.

It is because I have given you my full trust and confidence I can say these words."

"You--you mean, you love me?"

Her eyes fell from my face and her head was turned away, but there was no falter in her voice.

"I love you--are you sorry?"

"Sorry! I am mad with the joy of it; yet stricken dumb. Dorothy! Dorothy Fairfax, I have never even dared dream of such a message from your lips. Dear, dear girl, do you forget who I am? What my future must be?"

"I forget nothing," she said, almost proudly. "It is because I know what you are that my heart responds. Nor is your future so clouded. You are today a free man if we escape these perils, for whether Roger Fairfax be alive, or dead, he will never seek you again to hold in servitude. If alive he will join his efforts with mine to obtain a pardon because of these services, and we have influence in England. Yet, should such effort fail, you are a sailor, and the seas of the world are free. It is not necessary that your vessel fly the English flag."

"You give me hope--a wonderful hope."

"And courage," her hands firmly clasping mine. "Courage to fight on in faith. I would have that my gift to you, Geoffry. We are in peril still, great peril, but you will face it beside me, knowing that whether we live or die we are together. I am not afraid anymore."

She was like a child; I could feel her body relax in my arms as though relieved of its tension. I know I answered her, whispering into her ear words of love, and confidence, scarcely knowing myself what I said in that moment of unrestraint. I felt her eyes on my face and knew her lips were parted in a smile of content, yet doubt if they answered me. She seemed to yield unconsciously, her head upon my shoulder, her face upturned to the stars, while slowly all the intense fatigue of the day and night stupified mind and body. Almost before I realized her weariness, the eyes were closed and she was sleeping in my arms.

I held her closely, so awakened by what had passed between us, as to feel no desire to sleep myself. Dorothy Fairfax loved me. I could scarcely grasp the thought. I had dreamed of love, but only to repress the imagination as impossible. Yet now, voluntarily from her own lips, it had proven true. With eyes uplifted to the stars I swore fidelity, pledging solemnly all my years to her service; nor could I drive my thought away from the dear girl, sleeping so confidently upon my shoulder. Then slowly there came back memory of where we were, of what grave peril surrounded us, of my own responsibility. My eyes sought to pierce the gloom of the night, only to gain glimpses of black water heaving and tumbling on every side, the boat flung high on a whitened crest, and then hurled into the hollow beneath, as though it was a mere chip in the grasp of the sea. The skill of Watkins alone kept us afloat, and even his iron muscles must be strained to the limit. Forward the boat was a mere smudge, the men curled up asleep and no longer visible. All that stood out with any distinctness of outline was the lug sail, stiff as a board. I endeavored to turn my head, without disturbing the slumbering girl, to gain view of the steersman.

"How is she making it, Watkins?"

"A little stiff, sir, but she's a staunch boat. The sea's likely to go down after sunup."

"Well, you've had long enough trick--call one of the men aft. I'm not strong enough yet for that job."

"No, sir," and I caught the echo of a chuckle, "and yer have yer arms full. I kin hold on yere till daylight; 'twon't be long now."

"Make one of them help; who is the best man?"

"Schmitt for this sorter job."

I called him, and growling to himself at being awakened, the Dutchman crept past cautiously and wedged himself in beside Watkins. There was a few words of controversy between the two men, but in the end Schmitt held the steering oar and a few minutes later Watkins had slipped down into the boat's bottom and was sound asleep. And so the gray dawn found us.

CHAPTER XXVI
A FLOATING COFFIN

The laboring boat rested so low in the water it was only as we were thrown upward on the crest of a wave that I could gain any view about through the pallid light of the dawn. At such brief instants my eyes swept the far horizon, to discern nothing except the desolate, endless expanse of sea. A more dismal, gloomy view surely never unrolled itself before the eye of man. Everywhere the gray monotony of rolling waves, slowly stretching out into greater distance as the light strengthened, yet bringing into view no other object. It was all a desolate, restless waste in the midst of which we tossed, while above hung masses of dark clouds obscuring the sky. We were but a hurtling speck between the gray above and the gray below. How tiny the boat looked as my glance ranged forward with this memory of our surroundings still fresh in mind. The crest of the surges swept to the edge of the gunwale, sending the spray flying inboard. Occasionally drops stung my cheek and all the thwarts forward were wet with drizzle. The negro, Sam, alone was awake, baling steadily, his face turned aft, although scarcely glancing up from his labor. He looked tired and worn, a strange green tinge to his black face, as the dim light struck it. The others were curled up in the bottom of the craft, soaked with spray, yet sleeping soundly. The wind had lost its steadiness, coming now in gusts that flapped the sail loudly against the mast, but failed to awaken the slumberers. Depressed by the sight, my eyes sought the face of the girl whose head yet rested against my shoulder.

She lay there with tightly closed eyes, the long lashes outlined against her cheek, breathing softly. Between lips slightly parted her white teeth gleamed as she smiled from pleasant dreams. It was a beautiful face into which I looked, the cheeks faintly tinted, the chin firm, the rounded throat white as snow--the face of a pure, true woman, yet retaining its appearance of girlish freshness. Whatever of hardship and sorrow the past days had brought her, had been erased by sleep, and she lay then utterly forgetful of danger and distress. And she loved me--loved in spite of all dividing us--and in her rare courage had told me so. The memory thrilled my blood, and I felt my arm close more tightly about her, as I gazed eagerly down into the unconscious features. She was actually mine--mine; not even death could rob me of the treasure of her heart, while life offered me every reward. No doubt assailed me; I believed each whispered word from her lips, and the day dawned about us with rare hope. Not now would I yield to despair, or question the future.

Some sudden plunge of the boat caused the girl to open her eyes, and gaze half frightened up into my face. Then she smiled in swift recognition.

"Is it you, Geoffry? We are still alone at sea?"

"Yes, the night is ending; you have slept well."

She drew herself away from me gently, sat up and glanced about. "How tired you must be. I have been very selfish. There is nothing in sight?"

"Nothing."

"And the men are still asleep. Who are they?"

I named them as best I could, pointing out each in turn.

"Are they reliable--safe?" she asked. "You know them?"

"Not well, but they were selected by Watkins, as among the best on board the *Namur*. No doubt they will behave themselves."

"But they are pirates; they cannot be trusted."

"These fellows were not aboard the *Namur* from choice, but seamen captured on merchant ships and compelled to serve to preserve their lives. They are as eager to escape as we. Anyway I shall see to it that they do their duty. Sam!"

The negro looked up quickly.

"Yas, sah!"

"Call the others. Who knows where the food is stored?"

Watkins spoke up behind us.

"It's stored forward, sir, an' all safe; the water casks are lashed amidships."

"I'll see what we've got and serve out."

I crept forward cautiously, because of the erratic leaping of the craft, the men yielding me room to pass, and soon had Sam busily engaged in passing out the various articles for inspection. Only essentials had been chosen, yet the supply seemed ample for the distance I believed we would have to cover before attaining land. But the nature of that unknown coast was so doubtful I determined to deal out the provisions sparingly, saving every crumb possible. The men grumbled at the smallness of the ration, yet munched away contentedly enough, once convinced that we all shared alike. Watkins relieved the Dutchman at the steering oar, and I rejoined Dorothy. The silence was finally broken by one of the men forward asking a question.

"Could you tell us about where we are, sir?"

"Only as a guess," I answered frankly, my eyes traveling over the sea vista, "but will do the best I can. I have had no observation since we left the Capes, but Estada had his chart pricked up to the time he was killed, showing the course of the *Namur*. We were then about a hundred miles off shore and the same distance south. We have been sailing to the north of west since taking to the boat. That is the best course possible with this wind."

"Then a couple days should bring land, sir?"

"Ay, if figures are correct and this wind holds. But these are stormy waters, and we go by dead reckoning."

"That's near enough," he said stubbornly. "Even if you was astray fifty miles would make little difference. There's land to west of us, and plenty ter eat aboard till we get there--so why not eat it?"

I glanced about into the faces of the others forward, but received little encouragement--evidently the fellow was spokesman for his mates. The time had arrived for me to exhibit my authority, but before I could choose words, Watkins gave indignant utterance to a reply.

"Yer hed yer fair share with the rest ov us, didn't yer, Simms?" "O' course I did; but damn it, I'm hungrier then I wus afore--whut the hell's the use?"

"Let me tell you," I broke in, determined on my course. "It is not just the boat trip to be considered, although that may prove serious enough before we get ashore. If I am any judge we are going to have some weather in the next twenty-four hours, and may have to run before it to keep afloat. That's one point to think over. Another is that coast line west of us doesn't contain a dozen white settlements between the Capes and Florida, and you are just as liable to be hungry on land as sea. You've eaten as much as I have."

"Maybe I have, but by God, there is food enough there to last us a month."

"And it may have to do so. Now Simms, listen to what I say, and you others also. I am not going to repeat this. We're the same as ship-wrecked men, and I am in command of this boat. Whatever I say goes, and I've handled worse fellows than you are many a time. Grumble all you please; I don't mind that, but if you try mutiny, or fail to jump at my orders, I'll show you some sea discipline you will not forget very soon. You are with me, Watkins?"

"You bet I am, sir," heartily.

The Dutchman already half asleep, lifted his head.

"Mine Gott, I cud eat a whale," he growled rather discontentedly, "but what der difference say I do--dat wus best, ach."

Simms made no answer, sitting sullenly at the foot of the mast. I waited, thinking some other might venture a word, but evidently they had enough, and I was willing to let the affair rest. They had been shown that I meant to enforce discipline, and nothing remained but for me to carry out my threat if occasion arose. Meanwhile the least friction aboard, the better.

"All right, lads," I said cheerfully. "Now we understand each other and can get at work. We'll divide into watches first of all--two men aft here, and one at the bow. Watkins and I will take it watch and watch, but there is enough right now for all hands to turn to and make the craft shipshape. Two of you bail out that water till she's dry, and the others get out that extra sail forward and rig up a jib. She'll ride easier and make better progress with more canvas showing. How does she head, Watkins?"

"Nor'west, by west, sir."

"You can give two points more west, with the jib drawing--the sea is not quite so heavy?"

"Ay, ay, sir--she's riding fairly free, an' the wind is shifting nor'east. Thar won't be no storm terday."

The men worked cheerfully enough, finding sufficient to do to keep them busy for half an hour, and thus Dorothy and I watched them, whispering occasionally to each other, and commenting on the varied appearance of the fellows. They were rather an interesting lot in their way, the types familiar to me, but strange to her experience--sea scum, irresponsible, reckless, to be ruled by iron hand, yet honest enough according to their standards. The faces were coarse and dissipated, and many a half-smothered oath floated back to our ears, but I saw in them nothing to fear, or cause uneasiness. The sun had dissipated the clouds, while the swell of the sea had sufficiently subsided to permit of a wide view in every direction. The vista only served to increase our sense of loneliness and peril. We were a tiny chip tossed on the immensity of the waters, stretching away to the distant horizons. It was a vast scene of desolation, without another object to break its grim monotony--just those endless surges of gray-green water brightened by the touch of the sun. Again and again I swept my eyes about the circle in a vain effort to perceive something of hope; it was useless--we were alone on the boundless ocean.

I know not what we talked about during those hours; of all we had passed through together, no doubt; of our chances of escape and our dreams of the future. Her bravery and confidence increased my own courage. Knowing as I did the uncertainty of our position, I needed her blind faith to keep me hopeful. The men gradually knocked off work, and lay down, and finally I also yielded to her pleadings and fell into a sound sleep.

It seemed as though I scarcely lost consciousness, yet I must have slept for an hour or more, my head pillowed on her lap. What aroused me I could not determine, but Schmitt was again at the steering paddle, and both he and Dorothy were staring across me out over the port quarter, as though at some vision in the distance, sufficiently strange to enchain their entire attention.

"What is it?" I asked eagerly, but before the words were entirely uttered, a hoarse voice forward bawled out excitedly.

"There you see it; straight out agin that cloud edge. By God, it's a full-rigged schooner."

"Ay," boomed another, "a headin' straight cross our course astern."

I sat up, ignoring all else, thoroughly awake from excitement, gazing under hollowed hands in the direction the men pointed. For an instant I distinguished nothing but sea and sky, with patches of white cloud speckling the horizon. My heart sank with the belief that one of these had been mistaken for the sheen of a distant sail. Then as our boat was suddenly flung higher on the crest of a great wave, my straining eyes caught the unmistakable glimmer of canvas, could even detect its outline plainly delineated against the blue background. I reached my feet, clinging to the mast to keep erect and, as the boat was again flung upward, gained clearly the glimpse I sought.

"Ay, you're right, lads!" I exclaimed. "It's a schooner, headed to clear us by a hundred fathoms. Port your helm Schmitt--hard down man. Watch out the boom don't hit you, Miss Fairfax. Now, Sam, off with that red shirt; tie it on the boat hook, and let fly. They can't help seeing us if there is any watch on deck."

We swept about in a wide circle, shipping some water as we dipped gunwale under, but came safely out from the smother, headed straight across the bows of the oncoming vessel. All eyes stared out watchfully, Sam's shirt flapping above us, and both Watkins and Schmitt straining their muscles to hold the plunging quarter-boat against the force of the wind. A man forward on his knees growled out a curse.

"What the hell's the matter aboard there?" he yelled. "Did yer ever see a boat yaw like that, afore? Damn me, if I believe they got a hand at the wheel."

The same thought had leaped into my mind. The schooner was headed to pass us on the port quarter, yet yawing so crazily at times as to make me fearful of being run down. I could perceive no sign of life aboard, no signal that we had been seen. Indeed from where we crouched in the boat all we could see now was the bow with the jib and foresail. Not a head peered at us over the rail; in silent mystery it seemed to fly straight at us like a great bird, sweeping through water and sky. The sight angered me.

"Stand by, all hands," I cried desperately. "We'll board whether they want us or not. Slip across, Miss Fairfax, out of the way. Now, Watkins, run us in under those fore-chains; easy man, don't let her strike us. Lay hold quick lads and hang on for your lives. Give me that end of rope--ready now, all of you; I'll make the leap. Now then--hold hard!"

It was five feet, and up, my purchase the tossing boat, but I made it, one hand desperately gripping a shroud, until I gained balance and was flung inboard by a sharp plunge of the vessel. My head was at a level with the rail, yet I saw nothing, my whole effort being to make fast before the grip of the men should be torn loose. This done I glanced back into the upturned faces below.

"Hand in slowly lads; yes, let go, the rope will hold, and the boat ride safely enough. Let a couple of men come up till we see what's wrong with the hooker--the rest of you trail on."

"Am I to remain here, Mr. Carlyle?" "Yes for a few moments; there is no danger. You stay also, Watkins; let Schmitt and Sam come with me."

I helped them clamber up and then lifted my body onto the rail, from which position I had a clear view of the forward deck. It was unexpressibly dirty, yet otherwise shipshape enough, ropes coiled and the forward hatch tightly closed. Nothing human greeted me, and conscious of a strange feeling of horror, I slipped over onto the deck. The next moment the negro and Dutchman joined me, the former staring about wildly, the whites of his eyes revealing his terror.

"My Gawd, sah," he ejaculated. "Ah done know dis boat--it's shore de **Santa Marie**. "Ah's cooked in dat galley. What's done happened ter her, sah?"

"You know the schooner? Are you sure, Sam? What was she--a pirate?"

"No, sah; a slaver, sah," he sniffed the air. "Ah kin smell dem niggers right now, sah. Ah, suah reckon dars a bunch o' ded ones under dem hatches right dis minute-

-you white men smell dat odor?"

"I certainly smell something unpleasant enough. This is the **Santa Marie**; the name is on the stern of that boat yonder. When did you serve aboard here?"

"Three years back, sah, frum Habana to der African coast; Ah didn't want no more dat sorter sailorin'."

"But what could have happened? The boats are all in place, but no crew, I never saw anything like it at sea."

Schmitt's hand fell heavily on my sleeve and I glanced aside into his stolid face.

"Der's a feller on ther gratin' amidships, Captain," he said pointing aft. "But I just bet I know vat wus der trouble."

"What man?"

"Cholera," he whispered, "ve haf boarded a death ship."

CHAPTER XXVII
ON BOARD THE SLAVER

The terror of the two men as this thought dawned upon them in all its horror was apparent enough, and, in truth, I shared with them a vivid sense of our desperate situation. Nothing, not even fire was more to be dreaded than a visitation of this awful nature on shipboard. I had heard tales to chill the blood, of whole ships' crews stricken and dying like flies. Yet I dare not hesitate, or permit those under my command to flee in terror. Charnal ship though this might be, the danger to us was not so great, if we only remained in the open air, and used proper precaution in putting the dead overboard. We were in health, well nourished, and our stay aboard would be a short one. Even if the schooner was a floating sepulcher, it was safer by far than the cockleshell towing alongside.

"Let's find out the truth first, men," I said quietly. "Stay here if you want to while I go aft; only hold your tongues. There is no use giving up until we know what the danger is. Will you come with me, or remain where you are?"

The two exchanged glances, and then their eyes ranged along the unoccupied deck. I confess it was eery enough--the silence, the desolate vista, the wind-filled sails above, the schooner flying through the water as though guided by spectral hands, and that single motionless figure crouched on the grating amidships. It made my own nerves throb, and caused me to clinch my teeth, Sam turned his head, his frightened eyes seeking the scuttle leading into the forecastle. He was more frightened to remain where he was, than accompany me, but when he endeavored to say so, his lips refused to utter any sound. The terror in his eyes caused me to laugh, and my own courage came back with a rush.

"Afraid of dead men, are you? Then we'll face them together, my lads, and have it over with. Come on, now, both of you. Buckle up; there is nothing to fear, if you do what I tell you--this isn't the first cholera ship I've been aboard."

It was no pleasant job confronting us, although we had less dead men to handle than I anticipated. Indeed we found only five bodies on board, and as the slaver must have originally carried a large crew, it was evident the survivors had thrown overboard the corpses of those who succumbed first, until they also became too weak to perform such service. There were only two on deck, the fellow crouched on the grating, a giant, coal black negro, and a gray-bearded white man, his face pitted with smallpox, lying beside the wheel. Before he fell to the deck, he had lashed the spokes and still gripped the end of the rope in his dead hand. Determined on what was to be done, I wasted no time with either body. The two sailors hung back, so terrorized at the mere thought of touching these victims of plague, I steeled myself to the job and handled them alone, dragging the inert bodies across the deck, and by the exercise of all my strength launching them over the low rail into the sea. It was indeed a relief to know the deck was clear, and I ordered Schmitt to cut the lashings and take charge of the wheel. Sam was shaking like a leaf, his face absolutely green.

"What---what dey die of, sah--cholera?" he asked faintly.

"No doubt of it; but they are safely over the side now. There is nothing to be frightened about."

"But s'pose we gits it, sah; s'pose we gits it?"

"There is no reason why we should," I contended, speaking loud and confident, so both could hear. "We are all in good health and in the open air. See here, you men, stop acting like fools. We will take a look below, and then have the others on board."

"But Ah's suah feared, sah."

"At what? You are in no more danger than I am. See here, Sam, and you too, Schmitt, I am in love with that girl in the boat. Do you suppose I would ever have her come on this deck, if I believed she might contract cholera? You do as I say, and you are perfectly safe. Now Schmitt remain at the wheel, and you Sam come with me. There will be a dead nigger aboard unless you jump when I speak."

He trotted close at my heels as I flung open the door leading into the cabin. The air seemed fresh enough and I noted two of the ports wide open. A tall smooth-shaven man, with an ugly scar down one cheek, lay outstretched on a divan at the foot of the after mast, his very posture proclaiming him dead. His face was the color of parchment, wrinkled with age, but I knew him at once as Spanish. A uniform cap lay beside him, and I stopped just long enough to scan his features.

"Here, Sam, do you know this fellow."

The negro crept up behind me reluctantly enough, and stared at the upturned face over my shoulder.

"My Gaud, sah, he wus de ol' Captain."

"The one you served under? What was his name?"

"Paradilla, sah; damn his soul!"

"A slaver, I suppose; well, he's run his last cargo of niggers. Let's look into the rooms."

They were empty, all in disorder, but unoccupied. In what was evidently the Captain's room I discovered a pricked chart and a log-book, with no entry in it for three days. Without waiting to examine these I stowed them away in my pocket and returned to Paradilla, relieved to learn our labor aft was so light, and eager to have it over with. Some physical persuasion was necessary to compel Sam to assist me, but finally he took hold, and between us we forced the stiffened form of the Captain through the open after port, and heard it splash into the sea astern. Then I closed the cabin door, and led the way forward.

To my great relief the hold was empty, although the smell arising through the partially opened hatch was stifling, the reminder of a cargo lately discharged. There were two dead seamen in the forecastle, both swarthy fellows, with long Indian hair. I never saw a dirtier hole, the filth overpowering, and once satisfied that both men were beyond help, I was content to lower the scuttle and leave them there.

God! it was a relief to return once more to the open deck and breathe in the fresh air. Schmitt was holding the schooner close up in the wind, which, however, was barely heavy enough to keep the sails full. Yet at that the sharp-nosed craft was making the best of it, leaving a long wake astern, the waves cresting within a few feet of her rail as she swept gloriously forward. I leaned over, and hailed the boat, towing below.

"Come aboard, Watkins," I called sharply. "Pass the lady up first, and turn the boat adrift."

"What is she, sir?"

"An abandoned slaver. I'll tell you the story later. Come aboard."

"Ay, ay, sir."

I caught Dorothy's hands and aided her over the rail, the schooner rode steady and she stood still grasping me, her eager eyes on the deck aft. Then they sought my face questioningly, the seamen beginning to gather between us and the rail.

"Why was the vessel abandoned?" she asked. "What has happened? Do you know?"

"Yes; the story is plain enough," I explained, deeming it best to tell the whole truth. "This is a slaver, the **Santa Marie**, plying between Cuba and the African coast. Sam, the negro who came aboard with me, served as cook on board for one voyage. I do not know why they should be in these waters--driven north by a storm likely--but cholera was the trouble. The crew are all overboard, or dead."

"Overboard, or dead? You found them dead--the slaves also?"

"No; there were no slaves; the hold was clear. We found a few dead men, the last of the crew to survive. One man was lying beside the wheel; he had lashed it to its course before he died; and the Captain was in the cabin."

"And he was dead?"

"Yes, a tall, lean Spaniard; Sam said his name was Paradilla. We found five alto-gether, and flung their bodies over the side except two sailors in the forecastle."

Her eyes evidenced her horror, her lips barely able to speak.

"They--they died of cholera? All of them? There was no one left alive on board?"

"Not even a dog. It was a tragedy of the sea, of which we will never know all the truth. I have the log here in my pocket all written out until three days ago--

perhaps that was when the Captain died. But can you imagine anything more grim, more horrible, than this schooner, with all sails set, standing on her course with a dead man at the wheel?"

"And--and other dead men in cabin and forecastle!" her voice broke and her hands covered her eyes. "O Geoffry, must we stay aboard? The thought is terrible; besides, you said it was cholera."

"There is nothing we need fear," I insisted firmly, clasping the upraised hands and meeting her eyes frankly, "and I rely upon you to help me control the men. They are sailors filled with superstition, and will look to us for leadership. Please do not fail me. You have already passed through too much to be frightened at a shadow. This is a staunch vessel, provisioned and fit for any sea. We are far safer here than in the boat; it is as if God had sent us deliverance."

"Yet we face disease--cholera?" "I do not hold that a peril--not to us, if we use precautions. That is an ever-present sea danger, and I have read every book treating of the disease. So long as we are well fed and keep in the fresh air, we are not liable to suffer. The dead are overboard and every hatch closed. I will have the deck scoured from end to end. The bedding we need, and the food, is being brought up from the boat; we shall come in contact with nothing to spread the disease. You must meet this emergency just as bravely as you have the others; you will, will you not?"

Her eyes met mine smilingly, resolute.

"If you say so--yes. How can I help you?"

"Tell the men just what I have told you," I said gravely. "They will pay more heed to what you say, and will be ashamed to show less courage than you. Do you agree?"

We turned and faced them together, as they formed a little group against the rail. Their dunnage, together with a few boxes of provisions, and a couple of water casks, lay scattered about the deck, and now, their immediate task done, the fellows were sullenly staring around. Hallin was first to speak.

"Vot vas eet you say 'bout dis sheep? Eet haf cholera--hey?"

Dorothy took a step forward, and confronted them, her cheeks flushed.

"You are sailors," she said, speaking swiftly, "and ought not to be afraid if a girl isn't. It is true this vessel was ravaged by cholera, and the crew died; but the bodies have been flung overboard--Captain Carlyle risked his life to do that, before he asked us aboard. Now there is no danger, so long as we remain on deck. I have no fear."

The Swede shook his head, grumbling something, but before the revolt could spread, Watkins broke in.

"An' that's right, miss. I wus on the **Bombay Castle** when she took cholera, an' we hed twenty-one days of it beatin' agin head winds off the Cape. We lost sixteen o' the crew, but not a man among us who stayed on deck got sick. Anyhow these blokes are goin' ter try their luck aboard yere, er else swim fer it."

He grinned cheerfully letting slip the end of the painter, the released quarter-boat gliding gently away astern, the width of water constantly increasing, the light craft wallowing in the waves.

"Now bullies, jump fer it if yer want ter go. Why don't yer try it Ole? You are so keen about getting away, you ought not to mind a little water. So ye prefer to stay along with the rest of us. All right then, my hearties, let's hunt up something to work with and scrub this deck. That's the way to clean out cholera."

He led the way and they followed him, grumbling and cursing, but obedient. I added a word of encouragement, and in a few minutes the whole gang was busily engaged in clearing up the mess forward, making use of whatever came to hand, their first fears evidently forgotten in action. Watkins kept after them like a slave driver.

"That's the style; throw all the litter overboard. Bend your back, Pierre; now Ole, take hold here. What the hell are you men loafing for? Now, heave altogether."

I glanced astern, catching a fleeting glimpse beneath the main boom, of the disappearing quarter-boat, bobbing up and down in the distance; then my eyes sought the face of the girl. She met my gaze with a smile.

"They are all right now, are they not?" she asked.

"Yes, as long as they can be kept busy, and I will see to that. Let's go aft, and get out of this mess. I want to plan our voyage."

It was not difficult finding plenty for the lads to do, making the neglected schooner shipshape, and adjusting the spread of canvas aloft to the new course I decided upon. Fortunately we had men enough to manipulate the sails, real seamen, able to work swiftly. Sam started a fire in the galley, and prepared a hot meal, singing as he worked, and before noon I had as cheerful a ship's crew forward as any man could possibly ask for. The weather kept pleasant, but with a heavy wind blowing, compelling us to take a reef in the canvas, but the schooner was an excellent sea boat, and all alike felt the exhilaration of rapid progress. Dorothy and I glanced over the log, but gained little information. The vessel had been driven into the northwest by a succession of storms, and lack of provisions had weakened the crew, cholera broke out among them the third day at sea, the first victim being the cabin steward. With no medicine chest aboard and everything below foul, the disease spread rapidly. Within twenty-four hours sixteen bodies were thrown overboard and, in their terror, the remainder of the crew mutinied, and refused to work ship. Both mates died, and finally only three men were left alive--a negro known as Juan; the quarter-master, Gabriel Lossier, and the Captain, who was already lying sick and helpless in the cabin. That was the last entry barely decipherable.

As the sun reached the meridian I ventured again into the cabin, and returned with the necessary instruments to determine our position. With these and the pricked chart, I managed fairly well in determining our location, and choosing the most direct course toward the coast. Dorothy watched closely, and when I looked up from the paper, the men were gathered about the open door of the galley, equally interested. I ordered Watkins to send them all aft, and, as they ranged up across the narrow deck, I spread out the chart before them, and explained, as best I could, our situation, and what I proposed doing. I doubt if many were able to comprehend, yet some grasped my meaning, bending over the map and asking questions, pointing to this and that mark with stubby forefingers. From their muttered remarks I judged their only anxiety was to get ashore as early as possible, out of this death ship. Convinced this was also my object, they ventured forward cheerfully, as I rolled up the chart, and placed it in the flag locker.

One of the Frenchmen relieved Schmitt at the wheel, and, a little later, Sam served Dorothy and I on deck. The food was appetizing and well cooked, and we lingered over it for some time, while Watkins busied the men forward.

CHAPTER XXVIII
A NEW PLAN OF ESCAPE

Nothing occurred during the afternoon to disturb the routine work aboard, or to cause me any uneasiness. The swift slaver made excellent progress in spite of light winds, and proved easy to handle. Watkins found enough to occupy the crew on deck and aloft, and they seemed contented, although I noticed the fellows gathered together in groups whenever idle, and discussed the situation earnestly. While they might not be entirely satisfied, and, no doubt, some fear lingered in their minds, the fellows lacked leadership for any revolt, and would remain quiet for the present at least. I made one more trip into the desolate cabin, returning with pipes and tobacco, which I took forward and distributed, an ample supply for all the crew. As the men smoked, Watkins and I leaned over the rail, and discussed the situation.

Sunset brought clouds, and, by the time it was really dark, the entire sky was overcast, but the sea remained comparatively calm, and the wind steady. I judged we were making in the neighborhood of nine knots, and carefully pricked my chart to assure myself of our position. Even at that I was not entirely satisfied, although I kept this lack of faith hidden from the others. Dorothy, however, who kept close beside me much of the time, must have sensed my doubt to some extent, for once she questioned me curiously.

"Are you not sure of your figures?" she asked, glancing from the chart into my face. "That is three times you have measured the distance."

"It is not the figures; it is the accuracy of the chart," I explained. "It is not new, for the schooner evidently seldom made this coast, and it was probably only by chance that they had such a map aboard. Even the best of the charts, are not absolutely correct, and this one may be entirely wrong. I shall rely more on keeping a careful watch tonight than on the map; you see this cape? For all I know it may jut out fifty miles east of where it appears to be and we might run into shoal water at any minute."

She wrinkled her brows over the lines on the map, and then stared out across the darkening sea, without speaking.

It was a pleasant night in spite of the darkness, the air soft, and refreshing. We divided the men into watches, Watkins selecting the more capable for lookouts. I explained to these the danger, and posted them on the forecastle heads, ready to respond instantly to any call. I could see the glow of their pipes for some time, but finally these went out, one by one, and the growl of voices ceased. The schooner was in darkness, except for a faint reflection from the binnacle light aft, revealing the dim figure of the helmsman. Overhead the canvas disappeared into the gloom of the sky.

The locker was filled with flags, representing almost every nation on earth. Evidently the **Santa Marie** was willing to fly any colors, which would insure safety, or allay suspicion in her nefarious trade. I dragged these out, and spread them on the deck abaft the cabin, thus forming a very comfortable bed, and at last induced the girl to lie down, wrapping her in a blanket. But, although she reclined there, and rested, she was in no mood for sleep, and, whenever my restless wandering brought me near I was made aware of her wakefulness. Finally I found a seat beside her on a coil of rope, and we fell into conversation, which must have lasted for an hour or more.

I shall never forget that dark ship's deck, with no sound breaking the silence except the soft swirl of water alongside, the occasional flap of canvas aloft, and the creak of the wheel. Dorothy was but a shrouded figure, as she sat wrapped in her blanket, and the only other object visible was the dim outline of the helmsman. We seemed to be completely shut in between sea and sky, lost and forgotten. Yet the memory of the tragedy this vessel had witnessed remained with me--the helpless slaves who had suffered and died between decks; the dead sailors in the forecastle, their ghastly faces staring up at the beams above, and the horrible figure of Paradilla outstretched on the cabin divan. I was a sailor and could not feel that any good fortune would come to us from such a death ship. The memory brought to me a depression hard to throw off; yet, for her sake I pretended a cheerfulness I was far from feeling, and our conversation drifted idly into many channels.

This was the first opportunity we had enjoyed to actually talk with each other alone, and gradually our thoughts veered from the happenings of the strange voyage, and our present predicament, to those personal matters in which we were peculiarly interested. I know not how it occurred, for what had passed between us in the open boat seemed more like a dream than a reality, yet my hand found her own beneath the blanket, and I dared to whisper the words my lips could no longer restrain.

"Dorothy," I said humbly, "you were frightened last night. I cannot hold you to what you said to me then."

"You mean you do not wish to? But I was not frightened."

"They were honest words? You have not regretted them since?"

"No, Geoffry. Perhaps they were not maidenly, yet were they honest; why should I not have told you the truth? I have long known my own heart, and yours, as well."

"And you still repeat what you said then?"

"Perhaps I do not remember all I said."

"I can never forget--you said, 'I love you.'"

She drew a quick breath, and for an instant remained silent; then her courage conquered.

"Yes, I can repeat that--I love you."

"Those are dear, dear words; but I ought not to listen to them, or believe. I am not free to ask a pledge of you, or to beg you to trust me in marriage."

"Is not that rather for me to decide?" she questioned archly. "I give you my faith, Geoffry, and surely no girl ever had more reason to know the heart of a man than I. You have risked all to serve me, and I would be ungrateful indeed were I insensible of the sacrifice. Yet do not think that is all--gratitude for what you have done. I did not need that to teach me your nature. I make a confession now. You remember the night I met you on deck, when you were a prisoner, and told you that you had become the property of Roger Fairfax?"

"I could never forget."

"Nor I. I loved you then, although I scarcely acknowledged the truth even to myself. I went back to my berth to lie awake, and think until morning. A new world had come to me, and when the dawn broke, I knew what it all meant--that my heart was yours. I cared nothing because you were a prisoner, a bound slave under sentence. We are all alike, we Fairfax's; we choose for ourselves, and laugh at the world. That is my answer, Geoffry Carlyle; I give you love for love."

"'Tis a strange place for such a pledge, with only hope before us."

"A fit place to my mind in memory of our life together thus far, for all the way it has been stress and danger. And what more can we ask than hope?"

"I would ask an opportunity denied me--to stand once more in honor among men. I would not be shamed before Dorothy Fairfax."

"Nor need you be," she exclaimed impetuously, her hands pressing mine. "You wrong yourself, even as you have been wronged. You have already done that which shall win you freedom, if it be properly presented to those in power. I mean that it shall be, once I am safely back in Virginia. Tell me, what are your plans with--with this schooner?"

"To beach it somewhere along shore, and leave it there a wreck, while we escape."

"I suspected as much--yet, is that the best way?"

"The only way which has occurred to me. The men insist on it with good reason. They have been pirates, and might be hung if caught."

"And yet to my mind," she insisted earnestly, "that choice is most dangerous. I am a girl, but if I commanded here, do you know what I would do?"

"I shall be glad to hear."

"I would sail this vessel straight to the Chesapeake, and surrender it to the authorities. The men have nothing to fear with me aboard, and ready to testify in their behalf. The Governor will accept my word without a question. These men are not pirates, but honest seamen compelled to serve in order to save their lives; they mutinied and captured the bark, but were later overcome, and compelled to take the boats. The same plea can be made for you, Geoffry, only you were there in an effort to save me. It is a service which ought to win you freedom."

"But if it does not?"

"I pledge you my word it shall. If the Governor fail me, I will bear my story to the feet of the King. I am a Fairfax, and we have friends in England, strong, powerful friends. They will listen, and aid me."

"I am convinced," I admitted, after a pause, "that this course is the wiser one, but fear the opposition of the men. They will never go willingly."

"There is an argument which will overcome their fear."

"You mean force?" "No; although I doubt not that might suffice. I mean cupidity. Each sailor, aboard has an interest in the salvage of this vessel under the English law. You tell me the schooner was a slaver, driven out to sea by storm immediately after discharging a cargo of slaves. There must be gold aboard--perhaps treasure also, for I cannot think a slaver above piracy if chance arose. Let the crew dream that dream, and you will need no whip to drive them into an English port."

"Full pardon, and possibly wealth with it," I laughed. "A beautiful scheme, Dorothy, yet it might work. Still, if I know sailormen, they would doubt the truth, if it came direct from me, for I am not really one of them."

"But Watkins is, and he has intelligence. Explain it all to him; tell him who I am, the influence I can wield in the Colony, and then let him whisper the news to the others. Will you not do this--for my sake?"

"Yes," I answered, "I believe you have found the right course. If you will promise to lie down, and sleep, I will talk with Watkins now."

"I promise. But are you not going to rest?"

"Very little tonight. I may catch some catnaps before morning, but most of the time shall be prowling about deck. You see I have no officers to rely upon. But don't worry about me--this sort of life is not new. Good night, dear girl."

She extended her arms, and drew me down until our lips met.

"You are actually afraid of me still," she said wonderingly, "why should you be?"

"I cannot tell; I have never known what it was before. Somehow Dorothy, you have always seemed so far away from me, I have never been able to forget. But now the touch of your lips has----"

"Broken down the last barrier?"

"Yes, forever."

"Are you sure? Would you not feel still less doubt if you kissed me again?"

I held her closely, gazing down into the dimly revealed outline of her face, and this time felt myself the master.

"Now I am sure, sweetheart," I whispered, the note of joy ringing in the words, "that I have won the most precious gift in the world; yet your safety, and those of all on board is in my hands tonight. I must not forget that. I am going now to find Watkins, and you have promised to lie down and sleep."

"To lie down," she corrected, "but whether to sleep, I cannot tell."

I left her there, lying hidden and shapeless on the deck beneath the cover of the blanket, her head pillowed on the flags, and groped my own way forward, pausing a moment to gaze into the binnacle, and exchange a word with the man at the wheel. I found Watkins awake, seated on the forecastle steps, where I joined him, lighting my own pipe for companionship, our conversation gradually drifting toward the point I came to make. He listened gravely to what I had to say, with little comment, and was evidently weighing every argument in his mind.

"I've bin in Virginia, and Maryland, sir," he said at last seriously, "and if the young woman is a Fairfax, she'll likely have influence enough ter do just whut she says. They ain't over-kind ter pirates in them provinces o' late, I've bin told--but the savin' o' her life wud make a heap o' difference with the Governor. Yer know she's a Fairfax?"

"Absolutely. I told you the story that night in the forecastle, and I take more risk than any of you in giving myself up. I was bound in servitude to her uncle, Roger Fairfax, and am therefore a runaway slave."

"Well," he agreed, "I'll talk it over with the lads. It's a good story, an' I'd be ready ter take chances, but I ain't so sure, sir, on makin' 'em feel the same way. All most of 'em think about is ter escape bein' hanged. If they wus only sure thar wus treasure aboard, like you suspicion there may be, I guess most of 'em would face hell ter git their hands on a share of it."

"Then why not search, and see?"

He shook his head obstinately, and his face, showing in the dull glow of the pipe, proved that he, sturdy, intelligent seaman as he was, shared to no small extent the fears of the others.

"Not me, sir; I don't prowl around in no cholera ship, loaded with dead men--not if I never git rich."

"Then I will," and I got to my feet in sudden determination. "You keep the deck while I go below. Have you seen a lantern on board anywhere?"

"Ay, sir, there's one hangin' in the cook's galley. I hope yer don't think I'm a damn coward, Mr. Carlyle?"

"Oh, no, Tom. I know how you feel exactly; we're both of us sailors. But you see I've got to make this crew take the *Santa Marie* into the Chesapeake, and it's an easier job if I can find gold aboard."

"Yer've got to, sir?"

"Yes, I've given my promise to the girl. Light the lantern, and bring it here. Then we'll go aft together; if there is any specie hidden aboard this hooker, it will be either in the cabin, or lazaret. And, whether there is, or not, my man, the **Santa Marie** turns north tomorrow, if I have to fight every sea wolf on board single-handed."

CHAPTER XXIX
A STRUGGLE IN THE DARK

He came back with it swinging in his hand a mere tin box, containing a candle, the dim flame visible through numerous punctures. It promised poor guidance enough, yet emitted sufficient light to show the way around in that darkness below. So as not to arouse suspicion, I wrapped the thing in a blanket, and, with Watkins beside me, started aft. Dorothy must have been asleep already, for there was no sign of movement as we passed where she was lying. Neither of us spoke until my hand was on the companion door ready to slide it open.

"I'll not be long below," I said soberly. "And meanwhile you keep a sharp watch on deck. Better go forward and see that your lookout men are awake, and then come back here. Likely I'll have a story to tell you by that time. The wind seems lessening."

"Yes, sir; shall we shake out a reef in the foresail?"

"Not yet, Watkins. Wait until I learn what secret is below. An hour will make little difference."

With the lantern held before me, its faint light barely piercing the intense darkness, I stood on the first step leading down into the cabin, and slid the door back into place behind me. I had no sense of fear, yet felt a nervous tension to which I was scarcely accustomed. For the instant I hesitated to descend into the gloom of that interior. The constant nerve strain under which I had labored for days and nights, made me shrink from groping blindly forward, searching for the unknown. The very darkness seemed haunted, and I could not drive from my memory the figure of that dead Captain, whose life had ended there. It even seemed to me

I could smell foulness in the air; that I was breathing in cholera. Yet I drove this terror from me with a laugh, remembering the open ports through which the fresh wind was blowing; and cursing myself for a fool, began the descent, guided by the flickering rays of light.

I was conscious of a quickening pulse, as I peered about me in the gloom, every article of furniture assuming grotesque form. The rustling of a bit of cloth over one of the open ports caused me to face about suddenly, while every creak of the vessel seemed the echo of a human voice. A blanket in the form of a roll lay on the divan where I had found Captain Paradilla, and for a moment, as I stared at it, dimly visible in a ray of light, I imagined this was his motionless figure. Indeed, I was so strung up, it required all my reserve of courage to persevere, and traverse the black deck. My mind was fixed on a great chest in the Captain's stateroom, which, finding locked, I had not disturbed on my former visit. But first I explored the steward's pantry, in search of knife or hatchet. I found the latter, and, with it tucked into my belt, felt my way aft. It may have required five minutes to pry open the chest, and the reward was scarcely worth the effort. The upper tray contained nothing but clothing, and beneath this were books, and nautical instruments, with a bag of specie tucked into one corner, together with a small packet of letters. I opened the sack, finding therein a strange collection of coins, mostly Spanish, estimating the total roughly at possibly five hundred English pounds. Either this was Paradilla's private purse, or money kept on hand to meet the expenses of the voyage. I searched the room thoroughly, discovering nothing, finally concluding that if there was treasure on board, it must be concealed elsewhere. I did find, however, that which strengthened my suspicion, for, in rummaging hastily through a drawer of the rude desk, I came upon a bill of sale for a thousand slaves, dated two weeks before, but unsigned, although the parties mentioned within the document were Paradilla and a merchant of Habana, named Carlos Martinos. This would evidence the sale for cash of the late cargo of the *Santa Marie*--a goodly sum--but, whether the amount had been left ashore remained undecided. Only a careful search of the vessel could determine this.

However, this discovery nerved me to press forward with my exploration. All fear and dread had left me, and I went at the task coolly enough, and with a clear purpose. There remained aft two places unvisited--the lazaret and the port stateroom, which I had not previously entered, because of a locked door. I determined on breaking in here first, suspecting its use as a storeroom. There was no key in the lock, and the stout door resisted my efforts. Placing the lantern on the deck I succeeded finally in inserting the blade of the hatchet so as to gain a purchase sufficient to release the latch. As the door yielded, the hinges creaking dismally, a sharp cry, human in its agony, assailed me from within. It came forth so suddenly, and with so wild an accent, I stepped blindly backward in fright, my foot overturning the lantern, which, with a single flicker of candle went out. In that last gleam I saw a form--either of man, or boy--a dim, grotesque outline, fronting me. Then, in the darkness gleamed two green, menacing eyes, growing steadily larger, nearer, as I stared at them in horror. I could not move; I seemed paralyzed; I doubt if I even breathed in that first moment of overwhelming terror. Another cry, like that of a mad person, struck my ears, and I knew the thing was coming toward me. There was no other sound, no footstep on the deck; I merely felt the approach, realizing the increasing glare of those horrible eyes. They seemed to fascinate, to hold me immovable, the blood chilled in my veins. Was it man or beast? Devil from hell, or some crazed human against whom I must battle for life? The green eyes glared into my face; I could even feel the hot breath of the monster. I lifted my hand toward him, and touched--hair!

Even as the creature's grip caught me, ripping through jacket sleeve to the flesh, I knew what my antagonist was--a giant African ape. Horrible as the reality was, I was no longer paralyzed with fear, helpless before the unknown. This was something real, something to grasp, and struggle against, a beast with which to pit strength and skill. The sting of the claws maddened me, brought me instantly to life, and I drove my hatchet straight between those two gleaming eyes. I know not how it struck, but the brute staggered back dragging me with him in the clutch of his claws. His human-like cry of pain ended in a brutal snarl, but, brief as the respite proved, it gave me grip on his under jaw, and an opportunity to drive my weapon twice more against the hairy face. The pain served only to madden the beast, and, before I could wrench free, he had me clutched in an iron grip, my jacket torn into shreds. His jaws snapped at my face, but I had such purchase as to prevent their touching me, and mindless of the claws tearing at my flesh, I forced the animal's head back until the neck cracked, and the lips gave vent to a wild scream of agony.

I dared not let go; dared not relax for an instant the exercise of every ounce of strength. I felt as though the life was being squeezed out of me by the grasp of those hairy arms; yet the very vice in which I was held yielded me leverage. The hatchet dropped to the deck, and both hands found lodgment under the jaw, the muscles of my arms strained to the utmost, as I forced back that horrid head. Little by little it gave way, the suffering brute whining in agony, until, the pain becoming unendurable, the clinging arms, suddenly released their hold, letting me drop heavily to the deck.

By some good fortune I fell upon the discarded hatchet, and stumbled to my feet once more, gripping the weapon again in my fingers. I stood trembling, breathing hard, my flesh burning, peering about. The darkness revealed nothing, yet I knew I had been dragged within the stateroom, from which there was no escape, as I had lost all sense of direction. For an instant I could not even locate the brute. With an intense desire to escape, to place the door safely between me and my antagonist, I felt blindly about in the black void. Silently as I endeavored to move, I must have been overheard by the beast, for suddenly his jaws snapped savagely, and I saw once again the baneful glow of those horrible eyes. I knew enough of wild life to realize that now the ape feared me, and that my safer course was to attack. Acting on this impulse, determined to have an end, before he could grip me once more in those awful arms, and crush me into unconsciousness, I sprang straight toward him, sending the sharp blade of the hatchet crashing against the skull. The aim was good, the stroke a death blow, yet the monster got me with one jaw, and we fell to the deck together, he savagely clawing me in his death agony. Then the hairy figure quivered, and lay motionless. With barely strength enough for the task, I released the stiffening grip, and crept aside, rising to my knees, only to immediately pitch forward unconscious. It seemed to me as I went down that I heard voices, saw lights flashing in the outer cabin, but all these merged instantly into blackness.

When I came back once more to life I knew immediately I was upon the schooner's deck, breathing the fresh night air. I could see the outline of the helmsman in the little circle of binnacle light, a ray of which extended far enough to assure me of the presence of Dorothy. I watched her for some time, my mind slowly clearing to the situation, and, it was not until I spoke, that she became aware I had recovered consciousness.

"Dorothy."

"Yes, yes," she bent lower eagerly. "Oh, I am so glad to hear you speak. Watkins said you were not seriously hurt, but your clothes were torn into shreds, and you bled terribly."

"It was not a nightmare then; I really fought that beast?"

"Yes; but it is too horrible to think about--I--I shall never blot out the sight."

"You saw what occurred yourself?" I questioned in astonishment. "You actually came below? Then I did hear voices, and see a light, before my senses left me?"

"Yes; Watkins heard the noise of struggle, the cries of the brute, and woke me. At first he was afraid to go into the cabin, but I made him, rather than let me go alone. The only light we had was a torch, made from a rope end. We got there just as you fell. I saw you staggering on your knees, and that beast outstretched on deck, a great gash in its skull. Watkins says it was a chimpanzee."

"It was a huge ape of some kind, crazed with hunger no doubt." I sat up, aware of the smart of my wounds, but already convinced they were not deep or dangerous. "You did not look about? You took no note of what was in the room?"

"No," puzzled at my sudden interest. "I had no thought of anything but you. At first I believed you dead, until I felt the beat of your pulse. The light revealed little, until Watkins found the overturned lantern, and relit the candle."

"But I saw not even that much; the fight was in pitch darkness, yet I struck against things not furniture--what were they?"

"Oh, you mean that! I think it must have been a storeroom of some kind, for there were casks and boxes piled up, and a strange iron-bound chest was against one wall. I sat on it, and held the lantern while Watkins saw to your wounds. Then we carried you up here."

"That is the answer I sought. Yes, you must let me get up, dear. Oh, I can stand alone; a little weak from loss of blood yet, but none the worse off. Where is Watkins?"

"He went forward. Do you need him?"

"Perhaps it can wait until daylight. You know what I ventured below for?"

"To learn if there was treasure hidden aboard; you hoped such a discovery would induce the men to sail this schooner to the Chesapeake."

"Yes, and now I believe there is--hidden away in the locked room and guarded by that ape. In all probability no one but Paradilla knew the creature was on board, and he could have had no better guardian. No sailor would ever face the brute."

We may have talked there for an hour, Watkins joining us finally, and listening to my story. My wounds, while painful enough, were all of the flesh, and the flow of blood being easily staunched, my strength returned quickly. To my surprise the hour was but little after midnight, and I had so far recovered when the watch was changed, as to insist on Watkins going forward, leaving me in charge of the deck. I felt no desire for sleep, and so he finally yielded to my orders, and curled up in a blanket in the lee of the galley. The girl was harder to manage, yet, when I left her alone, she lay down on her bed of flags. Twice later she lifted her head, and spoke as I passed, but at last remained motionless, while I carefully covered her with an extra blanket.

The time did not seem long to me as I paced the deserted deck aft, or went forward occasionally to assure myself that the lookouts on the forecastle were alert. There was nothing to see or do, the sea and sky both so black as to be indistinguishable, and the breeze barely heavy enough to distend the canvas, giving the schooner a speed not to exceed six knots, I suspicioned a storm in the hatching, but nothing evidenced its near approach. However my thoughts busied me, and vanished all drowsiness. I believed I had won a way to freedom--to a government pardon. The good fortune which had befallen me in the salvage of this vessel, as well as our success against the pirates of the **Namur**, could scarcely be ignored by the authorities of Virginia, while the rescue of Dorothy Fairfax, and her pleading in our behalf, would commend us to mercy, and reward from the very highest officials. The money, the treasure, I personally thought nothing about, willing enough that it should go to others; but I was ambitious to regain my honor among men, my place of respectability in the world, for the one vital purpose which now dominated my mind--that I might claim Dorothy Fairfax with clean hands. My love, and the confession of her own, had brought to me a new vista, a fresh hope. It seemed to me already her faith had inspired me with new power--power to transform dream into reality.

I stood above her motionless figure as she lay asleep, and solemnly took a resolve. At whatever cost to myself, or others, the **Santa Marie** should sail in between the Capes to the waters of the Chesapeake. Be the result reward or punishment, liberty or freedom, the chance must be accepted, for her sake, as well as my own.

CHAPTER XXX
OPENING THE TREASURE CHEST

The dawn came slowly, and with but little increase of light. The breeze had almost entirely died away, leaving the canvas aloft motionless, the schooner barely moving through a slightly heaving sea, in the midst of a dull-gray mist. It was a dismal outlook, the decks wet, the sails dripping moisture, and nothing to look about upon but wreaths of fog. Even as the sun rose, its rays failed to penetrate this cloud bank, or yield slightest color to the scene. It was all gray, gloomy, mysterious--a narrow stretch of water, disappearing so suddenly the eye could not determine ocean from sky. The upper masts vanished into the vapor, and, from where I stood aft, I could but dimly perceive the open deck amidships. The light yet burning in the binnacle was hazy and dull.

There was to my mind a threat in the weather, expressed in the silence overhead, as well as in the sullen swell underfoot. We could not be far from the coast--a coast line of which I knew next to nothing--and, at any instant, the blinding fog encircling us might be swept aside by some sudden atmospheric change, catching us aback, and leaving us helpless upon the waters. Again and again I had witnessed storms burst from just such conditions, and we were far too short-handed to take any unnecessary risk. I talked with Harwood at the wheel, and waited, occasionally walking over to the rail, and peering out into the mist uneasily. It seemed to me the heave of water beneath our keel grew heavier, the fog more dense, the mystery more profound. Safety was better than progress, particularly as there was no real object any longer in our clinging to a westerly course. The sensible thing was to lay too until the enveloping fog blew away, explore that room below, and explain my plans to the men.

This determined upon I called all hands, and with Watkins in command forward, preceded to strip the vessel of canvas, leaving exposed only a jib sheet, with closely reefed foresail, barely enough to give the wheelsman control. This required some time and compelled me to lay hold with the others, and, when the last gasket had been secured, and the men aloft returned to the deck, Sam had the galley fire burning, and breakfast nearly ready. The lads, saturated with moisture, and in anything but good humor, were soon restored to cheerfulness, and I left them, sitting about on deck and returned aft, where Dorothy, aroused by the noise, stood, well wrapped up, near the rail.

Sleep had refreshed her greatly, her eyes welcoming me, a red flush on either cheek.

"Have you been up all night?"

"Yes, but I would hardly know it--a sleepless night means nothing to a sailor."

"But it was so selfish of me to sleep all those hours."

"I had you to think about; all we have said to each other, and our plans."

"What are they? You have determined?"

"To do as you suggested. It is the braver, and, I believe, the better way. The difficulty is going to lie in convincing the crew of their safety. I shall explore below before having a talk with them."

"In hope of discovering treasure to be divided?"

"Yes, that will have greater weight with those fellows than any argument, or promise. Here comes Sam with our breakfast; we will eat here from the flag locker."

The negro served us with some skill, and, discovering we were hungry, both did full justice to the well-cooked fare. The denseness of the fog hid the men from us, but we could hear their voices, and occasionally a burst of laughter. We were talking quietly together, and had nearly finished, when Watkins emerged through the mist, and approached respectfully.

"You did not like the look o' things, sir?" he asked, staring out into the smother astern.

"I've seen storms born from such fogs," I answered, "and know nothing of this coast."

"You think then it's not far away--out yonder?"

"It is all a guess; we made good progress most of the night, and I have no confidence in the chart. There are headlands hereabout, and we might be within hail of one at this minute. It is safer to lie quiet until the mist lifts. By the way, Watkins--"

"Ay, ay, sir."

"Miss Fairfax tells me that was a storeroom in which I fought the ape last night."

"It was, sir." "And she reports having seen a chest, iron-bound, among the other stuff. Did you notice it?"

He walked across to the rail, spat overboard, and came back, politely wiping his lips on his sleeve.

"Yes, sir, I did; it was stored ter starboard, an ol'fashioned sea chest, padlocked, an' looked like a relic, but a damned strong box. You think maybe there's gold in it?"

"Likely enough. I found about five hundred pounds in the Captain's room; but there must be more aboard, unless it was left behind in Cuba. My idea is that was why the monkey was locked up in there--to guard the treasure. Does that sound reasonable?"

He scratched his head, his eyes wandering from her face to mine.

"Yes, sir, it does. I've heard o' such things afore. A chimpanzee is better'n a big dog on such a job; thar ain't no sailor who would tackle the beast."

"That was my way of looking at it. So while we are lying here, and the lads are in good humor--hear that laugh--I am going to find out what's in the chest. After I know, I'll talk to the men. Do you agree?"

He nodded, but without speaking.

"Are you willing to go below with me?"

"I ain't overly anxious 'bout it, Mister Carlyle," he replied gruffly, plucking awkwardly at the peak of his cap. "I'm a seaman, sir, an' know my duty, an' so I'll go 'long if yer wus ter order me to. Yer know that; but I ain't fergot yet this yere is a cholera ship, an' it's goin' ter be as black as night down thar in thet cabin--"

"Don't urge him Geoffry," the girl interrupted, her hand on my sleeve. "Leave him here on deck, I am not in the least afraid, and all you need is someone to hold the light. Please let me do that."

I looked down into her eyes, and smiled.

"Suppose we should encounter another ape?"

"Then I would want to be with you," she responded quickly. "You are going to consent?"

"I suppose I am, although if there was the slightest danger my answer would be otherwise. Keep the men busy, Watkins, while we are gone--don't give them time to ask questions. You brought the lantern on deck?"

"Yes, sir; it's over there against the grating."

"Very well; we'll light up in the companion, so the flame will not be seen by the crew. Coming, Dorothy?"

She accompanied me cheerfully, but her hand grasped mine as we groped our way down the stairs into the dark cabin. A faint glimmer of gray daylight filtered through the glass from above, and found entrance at the open ports, but the place was nevertheless gloomy enough, and we needed what little help the candle afforded to find our way about. The memories haunted us both, and hurried us to our special mission. The door of the storeroom stood wide open, but the after ports were closed, the air within heated and foul. Dorothy held the lantern, her hands trembling slightly, as I stepped across and unscrewed both ports. The moist fog blew in upon me but was welcome, although I stared forth into a bank of impenetrable mist.

The dead ape lay just as he had fallen, with his hideous face upturned, and a great gash in the head. The hatchet with which I had dealt the blow, rested on the deck, disfigured with blood. The hugeness of the creature, its repulsive aspect in death, with savage teeth gleaming in the rays of the lantern, and long, hairy arms outspread, gave me such a shock, I felt my limbs tremble. For a moment I could not remove my eyes from the spectacle, or regain control of my nerves. Then I some way saw the horror, reflected in her face, and realized the requirements of leadership.

"He was certainly a big brute," I said quietly, "and it was a lucky stroke which finished him. Now to complete our work in here and get out."

I picked up the hatchet, and my glance sought the whereabouts of the chest. The light was confusing, and she stepped forward, throwing the dim yellow flame directly upon the object.

"This is what I saw--see; does it look like a treasure chest to you?"

"If it be not, I never saw one--and a hundred years old, if it is a day. What a story of the sea it might tell if it had a tongue. There is no way to find its secrets but to break it open. Place the lantern on this cask of wine; now, if I can gain purchase with the blade, it will be easily accomplished."

It proved harder than I had believed, the staple of the lock clinging to the hard teak wood of which the chest was made. I must have been ten minutes at it, compelled to use a wooden bar as lever, before it yielded, groaning as it finally released its grip, like a soul in agony. I felt the girl clutch me in terror at the sound, her frightened eyes searching the shadows, but I was interested by then to learn what was within, and gave all my effort to lifting the lid. This was heavy, as though weighted with lead, but as I finally forced it backward, a hinge snapped, and permitted it to drop crashing to the deck. For an instant I could see nothing within--no more indeed than some dimly revealed outline, the nature of which could not be determined. Yet, somehow, it gave me an impression, horrible, grotesque, of a human form. I gripped the side of the chest afraid to reach downward.

"Lift up the lantern--Dorothy, please. No, higher than that. What in God's name? Why, it is the corpse of a woman!"

I heard her cry out, and barely caught the lantern as it fell from her hand. The hatchet struck the deck with a sharp clang, and I felt the frightened clasp of the girl's fingers on my sleeve. Yet I scarcely realized these things, my entire attention focussed on what was now revealed writhin the chest. At first I doubted the evidence of my own eyes, snatching the bit of flaring candle from its tin socket, and holding it where the full glare of light fell across the grewsome object. Ay, it was a woman, with lower limbs doubled back from lack of space, but otherwise lying as though she slept, so perfect in preservation her cheeks appeared flushed with health, her lips half smiling. It was a face of real beauty--an English face, although her eyes and hair were dark, and her mantilla, and long earrings were unquestionably Spanish. A string of pearls encircled her throat, and there were numerous rings upon her fingers. The very contrast added immeasurably to the horror.

"She is alive! Surely she is alive?" the words were sobbed into my ear, trembling from Dorothy's lips, as though she could barely utter them. I stared into her face, the sight of her terror, arousing me from stupor.

"Alive! No, that is impossible!" and conquering a repugnance, such as I had never before experienced, I touched the figure with my hand, "The flesh is like stone," I said, "thus held lifelike by some magic of the Indies. I have heard of such skill but never before realized its perfection. Good God! she actually seems to breathe. What can it all mean? Who could the woman be? And why should her body be thus carried about at sea. Is it love, or hate?"

"Not love, Geoffry. Love would never do this thing. It is hate, the gloating of revenge; there can be no other answer--this is the end of a tragedy."

"The truth of which will never be known."

"Are you sure? Is there nothing hidden with her in there to tell who she was, or how she died?"

There was nothing, not a scrap of paper, not even the semblance of a wound exposed. The smile on those parted lips had become one of mockery; I could bear the sight no longer, and rose to my feet, clasping Dorothy close to me, as she still gazed down in fascination at the ghastly sight.

"We will never know. The man who could tell is dead."

"Captain Paradilla?"

"Who else could it be? This was his schooner, and here he alone could hide such a secret. There is nothing more we can learn, and the horror unnerves me. Hold the light, dear, while I replace the lid of the chest."

It required my utmost effort to accomplish this, yet I succeeded in sliding the heavy covering back inch by inch, until it fell finally into place. I was glad to have the thing hidden, to escape the stare of those fixed eyes, the death smile of those red lips. It was no longer a reality, but a dream of delirium; I dare not think, or speculate--my only desire being to get away, to get Dorothy away. My eyes swept about through the confusing shadows, half expecting to be confronted by other ghosts of the past, but all they encountered were the indistinct outlines of casks and boxes, and the hideous hairy figure of the ape, outstretched upon the deck. The candle fluttered in the girl's shaking hand, the yellow glare forming weird reflections, ugly shapes along the wall. God! what if it should go out, leaving us lost and groping about in this chamber of horrors? In absolute terror I drew her with me to the open door--then stopped, paralyzed; the half revealed figure of a man appeared on the cabin stairs.

"Stop! who are you?"

"Watkins, sir. I came below to call you. There's sumthin' bloomin' odd takin' place out there in the fog, Captain Carlyle. We want yer on deck, sir, right away."

CHAPTER XXXI
THE BOAT ATTACK

He waited for us just without the companion, but my eyes caught nothing unusual as I emerged into the daylight. I could barely see amidships, but thus far the deck was clear, and on either side hung the impenetrable bank of cloud, leaving sea and sky invisible. Simmes was at the wheel, with no other member of the crew in sight.

"What is it, Watkins? Where are the men?"

"Forrard, sir, a hangin' over the starboard rail. Thar's somethin' cursedly strange a happenin' in that damn fog. Harwood was the first ter hear the clatter ov en oar slippin' in a rowlock. I thought the feller wus crazy, till I heerd sumthin' also, an' then, sir, while we wus still a listenin' we both caught sound ov a Spanish oath, spoke as plain as if the buck was aboard."

"You saw nothing?"

"Not so much as a shadder, sir."

"A lost boat, likely--ship-wrecked sailors adrift in the fog; perhaps our other quarter-boat. No one hailed them?"

"No, sir; I told the men ter keep still till I called you. It might be a cuttin'-out party; this ain't no coast fer any honest sailors ter be huggin' up to, an' I didn't like that feller talkin' Spanish."

"But if their purpose is to take us by surprise," I said, "they'd be more cautious about it."

"Maybe they didn't know how near they was. 'Tain't likely they kin see us much better 'n we kin see them. The sea's got an ugly swell to it, an' the feller likely cussed afore he thought. Enyhow it wa' n't my place ter hail 'em."

"All right; where are they?"

"Straight off the starboard quarter, sir."

The crew were all gathered there, staring out into the mist, whispering to each other. Even they were indistinct, their faces unrecognizable, until I pressed my way in among them. I brought up beside Harwood.

"Hear anything more?"

"Not yet, sir," peering about to make sure of who spoke, "but there's a boat out yonder; I'll swear to that."

"How far away when you heard them?"

"Not mor'n fifty fathoms, an' maybe not that--the voice sounded clearest."

We may have been clinging there, a minute or two, breathlessly listening, our hands tensely gripping the rail. My coming had silenced the others, and we waited motionless, the stillness so intense I could hear the lapping of waves against the side, and the slight creak of a rope aloft. Then a voice spoke directly in front of me out from the dense fog, a peculiar, penetrating voice, carrying farther than the owner probably thought, and distinctly audible.

"Try the port oar, Pedro; we must have missed the damn ship."

I straightened up as though struck, my eyes seeking those of Harwood, who stared back at me, his mouth wide open in astonishment.

"You heard that?" I whispered. "Do you know who spoke?"

"By God, do I? Dead, or alive, sir, it was Manuel Estevan."

"Ay; no other, and alive enough no doubt. Lads, come close to me, and listen--they must not hear us out there. By some devil's trick the *Namur* has followed our course, or else yonder are a part of his crew cast away. They clearly know of us--perhaps had a glimpse through some rift in the cloud--and are seeking to board with a boat party. 'Tis not likely those devils know who we are; probably take us for a merchant ship becalmed in the fog, and liable to become an easy prey, if they can only slip up on us unseen. How are you, bullies? Ready to battle your old mates?"

"Those were no mates o' ours, sir," said Watkins indignantly. "They are half-breed mongrels, and no sailors; Estevan is a hell-hound, an' so far as my voice goes, I'd rather die on this deck than ever agin be a bloody pirate. Is that the right word, lads?"

The others grumbled assent, but their muttered words had in them a ring of sincerity, and their faces exhibited no cowardice. Harwood alone asked a question.

"I'm fer fightin', sir," he said grimly, "but what'll we use? Them lads ain't comin' aboard bare-handed, but damn if I've seed a weapon on this hooker."

"Dar's three knives, an' a meat cleaver in der galley, sah," chimed in Sam.

"We'll do well enough; some of you have your sheath knives yet, and the rest can use belaying pins, and capstan bars. The point is to not let them get aboard, and, if there is only one boat, we will be pretty even-handed. Pick up what you can, and man this rail--quietly now, hearties, and keep your eyes open."

It proved a longer wait than I expected. The fog gave us no glimpse of the surrounding water, and not another sound enabled us to locate the approaching boat. I felt convinced we had not been overheard, as no one had spoken above a whisper, and the men aboard had been noiseless in their movements about deck, I had compelled Dorothy to remain on the port side of the cabin, removed from all danger, and the only upright figure in sight was the man at the wheel. The rest of us crouched along the starboard rail, peering out into the mist, and listening for the slightest sound. They were a motley crew, armed with every conceivable sort of knife or war club, but sturdy fellows, ready and willing enough to give a good account of themselves. Watkins was forward, swallowed up in the smother of mist, but Schmitt held a place next me, a huge, ungainly figure in the dull light. So still it was I began to doubt having heard the voice at all--could it have been imagination? But no; that was impossible, for the sound had reached all of us alike. Somewhere out yonder, that boat was creeping along silently, seeking blindly through the fog to reach our side unobserved--those Wolves of the Sea had the scent.

I do not know how long the suspense lasted, but, I have never felt a greater strain on my nerves. Every deeper shadow increased the tension, imagination play-ing strange tricks, as I stared fixedly into the void, and trembled at the slightest sound. Once I was sure I heard the splash of an oar, but no one on deck spoke, and I remained silent. The faint creaking of a rope aloft caused my heart to thump, and when a loosened edge of canvas slapped the mast in a sudden breath of air, it sound-ed to me like a burst of thunder. Where were the fellows? Had they abandoned their search, confused by the fog; or were they still stealthily seeking to locate our position? Could there be more than one boat, and if not what force of men might such a boat contain? These questions never left me, and were alike unanswerable. Unable to withstand inaction any longer I arose to my feet, thinking to pass down the line with a word of encouragement to each man. A glance upward told me the heavy mist was passing, driven away by a light breeze from the south. Through the thick curtain which still clung to the deck, I could perceive the upper spars, already tipped with sunlight, and edges of reefed canvas flapping in the wind. The schooner felt the impulse, the bow swinging sharply to port, and I turned and took a few steps aft, thinking to gauge our progress by the wake astern. I was abaft the cabin on the port side when Dorothy called my name--a sudden accent of terror in her voice.

The alarm was sounded none too soon. Either fortune, or skill had served those demons well. Gliding silently through the obscuring cloud, hanging in dense folds of vapor to the water surface, propelled and guided by a single oar, used cautiously as a paddle, they had succeeded in circling the stern of the **Santa Marie**, unseen and unheard by anyone aboard. Not even the girl, unconscious of the possibility of approaching danger from that quarter, her attention diverted elsewhere, had her slightest suspicion aroused as they glided noiselessly alongside, and made fast beneath the protection of the after-chains. One by one, moving like snakes, the devils passed inboard to where they could survey the seemingly deserted deck. Some slight noise awoke her to their presence, yet, even as she shrieked the sudden alarm, a hand was at her throat, and she was struggling desperately in the merciless grip of a half-naked Indian.

Yet at that they were too late, the advantage of surprise had failed them. A half dozen had reached the deck, leaping from the rail, the others below clambering after their leaders, when with a rush, we met them. It was a fierce, mad fight, fist and club pitted against knife and cutlass, but the defenders knowing well the odds against them, angered by the plight of the girl, realizing that death would be the reward of defeat, struck like demons incarnate, crushing their astounded antagonists back against the bulwark. I doubt if the struggle lasted two minutes, and my memory of the scene is but a series of flashes. I heard the blows, the oaths, the cries of pain, the dull thud of wood against bone, the sharp clang of steel in contact, the shuffling of feet on the deck, the splash of bodies hurled overboard. These sounds mingle in my mind with the flash of weapons, the glare of infuriated eyes, the dark, savage faces. Yet it was all confusion, uproar, mingling of bodies, and hoarse shouts. Each man fought for himself, in his own way. I thought only of her, and leaped straight for her assailant with bare hands, smashing recklessly through the hasty guard of his cutlass, ignorant that he had even struck me, and gripped the copper devil by hair and throat. I knew she fell to the deck, beneath our feet, but I had my work cut out for me. He was a hell-hound, slippery as an eel in his half nakedness, strong as an ox, and fighting like a fiend. But for that first lucky grip I doubt my killing him, yet I had him foul, my grip unbreakable, as I jerked and forced his neck back against the rail, until it cracked, the swarthy body sliding inert to the deck. Whirling to assist the others, assured of the fellow's helplessness, I found no need. Except for bodies here and there the deck was clear, men were struggling in the chains; two below in the boat were endeavoring to cast off, and Schmitt, with Estevan helpless in his arms, staggered to the side, and flung the shrieking Spanish cur overboard out into the dark water. I heard the splash as he fell, the single cry his lips gave, but he never again appeared above the surface. Above the bedlam Watkins roared out an order.

"That's it, bullies! that's it! Now let her drop! We'll send them to hell where they belong. Good shot; she landed!"

It was the hank of a spare anchor, balanced for an instant on the rail, then sent crashing down through the frail bottom of the boat beneath. The wreck drifted away into the fog, the two miserable occupants clinging desperately to the gunwales. I lifted Dorothy to her feet, and she clung to me unsteadily, her face yet white.

"Is it all over? Have they been driven off?"

"Yes, there is nothing more to fear from them. Were you injured?" "Not--not seriously; he hurt me terribly, but made no attempt to use his cutlass. I--I guess I was more frightened than anything else. Is--is the man dead?"

"If not, he might as well be," I answered, glancing at the body; but not caring to explain. "It was no time for mercy when I got to him. Watkins."

"Ay, ay, sir."

"Have you figured up results?"

"Not fully, sir; two of our men are cut rather badly, and Cole hasn't come too yet from a smart rap on the head."

"None got away?"

He grinned cheerfully.

"Not 'less they swum; thar's six dead ones aboard. Four took ter the water, mostly because they hed too. The only livin' one o' the bunch is thet nigger 'longside the wheel, an' nuthin' but a thick skull saved him."

"Then there were eleven in the party. What do you suppose has become of the others aboard the *Namur*?"

He shook his head, puzzled by the question.

"I dunno, sir; they might be a waitin' out there in the fog. Perhaps the nigger cud tell you."

I crossed over to where the fellow sat on a grating, his head in his hands, the girl still clinging to my sleeve, as though fearful of being left alone. The man was a repulsive brute, his face stained with blood, dripping from a cut across his low forehead. He looked up sullenly at our approach, but made no effort to rise.

"What's your name, my man?" I asked in Spanish.

"Jose Mendez, Senor." "You were aboard the *Namur*?"

He growled out an answer which I interpreted to signify assent, but Watkins lost his temper.

"Look yere, you black villain," he roared, driving the lesson home with his boot "don't be a playin' possum yer. Stand up an' answer Mister Carlyle, or yer'll git a worse clip than I give yer afore. Whar is the bloody bark?"

"Pounding her heart out on the rocks yonder," he said more civilly, "unless she's slid off, an' gone down."

"Wrecked? Where?"

"Hell, I ain't sure--what's west frum here?"

"Off our port quarter."

"Then that's 'bout where she is--maybe a mile, er so."

"What about the crew?"

"They got away in the boats, an' likely mostly are ashore. We were in the last boat launched, an' headed out so far ter get 'round a ledge o' rocks, we got lost in the fog. Then the mist sorter opened, an' give us a glimpse o' yer topsails. Manuel was for boarding you right away, and the rest of us talked it over, and thought it would be all right. We didn't expect no fight, once we got aboard."

"Expected to find something easy, of course? Perhaps it would have been if you fellows in the boat had held your tongues. By any chance, do you know now who we are?"

He rolled his eyes toward Watkins, and then at Schmitt engaged in some job across the deck.

"Those two used to be on the *Namur*," he said, his tone again sullen. "Are you the fellers who locked us in between decks?"

"We are the ones, Jose. You were up against fighting men when you came in over our rail. What is it you see out there, Harwood?"

The seaman, who was standing with hollowed hands shading his eyes, staring forth into the swirling drapery of fog, turned at my call, and pointed excitedly.

"There's a bark aground yonder, sir; and by God, it looks like the *Namur*!"

Even as I crossed the deck to his side, eagerly searching the direction indicated, the wreaths of obscuring mist seemed to divide, as though swept apart by some mighty hand, and there in the full glow of the sun, a picture in a frame, lay the wrecked vessel. Others saw it as I did, and a chorus of voices gave vent to recognition.

"Damned if it ain't the old hooker!"

"She got what was coming to her all right, mates."

"Maybe that ain't hell, bullies! And she's lousy with treasure!"

"Come here, Sam! That's the last of the *Namur*."

CHAPTER XXXII
THE LAST OF THE NAMUR

Even from where we were, looking across that stretch of water, yet obscured by floating patches of mist, the vessel was plainly a total wreck, rapidly pounding to death on a sharp ledge of rock. Both masts were down, and, lifted as the bow was, it was easy to perceive the deck was in splinters, where falling spars and topmasts had crashed their way through. She must have struck the ledge at good speed, and with all sail set, for the canvas was overside, with much of the top-hamper, a horrible mess, tossed about in the breakers, broken ends of spars viciously pounding against the ship's side. The bows had caught, seemingly jammed in between rocks, the stern sunk deep, with cabin port holes barely above reach of the waves. It seemed probable that any minute the whole helpless mass might slide backward into the water, and be swept away. Not a living thing appeared on board, and, as the fog slowly drifted away, my eyes could discern no sign of any boat, no evidence of the crew, along the wide sweep of water. Little, by little, as the vista widened, and we still remained, watching the miserable wreck as though fascinated, we were able to distinguish the dark line of coast to the westward, and to determine that the unfortunate *Namur* had struck at the extremity of a headland, whose rocky front had pushed its way far out to sea. A voice not far distant aroused me.

"What was it you said Jack 'bout treasure on the old hooker? Hell, if it's there, why not get it afore it's too late?"

"It's thar, all right, Ole," and I knew the speaker to be Haines. "Ain't it, Mr. Carlyle?"

"Yes, lads, there must be money on board, unless those fellows took it with them in the boats. I know of fifty thousand pounds stolen in Virginia, and no doubt there is more than that."

"Perhaps they took the swag along with 'em, sir."

"That wouldn't be the way I'd figure it," broke in Watkins. "That nigger says the boat what attacked us was the last one ter git away, an' thar wa'n't no chest in her." If Manuel didn't stay aboard long 'nough ter git his fingers outer thet gold, none ov the others did. They wus so damned anxious to save their lives, they never thought ov nuthin' else, sir."

"But maybe they'll think about that later, an' cum back," insisted Haines, pressing forward. "Ain't that right, sir?"

"Right enough; only they will not have much time to think it over, from the look of things out there," I answered. "The bark is liable to slide off that rock any minute, and go down like a stone. What do you say, bullies? Here is a risky job, but a pocket full of gold pieces, if we can get aboard and safely off again, Who'll go across with me?"

There was a babel of voices, the men crowding about me, all else forgotten as the lust of greed gripped their imaginations.

"Stand back, lads! I cannot use all of you. Four will be enough. I choose Haines, Harwood, Ole Hallin and Pierre. Lower that starboard quarter-boat you four, and see to the plugs and oars. No Watkins, I want you to remain in charge here. There is plenty to do; get those bodies overboard first, and clean up this litter; then shake out the reef in the foresail, and stand by--there is wind coming from that cloud yonder, and no time to waste. You'll not lose anything of what we bring back; it'll be share and share alike, so fall too, hearties."

"Shall we lower away, sir?"

"Ay, if all is fast I'll be with you in a minute; get aboard, Ole, and ward her off with a boat hook; easy now, till she takes water."

I paused an instant to speak to Dorothy, seated on the flag locker, explaining to her swiftly my object in exploring the wreck, and pledging myself not to be reckless in attempting to board. I read fear in her eyes, yet she said nothing to dissuade me, and our hands clasped, as I led her to the side, where she could look down at the cockleshell tossing below.

"It will mean much if we can recover this pirate hoard," I whispered, "freedom, and a full pardon, I hope."

"Yes, I know, Geoffry; but do not venture too much. You are more to me than all the gold in the world."

"I shall not forget, sweetheart. The sky and sea are almost clear now, and you can watch us from here. In a short time we shall be safely back again."

I slipped down a rope, and dropped into the boat, taking my place with a steering oar at the stern, and we shot away through the green water. The men yet lined the rail watching us enviously, although Watkins' voice began roaring out orders. Dorothy wraved her hand, which I acknowledged by lifting my cap. The schooner, with her sharp cutwater and graceful proportions made so fair a sea picture, outlined against the blue haze, I found it difficult to remove my gaze, but finally my thought concentrated on the work ahead, and I turned to urge the oarsmen to a quicker stroke.

The distance was greater than I had supposed it to be from the deck of the *Santa Marie*, nor did the dark cloud slowly poking up above the sea to the southeast ease my anxiety to get this task over with, before a storm broke. The *Namur* proved to be a more complete wreck than our distant view had revealed, and lying in a more precarious position. While the sea was not high, or dangerous, beyond the headland, the charging billows there broke in foam and were already playing havoc with the stranded vessel, smashing great spars, entangled amid canvas and cordage, about so as to render our approach extremely perilous. We were some time seeking a place where we might make fast, but finally nosed our way in behind the shelter of a huge boom, held steady by a splinter of rock, until Harwood got the hank of his boat hook in the after-chains, and hung on. It was no pleasant job getting aboard, but ordering Haines to accompany me, and the others to lie by in the lee of the boom, I made use of a dangling backstay, and thus hauled myself up to a reasonably secure footing. The fellow joined me breathless, and together we perched on the rail to gain view of the deck.

It was a distressing, hopeless sight, the vessel rising before us like the roof of a house, the deck planks stove in, a horrible jumble of running rigging, booms and spars, blocking the way forward. Aft it was clearer, the top-hamper of the after mast having fallen overboard, smashing a small boat as it fell, but leaving the deck space free. There were three bodies tangled in the wreckage within our sight, crushed out of all human resemblance, and the face of a negro, caught beneath the ruins of the galley, seemed to grin back at me in death. Every timber groaned as the waves struck, and rocked the sodden mass, and I had no doubt but that the vessel had already broken in two. I heard Haines utter an oath.

"By God, sir, did you ever see the like! She can't hang on here."

"Not, long surely," I admitted. "A bit more sea, and she breaks into kindling wood. If there is any salvage aboard, my man, it will be done in the next twenty minutes."

"There is no hope o' gittin' forrard, sir--look at that damn litter, an'--an' them dead men."

"It isn't forward we need to go, Haines; it's aft into the cabin, and that seems a clear enough passage--only the water down there may be too deep. Let's make a try of it."

He was evidently reluctant, but sailor enough to follow as I lowered myself to the deck, clinging hard to keep my footing on the wet incline. A light spar had lodged here, and by making this a species of bridge, we crept as far as the companion, the door of which was open, and gained view of the scene below. The light was sufficient to reveal most of the interior. From the confusion, and dampness the entire cabin had evidently been deluged with water, but this had largely drained away, leaving a mass of wreckage behind, and a foot or two still slushing about the doors of the after staterooms. It was a dismal hole in the dim light, more like a cave than the former habitation of men, but presented no obstacle to our entrance, and I led the way down the stairs, gripping the rail to keep from falling. Haines swore as he followed, and his continual growling got upon my nerves.

"Stop that infernal noise!" I ordered, shortly, looking him savagely in the face. "I've had enough of it. You were wild to come on this job; now do your work like a man. Try that room door over there; slide down, you fool, the water isn't deep. Wait a minute; now give me a hand."

"Is the gold in here, sir?" he asked with interest.

"More than likely; this was the Captain's room. See if it was left locked."

The door gave, but it required our combined efforts to press it open against the volume of water, slushing about within. While the stern port was yet slightly above the sea level, the crest of breaking waves obscured the glass, leaving the interior darker than the outer cabin. For a moment my eyes could scarcely recognize the various objects, as I clung to the frame of the door, and stared blindly about in the gloom. Then slowly they assumed shape and substance. Screwed to the deck the furniture retained its place, but everything else was jammed in a mass of wreckage, or else floating about in a foot of water, deepening toward the stern. There were two chests in the room, one of which I instantly recognized as that of Roger Fairfax. The sight of this made me oblivious to all else, urged on as I was, by a desire to escape from the doomed wreck as soon as possible.

"There's the chest we want Haines," I cried, pointing it out. "Have the lads back the boat up to this port; then come down, and help me handle it."

He did not answer, or move; and I whirled about angrily.

"What is the matter with you? Did you hear what I said?"

"Yes, sir," his voice trembling, "but--but isn't that a man over there--in the bunk? Good God, sir; look at him!"

The white, ghastly face stared at us, looking like nothing human in that awful twilight. I actually thought it a ghost, until with desperate effort, the man lifted himself, clinging with gaunt fingers to the edge of the bunk. Then I knew.

"Sanchez! You! those damn cowards left you here to die!"

"No one came for me," he answered, choking so the words were scarcely intelligible. "Is that what has happened; the bark is wrecked; the crew gone?"

"Yes, they took to the boats--Manuel with them."

"Manuel!" his enunciation clearer from passion, "the sneaking cur. But I cannot see your face; who are you, and what brought you here?"

"I'll tell you frankly, Captain Sanchez," and I stepped closer. "We risked coming aboard to save that chest--Roger Fairfax's chest--before it went down. This vessel has its back broken, and may slide off into deep water at any minute. We must get you out of here first."

"Get me out!" he laughed hideously. "You pretend to place my safety ahead of that treasure. To hell with your help. I want none of it. I am a dead man now, and the easiest way to end all, will be to go down with the ship--'twill be a fit coffin for Black Sanchez. By God! I know you now--Geoffry Carlyle?"

"Yes, but an enemy no longer."

"That is for me to say. I hate your race, your breed, your cursed English strain. The very sound of your name drives me mad. I accept no rescue from you! Damn you, take your gold and go."

"But why?" I insisted, shocked at the man's violence. "I have done you no ill. Is it because I interfered between you and Dorothy Fairfax?"

He laughed again, the sound so insane Haines gripped my sleeve in terror.

"That chit! bah, what do I care for her but as a plaything. No, my hate runs deeper than that. How came you here--in the boat stolen from the *Namur*?"

"No Captain Sanchez. The day after we left the ship, we boarded a schooner found adrift, the crew stricken with cholera, with not a man left alive on deck, or below. She lies yonder now."

"A schooner! What name?"

"The *Santa Marie*--a slaver."

"Merciful God!" and his eyes fairly blazed into mine, as he suddenly forced his body upward in the bunk. "The *Santa Marie* adrift! the crew dead from cholera? And the Captain--Paradilla, Francis Paradilla----what of him?"

"He lay alone on a divan in the cabin--dead also."

He tried to speak, but failed, his fingers clawing at his throat. When he finally gained utterance once more, it was but a whisper.

"Tell me," he begged, "there was no woman with him?"

I stared back into the wild insanity of his eyes, trying to test my words, suddenly aware that we were upon the edge of tragedy, perhaps uncovering the hidden secret of this man's life.

"There was no woman," I said gravely, "on deck or in the cabin."

"What mean you by saying that? There was one on board! Don't lie to me! In an hour I am dead--but first tell me the truth. Does the woman live?"

"No, she died before. We found her body in a chest, preserved by some devilish

Indian art, richly dressed, and decked with jewels."

"English?"

"I judged her so, but with dark hair and eyes. You knew her?"

"In the name of all the fiends, yes. And I know her end. He killed her--Paradilla killed her--because she was as false to him as she had been to me. Hell! but it is strange you should be the one to find her--to bring me this tale, Geoffry Carlyle!"

"Why? What is it to me?"

"Because she is of your line--do you know her now?" "No; nor believe it true."

"Then I will make you; 'tis naught to me anymore; for I am dead within the hour. You go back to England, and tell him; tell the Duke of Bucclough how his precious sister died."

"His sister! Good God, you cannot mean that woman was Lady Sara Carlyle?"

"Who should know better than I?" sneeringly. "Once I was called in England, Sir John Collinswood."

He sank back, exhausted, struggling for breath, but with eyes glowing hatred. I knew it all now, the dimly remembered story coming vividly back to memory. Here then was the ending of the one black stain on the family honor of our race. On this strange coast, three thousand miles from its beginning, the final curtain was being rung down, the drama finished. The story had come to me in whispers from others, never even spoken about by those of our race--a wild, headstrong girl, a secret marriage, a duel in the park, her brother desperately wounded, and then the disappearance of the pair. Ten days later it was known that Sir John Collinswood had defaulted in a large sum--but, from that hour, England knew him no more. As though the sea had swallowed them both, man and woman disappeared, leaving no trace behind.

The face I gazed dumbly into was drawn, and white with pain, yet the thin lips grinned back at me in savage derision.

"You remember, I see," he snarled. "Then to hell with you out of here, Geoffry Carlyle. Leave me to die in peace. The gold is there; take it, and my curse upon it. Hurry now--do you hear the bark grate on the rocks; it's near the end."

CHAPTER XXXIII
BEFORE THE GOVERNOR

The sound startled me; I imagined I heard the keel slipping, yet before we had reached the door opening on deck, the slight movement ceased. My hand gripped the frightened Haines.

"Tell them in the boat to do as I said; then come back here."

"My God, sir, she's a goin' down."

"Not for some minutes yet. There are thousands of pounds in that chest; you've risked life for less many a time. Jump, my man!"

The boat lay in close, bobbing up and down dangerously, yet held firmly beneath the opened port. Pierre warped her in with a rope's end, leaving the other two free to receive the box, as we cautiously passed it out within grasp of their hands. It was heavy enough to tax the strength of two men to handle it, but of a size and shape permitting its passage. Sanchez had raised himself again, and clung there to the edge of the bunk watching us. Even in the darkness caused by the chest obscuring the port, I felt the insane glare of his eyes fastened upon me. Once he attempted to speak, but his voice failed him.

"Now let down easy, lads," I called. "No, place it amidships; get it even, or you go over. Wrap your line about the thwart, Pierre, and take a hand. Ay! that's better. Watch out now; we'll drop this end--Lord, but I thought it was gone! Fix it to ride steady, and stand by--we'll pass a wounded man out to you!"

I stepped across to Sanchez, slushing through the water, and barely able to keep my feet. No matter who the brute was, he could not be left there to die like a rat alone. Willingly, or not, the fellow must be removed before the bark went down. He saw me coming, and drew back, his ghastly face like a mask.

"No, you don't--damn you, Carlyle!" he snapped angrily. "Keep your hands off me. So you want me to die with my neck in a noose, do you? Well, you'll never see that sight. I was born a gentleman, and, by God! I'll die like one--and go down with my ship. Get out of here now--both of you! You won't? Hell's fire, but you will, or else die here with me! I'll give you a minute to make your choice."

He left no doubt as to his meaning, his purpose. From somewhere beneath the blanket, the long, black muzzle of a pistol looked straight into my eyes. The hand holding it was firm, the face fronting me savagely sardonic.

"I'd like to kill you, Carlyle," he hissed hatefully. "By God, I don't know why I shouldn't, the devils in hell would laugh if I did--so don't tempt me too far. Get out of here, damn you! Every time I look at you I see her face. If you take a step nearer, I pull the trigger--go!"

I heard Haines scrambling back up the sharp incline of deck, and realized the utter uselessness of attempting to remain. Any instant might be our last; the man crazed, and probably dying, would kill me gladly. He had chosen his fate--what was it to me? I turned, and worked my way upward to the companion steps, half expecting every instant to be struck by a bullet from behind. At the door I paused to glance below; through the semi-darkness I could see his eyes glaring at me like those of a wild beast.

"You refuse still to let me aid you, Sanchez?"

"To hell with you! Leave me alone!"

It was a hard pull back to the **Santa Marie**, for the sea had grown noticeably heavier, while the weight of the chest sank the boat so deeply in the water, as to retard progress and keep one man bailing. The cloud in the southwest had already assumed threatening proportions, and I urged the oarsmen to greater exertions, anxious to get aboard before the coming storm broke. It was hard to keep my gaze from the doomed **Namur**, but I could detect no change in her position, as we drew in toward the waiting schooner. Harwood alone questioned me, and I told him briefly what had occurred within the cabin, and his comment seemed to voice the sentiment of the others.

"He made a bloomin' good choice, sir. That's how the ol' devil ought ter die-- the same way he's sent many another. It beats hangin' at that."

Dorothy greeted me first, and we stood close together at the rail, as the men hoisted the chest on deck, and then fastened the tackle to the boat She said nothing, asked nothing, but her hands clung to my arm, and whenever I turned toward her, our eyes met. I did not find the courage to tell her then what we had found aboard the **Namur**, although I could not prevent my own eyes from wandering constantly toward the doomed vessel. The rising sea was slapping the submerged stern with increasing violence, the salt spray rising in clouds over the after rail. Watkins approached us, coming from among the group of sailors forward.

"There's a smart bit of wind in those clouds, sir," he said respectfully, "an' I don't like the look o' the coast ter leeward. Shall we trim sail?"

"Not quite yet, Watkins. It will be some time before the gale strikes here. The bark is going down, presently."

"Yes, sir; but the men better stand by." He glanced from my face to that of the girl, lowering his voice. "Harwood tells me Sanchez was aboard, sir, and refused to leave?"

"Very true; but he was dying; no doubt is dead by now. There was nothing to be done for him."

"I should say not, Mr. Carlyle. I wouldn't lift a finger ter save him frum hell."

There was a sudden cry forward, and a voice shouted.

"There she goes, buckies! That damn Dutchman's done with. That's the last o' the *Namur*!"

I turned swiftly, my hand grasping her fingers as they clung to the rail. With a rasping sound, clearly distinguished across the intervening water, as though every timber cried out in agony to the strain, the battered hulk slid downward, the deck breaking amidships as the stern splashed into the depths; then that also toppled over, leaving nothing above water except the blunt end of a broken bow-sprit, and a tangle of wreckage, tossed about on the crest of the waves. I watched breathlessly, unable to utter a sound; I could only think of that stricken man in the cabin, those wild eyes which had threatened me. He was gone now--gone! Watkins spoke.

"It's all over, sir."

"Yes, there is nothing to keep us here any longer," I answered still dazed, but realizing I must arouse myself. "Shake out the reef in your mainsail, and we'll get out to sea. Who is at the wheel?"

"Schmitt, sir--what is the course, Captain Carlyle?"

"Nor'west, by nor', and hold on as long as you can."

"Ay, ay, sir; nor'west by nor' she is."

I yet held Dorothy's hand tightly clasped in my own, and the depths of her uplifted eyes questioned me.

"We will go aft, dear, and I will tell you the whole story," I said gently, "for now we are homeward bound."

    *   *   *   *   *

I write these few closing lines a year later, in the cabin of the **Ocean Spray**, a three master, full to the hatches with a cargo of tobacco, bound for London, and a market. Dorothy is on deck, eagerly watching for the first glimpse of the chalk cliffs of old England. I must join her presently, yet linger below to add these final sentences.

There is, after all, little which needs to be said. The voyage of the **Santa Marie** north proved uneventful, and, after that first night of storm, the weather held pleasant, and the sea fairly smooth. I had some trouble with the men, but nothing serious, as Watkins and Harwood held as I did, and the pledge of Dorothy's influence brought courage. I refused to open the chest, believing our safety, and chance of pardon, would depend largely on our handing this over in good faith to the authorities. Watkins and I guarded it night and day, until the schooner rounded the Cape and came into the Chesapeake. No attempt was made to find quarters below, the entire crew sleeping on deck, Dorothy comfortable on the flag locker.

It was scarcely sunrise, on the fifth day, when we dropped anchor against the current of the James, our sails furled, and the red English colors flying from the peak. Two hours later the entire company were in the presence of the Governor, where I told my story, gravely listened to, supplemented by the earnest plea of the young woman. I shall never forget that scene, or how breathlessly we awaited the decision of the great man, who so closely watched our faces. They were surely a strange, rough group as they stood thus, hats in hand, waiting to learn their fate, shaggy-haired, unshaven, largely scum of the sea, never before in such presence, shuffling uneasily before his glance, feeling to the full the peril of their position. Their eyes turned to me questioningly.

Opposite us, behind a long table, sat the Governor, dignified, austere, his hair powdered, and face smoothly shaven; while on either side of him were those of his council, many of the faces stern and unforgiving. But for their gracious reception of Dorothy, and their careful attention to her words, I should have lost heart. They questioned me shrewdly, although the Governor spoke but seldom, and then in a kindly tone of sympathy and understanding. One by one the men were called forward, each in turn compelled to tell briefly the story of his life; and when all was done the eyes of the Governor sought those of his council.

"You have all alike heard the tale, gentlemen," he said. "Nothing like it hath ever before been brought before this Colony. Would you leave decision to me?"

There was a murmur of assent, as though they were thus gladly relieved of responsibility in so serious a matter. The Governor smiled, his kindly eyes surveying us once more; then, with extended hand he bade Dorothy be seated.

"The story is seemingly an honest one," he said slowly, "and these seamen have done a great service to the Colony. They deserve reward rather than punishment. The fair lady who pleads for them is known to us all, and to even question her word is impossible. Unfortunately I have not the power of pardon in cases of piracy, nor authority to free bond slaves, without the approval of the home government; yet will exercise in this case whatsoever of power I possess. For gallant services rendered to the Colony, and unselfish devotion to Mistress Dorothy Fairfax, I release Geoffry Carlyle from servitude, pending advices from England; I also grant parole to these seamen, on condition they remain within our jurisdiction until this judgment can be confirmed, and full pardons issued. Is this judgment satisfactory, gentlemen?"

The members of the council bowed gravely, without speaking.

"The chest of treasure recovered from the sunken pirate ship," he went on soberly, "will remain unopened until final decision is made. As I understand, Master Carlyle, no one among you has yet seen its contents, or estimated its value?"

"No, your excellency. Beyond doubt it contains the gold stolen from Roger Fairfax; and possibly the result of other robberies at sea.

"The law of England is that a certain percentage of such recovered treasure belongs to the crown, the remainder, its true ownership undetermined, to be fairly divided among those recovering it."

"Yet," spoke up Dorothy quickly, "it must surely be possible to waive all claim in such cases?"

"Certainly; as private property it can be disposed of in any way desired. Was that your thought?"

"A Fairfax always pays his debt," she said proudly, "and this is mine."

There was a moment's silence as though each one present hesitated to speak. She had risen, and yet stood, but with eyes lowered to the floor. Then they were lifted, and met mine, in all frank honesty.

"There is another debt I owe," she said clearly, "and would pay, your Excellency."

"What is that, fair mistress?"

She crossed to me, her hand upon my arm.

"To become the wife of Geoffry Carlyle."

The Codes Of Hammurabi And Moses
W. W. Davies

QTY

The discovery of the Hammurabi Code is one of the greatest achievements of archaeology, and is of paramount interest, not only to the student of the Bible, but also to all those interested in ancient history...

Religion   ISBN: *1-59462-338-4*   **Pages:132**

MSRP $12.95

The Theory of Moral Sentiments
Adam Smith

QTY

This work from 1749. contains original theories of conscience amd moral judgment and it is the foundation for systemof morals.

Philosophy ISBN: *1-59462-777-0*   **Pages:536**
MSRP $19.95

Jessica's First Prayer
Hesba Stretton

QTY

In a screened and secluded corner of one of the many railway-bridges which span the streets of London there could be seen a few years ago, from five o'clock every morning until half past eight, a tidily set-out coffee-stall, consisting of a trestle and board, upon which stood two large tin cans, with a small fire of charcoal burning under each so as to keep the coffee boiling during the early hours of the morning when the work-people were thronging into the city on their way to their daily toil...

Pages:84

Childrens   ISBN: *1-59462-373-2*   *MSRP $9.95*

My Life and Work
Henry Ford

QTY

Henry Ford revolutionized the world with his implementation of mass production for the Model T automobile. Gain valuable business insight into his life and work with his own auto-biography... "We have only started on our development of our country we have not as yet, with all our talk of wonderful progress, done more than scratch the surface. The progress has been wonderful enough but..."

Pages:300

Biographies/   ISBN: *1-59462-198-5*   *MSRP $21.95*

The Art of Cross-Examination
Francis Wellman

QTY

I presume it is the experience of every author, after his first book is published upon an important subject, to be almost overwhelmed with a wealth of ideas and illustrations which could readily have been included in his book, and which to his own mind, at least, seem to make a second edition inevitable. Such certainly was the case with me; and when the first edition had reached its sixth impression in five months, I rejoiced to learn that it seemed to my publishers that the book had met with a sufficiently favorable reception to justify a second and considerably enlarged edition. ..

Pages:412

Reference   **ISBN:** *1-59462-647-2*   *MSRP $19.95*

On the Duty of Civil Disobedience
Henry David Thoreau

QTY

Thoreau wrote his famous essay, On the Duty of Civil Disobedience, as a protest against an unjust but popular war and the immoral but popular institution of slave-owning. He did more than write—he declined to pay his taxes, and was hauled off to gaol in consequence. Who can say how much this refusal of his hastened the end of the war and of slavery ?

Law   **ISBN:** *1-59462-747-9*   **Pages:48**

MSRP $7.45

Dream Psychology Psychoanalysis for Beginners
Sigmund Freud

QTY

Sigmund Freud, born Sigismund Schlomo Freud (May 6, 1856 - September 23, 1939), was a Jewish-Austrian neurologist and psychiatrist who co-founded the psychoanalytic school of psychology. Freud is best known for his theories of the unconscious mind, especially involving the mechanism of repression; his redefinition of sexual desire as mobile and directed towards a wide variety of objects; and his therapeutic techniques, especially his understanding of transference in the therapeutic relationship and the presumed value of dreams as sources of insight into unconscious desires.

Pages:196

Psychology   **ISBN:** *1-59462-905-6*   *MSRP $15.45*

The Miracle of Right Thought
Orison Swett Marden

QTY

Believe with all of your heart that you will do what you were made to do. When the mind has once formed the habit of holding cheerful, happy, prosperous pictures, it will not be easy to form the opposite habit. It does not matter how improbable or how far away this realization may see, or how dark the prospects may be, if we visualize them as best we can, as vividly as possible, hold tenaciously to them and vigorously struggle to attain them, they will gradually become actualized, realized in the life. But a desire, a longing without endeavor, a yearning abandoned or held indifferently will vanish without realization.

Pages:360

Self Help   **ISBN:** *1-59462-644-8*   *MSRP $25.45*

QTY

The Rosicrucian Cosmo-Conception Mystic Christianity *by Max Heindel* ISBN: *1-59462-188-8* **$38.95**
The Rosicrucian Cosmo-conception is not dogmatic, neither does it appeal to any other authority than the reason of the student. It is: not controversial, but is: sent forth in the, hope that it may help to clear.. New Age/Religion Pages 646

Abandonment To Divine Providence *by Jean-Pierre de Caussade* ISBN: *1-59462-228-0* **$25.95**
"The Rev. Jean Pierre de Caussade was one of the most remarkable spiritual writers of the Society of Jesus in France in the 18th Century. His death took place at Toulouse in 1751. His works have gone through many editions and have been republished... Inspirational/Religion Pages 400

Mental Chemistry *by Charles Haanel* ISBN: *1-59462-192-6* **$23.95**
Mental Chemistry allows the change of material conditions by combining and appropriately utilizing the power of the mind. Much like applied chemistry creates something new and unique out of careful combinations of chemicals the mastery of mental chemistry... New Age Pages 354

The Letters of Robert Browning and Elizabeth Barret Barrett 1845-1846 vol II ISBN: *1-59462-193-4* **$35.95**
by Robert Browning and Elizabeth Barrett Biographies Pages 596

Gleanings In Genesis (volume I) *by Arthur W. Pink* ISBN: *1-59462-130-6* **$27.45**
Appropriately has Genesis been termed "the seed plot of the Bible" for in it we have, in germ form, almost all of the great doctrines which are afterwards fully developed in the books of Scripture which follow... Religion/Inspirational Pages 420

The Master Key *by L. W. de Laurence* ISBN: *1-59462-001-6* **$30.95**
In no branch of human knowledge has there been a more lively increase of the spirit of research during the past few years than in the study of Psychology, Concentration and Mental Discipline. The requests for authentic lessons in Thought Control, Mental Discipline and... New Age/Business Pages 422

The Lesser Key Of Solomon Goetia *by L. W. de Laurence* ISBN: *1-59462-092-X* **$9.95**
This translation of the first book of the "Lernegton" which is now for the first time made accessible to students of Talismanic Magic was done, after careful collation and edition, from numerous Ancient Manuscripts in Hebrew, Latin, and French... New Age/Occult Pages 92

Rubaiyat Of Omar Khayyam *by Edward Fitzgerald* ISBN:*1-59462-332-5* **$13.95**
Edward Fitzgerald, whom the world has already learned, in spite of his own efforts to remain within the shadow of anonymity, to look upon as one of the rarest poets of the century, was born at Bredfield, in Suffolk, on the 31st of March, 1809. He was the third son of John Purcell... Music Pages 172

Ancient Law *by Henry Maine* ISBN: *1-59462-129-2* **$29.95**
The chief object of the following pages is to indicate some of the earliest ideas of mankind, as they are reflected in Ancient Law, and to point out the relation of those ideas to modern thought. Religion/History Pages 452

Far-Away Stories *by William J. Locke* ISBN: *1-59462-129-2* **$19.45**
"Good wine needs no bush, but a collection of mixed vintages does. And this book is just such a collection. Some of the stories I do not want to remain buried for ever in the museum files of dead magazine-numbers an author's not unpardonable vanity..." Fiction Pages 272

Life of David Crockett *by David Crockett* ISBN: *1-59462-250-7* **$27.45**
"Colonel David Crockett was one of the most remarkable men of the times in which he lived. Born in humble life, but gifted with a strong will, an indomitable courage, and unremitting perseverance... Biographies/New Age Pages 424

Lip-Reading *by Edward Nitchie* ISBN: *1-59462-206-X* **$25.95**
Edward B. Nitchie, founder of the New York School for the Hard of Hearing, now the Nitchie School of Lip-Reading, Inc, wrote "LIP-READING Principles and Practice". The development and perfecting of this meritorious work on lip-reading was an undertaking... How-to Pages 400

A Handbook of Suggestive Therapeutics, Applied Hypnotism, Psychic Science ISBN: *1-59462-214-0* **$24.95**
by Henry Munro Health/New Age/Health/Self-help Pages 376

A Doll's House: and Two Other Plays *by Henrik Ibsen* ISBN: *1-59462-112-8* **$19.95**
Henrik Ibsen created this classic when in revolutionary 1848 Rome. Introducing some striking concepts in playwriting for the realist genre, this play has been studied the world over. Fiction/Classics/Plays 308

The Light of Asia *by sir Edwin Arnold* ISBN: *1-59462-204-3* **$13.95**
In this poetic masterpiece, Edwin Arnold describes the life and teachings of Buddha. The man who was to become known as Buddha to the world was born as Prince Gautama of India but he rejected the worldly riches and abandoned the reigns of power when... Religion/History/Biographies Pages 170

The Complete Works of Guy de Maupassant *by Guy de Maupassant* ISBN: *1-59462-157-8* **$16.95**
"For days and days, nights and nights, I had dreamed of that first kiss which was to consecrate our engagement, and I knew not on what spot I should put my lips..." Fiction/Classics Pages 240

The Art of Cross-Examination *by Francis L. Wellman* ISBN: *1-59462-309-0* **$26.95**
Written by a renowned trial lawyer, Wellman imparts his experience and uses case studies to explain how to use psychology to extract desired information through questioning. How-to/Science/Reference Pages 408

Answered or Unanswered? *by Louisa Vaughan* ISBN: *1-59462-248-5* **$10.95**
Miracles of Faith in China Religion Pages 112

The Edinburgh Lectures on Mental Science (1909) *by Thomas* ISBN: *1-59462-008-3* **$11.95**
This book contains the substance of a course of lectures recently given by the writer in the Queen Street Hail, Edinburgh. Its purpose is to indicate the Natural Principles governing the relation between Mental Action and Material Conditions... New Age/Psychology Pages 148

Ayesha *by H. Rider Haggard* ISBN: *1-59462-301-5* **$24.95**
Verily and indeed it is the unexpected that happens! Probably if there was one person upon the earth from whom the Editor of this, and of a certain previous history, did not expect to hear again... Classics Pages 380

Ayala's Angel *by Anthony Trollope* ISBN: *1-59462-352-X* **$29.95**
The two girls were both pretty, but Lucy who was twenty-one who supposed to be simple and comparatively unattractive, whereas Ayala was credited, as her Bombwhat romantic name might show, with poetic charm and a taste for romance. Ayala when her father died was nineteen... Fiction Pages 484

The American Commonwealth *by James Bryce* ISBN: *1-59462-286-8* **$34.45**
An interpretation of American democratic political theory. It examines political mechanics and society from the perspective of Scotsman James Bryce Politics Pages 572

Stories of the Pilgrims *by Margaret P. Pumphrey* ISBN: *1-59462-116-0* **$17.95**
This book explores pilgrims religious oppression in England as well as their escape to Holland and eventual crossing to America on the Mayflower, and their early days in New England... History Pages 268

QTY

The Fasting Cure *by Sinclair Upton*   ISBN: *1-59462-222-1*   **$13.95**
In the Cosmopolitan Magazine for May, 1910, and in the Contemporary Review (London) for April, 1910, I published an article dealing with my experiences in fasting. I have written a great many magazine articles, but never one which attracted so much attention... New Age/Self Help/Health Pages 164

Hebrew Astrology *by Sepharial*   ISBN: *1-59462-308-2*   **$13.45**
In these days of advanced thinking it is a matter of common observation that we have left many of the old landmarks behind and that we are now pressing forward to greater heights and to a wider horizon than that which represented the mind-content of our progenitors...   Astrology Pages 144

Thought Vibration or The Law of Attraction in the Thought World   ISBN: *1-59462-127-6*   **$12.95**
by William Walker Atkinson   *Psychology/Religion Pages 144*

Optimism *by Helen Keller*   ISBN: *1-59462-108-X*   **$15.95**
Helen Keller was blind, deaf, and mute since 19 months old, yet famously learned how to overcome these handicaps, communicate with the world, and spread her lectures promoting optimism. An inspiring read for everyone...   Biographies/Inspirational Pages 84

Sara Crewe *by Frances Burnett*   ISBN: *1-59462-360-0*   **$9.45**
In the first place, Miss Minchin lived in London. Her home was a large, dull, tall one, in a large, dull square, where all the houses were alike, and all the sparrows were alike, and where all the door-knockers made the same heavy sound...   Childrens/Classic Pages 88

The Autobiography of Benjamin Franklin *by Benjamin Franklin*   ISBN: *1-59462-135-7*   **$24.95**
The Autobiography of Benjamin Franklin has probably been more extensively read than any other American historical work, and no other book of its kind has had such ups and downs of fortune. Franklin lived for many years in England, where he was agent...   Biographies/History Pages 332

Name	
Email	
Telephone	
Address	
City, State ZIP	

☐ **Credit Card**   ☐ **Check / Money Order**

Credit Card Number	
Expiration Date	
Signature	

Please Mail to: Book Jungle
PO Box 2226
Champaign, IL 61825
or Fax to: 630-214-0564

ORDERING INFORMATION

web*: www.bookjungle.com*
email*: sales@bookjungle.com*
fax*: 630-214-0564*
mail*: Book Jungle PO Box 2226 Champaign, IL 61825*
or PayPal *to sales@bookjungle.com*

Please contact us for bulk discounts

DIRECT-ORDER TERMS

**20% Discount if You Order
Two or More Books**
Free Domestic Shipping!
Accepted: Master Card, Visa,
Discover, American Express

www.ingramcontent.com/pod-product-compliance
Lightning Source LLC
Chambersburg PA
CBHW080901020726
47502CB00008B/2304